The next day I felt pretty good for a change, so I jumped into a pair of pants and a windbreaker and rode my motorcycle to work.

I saw Gus pulling into his parking space under the tangerine tree.

"Where in God's name have you been, Jordan?" he yelled, frowning from under his visor. "Bill sent me to find you but you'd already left the house. Audrey's missing."

"How can that be?"

"The Armats say she didn't sleep in her bed last night. She's gone. They're ready to call out the National Guard."

"She's been gone a few hours and they're putting her picture on a milk carton? Are they sure she's gone? Maybe she went for an early walk?"

Gus pointed toward the villas. "They're waiting for us. Apparently she left a note."

"This is ludicrous," I said. "These people do nothing but overreact. No wonder Audrey's like she is."

"Well, Mrs. Armat is blaming us for what she is referring to as Audrey's disappearance."

"Audrey was here maybe one day and this woman is blaming us?"

"That's right," said Gus. "And I hate to tell you this, Jordan, but she's especially blaming you."

THE TOTAL ZONE

**Martina Navratilova
and Liz Nickles**

BALLANTINE BOOKS • NEW YORK

Copyright © 1994 by Martina Navratilova and Elizabeth Nickles

All rights reserved under International and Pan-American Copyright Conventions. Published in the United States by Ballantine Books, a division of Random House, Inc., New York, and simultaneously in Canada by Random House of Canada Limited, Toronto.

This is a work of fiction. The characters, incidents, and dialogues are products of the authors' imaginations and are not to be construed as real. Any resemblance to actual events or to actual persons, living or dead, is entirely coincidental.

Library of Congress Catalog Card Number: 94-10182

ISBN 0-345-38867-4

This edition published by arrangement with Villard Books, a division of Random House, Inc. Villard Books is a registered trademark of Random House, Inc.

Manufactured in the United States of America

First Ballantine Books Edition: July 1995

10 9 8 7 6 5 4 3 2 1

To all those fourteen-year-olds who play tennis—
or any other sport for that matter—
for one reason only—
because they love it.

—MARTINA NAVRATILOVA

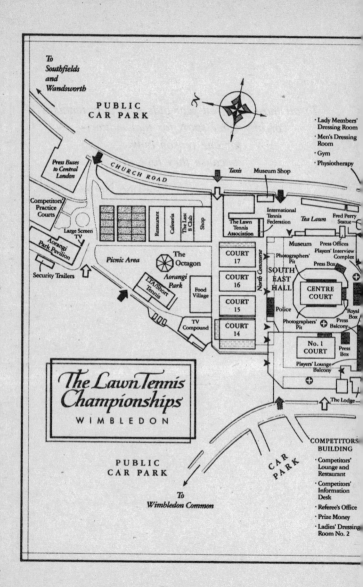

To
Southfields
and
Wandsworth

PUBLIC
CAR PARK

· Lady Members'
Dressing Room
· Men's Dressing
Room
· Gym
· Physiotherapy

CHURCH ROAD

Taxis   Museum Shop

Press Buses
to Central
London

Competitors'
Practice
Courts

Large Screen
TV

Restaurant

Cafeteria

The Last
8 Club

Shop

The Lawn
Tennis
Association

International
Tennis
Federation

Tea Lawn

Fred Perry
Statue

Museum

Photographers'
Pit

Press Offices

Players' Interview
Complex

Press Box

Aorangi
Park Pavilion

Picnic Area

The
Octagon

Aorangi
Park

Security Trailers

LTA/Short
Tennis

Food
Village

COURT
17

COURT
16

COURT
15

COURT
14

North Concourse

SOUTH
EAST
HALL

CENTRE
COURT

Police

Royal
Box

Press
Balcony

TV
Compound

Photographers'
Pit

No. 1
COURT

Press
Box

Players' Lounge
Balcony

The Lawn Tennis
Championships
WIMBLEDON

The Lodge

COMPETITORS
BUILDING

· Competitors'
Lounge and
Restaurant
· Competitors'
Information
Desk
· Referee's Office
· Prize Money
· Ladies' Dressing
Room No. 2

PUBLIC
CAR PARK

CAR
PARK

To
Wimbledon Common

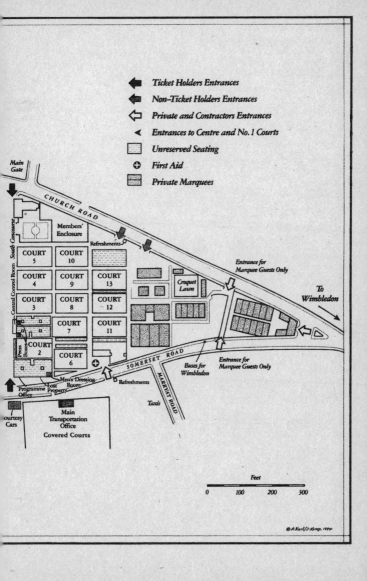

Ticket Holders Entrances

Non–Ticket Holders Entrances

Private and Contractors Entrances

Entrances to Centre and No. 1 Courts

Unreserved Seating

First Aid

Private Marquees

Main
Gate

CHURCH ROAD

Members'
Enclosure

Refreshments

Entrance for
Marquee Guests Only

To
Wimbledon

Central Control Room

South Concourse

COURT 5

COURT 10

COURT 4

COURT 9

COURT 13

COURT 3

COURT 8

COURT 12

Croquet
Lawn

COURT 7

COURT 11

Press
Room

COURT 2

COURT 6

SOMERSET ROAD

MARRYAT ROAD

Men's Dressing
Room

Refreshments

Buses for
Wimbledon

Entrance for
Marquee Guests Only

Programme
Office

Lost
Property

Taxis

Courtesy
Cars

Main
Transportation
Office
Covered Courts

Feet

0   100   200   300

© A. Karl/J. Kemp. 1994

ACKNOWLEDGMENTS

We wish to thank all the people in the tennis community who gave us access, shared their expertise, and helped make the book as accurate as it is.

ONE

The last time I was in front of the TV cameras, millions of people saw me get annihilated by a sixteen-year-old girl with her hair in pigtails and braces on her teeth. I never went back to Wimbledon, or any other tennis tournament for that matter, although not entirely as a personal choice. Now I was in front of the cameras again, and it all came back in the blitz of flashes—the headiness of the attention, the cheers of the crowd, the adrenaline that raced through my body as I braced to run the gauntlet. Except this time I wasn't playing for the crowd; I was in it. I wasn't out to win; I was out of the game. And I wasn't getting an award; my former opponent—now my client—was. I walked purposefully ahead on the red carpet, joining the crush of celebrities, entourage members, and wannabes, simultaneously hoping that somebody would recognize me and dreading the prospect. Suddenly I felt a hand wrench my shoulder and reach past my neck with a sharp chop to my throat. Something shoved the small of my back. A metal object grazed my skull, and a heavy combat boot smashed down on my instep, tripping me to my knees. A blinding light flashed before my eyes.

Paparazzi.

An exclusive shot of a major star was worth thousands of dollars, and these guys would probably kill for it. The legitimate press was one thing. The tabloid guys, however, were a whole other breed. If they didn't get a shot, they'd create it by stripping one star's head onto another's body, or whatever it took. Nothing personal. I was irritated, and a little shaken, but I knew I was not the intended prey—a shot of me was worth about five cents, if my mother had change in her purse. I was just blocking somebody's viewfinder.

I was rescued by a Garden security officer, who grabbed the photographer and yanked him unceremoniously off me. "Where's your pass, mister?" he grilled the man, as another guard raced to offer me a hand and two or three more men in uniform materialized.

"Media," the photographer mumbled.

"You don't have a pass. Get over here," commanded the guard, as he and his uniformed friends formed a wedge, lifted the photographer up by the elbows, and deposited him back behind the velvet rope.

"Are you all right, miss?" asked the guard who'd helped me up. He held his walkie-talkie at the ready.

"I'm fine. It was an accident. I think." I'd escaped pretty much unscathed, except that I'd ripped my stockings when I fell and a huge run was making its jagged way down the length of my left leg. And, of course, I'd skinned my knee. But then, that was in character.

There are some people, like Fred Astaire, Ginger Rogers, fashion models, and society page habitués, who can wear formal gowns and tuxedos as comfortably as a T-shirt and jeans. I, Jordan Myles, am not one of them. I blame this on the fact that, until a few years ago—five years ago, to be exact—I spent most of my life at a dead run across a tennis court in Nikes, ankle socks, shorts, and a T-shirt, clutching a racket, not an evening bag. Even when I was the number-three player on the women's tour, where events like awards dinners, fund-raisers, charity benefits, and testimonials were part of the schedule, for the most part my focus was on my training. When I had to show up at an event, I fell back on my uniform—biannual variations on a black synthetic dress that packed well, could be de-wrinkled in shower steam, rinsed out in a bathroom sink, hung up to drip-dry, and worn that night, if necessary. As any woman who's ever played on the tour can attest, it's not your opponent that's your worst nightmare—it's your laundry.

But tonight was different. Everyone in the world of sports, which meant a major percentage of my old friends, not to mention my current and potential clients, was going to be at the Sports Network Awards, an event they accurately refer to in the press as "star-studded" and "glittering," so I did make a particular and extensive effort—well, extensive for me, anyway. Before I flew to New York from Palm Springs for the awards, I bought a simple navy blue cocktail dress with an interesting backless look, and tonight I spent some time attacking my short, curly black hair with its natural enemy, the blow-dryer. I never use much makeup, because frankly I do look better without it. My eyes are dark hazel, my color naturally high, my nose, which was once broken in a midcourt collision, beyond the ministrations of any over-the-counter beauty products. Things had looked promising until I had to deal with one critical issue women's evening wear has yet to address, which is where to put your beeper.

I'm a physical therapist at the Desert Springs Sports Science Clinic, and it's part of my job never to be unreachable. It's important to our clients that we are available at all times—many of them are high-profile celebrities who call in questions or problems from a mixed bag of time zones. In a crowd you can't hear a beeper in your purse, so I compromised by putting on a jacket and clipping the beeper to the pocket. The jacket covered up 90 percent of the dress, but what are you going to do?

Actually, who was going to care? Certainly not my escort—he had the proper perspective, having first met me in a hospital gown in traction, with pins and staples piecing my leg together after the mountain-climbing mishap that didn't kill me but managed to abruptly end my career in professional tennis when I was twenty-two. Officially, Gus is Dr. Augustus Laid-law, director and cofounder of the Springs, my associate on the staff and one of the most brilliant, if controversial, sports psychologists in the world. Unofficially—very unofficially—he's a friend I'm involved with, and have been in varying degrees since he helped me get back on my feet, in more ways than one, after the accident. It's a complicated relationship, something you can't really label. Occasionally, when she thinks enough time has elapsed since the last time she shook the trees in hopes that some information would fall out, my mother will ask the usual discreet questions all mothers of single daughters ask. I never have the answers. What is Gus to me? A friend, a mentor, an associate, a lover, a role model, a doctor, a teacher, a conscience, a nemesis, a jerk. At any given moment, one or more of the above may apply.

I always tell myself things are as good as they were when I was playing tennis—in some ways, better. I have a stable life, a predictable if not astronomical income, a home of my own, friends, a profession I believe in that helps others. I'm a founding staff member of the Springs, an exciting new sports medicine clinic that helps athletes from every sport make the best of their minds and bodies. My failed marriage is in the past, if you can call something that only lasted six months, and which was therefore history almost the minute it began, a marriage. And there's Gus. In other words, I've gotten on with my life.

Which brought me to the Paramount Theater at Madison Square Garden for this convergence of the best and brightest in sports. It's sort of ironic, because, for so many years, the Garden was a regular part of my life—an every-November stopover for the Virginia Slims Championships, the punctuation at the year's end of the women's tour. I don't know if I will ever get over feeling disconnected about being in New York and putting on a fancy outfit instead of baggy sweats and a T-shirt. Or drop the habit of feeling guilty when I eat a giant slice of tiramisù at Contrapunto. Or stop feeling strange about pulling out a business card that says *Jordan Myles, Physical Therapist*—or about having a business card, period. I have to keep reminding myself that things are different now.

All the big names were slated to be here tonight. I scanned the crowd milling through the vast entrance to Madison Square Garden, up the escalators and into the Paramount Theater, for Gus, who was flying in from a corporate speech in Detroit. At the top of the escalators, there is an Art Deco–ish lobby; here the entering crowd merged with the people spilling out from the glass-enclosed Play-by-Play Lounge, were a VIP dinner had been held for tonight's honorees and their guests. Through the glass, I could see the flicker of candles and white tablecloths and garlands of balloons and ribbons hanging from the ceiling. I spotted Ollie Cedars, the heavyweight title contender, his huge bulk and orbiting entourage parting the crowd. Ollie waved, revealing a massive diamond-studded watch. Behind us, cries of "Mi-chael! Mi-chael!" signaled that Michael Jordan had arrived. Smiling to the bank of photographers, who obliged with a blinding flash of lights, was Linsey Marks, blond, in a white beaded gown, living up to her reputation as the glamour girl of golf. Billie Jean King walked in, and just behind her were country-music star Allie Trask and rapper Mr. Huge. A famous football star rode up the escalator with a gorgeous woman clinging to each arm. His public appearances and macho press coverage are always designed to mask the fact that he's known in sports circles to be gay.

Barricaded behind another storm of camera flashes, her back pressed to the wall, was Mariska Storrs, her hair slicked back and sleek as her tuxedo. I wondered if I should rescue her, but if there's anybody who knows how to handle the press it's Mariska. Mariska, who has won more Grand Slam titles than any woman in history, is one of those people who has achieved a pinnacle so rarefied that her last name is an unnecessary appendage. She has true charisma, but has sustained the public's interest for this long because of sheer talent and ability; if you have charisma without ability, nobody cares. Since her highly publicized escape from behind the Iron Curtain almost twenty years ago, she's probably racked up more sports coverage—and gossip items—than all her rivals combined. Her unbroken string of seven consecutive Wimbledon singles wins is countered by overblown reports of her affairs with, variously, a British rock star, a top fashion model, and a housewife. Every year for fifteen years she's re-earned her spot in the standings by winning at least one Grand Slam tournament, and last year *Sports Illustrated* named her "Athlete of the Nineties." She's known for being an aggressive, tough—even brutal—player, and her media personality somewhat reflects this. In interviews she can come across like a sharp stick in the eye, but the upside is, she's always been uncondescendingly honest. Needless to say, some of the players are intimidated by her. Tonight, typically, Mariska moved through the crowd, acknowledging the rest of the world with an unapproachable, practiced smile, an expression engineered to get her through the evening and disguise the fact that her mind is somewhere else entirely. On the court she is laserlike in her intensity, but off the court she tends to be unfocused, with a short attention span, almost like a child. She wants what she wants when she wants it. Period. You can find yourself talking to Mariska one minute, then conversing with thin air the next, because when she's had enough of listening to what you have to say, she's finished—even if you're not. Many people here tonight had been the victims of her legendary temper, or cut off by her abruptness. There were probably a couple dozen others who had phone calls in to her that would never be returned. Then there were those who are just plain scared of her, petrified in her presence—not just fans, but players, press, and even officials. Of course, whether they like her or not, virtually everyone is in awe of Mariska's achievements, a fact that only magnifies her flaws, real or perceived. She is very much aware of this. "Everybody always complains that I make all the decisions," Mariska once said to me, "but the fact is that everybody defers to me because they want to make sure I approve of what's happening, or they want to make sure that I'm having a good time. So it just ends up that way."

But of all the women in tennis, Mariska is the one who helped me the most. When I was playing, she took the time to give me tips on rackets and grips—attention many top players won't give to a lesser player on the tour. After my accident, she visited the hospital, sat by the bed, and talked me back from the despair that can only come from losing a career you can't imagine not having. Not that she was Florence Nightingale—she wasn't. Mariska's bedside manner consisted of about twenty sympathetic seconds followed by a barrage of orders: "Get moving—oh, you can't move? Well, wiggle! Get off your butt! Stop feeling sorry for yourself! Stop whining! Grow up!" I was trapped in a bed with bars—I had to listen.

Then two years ago when Gus opened the Springs, Mariska became his charter client, thereby triggering an avalanche of business and landing us a feature story in *Time* magazine. Tonight, Mariska was being honored with a Lifetime Achievement Award, and there's no one who deserved it more. "I've been in the twilight of my career for longer than most people have careers," she often joked, and with no sign of retirement on the horizon, it's the truth. All comers continue to find themselves staring uncomfortably across the net at a demolition machine. If I'd gone to a Gypsy fortuneteller ten years ago, I'd have laughed her out of business if she'd peered into her crystal ball and predicted that I would leave tennis long before Mariska, who was even then, in her mid-twenties, the grand old lady.

"Jordan!" That voice. Smooth as café au lait and equally capable of scalding you to death. It is a deep, professionally honed voice I'd heard say my name many times, with many emotions, starting with a fascination that led to the altar and ending when he said goodbye and walked out on me once and for all. Yes, lunging through the sea of sequins, trailed by a videocam crew and a big-haired ex–Miss America with a microphone, was its possessor, Tim Tulley, cable network sportscaster, commentator, and my ex-husband. He still looked the same—better, actually. Wavy blond hair, green eyes, cleft chin like the kind usually reserved for statues, body only slightly less perfect than his tan. I almost felt sorry for Miss America. It must be devastating to win the pageant and then a few scant years later end up working with a man who was better-looking than you.

I certainly could see what I saw in Tim, but in retrospect I had been insane to marry him. Being competitive myself, I had liked his ambition, his aggressiveness. But there was a downside I hadn't counted on. A man like Tim is perpetually on the Stair-Master of Life—always stepping up to the next, better thing in any category, including job, home, apparel, and women. When I was a rising player, we shared a reasonable number of interests. We were both on the way up, we both liked sports obsessively, we both tended to travel a lot, although usually in different directions. There was also a certain element of opposites attracting, because in many ways we had absolutely nothing in common. For instance, for all his chiseled muscles and sports mania, Tim was totally uncoordinated. In the gym, his trainer had to hand him his weights or he would have dropped them on his foot. Still, things worked out fine for a while. But when I had some really big decisions to make, like would I stay on the tour and go for it or give it up and have another kind of career and possibly think about a family, I had to discuss it with Tim by fax. He'd gotten a promotion, he was unreachable on the road, and he just wasn't there for me. And in fairness, I suppose he could say the same about me. We probably should have had a date, not a marriage. Tim told me he wanted a divorce when I was in the hospital. Bad timing, he said, but he'd wanted to tell me about Ashley for some time. Ashley was his co-reporter at the station at the time. Apparently she was a co–many things at the time. Well, at least he didn't fax me the news.

I wondered whatever had happened to Ashley. Now it appeared that Tim had moved on to beauty queens, climbing to the top of the hairspray hierarchy. God, I hoped he wasn't involved with this one. I couldn't imagine having been married to a man who went on to date a woman who wore a crown and a sash.

They were coming closer. I found myself raising my eyebrows and waving my fingertips, as if to a cocktail-party acquaintance. Like such acquaintances, we are always cordial. But Tim was in a hurry. The crowd was no match for his flying wedge of equipment, and mouthing "Catch you later," his hand cupping Miss America's elbow as if she were a vessel that required steering, Tim passed me in the tidal wave of media racing to catch up with Shaquille O'Neal.

A sudden surge propelled me into the theater lobby, where I found myself standing next to XuXu Martin

Lopez, who is ranked number four in women's tennis, and her mother. Maria Lopez straightened the shoulders of her daughter's dress as if she were preparing her gown for her wedding procession. The Lopezes, mother and daughter, always travel together.

"Hi, Jordan," XuXu beamed at me. Her English is heavily accented but fluent. "You are looking very good. Strong! Soon maybe you play again?"

We both laughed, knowing that wasn't going to happen, but I appreciated the encouragement. In a match she could be a pit bull. She had a typical clay-courter style. Small and pugilistic, she was a retriever and a counterpuncher rather than a creator, covering the court on bandy legs so tenacious you had to pry the points from her. XuXu would have made a wonderful heat-seeking missile. If she had an opportunity, she'd try to smash the ball right in your face, or go for your body instead of the open court. This would cost her points when you ducked and the ball went long, but she didn't seem to care. Next time you played XuXu you'd look across the net and she'd be gunning for you again. Privately, however, XuXu was always warm and friendly. I thought that had a lot to do with her stable home life. Tennis was a family tradition—her father had been one of the top players on the men's tour—but Mrs. Lopez, or Mama, as everyone calls her, was just that: a mother-in-residence. Somehow, without ever speaking a word of English, Mama Lopez always made her point unmistakably clear, which was that she was there to aid and protect her daughter, and she did that job very well. As a teenager on the tour, I'd envied girls like XuXu, whose parents traveled with them. Sometimes my mother made it to the big matches, but after my father died when I was fifteen, more often than not she stayed home in Pasadena with my sister, and except for my coach I was pretty much on my own.

Suddenly Mama Lopez waved excitedly and started chattering in Spanish, and I looked in the direction of her beckoning fingertips to see Marion Stryker, the venerable general manager of the Women's Tennis Association, a fixture on the circuit. Elegant and serene, Marion glided through the crowd like a queen, trailed by the assistant manager, Kanga Cheyne. Marion nodded and smiled to the Lopezes, relegating me to a slight lift of an eyebrow, as though she couldn't quite place me, although of course she could. No one involved with tennis will ever forget the huge buildup she orchestrated for me as the next phenom, the girl who was supposed to follow in the footsteps of Kelly Kendall, America's sweetheart, and become the challenger to Mariska's throne. I was a major disappointment to Marion. I turned out to be neither cute nor all-American, and after a while I started losing my matches, and then I fell off a mountain and never played again. These events had their tragic aspects, but from Marion's point of view, I suppose, it was a lot of time and money invested in building a crowd draw and nothing to show for it. In retrospect, however, she should thank me. My abrupt departure from the scene, my literal fall from grace, left the door wide open for somebody not only more talented but more eminently promotable, somebody the media could latch on to and the crowds would clamor for—specifically, Audrey Armat, the dazzling sixteen-year-old who was currently the number-four woman player in the world, and rising fast.

"There you are!" Mariska, having escaped the photographers, now made her way against the tide of the crush to give me a quick hug. "So how's it going out there in the desert?" Her Russian accent was faint, diluted by many years of Americanization.

"Our new golf course is great. Come out and we'll play," I said, grinning. "We'll play from the blue tees."

"The pro tees? When did you take up golf?"

"Just. But I'll still beat you." The competitive urge never dies. I would play tiddleywinks for blood. Of course, so would she.

"Please. You have more pins in that leg than there are in that fancy new course of yours."

"I'll limp through it." Actually, I was running a couple of miles a week and I felt amazingly good, better than I had ever imagined I could.

"You're on," said Mariska.

"Where's Audrey?" A young woman in a black minidress with a silver plastic Sports Network badge dangling from a chain around her neck appeared beside us. She wore a high-tech remote headset and a small black nylon fanny pack, carried a clipboard, and was accompanied by a distinguished-looking white-haired gentleman I recognized as Milton Bevins, a tour regular. Milt—Uncle Miltie, as the girls called him—had spent years rotating his attentions from player to player, playing fairy godfather and showering various ones in turn with expensive gifts. These days he was attached to Audrey's entourage. Mariska had told me that he once tried to give her a car, and one of the stars of the men's tour had reportedly framed an uncashed $100,000 gift check from Milt, which he swore the bank verified as good. It was rumored that Uncle Miltie had a multimillion-dollar trust fund and a $6 million-a-year annuity with which to facilitate his largesse.

"The producer is looking for Audrey. She missed the rehearsal," said the fanny-pack woman, clearly disgruntled.

"I haven't seen her tonight." Mariska shrugged. She didn't look around the room or devote a fragment of energy to wondering where anybody else might or might not be. Having burned the shoelaces off virtually every up-and-coming young woman player in the past decade, including myself, she seemed to view the never-ending roster of challengers as simply a passing parade. History had yet to prove her wrong, although to my mind her seeming disinterest signaled that, underneath the veneer, she was very aware of her vulnerability. How can you not be, I wondered, when there's no place to go but down?

The fanny-pack woman and Uncle Miltie took off in another direction in search of Audrey. When she made her appearance, Audrey was bound to garner a lot of attention. She always did. The promotions for tonight's event had all prominently featured the fact that she would accept an award as Most Promising Young Female Tennis Player. That was an understatement. This was a girl who by her fifteenth birthday had won ten tournament titles in two years, and this year, at sixteen, nailed the Australian Open for her first Grand Slam victory, setting her up against Mariska for what the media publicized as the Duel of the Grand Slams. The fact that she was strikingly pretty, with strawberry-blond hair and an aloof yet dynamic presence, drew the media like a magnet. Audrey's skills went beyond the basics of playing a brilliant game. She didn't just play matches, she gave performances, feeding the hungry crowd with carefully measured doses of virtuosity combined with a sweetness that was irresistible to fans and the media alike. I'd heard she had a sportswear line, a racket endorsement, and a soft-drink endorsement contract in the works. And she wasn't even out of high school.

I didn't know Audrey beyond a nodding acquaintance, but admittedly all the fuss made me a bit curious. "Do you think Audrey's going to live up to everybody's expectations?" I asked Mariska. I'd seen Audrey play, but of course I'd never played her. Mariska had, many times, and once or twice she'd even lost to her, so she certainly had a basis for comparison.

Mariska frowned slightly. "I don't know. She's good. She can beat me." She paused. "But I feel sorry for her."

"Sorry?" I wanted to understand what Mariska meant, because she had a well-known ability to psych out her opponents, on and off court. It was one of the secrets to her game, how she consistently "routined"—managed to routinely rout—younger, potentially stronger and faster players. Did she mean she felt sorry for what she, better than anyone, knew must lie ahead in a tennis career? A career that is rewarding and terrifying at the same time— the punishing effort, the unending hours of practice, the hotel-room existence, the sacrifice of a social life, the litany of injuries, the expense, the unavoidable zigzags of ecstasy and heartbreak cloaked in the tantalizing promise of glamour that only occasionally, and for the very few, materializes for any duration. Was she responding to expectations that the media were putting on Audrey before the young girl had a real chance to grow up? Or was this just professional competitiveness seeping through? I didn't find out then, because the crowd moved into the theater and Gus was there.

"I changed into my tux in the airport men's room," he said, running a hand through his shaggy, sandy hair. He leafed through a glossy program of the night's events. "But at least I'm here. God knows if I'll ever see my bag again. I tipped the taxi driver to take it to the hotel, but I'm not sure he spoke English. Mariska, if I'd known you looked so much better than me in a tux, I wouldn't have bothered."

"Maybe you should have cleared your outfit with me beforehand, Dr. Gus," she admonished. "But I like the cowboy boots."

Although Gus looked pretty good to me, with his 6'3" thin frame, angular face, and hazel eyes that at the moment seemed gray behind his glasses, he was right. She did look better in a tux. It was part of Mariska's androgynous appeal, an element of her charisma. Gus, like me, was in his natural element outdoors, in denim and khakis, with his sleeves short or rolled up, without a tie. He claimed he had medical evidence that neckties cut off circulation to the brain and shaved several points off your IQ. Even when he was appearing at industry gatherings or giving speeches, his tie was usually in his pocket, and more than once at a fancy restaurant I'd seen the maître d' slip Gus the house tie so that he could be seated.

Gus's love of the outdoors was one reason he chose to apply his psychology specialty to sports. When he entered the field, it had not been a field as such—just a handful of experimenters. He had grown up with the profession, molded elements, made discoveries, accepted challenges, built a practice. His work in helping

Mariska intensify her game and escalate her performance level by monitoring her mental and emotional attitude had brought him to national prominence. After they worked together, Mariska rallied for an incredible midcareer resurgence to win yet another string of Grand Slam titles. Of course, as he always stressed, and was absolutely adamant about, Mariska had done it herself, but there's no doubt Gus was a factor.

"How'd it go in Detroit?" I asked.

"Car people," he said. "They're into golf. I made the Arnold Palmer analogy." A firm nod indicated that it had been a satisfactory speech.

The link between Arnold Palmer and cars was not immediately obvious, even to me, but you can be certain that Gus made it and the audience loved it. He has an amazing talent for linking any activity, state of mind, or business situation to a sports scenario, a knack that resulted in his best-selling book, *Play to Win*, and a constant demand for him to appear on the corporate speaking podium.

Moving into the huge auditorium toward our seats was slow going. Every couple of feet someone reached out to shake Mariska's hand or congratulate her on her award, and several Springs clients, including Jake Stoppard, the Forty-Niners' quarterback, blocked the aisle to greet Gus and me.

"Do you have your acceptance speech written?" I asked Mariska as we finally took our seats.

"Oh God," she said, shuddering. "They just told me today that I had to say something, can you believe it? I wrote down a few notes on some cards, but ..." She shook her head nervously. Mariska could face any opponent across the net, but facing a microphone was something else.

"Maybe you should make the tennis-automotive link," I said, jabbing Gus with my elbow. "Works every time."

"Will everyone please take their seats," a voice announced over the loudspeaker. A band on a riser to the right of the stage began a crashing overture. I showed an usher our tickets: Section 100, Center Aisle A. He pointed us to the area just in front of the stage, where the stars who were going to receive awards were taking their seats. Ours were in the third row.

"They have to start on time," said the woman in the seat next to me to nobody in particular. "It's live TV."

An entertainer I didn't recognize came out on the stage and introduced himself as the warm-up act. Brandishing a cigar, he told the audience the ground rules: "No leaving, no flash photography, no waving to the camera if it points at you, 'cause you'll look like a putz." The stage was set up in a quasi-Greek-classic look, with three giant video monitors, each encased in a massive column. A long table held the awards, several dozen shimmering Lucite obelisks guarded by a man in a black jumpsuit and white gloves. There was an especially vibrant rendition of "New York, New York," and an announcer boomed, "Welcome to the fifth annual Sports Network Awards, with special guest, Bill Murray." Bill bounded onstage in a Chicago Cubs cap, a baseball shirt under his tuxedo.

Then I felt it. A familiar vibration, this time inside my jacket, on my thigh. The beeper. Simultaneously, Gus motioned to his tuxedo pocket. His beeper. The two of us rose in unison.

Instantly, a producer in black tie and headphones crouched in front of us and yanked us down. "You can't leave now," he hissed. "You're in the front section. It won't look good on camera."

"Sorry," I said. "It's an emergency."

He probably wished he could get Ollie Cedars, who was on Gus's left, to throw himself in front of us and block our path, but we edged past him and headed toward the aisle. As we left, I heard the producer whisper frantically, "Get some fillers in here!" A man and woman in evening dress materialized from thin air and stepped in front of us, taking our seats almost before we'd left them.

"I wonder what they're serving at the party afterward," I whispered.

"Probably just your basic McSmoked salmon, pâté de foie gras, Dom Pérignon," said Gus wistfully.

"Ugh," I pronounced. "Foie gras. Do you know where that comes from? They take these geese and force-feed them with tubes . . ."

"Spare me the lecture. Then again, it could be a wrong number. Or something that can wait till tomorrow. There's always that possibility."

"Maybe two hundred grams of solid goose fat is good for you. There's always that possibility, too." I leaned against the lobby wall as we both pulled out our cellular phones. "If this isn't life-or-death, I'm going to kill Tony."

I got through first. Tony, my administrative assistant, was breathless. "Jordan, I hope you're packed," he said. "You and Gus have to get back to the Springs right away, tonight." There was a dramatic pause.

"Why? What's the crisis?" Tony's flair for the theatrical could not be underestimated.

"A VIP client is arriving tonight on an emergency basis. Strictly hush-hush." I could hear the computer keys clicking furiously in the background as Tony typed. He is one of those fast-motion people who are always doing two things at once, which makes him a particularly valuable assistant. "It's an unusual circumstance, I admit," Tony continued, lowering his voice conspiratorially as if he were worried that the line might be tapped, "and I don't have all the details, but the client is insisting on immediate attention from Dr. Laidlaw, and Mr. Stokes thinks it would be best if you were available, too."

Bill Stokes, a former Olympic gold medal–winning marathoner who once had his face on a cereal box, is the cofounder of the Springs and Gus's partner. Ten years ago they teamed up to develop and patent Pro-Aide, an electrolyte and nutrient energy replacement drink for athletes which they sold to a soft-drink company for millions of dollars. They then used the money as seed capital to found the Springs.

"Who is the client?"

"Frankly, I don't know. They wouldn't tell me—it's that secret. Dr. Laidlaw will probably have the details."

"But, Tony, how are we going to get out tonight? We don't have plane reservations and Gus doesn't even know where his suitcase is."

"The client has sent a private jet to the Marine Terminal at La Guardia. It's waiting on the tarmac with orders to take off as soon as you arrive. Your car is in front of the theater right now to take you straight to the airport. Obviously, it's a matter of utmost urgency. Let me worry about the luggage. I'll call your hotel. The Intercontinental, wasn't it? The concierge will arrange to have your bags packed and then FedEx your stuff back here. There wasn't any medicine in there that you needed or anything, was there?"

"No. But I'm not exactly in my travel clothes."

"No time to change. Happy trails."

"Till we meet again." I pushed the END and CLEAR buttons, turned the phone off, and returned it to my purse.

Gus was still talking, and I could make out snatches of conversation. "Right. Right. Are you sure? Actually, I'd prefer a one-on-one situation, Bill. I see. I suppose so, Bill. Yes." He paused to search his pockets, pull out a wadded paper cocktail napkin from some event long past, and scribble a note on it. "Fine. We're leaving now."

We retraced our steps out of the lobby and down the escalators.

"I can't stand the suspense," I said. "Who's the mystery client?"

"Audrey Armat."

"Audrey!" That explained why they wanted me. I was the point person for women's tennis. "But she's supposed to be getting an award on live television in fifteen minutes."

"Global Sport will handle the situation. They've got plenty of coverage here tonight. They'll arrange for somebody to accept for Audrey." Global Sport, the biggest and most powerful sports talent agency in the world, was capable of handling any situation, from a press conference to Desert Storm.

"And what's the emergency? Audrey has a pimple?"

A Town Car was waiting at the curb on Sixth Avenue. A light summer rain had started, and the driver got out with an umbrella and held it over us as we climbed into the backseat.

"Her game is slipping."

"Well, that's not a good thing. I'm sure it's a serious problem, and we can probably help. But we're supposed to rush out in the dead of night, fly across the country, and put her in serve-and-volley ICU?"

"Something like that." The car turned and headed for the Midtown Tunnel. In the darkness I could see Gus's jaw clenching and unclenching, something he did when he was trying to figure things out. "It's bizarre. I don't get it, either, but we won't know much till we get there. Bill shorthanded the explanation. I don't think even he has the story." Gus squinted at the scribbles on the cocktail napkin, as if they contained the answer. "What do you know about Audrey?"

"Well, I remember seeing pictures of her in *People* magazine when she was a little kid, four or five years old, whacking at tennis balls with a sawed-off racket. By the time she was nine, they had 'star' written all over her. By the time she was ten, she had a clothing deal."

"What about her game?" Gus asked.

"Her game is incredible. A hundred-plus-mile-an-hour serve. Best second serve in women's tennis, and a running forehand down the line that most pros only dream about. A real power game. She was just coming onto the tour when I was leaving—but I've watched her play. Totally consistent, and what she can't put away she runs down. Lots of endorsements, even before she turned pro. Off the court, she sort of keeps apart from the other players, but that's to be expected. She's young. Travels with her family. Her father's her coach, and she has a twin brother who's her hitting partner. I've never met him. Anyhow, she pulled a hamstring muscle a few months ago. Then, in February, she played a terrible final at the Lipton, and had just lost in the first round at Amelia Island. I assumed the leg was bothering her. Maybe it's worse, and they're worried about Wimbledon. But why can't this hold till morning? Or at least until we eat dinner and change clothes?"

"Apparently her family is very concerned that she get immediate attention."

In other words, the mother was hysterical. Corinne Armat's tantrums were legendary. I had personally witnessed one. Three years ago, when I was on the staff of the Women's Tennis Association, I was what they call a primary health-care provider for the women's circuit, one of the people who travel from tournament to tournament giving on-premises physical therapy. I was working Wimbledon when Audrey made the semis. It was one of those rain-soaked Wimbledons, and I'd taken a break to dash to the players' lounge for some of the legendary strawberries and cream and a cup of hot tea. I was dripping wet, standing with my tray in the cafeteria checkout line. Mrs. Armat was in front of me—God, I'll never forget her outfit. Two prints that didn't match and a huge gold lamé Chanel purse with handles, like a shopping bag—anyway, she was complaining that the carrots and peas were not organic, that she refused to put pesticides in her daughter's system, and I remember standing there as the dampness seeped down to my skin while she kept up this tirade.

Somehow, heading back to the airport at nine o'clock

at night, dinnerless, for a six-hour flight in a cocktail dress and heels that suddenly had taken on the ability to strangle feet where they stood, I had a premonition that I might soon be able to empathize all too well with those unfortunate vegetables.

"Gus," I said, kicking off my shoes, "this mother is one step from the edge. A major prima donna."

Gus laughed softly in the darkness. "Nothing we can't handle, I'm sure. Haven't we seen our share of prima donnas in this business?"

"The golfer who wanted me to baby-sit her pet monkey . . ."

"Now, there's a real nut case." Gus burst out laughing, and so did I, because my own dog has gotten more than her fair share of star treatment—but then, she is a dog, and not your average dog. And now that I'm on the other side of the fence, a lot of things that I used to take for granted seem pretty ridiculous to me. "How about the baseball player who complained about the mixed nuts on the Learjet that we sent for him?"

"The coach who wanted us to install a special bathtub for his three-day stay at the clinic?"

"And his girlfriend, who was on the lemon diet?"

"Maybe we could make a board game of this."

"How about, roll the dice: if you like Monopoly, you'll love Idiosyncrasy?"

We laughed again, but we were both on the alert. Knowing Corinne Armat, I was actually very uneasy. I had the feeling that we were about to take off straight into a whirlwind that could turn into a full-fledged hurricane.

TWO

In the way things always happen when you travel, the light summer shower that started when we left for the airport transformed itself into a raging thunderstorm, and so, after a long and unwelcome weather delay, it was three o'clock in the morning, Pacific Standard Time, when we finally arrived at Palm Springs Regional Airport, and even then I wasn't able to go home. The vigilant Tony, baseball cap pulled to the top of his wire-rimmed glasses, had met us at the plane and hurried us into one of the Springs' fleet of white Jeep Cherokees.

At this hour it was about a twenty-minute trip to Indian Wells, where the clinic was located on the edge of the desert. We cut straight across Gene Autry Trail, missing the town of Palm Springs itself. I love the fact that in Palm Springs you can drive on streets named after celebrities: Gerald Ford, Frank Sinatra, Bob Hope, Dinah Shore, Gene Autry. It's kind of wild to tell a friend, "I'll meet you at Bob Hope and Dinah Shore." We headed east on the highway, past the shopping centers, car dealers, fast-food places, developments, through Rancho Mirage, past the cappuccino place and the dried-fruit shop that makes the best date milk shakes in the world, because they are probably the only date milk shakes in the world, through Desert Palm and past the great resorts, and, finally, just before hitting the desert and miles of sand and scrub, reached Indian Wells. A velvety night sky was slung across the desert, and an almost full moon silhouetted the spiky shrubbery and white stucco buildings against the rugged shape of the Chocolate Hills as we passed through the security gate and down the palm tree–lined drive. Even in the dead of night it was an impressive facility, a beautiful place as well as one of the world's most advanced multisport training centers. The lushly landscaped grounds included fifteen tennis courts with Deco turf, hard Har-Tru, red clay and grass surfaces, rebound Ace, and even an indoor Supreme court; a regulation basketball court; a baseball and a softball field; a soccer field; a 500,000-gallon superpool; and a new eighteen-hole golf course. We drove past the cutting-edge fitness center that also housed physical-therapy facilities and the technical core for computerized nutritional profiling and tracking and videotaped motion analysis of golf swings and tennis strokes. The staff buildings, next to the parking lot we now pulled into, contained the offices of the cream of a crop culled from all aspects of medicine, including sports psychologists, rehabilitationists, acupuncturists, homeopathic specialists, licensed nutritionists, an osteopath, and a visiting professor of kinesiology and bioengineering. This was a multimillion-dollar operation, highly capitalized: Gus and Bill had staked their careers and their fortunes on its success, and so far it had shown a strong beginning and steady growth.

Bill was waiting in his office, which was the largest in the complex. During the day there was a sweeping view of the grounds and the mountains beyond, but tonight there was just the nothingness of blackness beyond the windows and our own reflections on the glass, four people struggling to stay awake. I was glad I'd been able to get a few hours' sleep in on the plane, because we weren't wasting any time here on the amenities, or even the necessities.

"Well, I'm glad you dressed for the occasion," Bill said, lowering his glasses. "Nice outfit. Maybe we should instate a formal dress code. Appeal to the fashion element."

"Ha ha." My sense of humor must have been sleeping. I kicked off my shoes.

As always, Bill did not seem rumpled or even wrinkled. I wondered just how he achieved this permanent state of permanent press. He wore khakis and a fresh pink cotton shirt with French cuffs and cuff links featuring the Springs' palm-tree logo, a white Springs windbreaker tied loosely around his shoulders. His buff suede shoes did not have a scuff on them. He sported his trademark crew cut, a style he had not changed since his days on the Olympic team, his hair now grayed into distinction. After he won an Olympic gold medal in his early twenties, Bill had effortlessly made the leap to the Wheaties box, then on to the U.S. Olympic Committee and then the corporate world, buoyed by his expansive personality, keen intelligence, and an innate knack for public relations and fund-raising. Gus and Bill are very different, but they share the characteristic of being among the small percentage of people who routinely make their dreams reality. Within five years of the day they met, they broke ground for the Desert Springs Sports Science Clinic. Six months later, they recruited me to join them.

"Tony," Bill said, "how's that coffee coming?"

"I'm improvising," he yelled from down the hall.

"No coffee for me," I called out. I try to avoid caffeine, although in this case, I must admit, I would have appreciated its effects. In my experience, a call for coffee at three-something A.M. is never a good sign. The Springs has its own health-food kitchen, store, and juice bar, and we grow our own organic fruits and vegetables on the premises, but none of that was available now.

"This had better be good," said Gus through a yawn. "Or at least life-and-death." He dropped into a chair and propped his feet up on a wastebasket. For as long as I've known him, Gus has always been looking for a place to put his feet.

I leaned against the wall, hoping it would hold me up, and accepted a paper cup of orange juice and a Twinkie from Tony. I'm a vegetarian on principle, due to my love of animals, but as far as I know, there's never been a Twinkie with a face.

"As you both know, Audrey Armat is here with her parents. Her brother is also here—he's her twin; they're very close and he's her only hitting partner. As for the red alert, I admit this is not usual procedure, and I apologize to both of you for bringing you here in the middle of the night. But the Armats are insisting on getting to work at seven A.M."

I rechecked my watch. That was in three and a half hours.

"What's the urgency, as you see it, Bill?" asked Gus.

"Well, frankly, I can't put my finger on it, and that's exactly why I think it might be urgent, besides what the parents are demanding. I got a call from Ted Robb at Global Sport. He's Audrey's commercial agent, the liaison with her sponsorship deals. Those guys always put on a front like everything's fine and dandy, but you know that if you hear from them it's not just to get your address for their Christmas-card list. Ted was concerned, and he downplayed it, but I got the distinct impression that they made a very strong suggestion to the Armats that Audrey should come here for a little fine-tuning before the big Grand Slams. That's what they're shooting for—the high-visibility tournaments. And sponsors don't go for losing players. Apparently, her father saw the light."

"Emilio Armat, Audrey's father, is also her coach," I said. "He's always been her only coach. From what I see, the family's a pretty closed unit. There's no entourage, no outsiders. Maybe just Ted Robb for the endorsement deals, because you can't get along in tennis without the cooperation of Global Sport. They control too many of the major tournaments, and of course they represent all the big players." I knew about this personally: Global Sport had once represented me.

Bill flicked on his computer and punched the keyboard to bring up a file. "Audrey's record has been astonishingly good, until recently."

Gus leaned behind the computer monitor. "Let's have a look at her rankings since she turned pro three years ago—she was number fourteen in 1991, number eight in 1992, and number four in 1993. Ten career wins, including one Australian Open."

"She pretty much started at the top," I said. "Audrey was born in the top fifteen." I unwrapped the Twinkie, bit off the spongy end, and sucked the plastic cream. It was amazing how, at this hour, I could fool myself into believing that the stuff tasted like a semblance of an edible food product. Clearly, I had become a zombie. Disgusted with myself, I tossed the Twinkie into the wastebasket. Hopefully, it was at least biodegradable.

"Ten tournament wins, two of them Grand Slams," Gus noted.

"She hasn't won Wimbledon yet, or the U.S. Open. Those are on the agenda for this year, if you believe the press," I said.

"Not much of a doubles player, is she?"

"She could be, but her father concentrates her career on singles. That's where the glamour is. And the money."

"What about personal details?" asked Bill. "Any boyfriend on the scene?"

"Actually, she's supposedly had a thing going with Alex Bracht, one of the top-ranked men," I said. "Of course, at Audrey's age that could mean a lot or it could mean nothing. But I seem to recall reading that he gave her a ring of some sort." The two of them had been a teen-swoon-type item for over a year, with lots of holding-hands- and close-dancing-type pictures in the tabloids. But then again, the professional tennis circuit is hardly conducive to romance. The men and the women don't interact all that much, you don't meet anybody else—in fact, armed guards keep most of the male population away from you—and the practice schedule precludes just about any discretionary time. Unlike other sports, pro tennis is a year-round commitment. Between the Grand Slam circuit, exhibitions, satellite matches, and, for many players, team tennis, there is no real "season," just a nonstop cavalcade of constant events and a few scattered weeks off.

"What do you know about the boyfriend?" asked Bill intently.

"Alex is one of the tennis brat pack, Mr. Macho, Mr. Tantrum, Mr. Throw Your Racket. A bad boy. Bleaches his hair. Makes a big deal out of changing his shirt between sets. Very showy. They don't seem like the same type, but then, opposites attract."

"How long has Bracht been in the picture?" asked Gus.

"I'm not sure, but I think for a while."

"Did they have a fight recently? Break up? Teenage girls have lots of boyfriend problems."

I hope Gus didn't have to get a medical degree to learn that. "You know, there's something else," I said. "Audrey pulled a muscle a few months ago. If it didn't heal properly, that could certainly account for a performance problem. That's easy to check out."

"Emilio Armat told me that as he sees it, it's mental—Audrey's motivation is falling off," said Bill.

"We see it all the time," said Gus. "It doesn't have to be a boyfriend or a physical injury. There's always a cycle of stress and de-motivation. Peak performance is a question of controlling the cycle, picking your moments, so you don't fall apart, say, in the finals at the U.S. Open. It's one thing to possess the physical skills, but can you always count on them when the pressure is on?"

Bill nodded. "True. But if the slide continues, and she can't pick her moments, and she loses the big ones this summer, apparently there are some major endorsement opportunities at stake. Seven figures. The Armats want to nip it in the bud, and they feel there's not a moment to waste. I thought it would be good for us to be as responsive as possible. This is the kind of business we need." He didn't have to add that as a new business, we had to build our client list, and Audrey Armat was a showcase client.

"I can't believe they're here, to tell you the truth," I interrupted.

Bill was surprised to hear me say this. "Why not? We are the best. Where else are they going to go?"

"It's not us—don't get me wrong—it's them. The Armats have never gone outside their own family for anything. Ever. Well, Global Sport may be the one exception—they're their bridge to the sponsors. For example, Audrey never dishes the dirt with the girls on the tour. It's like she's her parents' creation, there's this invisible shield they've set up around her and nobody's allowed to pass through it, for fear of breaking the image. They pulled her out of classes—she's tutored by her parents and they fax her homework in to some private school. She won't even hit with anybody except her brother, which is the next best thing to hitting to herself, since he's her twin. Frankly, bringing her here doesn't add up."

"They've exhausted the options, I suspect," said Bill. "And I'm sure Ted Robb made it clear that there's a lot at stake, in the way only agents can. Mrs. Armat seemed especially—shall we say—nervous. It's a very stressful situation."

I could well imagine.

"She may be a champion, but she's a teen," said Gus. He had written a well-received book on parent coaching techniques. "Rebellion is very common at this stage."

"I read that she threw her racket in a match a few weeks ago," I said. "That's unusual enough for her that it made the news."

Gus nodded. "At this age, they're synthesizing everything. It puts them under a lot of pressure. They're becoming more aware, less instinctive. There's an awakening that's sexual, among other things. Their needs change. They even start to eat differently— Let's put Joan on call." Joan Edgemont was our nutritionist. Tony made a note and rushed out of the room, probably to phone the poor woman. "Audrey's at the point developmentally where authority figures like parents are losing their grip on her. I suspect the Armats can't do it alone anymore, and that's why they're here."

"Well," I said, "we're authority figures, too, aren't we?"

"We're not relatives," Gus said. "And, for God's sake, the last thing we should do is take the authoritative approach."

"Good," said Bill, handing out a set of computer fact sheets on Audrey's background to each of us. "That's why I felt it was important for us to meet before we're face-to-face with Audrey tomorrow morning. Gus, will you brief us on how to approach this?"

Gus stretched in his chair. "First of all, it's a game. Don't dictate or preach—that's disastrous with teens. Make everything a game if you can. Keep it fun, make her want to cooperate. And, Bill, as I said on the phone, I'd frankly prefer not to have the parents be part of this."

Bill sighed. "Understood. But I'm afraid that's not an option. These parents have an iron grip."

"That's probably a big part of the problem. But maybe if we talk to them we can get them to back off while she's here. At least they can understand that tennis may be an individual sport, but this is a team effort, and as parents they have to be able to remain objective to make the team effective."

Bill turned to me. "Now, Jordan. You'll be in charge of Audrey's physical therapy, so you'll be alone with her in the training room. Obviously, the parents aren't going to be holding her hands while you're working on her leg muscles. And you've been a young player yourself. Maybe you'll be able to get her to open up."

"Of course, first I'll want to determine that she's healthy," I said. "But it's possible she'll talk to me." That kind of thing was not uncommon. As a physical therapist you literally have another person in your hands. You're invading their space, communicating at every level. People feel comfortable with you, and a security factor sets in. People drop their guard, talk, tell you things—often not overtly, but you learn to watch and listen. This is a critical point of trust, and something I would never abuse.

"We'll follow the usual protocol—do a medical and nutritional workup first," said Gus. "Then we'll talk, and get her out for some on-court work. We'll look for any imbalances, chronic over- or undertraining. Motivation problems are usually a symptom of imbalance. And that's the window. When you're not motivated, when you pull out that cornerstone, the whole thing collapses."

Bill stood up. "Jordan, whether this thing turns out to be psychological or physical or a combination, you'll be our point person on this. We'll all back you up, but it's you this girl's going to feel most comfortable with. I've arranged to clear your schedule while she's here so you can give Audrey a hundred percent of your attention." He handed me a thick file. "What's not in here is on-line on our computer system. Familiarize yourself. I want you to know every shot she's ever made, every match she's won, get it down cold. At least it's a starting point." He checked his watch but registered no emotion at the ungodliness of the hour or the thickness of the file. "Okay, I think we know where to get started. Let's go home and get some rest. See you all back here at seven."

"What you've just said is a total contradiction, Bill," I mumbled.

"What, Jordan? I can't hear you." He loped out of his office without showing a shred of fatigue, much less deafness. The man could probably have gone straight out and won a decathlon.

I quickly made some calculations. My town house was in a small complex about ten minutes from the Springs. I probably had time to go home, take a shower, wash my hair, lie down for half an hour, walk and feed A.M., do a few stretching exercises, which I never miss, no matter what, take a shower, eat a bite of something, get dressed, and make it back here by seven. I probably couldn't sleep anyhow. I was too revved up.

"Can I drop you at home, Jordan?" asked Tony, stifling a yawn.

"Thanks, but I'll take one of the Jeeps from the fleet. Gus, I can give you a ride if you want."

"Great," he said. Gus needed a shave, and he looked asleep on his feet, for which I didn't blame him. He'd also had the Detroit speech on his itinerary today. Or by now I guess it was yesterday. It had been a long haul. Hours like these were one reason why Gus's marriage hadn't worked out, he'd told me—but I had a feeling that if Gus had a job that didn't require eighty hours a week, he'd be bored and change jobs.

"I stopped by your place earlier tonight and walked and fed A.M.," said Tony. "She'll be glad you're back early."

I smiled. Tony has my keys, and I know he'd do anything—not for me, but for A.M. A.M., or Alice Marble, as her full, unpedigreed name reads, in honor of the legendary tennis champion, is my Jack Russell terrier—or, let's be realistic, I am her human. She usually goes everyplace with me, and the staff at the Springs has adopted her. She's much more popular than her owner. With most people, that is.

"That dog gets better treatment than your clients, and certainly than your friends," grumbled Gus as we headed for the parking lot.

"Why not? I don't see my clients or my friends licking my toes. In fact, I don't see you doing that, either."

"Thank God for that."

I dropped Gus off, and it was five o'clock when I finally turned into the Sandstone Canyon Villas, as my complex is called, and waved to Sammy, the guard. I live in a gated community of town house condominiums on the edge of a golf course. The buildings are chocolate and beige stucco with red terra-cotta tiled roofs and balconies with curlicue wrought iron, a sort of combination of modern and Moorish. Without a doubt I'm the youngest person in the complex. My youngest neighbor is in his seventies. It's an expensive, safe, easy place to live, with great weather and golf course and tennis access, hallmarks of a retirement community. But that's exactly why I like it. I'm not up for socializing with a lot of thronging singles, listening to the noise of screaming kids or mowing any lawns. If it grows, it grows, and I'm happy to look at it, but I'm not going to go out there and weed it. To me that's part of the beauty of the desert and the mountains. You don't have to landscape them or decorate them. They're just there, better than anything you'd ever imagine.

I put the key in my lock. Behind the door, I heard the welcoming committee barking on cue.

"Honey," I called out, "I'm home."

As the door swung open, A.M. made a vertical leap into my arms, tongue lapping, stubby tail wagging furiously. I was home. That might not mean much to most people, but until I bought the town house, my entire adult life had consisted of a crash pad level of domesticity. My previous homes, in Miami and then St. Petersburg, had been rooms in apartments shared with three other women. I was on the road so much in my job with the WTA that it didn't make sense to carry a lease and buy furniture for a place I was never in. So that house was just one more stop along the way. After the divorce, I wanted to travel light. For the six months that I was married to Tim I'd simply moved into his place, a bride's paradise of leather upholstery and shag rugs so thick you could have mowed them. I should have known: the apartment reflected his permanent bachelor mentality. Before that I had a token home, my mother's, but my real life was nomadic—traveling the globe and pitching my tent in an endless series of hotel rooms, then tearing down camp and moving on to the next, going back to the same places year after year, occasionally renting a furnished apartment or house. It wasn't that I couldn't afford anything more—I had a comfortable, if not bulging, nest egg set aside from my winnings at an age when most girls had their life savings in a piggybank—but I never had the feeling of staying in one place long enough to put down roots. One of the reasons Wimbledon was my favorite tournament was that I loved the house I rented there for the two weeks of the championships, a little brick Tudor with a tiny English garden. Now, at last, I had a house of my own.

I'm really proud of my house. It's simple but comfortable. I decorated it myself in colors that reflect the desert—earth tones of browns, beige, rose, and red. I had the living room ceiling sponge-painted to resemble clouds drifting across the desert sky. There's no leather, of course, and I've tried to use natural materials and colors wherever possible. One of the reasons I bought this house is the fact that the builder was ecologically sensitive. For instance, there are water-saver shower heads and plumbing fixtures in the bathroom, there are built-in recycling bins in the kitchen, and there's a place to compost my garbage in the garden. I'm trying to do my part. I use rechargeable batteries and recycled toilet paper, and there is no Styrofoam in my cupboards.

I went into the kitchen, squeezed a couple of oranges in my juicer, and made a bowl of custom-mixed granola and soy milk. I picked up the remote control and flicked on CNN. It's a habit I picked up on the road. Since it's on twenty-four hours a day, you can get it anytime, and watching it provided a small measure of constancy and the sound of a human voice when I moved from city to city, hotel room to hotel room—and, best of all, it's always in English. A breakfast bar of Mexican tiles separates my kitchen from the combination dining area/living room, and I pulled up a bar stool to watch whatever was on. The living room has a double-height ceiling, a peach canvas-covered U-shaped couch, the white rug I bought in Greece, and the glass and brass coffee table with spiky sprays of dried flowers. The curtains were closed, but I had a nice patio outside. It was designed for entertaining, which I almost never do. But if I ever do decide to have somebody over, I'm in great shape. Over the kitchen cabinets is a honeycomb of wine racks that hold my wines from the different regions of Europe where I've played or worked on the tour, and I must say, it would be the envy of even the snobbiest wine connoisseur.

The glass shelves bracketing the stone fireplace are lined with books, cassettes, and photo albums. There are about two hundred trophies there—a conglomeration of engraved silver plates, wood and brass plaques, little rackets mounted on stands, crystal obelisks, engraved bronze tennis balls, and tiny statuettes. These were all trophies I won before I turned pro. When my mother moved into a smaller apartment two years ago, she boxed them up and sent them to me.

"It seems like such a shame to throw them out," she'd said. I'd just moved into the town house and there was a lot of empty shelf space to fill, so I kept them. Mom put the trophies from my professional career in storage somewhere. I really don't want anything to do with them. Those trophies seemed to taunt me with evidence of career promise unfulfilled, commitment left unmade, while the junior ones—collected when tennis was still fun, a game, not a job—had some sort of sentimental value.

I'd won many of the trophies in the shelf unit when I was about Audrey's age. I'd started at age ten—late, for tennis—and my mother had insisted that I finish high school and go to college. As I grew older, moved up in the ranking and turned pro, it became harder and harder to choose one path or the other, so I chose both. It didn't work, but at least I'd had a childhood. I'm not saying it was normal to be in the quarters of the French Open one week and back in high school taking finals the next, but it seemed normal to me at the time, because that was what I knew. Audrey didn't even have that much, but like me, she probably didn't question it.

Killing the next three hours was not hard. I let A.M. trot around outside for about five minutes. Then I trudged upstairs and lay down on the bed for a minute to read my briefing papers. I made a point of avoiding the den, which is my euphemism for the second upstairs bedroom. I knew that if I looked in there all I'd see was the monster pile of paperwork and bills that was heaped on my desk. I hate sitting in a closed room, even in my own house, picking over administrative details. When I was on the tour I had an agent, a lawyer, an accountant, and my mother to take care of these things. Now I have to think about mortgages and insurance policies and water bills and vet bills and all the minutiae of the real world, and it drives me crazy. I've decided I'm in denial about all this, which is good, since admitting the problem is the first step toward solving it. The second step is to close the door on it, which is what I usually do until one of those bills comes in with a "Final Notice" stamp on the envelope. Once, they actually turned off my phone. It's too bad, because the den is otherwise a nice room, with a balcony, and a soft love seat that converts into a guest bed. In case I ever get nostalgic, which I don't, there's also my Wall of Keys, where I hammered in about a hundred hooks and hung my collection of hotel keys. This started by accident, when I forgot to return a key, then grew to collection status. I also have all my laminated player's passes from tournaments I have played. When I retired from the circuit, my friend Cassie took them and had them made into a giant, framed collage. That's on another wall.

My bedroom is less emotionally conflicting. It features my treasured Italian pottery, each piece of which I personally dragged back from some off-the-beaten-track-type craft shop somewhere in the countryside outside Rome. There's a huge urn on the floor by my bed, some nesting bowls on top of my armoire, and a flat glazed tray on top of my dresser, where I toss my keys, wallet, and tickets. There's a beautiful view of the San Jacinto range, with its sometimes snowcapped peaks, but I like to sleep late, so there are heavy blackout curtains that eliminate all sense of time, weather, and season when you draw them. The bed is made of extremely sturdy stripped bleached wood logs—nothing tropical— with a striped beige and rose spread. Actually, I dislike this spread. It weighs so much I barely bother to take it off the bed. Hanging it over its stand is like dragging a carcass across the floor. Tonight I didn't even get around to turning it back. I fell asleep and woke up two hours later purely by instinct, with barely enough time to shower and throw on pants and a blouse and sweater. The new backless navy blue dress, whose lack of a back had never been seen outside the store where I bought it, went back into the closet for another millennium.

T H R E E

A.M. and I made it to the clinic by 6:45. It was already a sparkling day, bright, with a light wind fanning the palm fronds and the splashes of vermillion bougainvillea that tumbled over the stucco walls. I flagged Tony in the parking lot as he passed by on a golf cart.

"God, what a zoo yesterday," he said.

"Yeah, it did run late."

"Well, the early part was worse." He grimaced. "That Corinne Armat—what a piece of work."

"So I've heard." I punched my code into the security system and we let ourselves into the glass lobby of the building.

"First she refused to fill out the releases—she says she never signs anything that their lawyer hasn't looked over. Then we didn't have the right kind of water available for Audrey. Then there was the whole thing about getting you and Gus back here. She referred to the people on the staff as a "skeleton crew," as if she were getting the second string or something. It was really ridiculous."

"So what are you going to do?"

Tony pulled a list out of his pocket and waved it.

"Mrs. A's orders: I'm going to make sure every raspberry, melon slice, and kiwi on the goddamn fruit plate is fucking organic, and God help them if they made the ice cubes out of tap water." He veered off purposefully toward the kitchen.

My office is small, but it has its features. There's a view of the inner atrium courtyard with its homage to the desert, a sandscape complete with botanically accurate flora, and a collection of framed pictures of A.M. with various sports stars. The real dog sat under the desk, on a towel at my feet. I was at the computer, scrolling through the files Bill had given me, when he appeared in the doorway with our newest clients.

"And this is Jordan Myles, who'll be handling the physical therapy portion of our program," Bill said as I jumped to my feet. "I'm sure you've met on the tour."

Corinne Armat squinted her eyes as if to edit the memory. She was a tiny, small-boned woman who nonetheless gave the impression that she could move pianos in her spare time. She was one of those women who obviously had been very attractive once, maybe twenty years ago, and she'd tried to freeze her look at that point in time. Her red hair was lacquered into a permanent seventies rerun "wings" style. She wore a yellow quilted Chanel bomber jacket, a Chanel waist purse, stirrup pants, and yellow suede heels.

"She's the tennis player?" she asked. From the way she said it, I could tell that it was Bill who had wanted me here, certainly not the Armats.

"Former," I said, trying to keep things breezy. "In a previous life."

"Jordan is our top physio," said Bill. "Here at the Springs we follow what we call the Total Body System, which is a total training program. We interrelate the player's psychology and physiology with their natural talent and skills. And Jordan certainly empathizes with the players, having been one herself."

Mrs. Armat pursed her lips as if sucking an invisible straw. "We thought we made it clear that we wanted Audrey's little visit here kept strictly confidential. With someone so closely aligned to the tennis community involved . . ." She cast a glance at me, as if it were obvious to all but the most obtuse that I was an information leak waiting to burst. Her false eyelashes were so thick I thought her eyelids were in danger of dropping shut at any moment. "How can we be sure that will be the case?"

Yes, I had indeed recalled her accurately. "Mrs. Armat," I said succinctly, "we're all professionals."

Emilio Armat stepped diplomatically in front of his wife, looked around the office expansively, took my hand, and shook it warmly. A heavy gold signet ring gleamed on his finger. Audrey's father was known as one of the most handsome and charming men in tennis, and his smile and sunny nature seemed to bear that out. He was over six feet tall, deeply tanned, about forty-five, with curly salt-and-pepper hair, piercing navy blue eyes, a cleft chin, and deep dimples that appeared when he smiled. His custom-tailored golf shirt revealed muscular arms and a tapered waistline that had probably not expanded an inch in twenty years. Around his neck were several heavy gold chains, including one with a large gold A^2 insignia, studded with diamonds. "I look forward to working with you, Jordan," he said. His voice was measured, with a faint accent of indeterminate origin, as if English were his second language, or he had taught himself grammar through a mail-order course. "You were a very talented player. I have studied tapes of your finals match at Wimbledon."

I tried not to wince. That match had been both my finest hour and biggest horror. It was a textbook case of snatching defeat from the jaws of victory. "I'm looking forward to working with Audrey, too," I said.

Audrey, dressed in a pink warm-up suit, was leaning against the door frame. She was even taller than I am, but the coltishness often seen in young girls was replaced by a fluidity of line apparent even now. She was pretty and strawberry-blond, her hair tied in a high ponytail, mirrored sunglasses hiding her trademark turquoise eyes. She hesitated a moment, then straightened her shoulders, raised her head, removed the sunglasses, and smiled brilliantly, as if going onstage. She had her father's dimples—and, with these simple gestures, an unmistakable flash of star power that she seemed to be able to flip on with some inner switch.

"Hi, Jordan," she said sweetly. She walked toward me with her hand outstretched, and her handshake was firm.

"How're you doing, Audrey?"

"I guess you know how it goes." She sighed and pointed to her leg. "My knee is still giving me trouble. It really hurts. You'll see."

"Don't worry. We'll figure it out." I tried to sound reassuring.

"This is Audrey's brother, my son E.J.," said Emilio, fairly pushing a sullen young man into my office.

E.J. nodded perfunctorily. "H'llo," he mumbled. I reached out for a halfhearted handshake. Looking at him was disconcerting—he was like a photo negative of his sister. They were the same height and build. Their faces were almost identical—similar carved features and bowed lips; but where Audrey's hair was fair, E.J.'s was black, like his father's once must have been, and his skin and eyes were dark. A shock of hair escaped from a ponytail about the same length as his sister's and hung over his eyes, and he peered out through it listlessly. The main difference between the two was not in coloration or sex, but energy level. Audrey seemed a palomino colt, collected and conditioned, with a pale aura of power beneath her little-girl charm. On the other hand, it was difficult to imagine her brother summoning the energy to pick up a tennis racket, much less function as the hitting partner of his world-class sister.

"This way, Audrey," commanded Corinne Armat, her voice the verbal equivalent of a yank at the ear, and the foursome, flanked by Gus and Bill, moved on to the next stop on the tour. Emilio Armat turned, shrugged, and smiled over his shoulder at me, as if apologizing for his wife's abruptness. "We will see you shortly," he said.

I brought Audrey's schedule up on my computer. Our first session with Gus wasn't for a while, so I decided to spend a little time going over the records and preparing myself as well as I could. Tennis is not a trauma sport, but it certainly has its share of injuries, some of them quite complex. Audrey's record included the various requisite blisters—a common problem in tennis because of all the sliding—and some incidents of heat exhaustion; her recent problems involved a pulled hamstring, and now a new one, patellar tendinitis, a condition aggravated by changing direction and pushing off, and playing on hard surfaces afterward. These injuries seemed minor, and par for the course in an athlete of Audrey's level and age, but I noticed an unusually high number of medical and physiotherapy visits or consultations. Eleven so far this month. Ten the month before. Eight the month before that. Before the knee, it was her ankle. Before the ankle, the rotator cuff. Before that, headaches, wrist problems, all minor things that got better only to be replaced by other problems. And there was an extensive list of referral doctors and therapists. There was nothing really serious—but on paper this girl sounded like a budding hypochondriac. Puzzled, I tapped my pencil on the glass desktop. Sometimes you find that the psychology behind the complaint is more important than the specific complaint. The question was how to categorize this. As I saw it, the choices were: legitimate; the result of paranoia; the result of someone else's overprotectiveness; or cries for help. Paranoia, overprotectiveness, or cries for help due to what, I couldn't tell.

Whatever, I didn't like any of the last three possibilities, because, number one, it would be very difficult, if not impossible, to prove any of these armchair theories and, number two, it wasn't my job to prove them. I was here to deal with the first option, a legitimate physical problem. I liked it even less when Bill called, told me to come immediately to Gus's office, and, as I headed there, I could hear Corinne Armat's voice—something anyone in a two-mile radius could have done. Along the hallway, the secretaries pretended not to listen. Sheila, Gus's secretary, sat just outside his door. I motioned silently toward the room, and she answered with a roll of her eyes.

"Nobody tells us what we can and can't do with our

daughter," Mrs. Armat was yelling. "She is a minor. She needs our protection. If you think I'm going to turn her over to strangers, however qualified they might be, and go for a nature hike and a manicure like these women out here who walk poodles at the fat farms, you've got another thing coming."

I opened the door a crack and stood just outside the office, waiting for a break in the diatribe.

"Now, Corrie, I'm certain they have Audrey's best interests at heart," Emilio said soothingly. "They just do not understand that we are a team." He brandished his necklace with the A^2 insignia. "The A team. Doctor, our family is like a precision machine. You cannot tune one part and ignore the others." He gestured toward E.J., who was leaning against the corner wall.

"Come in, Jordan," said Gus, sounding rather grateful for the diversion, which I now realized I was supposed to be.

"You do not know Audrey," her mother stated firmly. "She needs her family around her. We are her family. We are her parents. It's we who have sacrificed. We do everything. All this girl has to do is put on an outfit and play tennis. We make it possible. We gave up our lives so that she could play this game. Our role is not going to change just because we are here under this roof."

Audrey sat erectly on her chair, as if she had pulled an invisible curtain around herself that deflected the vibrations within the room and left her unscathed. E.J., his gaze half-lidded, gnawed at his nails and picked at his cuticles, which, I noticed, were bleeding.

Bill stepped in, his head cocked thoughtfully. "Let's clarify: Our mission here—is it to fulfill your dream or ours, or to be sure that your child emerges a healthier, happier person?"

Audrey still said nothing. Her eyes were on the floor, as if she were finding the thread count of the carpet fascinating.

Emilio Armat crossed his arms. "Are you a parent, Doctor?"

"No," Gus admitted.

"Ah," said Mr. Armat indulgently. "Of course. You cannot identify. But you certainly must understand our position. It hasn't been announced yet, but we have lined up a soft drink sponsorship, and one of the major cosmetics companies is going to launch a new teen fragrance, named for Audrey. All this, of course, hinges on keeping Audrey's career on track."

"It's a simple matter. Audrey seems to be losing some of her motivation," stated Mrs. Armat. "Certainly her skills are not in question. My husband has trained this girl from the cradle."

Emilio Armat corrected the thought. "From *before* she was born! And she is a very motivated girl, so it's hard to detect. But we've heard so much about your wonderful mental toughness program, Dr. Laidlaw. You know, I read your book. And I totally agree with the part where you say that it makes no sense that fifty percent of the game is mental, yet most athletes spend only about five percent of their total training time refining their mental skills. In my opinion, Doctor, you have hit the nail on the head."

"Assuming you know how to adapt your theories for a young person and her family," interrupted Mrs. Armat.

"Mrs. Armat," Gus said, "no one is trying to disagree, challenge you, or criticize in any way. I think we all agree that the first step is to assure that Audrey gets as nutritionally and biomedically precise as she can. But before there can be any kind of attitudinal change, there has to be complete self-awareness on the part of Audrey and everyone she's working with."

"Well," Bill said diplomatically, "before we prejudge anything, why don't we just get Audrey started with the program? If there are any problems or questions, we can deal with them as they arise." He patted Mr. Armat on the back, assuming a camaraderie that did not exist; at this moment civility barely existed in the room. But that was Bill's way. His mere presence could determine a mood, turn an attitude around, whether he was dealing with a child or a board of directors. It was his talent. But then he hadn't come head to head with Corinne Armat before.

She gazed icily at him, then took out an ultralong cigarette, inclined her head toward Emilio, who lit it with a flick of a slim gold lighter, and inhaled heavily. "I wish I could stop smoking," she said to no one in particular as she exhaled, waving the smoke away with the cigarette, its tip marked with bright orange lipstick. A huge diamond flashed as she moved her hands. "But all this pressure, as you see." She sighed and pointedly checked her watch. "We might as well begin. This is costing enough per minute."

I didn't see Audrey for the next couple of hours. She began with a routine physical, including the prerequisite electrocardiogram, vital statistics, and blood work. Next on the agenda was nutritional therapy and rehab with Joan Edgemont. Joan's routine involved giving Audrey a diary to record every bite she ate for the next five days. While most sports nutrition programs focus on chemistry, which tends to bore young athletes into ignoring it, the Springs' approach starts with something they care about: food. Sometimes, you think you know what you eat, but putting everything that goes into your mouth down on paper, then reading what you wrote later, can be a big surprise. Maybe you eat well on game days, for instance, but on rest days your diet tests out at 50 percent fat. The Springs' nutritional workup is very precise. It's not enough to say you had a hamburger for lunch; you have to practically write a paper on that hamburger—was it from McDonald's or Wendy's? A Big Mac or a Quarter Pounder? Did you have a bun or trimmings? What kind and how much? This information is then fed into the computer, and Joan's custom program spits out a complete assessment of your food intake, including vitamins, minerals, water, fat (poly- and monounsaturated), carbohydrates, protein, and cholesterol. Joan calls this "feeding your Ferrari"—if you don't eat well, you're going to have engine trouble. I assumed this phase of Audrey's program went well enough—although I was later to learn otherwise.

At eleven o'clock Audrey, her parents, and E.J. arrived on schedule for her mental-toughness workup. I was there not because I'm an expert in this area, but as part of the team.

"Parents are a key element of the team, as you rightly pointed out, Emilio," Gus said after we were settled in, Audrey cradling a huge bottle of mineral water that she seemed to carry everywhere with her like a security blanket.

The Armats nodded in unison. No argument there.

"All the studies have shown that parents are powerful motivators for young athletes, at any level. But sometimes, to escalate progress to the next level, parents have to step back in order for the team approach to be as effective as it can be."

Both Armats visibly tensed, but Gus continued. "The time comes for the parent to become a supporter rather than a motivator. The best results might occur when Audrey is free to concentrate on herself."

Mrs. Armat leaned forward in her chair. "Step back? Are you serious, Doctor? Our instinct is to remain closer than ever, frankly. Audrey needs us."

"Well, that's your perception at this time."

"That is a fact, Doctor."

"What do you think, Audrey?"

Audrey's face flushed. "I think my parents know what works for me."

"We're going to be analyzing Audrey's mental attitude," Gus said, boldly plowing onward. "We'll talk about visualization techniques that could help Audrey control her physiological state. We have to identify what she does to get into the total zone state, the state of flow, as it were, when she is at her performance peak. Audrey has to do this herself, I'm sure you'll agree."

"Up to a point, Doctor," warned Corinne Armat. "If you put too much pressure on Audrey, she won't respond well."

"It's all a question of balance," emphasized Gus. "I have a little game here. Three questionnaires—one for each parent and one for you, Audrey. Maybe we could start by taking a few minutes for each of you to fill yours out. This isn't like a test in school. It's just top-of-mind answers. We'll compare and contrast your answers. Page two asks you to draw up a list of parents' strengths and weaknesses. Question four deals with how the parents react under pressure."

Corinne Armat burst into laughter. "I've never heard of anything so ridiculous in my entire life! Have you, E.J.?"

E.J. shrugged and snapped his gum, but he might as well have been doing handstands in the corner. The question was purely rhetorical; neither Corinne nor Emilio glanced at him.

"*Our* strengths and weaknesses? How *we* react to pressure? Who knows? Personally, allow me to confide in you that I have never played Steffi Graf. Really, Doctor! We are not here to discuss Emilio and myself. The subject here is Audrey." Corinne took out a Kleenex, rolled it into a point, and dabbed carefully at the corners of her mouth.

"We're talking about working together as a group to communicate better," explained Gus. But the rest of the meeting was strained. The Armats refused to fill out the questionnaires. And before she answered any of Gus's questions, Audrey glanced at her father, who cued her with an imperceptible nod or expression. The strangest part was, she didn't seem to mind. Most teenagers can sniff out adult manipulation like bloodhounds at a customs bust, and their usual reaction is to confront, to sulk, to argue, to react. I watched Audrey intently, but she showed none of these tendencies. She seemed docile, cooperative, and totally unwilling to contradict her parents or make waves on her own behalf. The sure-footed star of the tennis court had given way to the submissive daughter, when of all teenagers in the world she was one of those most entitled to speak for herself. The Armats, I thought, had her very well trained indeed. I couldn't even train A.M. to do a simple trick without her cooperation.

Audrey and her brother went back to their villa for lunch, while her parents, Gus, Bill, and I all had lunch together in the Springs' on-premises café. We took over a large table, and I found myself sitting next to Emilio Armat.

"It's not easy being a young person on the tour, I know," he said. "And you know."

"Audrey's so successful," I said. "You must be very proud."

"Proud, of course. And I am anxious for her to spend time with you. She needs to see how others handled the situation, to learn and grow."

"She'll have to learn from her own experience," I said. "Everyone is different."

"But you were a very mature player," said Mr. Armat. "I have been told."

"Being old before your time is no fun."

Mr. Armat looked at me appraisingly. "As I understand it, you were just coming into your own, incorporating serve and volley into your game. You had won three Grand Slams . . ."

"But two were the French and the Australian Open on years nobody else was playing."

"I hope you count that second Australian, the one where they *did* come." Mr. Armat laughed heartily and patted my arm. It was easy to talk to him. His eyes seemed warmly sympathetic, as if his sole purpose in life at that moment was to hear anything I had to say about myself. Unlike his wife, who had launched into a monologue at the other end of the table, he actually listened, watching me intently, nodding supportively as I found myself telling him the entire story of my fall and recovery.

"You were brave to keep involved with tennis," Emilio said. "That took courage. The kind of courage we wish for Audrey to someday have."

"Audrey obviously has plenty of courage already. Otherwise, she wouldn't be the champion she is."

"That is the courage of the game," Emilio said thoughtfully. "We are talking about the courage of life."

We talked about his life—his boyhood struggles in a poor family, his lack of formal schooling. "I sent away for a course to learn electronics," he said proudly. "I can wire anything."

"Where did you learn tennis?" I asked.

"By watching. I worked at a local club. Frankly, I saw tennis was a way to cut through the social strata, a way to a nice life, if you played well. But that was just the beginning. Later, I watched all the greats—on TV or on videotapes. I tell Audrey, to watch is to learn."

By the time the dishes were cleared, I'd actually begun to warm to Emilio Armat and, what's more, I owed him twenty dollars. "So you count up everybody's numbers," he explained. "The key to liar's poker is to bluff, and hope nobody calls you on it right away."

"Emilio!" yelped Mrs. Armat as she saw me opening my wallet. "Don't take that poor girl's money!"

"My dear," he announced, "today I am teaching, not hustling."

Everyone laughed, and the tension of the morning seemed broken. Bill had then taken Audrey to the video studio, where he and Mickey Gomez, our tennis pro, had analyzed recent tapes of her matches, focusing on her serve and return, dissecting her power game freeze-frame by freeze-frame, measuring angles and velocities, looking for patterns. Audrey's entire game was put under the microscope as Mickey looked for what happened emotionally in a situation as well as technically. Emilio Armat was at Mickey's elbow, simultaneously checking Audrey's opponent's game, figuring out where they were serving, where they were passing, and their favorite shots. Special attention was given to the big points, because this is how you determine patterns. Players revert to their patterns on the big points; that's when they turn instinctively to their strengths, and you have to ask yourself—when the chips are down, where do they go? Down the line? Crosscourt? And you begin to strategize.

Corinne and Emilio Armat stayed with Audrey every step of the way, as E.J., who according to the omniscient Tony looked bored out of his mind, resorted to playing a pocket Nintendo game with an anesthetized expression on his face.

"But that Audrey's a real sweetheart," Tony said. "So soft-spoken and cooperative. You'd never guess she was a star."

"She's an incredible natural athlete, and she has all the strokes. At this point, unless there's an injury, which we'll know better later, it's mental," I said.

It was four o'clock before Audrey got to me for our session. For the first time, we were alone. The training table does not have room for more than one subject. Sitting on the edge of my table, she showed me her left leg, which was swathed in an elastic bandage. I unwrapped the bandage and found a batch of diodes and magnets, held in place with small round Band-Aids, dotted along her leg from shin to knee.

"Tell me what's been going on," I said.

"The pain just won't go away," Audrey said, gingerly flexing the knee.

I asked Audrey how she was sleeping.

"Not too well," she admitted. "I'm tired, but I can't get to sleep. I know I have to get through this period. I'll do anything. Maybe I should change my vitamins. Maybe my resistance is down."

It seemed like a good time to bring in my heavy artillery. I whistled, and A.M. trotted in and jumped up onto the examining table.

"This is my assistant," I said as she licked Audrey's hand. "Is it okay if she examines you?"

For the first time, Audrey smiled a real smile, not a PR creation. She delightedly tickled A.M. behind her ears. The two of them got along immediately.

"I've never had a pet," Audrey said wistfully. "It must be fun. I love animals."

"So get yourself a dog," I said. "It's obvious animals like you, too. Shake, A.M."

Soon they were having a rowdy tug-of-war with an elastic bandage. Now that Audrey had finally relaxed, I decided to go for it. "You know, Audrey, you've had a battery of tests, including an MRI. You've had everything short of surgery. Nobody can find the problem."

A.M. brought out a roll of athletic tape which she presented to Audrey to throw for her. This worked pretty well as a diversion until I started removing the little Band-Aids and the forest of magnets and diodes.

"What are you doing?" Her voice seemed panicky.

"I don't think you need these." It was a risk, I'll admit. I didn't know as much as I was letting on—not yet. I was testing Audrey's reaction. "I really feel that by now you should have been progressing in this area. I think these are a crutch." I looked her straight in her turquoise eyes. Tears were welling up.

"It hurts," she said. "It really hurts. I don't think I can play, I—"

She seemed distraught. "Audrey," I said. "Is there something you've been trying to say? Sometimes, with all the pressure that's on you, it can be hard to level with people. I know that." Maybe she was burning out. The signs were certainly there. "Maybe you need to take some time off. Have you discussed that possibility with your folks?"

"I'm not sure what I'd do," she murmured.

"Lie around, do nothing, go to the mall."

"I've never been to a mall."

"You're kidding. Well, you're not missing a great cultural experience—it's no big deal. You just hop in the car, drive down, and go shopping."

"My mom keeps my driver's license and the car keys in her purse." Audrey sighed.

I didn't even want to get close to that one. So I said, "Well, there are other things to do."

She laughed. "All I do is work out, practice, and play my matches. Oh, and press conferences."

"How'd you like school?"

"I never felt like I was part of it, so I guess I don't miss it. You went to college," Audrey said. "What's college like?"

"Hard, but fun," I said. "Every college is different. Why don't you visit some campuses and see for yourself?"

She shook her head. "I could never do that to my parents, after all they've done for me. Besides, I'd never get in." She laughed. "My brother does my homework for me." The tears started, rolling down her cheeks and splashing onto A.M., who was now in her lap. Something was definitely hurting this girl, and it wasn't just her knee.

"Audrey?"

"I guess I'm just tired. Can we wrap this up?"

"I'm just going to give you a few simple exercises," I said. "We'll start with basic stretches." I handed her a heavy, oversized rubber band designed for resistance work and demonstrated the movements. "First you need to get moving again. The muscles may have tightened up on you."

Whatever it was, Audrey never opened up further. I wasn't too worried—we had nine more days together, and I didn't want to put pressure on her yet, physically or emotionally. Our session ended with me massaging her back and shoulders, icing her knee, and talking about what we'd do tomorrow, once she'd tried the stretches, and A.M. fetching some more rolls of tape on command. I felt confident that before her stay at the Springs was over, Audrey would tell me what was really bothering her.

Then it was time for a papaya smoothie at the juice bar and home. Home consisted of the dreaded weekly laundry ritual, a bike ride with A.M. jogging alongside, a salad, and bed by 9:30. Just before I turned out the light, I unplugged the phone and neglected to locate my beeper. It was that or not live to see morning.

* * *

The next day I felt pretty good for a change, so I jumped into a pair of pants and a windbreaker and rode my motorcycle to work. This is always a special treat for A.M., who comes along in a special canvas saddle-bag.

I saw Gus pulling into his parking space under the tangerine tree.

"Where in God's name have you been?" he yelled, frowning from under his visor. "Nobody answered your phone or your beeper. Bill sent me to find you but you'd already left the house."

"Oh, God. I left it in my jacket from New York. Sorry. What's the disaster du jour?" I hoisted A.M. down from her perch, and she jumped and wagged at Gus, who gave her a distracted pat.

"Audrey's missing."

"How can that be?"

"The Armats say she didn't sleep in her bed last night. She's gone. They're ready to call out the National Guard."

"She's been gone for a few hours and they're putting her picture on a milk carton? Are they sure she's gone? Maybe she went for an early walk?"

Gus pointed toward the villas. "They're waiting for us. Apparently she left a note."

"This is ludicrous," I said hotly as we made our way down the winding, palm tree–lined path. It was a chilly morning, so I zipped up my windbreaker and turned up the collar. "These people do nothing but overreact. No wonder Audrey's like she is. I haven't told you what I found in her chart. Or how she started crying in the training room. She was ready to have a breakdown of some sort from all this hype." I was especially upset that Audrey had apparently taken off unannounced, because I'd felt so close to getting through to her.

"Well, you'd better be prepared," Gus said. "Mrs. Armat is blaming us for what she is referring to as Audrey's disappearance. This could get nasty."

"Audrey was here maybe one day and this woman is blaming us?"

"That's right," said Gus. "And I hate to tell you this, but she's especially blaming you."

FOUR

Inside the whitewashed villa, aptly named Agua Caliente (Spanish for "hot water") in honor of the ancient mineral springs on which the city rests, the hysteria was tangible. It was an unfamiliar atmosphere in this luxurious setting. The villas had been custom designed to accommodate the clients' every wish and whim—from refrigerators prestocked with their favorite foods to the Springs' own line of herbal bath products artfully arranged in the marble-and-natural-wood bathrooms, which had wood-burning fireplaces, sunken whirlpool tubs, and showers the size of walk-in closets with six adjustable heads. Emilio Armat stood gazing out the picture window that overlooked the walled patio and golf course beyond. His hands were jammed into his pockets, his muscles tensed. Colonel Eddie Simms, head of security, sat frowning in his uniform at a round, bleached wood table pulled up to an upholstered sisal banquette, his mobile phone glued to his ear. A walkie-talkie propped in front of him emitted bursts of static. Joan Edgemont, her blond hair pulled back in a ponytail, stared intently at a notebook in her lap. Corinne Armat paced rhythmically back and forth across the marble floor, her antelope suede boots clicking with every step. She wore a beaded white suede jacket with long fringed trim that swung rhythmically as she walked, topping tight white stretch pants. A coordinated beaded clip held her hair in a soufflé-like puff on top of her head. In one hand she held a lit cigarette in a holder, in the other an ashtray heaped with half-smoked, orange-lipstick-tipped butts. She smashed the latest cigarette out in the heap, breaking it in half and spilling a filmy trail of ashes onto the floor. Her mouth etched a bright orange slash across her tightly drawn face. Only Bill looked at ease. In fact, he resembled a Ralph Lauren ad, sitting casually with his legs crossed, one arm draped across the back of a cushiony club chair, the collar of his yellow shirt stylishly upturned beneath his navy cashmere sweater vest. All heads turned in our direction as Gus and I walked into the room. I hoped they didn't think I had any answers.

Eddie Simms folded his phone and rose to greet me. I motioned for A.M. to sit and wait in the entrance hall. I hadn't had many dealings with the Colonel before, except for the routine security briefings he'd given the entire staff. With so many celebrities and notables coming and going, the Springs was extremely security conscious. No one without an employee or approved supplier photo ID or an appointment written in the guard's book could get through the front gate. There were six security checkpoints within the complex, each manned by an armed guard, and a central station with video surveillance cameras that swept the main buildings. I knew that until a few years ago Simms had been a career army intelligence officer—in fact, Bill had met him in the service. A result of all the cutbacks and base closings, Simms's retirement had coincided with the opening of the Springs, a fortunate coincidence for Bill, who had signed the Colonel on as head of clinic security. The "Colonel" title was, at this point, strictly honorary, but it fit Eddie Simms so well that nobody could imagine him being just plain "mister."

The Colonel flipped open a small spiral notebook and glanced at Bill. "All right," he said, his voice commanding the scattered attention of the room. "I think we're all here."

Bill nodded imperceptibly.

Corinne Armat strode over to the accompaniment of staccato heel clicks. "It's a very simple matter, Sergeant."

"Colonel."

"Colonel." She stopped, automatically reapplied a fresh ring of orange lipstick, and blotted her lips together, replacing the lipstick tube cap as if she were snapping a bullet into a gun. "My daughter has disappeared. She is psychologically vulnerable now, thanks to the pressure she has been subjected to here . . ." She glanced contemptuously in my direction. "It has obviously pushed her over the edge."

"Let's not make any assumptions, Mrs. Armat," said the Colonel. He glanced at his notebook. "Audrey has not been gone long enough to jump to conclusions."

"Audrey is gone. That is my conclusion, and my husband's, and as her parents, ours are the only conclusions that matter," hissed Mrs. Armat. She spun on her heel and continued pacing. "She has never been unaccounted for for so much as one minute. Where would she go? She knows no one in Palm Springs."

"Maybe she went for a drive with somebody," suggested the Colonel. "Teenagers have been known to do that. And the guards don't check everybody who leaves, just the people coming in."

"If she wanted to drive someplace, she would have asked me."

I could imagine being this woman's daughter, having to ask for my keys and driver's license, waiting for her to say yes or no, then dole it out of her purse. Not a pretty thought.

The Colonel scribbled a note. "Well, it's possible she went for a walk . . ."

"I doubt it. Her knee was bothering her. There's also a note. Emilio!" Orange fingernails snapped imperiously. "Read them the note."

Mr. Armat took an envelope from his pocket and pulled out a small piece of paper. "She went back to the villa to change, and when she didn't come back we went to look for her. This was on her bed," he said slowly. "I will read it: 'Don't even try to look for me. I can't go on like this.' It's in her handwriting, of course." He showed the note to the Colonel, who studied it briefly, then passed it to Gus, who passed it around the room. I stared briefly at the writing, in felt-tipped pen, scrawled, it appeared, hastily and carelessly. One end of the paper appeared to have been ripped off. Then I handed it back to Emilio Armat, who stuffed the note back into his pocket. "The thing is, we still have a chance to find her now. If we wait, who knows where she will go, or what foolish thing she might do. Audrey is not very mature about anything except her tennis game, I'm afraid." He shook his head sorrowfully. "What can we do about our children?" he asked rhetorically. "We give them everything, sacrifice everything . . . Perhaps if we did less . . ." He sighed. "But of course, we do it for love. I trained Audrey from birth, and I trained her myself. Even as a baby, her coordination was obvious, as was her brother's. I hung a tiny racket over each of their cribs. I had a job at the country club—a good job, a management position." He absent-mindedly cracked his knuckles. "I walked by those tennis courts on the way to work every day, and then on my way home, and I saw clearly that this was the path. If only one of my children could be molded ... E.J., he was talented, but, well, Audrey rose to the occasion spectacularly, like the champion she has always been. She threw a perfect spiral when she was four years old. You should have seen her at five years old, doing wind sprints after three hours of practice. She ran faster than any of the girls, and the boys, too. And when other kids gave up when things got difficult, she wanted more." He sighed. "Well, now her focus seems to be gone. Maybe growing up was not so good for her."

"You can't stop a child from growing up," said Gus. "It's not exactly something you can blame yourself for, either."

Emilio Armat seemed perplexed. "Always before, Audrey could focus, concentrate, play her game. But recently, she has drifted. And when she drifts, she loses. She could not get into the zone anymore. It seemed to close off for her, where, before—well, she owned it. That upset her terribly—clearly, more than we knew."

The zone—a mystical phenomenon with which I had a passing acquaintance. It's the metaphysical place where your state of mind harmonizes perfectly with your athletic skills, and you can do no wrong. The ball is as big as a watermelon. You have time, you have the shots, you have the skill. It all comes together when you're in the zone, and nothing else exists. It's the athlete's dream state, the winning state. When you're in the total zone, you can't lose.

"Shut up, Emilio," snapped Mrs. Armat. "This is no time to get mystical. It's time for action. Now. Let me recap the situation as I see it. Counting back, Audrey spent yesterday morning with us, going over routine information about her health and her game. Am I correct, Dr. Edgemont, that all she discussed with you was her diet?" She drilled Joan with a look.

"Well, Audrey started filling out her diet diary. I have a copy here," said Joan. "Every client does it."

"And," continued Corinne Armat, as if she were a prosecutor facing down Perry Mason, "I don't imagine that the confession that she ate french fries caused her any psychological trauma, do you, Dr. Edgemont?"

"I should say not," said Joan. "That's a very minor detail. Audrey is in good health. We ran the routine physical tests, as you know, and the blood chemistries aren't in yet, but we imagine they will check out."

"Audrey didn't have any drug history, did she?" asked the Colonel. "Or steroid usage, perhaps?"

Mrs. Armat lifted her chin indignantly. "Absolutely not! I resent that question! She wouldn't even take an aspirin."

"It's a routine question, Mrs. Armat. I did see some things in the refrigerator." The Colonel walked over into the kitchen, and the rest of us followed. He stopped at the refrigerator. "What's this?" He pointed to a note taped to the door that said, in large letters, YOU'RE FAT!!!

"Just a reminder to Audrey," said Mrs. Armat. "It's nothing."

The Colonel opened the door, and we could see the

top shelf crammed with dozens of bottles, jars, and glass pharmacy vials. "And what's all this, if you don't mind my asking?"

"Audrey's vitamins," said Emilio. "In the brown glass bottle with the stopper is an herbal derivate for bronchial support. Then there's this one—evening prim-rose oil. Flaxseed oil. Vitamin E—four hundred units. Vitamin C. Beta-carotene. Choline. This one's a homeopathic anti-inflammatory. Milk thistle for the knee. This one's for lymph drainage. These are marine lipid concentrates. Biotics. And in this plastic bottle, a mineral toddy of seven major and fifty-three trace minerals distilled from prehistoric plant deposits. Oh, and that's carob milk over there. And a bunch of dried bananas, some dried apricots, mineral water, and a package of rice cakes."

"How often does she take these vitamins and minerals?" asked the Colonel. "There must be twenty different supplements in here."

"There are, and she takes them all every day," answered Emilio. "It's part of her normal regimen. We discussed it with her personal physician and nutritionist and with Dr. Edgemont. These things are all natural, and nothing that would affect her behavior, I assure you."

"That's true," agreed Joan. "Many of our athletes have extensive vitamin programs. There may be some controversy over their efficacy, but certainly no harm or mood-altering impact."

The group migrated back to the living room, where-upon Corinne Armat flashed her laser eyes in my direction. "Now, what about Audrey's physiotherapy session? This was the only time Emilio and I didn't accompany her, and when I met her outside when it was over, I noticed Audrey had been crying. Her eyes were red and swollen, and she wouldn't talk to me. She went back to her room and locked herself in. I couldn't believe it. We're best friends, Audrey and me. This morning, when she still didn't answer, I had security open the door with their key, and she was gone. The bed hadn't even been slept in! I'd like to know what went on in that session, Ms. Myles." Mrs. Armat jabbed a finger in my direction. "I'd like to know why my daughter was in tears. What was said that put her under so much stress that she was driven away? How was she made to feel that she couldn't confide in her own mother?" Tears glittered in Mrs. Armat's eyes. "If you'll recall, Bill, I stated up front that I was not completely comfortable with Ms. Myles's background."

I felt a migraine pounding behind my eyes.

But Mrs. Armat wasn't finished yet. "As I see it, it's simple. Audrey had a very disturbing session with you, Ms. Myles. Something happened in that session that caused my daughter to behave in a way that is completely unlike her. She is not a runaway or a drug addict." Her eyes clouded with indignation. "I think we deserve some answers. What, if I may ask, did you say to Audrey?"

"Thank you for giving me a chance to speak, Mrs. Armat," I said, trying to remain as controlled as possible. Getting into hand-to-hand combat with this woman was definitely not a good idea. "I appreciate and share your concern for Audrey. The fact is, I can't imagine that there was anything in our session that put her under any pressure at all, much less the kind that note implies. However, according to her chart she's had an unusual number of minor medical complaints and follow-up visits, and I asked her about that."

"Audrey is a champion," defended Mr. Armat. "We must safeguard her condition at all times. Act preventively."

"Yes, that's true," I acknowledged. "But, to be frank, this seemed excessive. And when I asked her about it, she did get defensive and upset."

"I knew it!" Corinne Armat pounced. "Of course—don't you see? You made Audrey feel paranoid. She's a very sensitive child. This was totally irresponsible on the part of this facility and, in particular, Bill, your staff." She whirled on her husband. "Emilio, perhaps our baby knew best after all—to leave this place. I only hope that Audrey has removed herself from this hostile environment and for the security of her home. We had best leave ourselves at this point."

"Just a minute," I said. "What if Audrey comes back here? Maybe she's just being emotional for the moment."

"She won't come back to this place, I can assure you," said Mrs. Armat flatly. "Emilio, you'd better call Ted Robb at Global Sport. He'll have to finesse that phone interview with *Sports Illustrated* that Audrey was supposed to do tonight. I can only hope she turns up in time for the cover shoot."

"Now, Corinne," interjected Bill, "we all have to remember that Audrey is not a baby. She's a young woman. Surely she'll be able to get this out of her system and things will return to normal."

"That's totally untrue," Mrs. Armat countered. She opened her purse, pulled out a sheaf of plane tickets, and opened one to check an itinerary. "You know as well as

I do. Audrey has always been totally protected by us, so she can concentrate on her game. She's never even written a check, or made a plane reservation. She's completely unprepared to deal with the outside world." She slapped the tickets into her husband's hand. "Emilio, call the airport. We have to leave for home immediately. Audrey will know to find us there."

"Where's E.J.?" I asked, suddenly realizing that he wasn't there. Nobody had mentioned him yet, although he was Audrey's constant companion. "Maybe she's with him."

Corinne Armat brushed off the question with a wave of her hand. "E.J. went ahead to the airport."

"What about her boyfriend?" asked Gus. "Could she have gone to see him?"

"I can't imagine it," said Emilio with finality. "Besides, I called him immediately. He hasn't talked to Audrey in two weeks."

The Colonel looked resigned. "All I can tell you, Mr. and Mrs. Armat, is that if she drove off the complex, we'll have that on our security videos. It might give the police some clues to where she went, or with whom, although I doubt they'll classify her as missing—she's been gone such a short time."

"Of course," said Gus calmly. "You're right. The police should be notified immediately. The press may lead us to her, too—they'll certainly be all over the case."

Emilio held up his hand insistently. "No press. And, we have decided, no police. And no lawyers." He paused and glanced at his wife. "Yet. For now, this is a private family matter."

"But she is Audrey Armat." Gus can outrationalize any argument. "Once this becomes a police matter, the press will be very interested. And it will be a matter of public record."

"Until we ascertain what has happened, we can't risk making Audrey's situation public," Emilio said. He walked over to his wife's side and tucked her hand sympathetically under his arm. "Or even calling the police. But if Audrey is harmed in any way or misses one tournament or loses as much as one patch deal, we will hold your organization totally responsible." His jaw twitched. "May I remind you of the economics. A patch deal alone is fifty thousand dollars. As it is, we will probably be losing a cover story with *Sports Illustrated*. And I cannot imagine how the perfume company would react if they heard about this—Audrey is the role model to millions of young girls, a lovely, romantic figure. Lovely, romantic figures of young girls with multimillion-dollar contracts don't go running off and getting into trouble without their parents!" His face tightened momentarily, then, with a studied effort, he spoke calmly. "This could be disastrous."

"And not only for us," said Corinne Armat, layers of heavy pancake makeup failing to mask her fury. "Don't think I won't see that you all lose your licenses for negligence and malpractice, across the board. I promise you that. It will become my mission in life, I swear to God." Her voice trembled and she started to cry, and her husband took her in his arms and patted her back. "We have to find Audrey," she sobbed plaintively. Then she collected herself, pulled back, and stared at Emilio.

"This is your fault," she whispered. "Yours!" Her mascara was running, leaving dark smears under her eyes, and she sniffled and dabbed at them with the back of her hand, staining the white suede of her sleeve. One of her false eyelashes had come unglued and was dangling perilously.

"I think you had all better leave," Emilio said quietly.

The room was cleared in a matter of seconds. As we left, I could hear an argument erupting.

Emilio's voice barked out, "Learn to keep your big mouth shut, for once! This is a private family matter."

I looked back and saw his face. It was contorted and ugly, with no trace of the smooth operator. Corinne Armat was white, like a crumpled tissue. I supposed I couldn't blame them for falling apart. The pressure was terrible.

It felt good to breathe again outside, and we stood there silently in a little group feeling stunned, almost suffocated from the atmosphere in the villa, like fish that had been yanked out of water and clubbed on the dock.

"Whew!" said the Colonel finally, blotting his forehead with his sleeve. "That was one tough lady. Too bad she's not the one playing tennis."

"Oh, but she is," said Gus. "That's the thing about these parents. In their minds, it's they who are playing. A sort of psychological virtual-reality state. The young person is just a means to the end, which is fulfilling the parents' dream. It's as if the parents were on the court themselves—at least that's how they feel. With this kind of parents, the child is their entire career, their entire selves. Emilio Armat—what did he do before he became Audrey's coach?"

"I think he was a maintenance engineer at a fancy country club that had tennis courts," I said, leaning down to pick up A.M. and tuck her under my arm.

"And to which he could probably never belong, even

if he could have afforded the membership fee," said the Colonel.

"I thought he had a management position," said Bill.

"Maybe he managed the maintenance department."

I closed my eyes, hoping I could erase the problem somehow. "I think these people are overreacting, to say the least. Are we absolutely sure she's gone?" I said.

Suddenly there was a slam from the Armats' villa. Emilio and Corinne, carrying a few pieces of hand baggage, hurried out the door and into a rented Jaguar sedan, then sped off in the direction of the exit to the complex.

"We've got to handle this very carefully," said Bill, observing their departure with concern. "This is a highly sensitive time for our organization. As you may or may not be aware, the Southwestern Bank has taken an ownership position in return for majority funding of the new golf course and players' training complex. These are bankers, they really go by the book. We wouldn't want to make them uncomfortable with some sort of negligence suit. Not to mention what it would do to our client roster. Litigation would be blowing things out of proportion—you know that, and I know it, and maybe, in their hearts of hearts, the Armats know it, too. But the public won't. We can't afford this kind of thing, now or ever. In thirty-five years in the sports industry, I've never been involved in any legal action, and I'm not about to start now. We are going to make every effort to get to the bottom of this, even if this young woman just ran off to get a glass of water. Jordan, why don't you tell us your version of what went on with Audrey?"

"What I saw is a recent history of complaining about

minor injuries that borders on hypochondria. And when one thing dies down, there's another problem. Serial complaints. Some of them are valid, but we're talking about dozens of visits to doctors and therapists. The referral file was an inch thick. She wasn't sleeping well, and there have been some uncharacteristic temper outbursts. Her knee, on the other hand, seemed far better than she wanted it to be. What about her nutrition, Joan?"

"Pretty good. Too good. She's never even had a Big Mac."

"I don't believe it," I said. "How can you grow up in America and not have a Big Mac?"

"Her parents monitored her diet," Joan said. "And, apparently, that was that."

"Tell us some more about the knee," said Gus.

"Healed—or it should have been. But she claimed it still hurt. She's had CAT scans and X rays and sonograms—there's no physical reason for it. I'm not a psychologist, and I'd have to check with the specialists, but it seemed like textbook behavior for something else. If you read between the lines in a lot of these cases, someone is silently crying for attention."

"It's ironic," Joan commented. "You're talking about a girl who has the adulation of millions of fans. You'd think she gets plenty of attention."

"Well, it's obviously the wrong kind of attention. The question isn't so much what's happening, but why. And when I asked Audrey about it, she broke down." The whole thing was really disturbing. If Audrey hadn't behaved as she had the previous day, I might have been less concerned about her bolting the clinic—even if that's what actually happened. But I suspected that the

Armats were right—something, or someone, had triggered a rebellion. Something was very off here—and it wasn't her serve.

And I'm not big on intuition, but there was another major element missing in this equation—Audrey's brother.

"I wonder if E.J. was really at the airport," Gus said.

I turned around and headed back to the villa. "Let's find out."

Wherever he was, I felt sorry for him. "Poor E.J. Twin brother–slash–gofer. Here's a kid with a reason to have an inferiority complex, if there ever was one. I bet there's more to his story than meets the eye."

After ringing the doorbell and knocking for three or four minutes on the door of the darkened building, it was clear that nobody was racing to answer.

The villas used a code punch system rather than keys, and since the Colonel had the code we were back inside almost instantly.

I parked A.M. back in the foyer and left her with a chew toy that I keep in my pocket for emergencies. Colonel Simms checked upstairs while the rest of us milled around the ground floor. The smell of Corinne Armat's stale smoke hung thickly in the air. Nobody knew quite what we were looking for, or what to do. The Springs was not geared for crisis management. "No sign of life up here," the Colonel called down the stairs. "And I talked to my gate man. He didn't see anybody leave the complex, but the mechanics report one of the Jeeps is unaccounted for."

"That's interesting," said Gus. "It sounds like Audrey and E.J. went for a ride somewhere."

I found myself wandering up the curved, carpeted

stairway. There were three bedrooms on the second floor. One, obviously E.J.'s, had men's jeans, T-shirts, shorts, shoes, underwear, and various tennis and gym bags strewn about the room. It certainly didn't look as if he'd packed anything before he left.

Next door was the room Audrey had used. I flicked on the light. The bed was neatly made. Her closet was empty, except for tennis clothes and rackets and their cases. Twelve custom rackets, neatly sealed in plastic, were stacked on the floor of the closet in two piles of six. Her makeup kit was gone, but a small, purse-size cosmetics case remained on the vanity counter. I unzipped it: Tylenol, sunscreen, lip balm, and a pair of calipers, the kind that are used to measure body fat. Very utilitarian, and obviously forgotten. I closed the bag. Housekeeping would send it to her with the rest of the Armats' things.

In the master suite, the Armats' bags were closed and tagged. The two queen-size beds were still rumpled. I ran my finger aimlessly along the empty dresser top and glanced at the wastebasket. On a whim, I went through it—this was totally out of character; I've never been much for going through other people's things, much less their garbage. Here's what I found: envelopes, two Kleenexes, today's newspaper. Then, as I crouched down to put the wastebasket back, I saw a tiny wadded scrap of paper, half buried in the carpet. Unfolding it, I saw a fragment of what looked like Audrey's handwriting, or at least something that seemed at first glance to match the handwriting on the note her parents had shown us. "I hate you," it said.

So much for the Brady Bunch.

Downstairs, I smoothed the small scrap of paper out

on top of the dining room table. "From what I saw, it looks like Audrey's writing to me," I said. "Same felt-tipped pen."

"I can get an associate of mine to do a handwriting analysis," said the Colonel. "Just get me some of the paperwork Audrey filled out while she was here."

Gus shook his head. "If Audrey wrote this note, it's a very sad situation."

"If this is really Audrey's handwriting," I said, "the Armats didn't want anybody to see the entire note. But obviously they wanted everybody to see the first part of the note. They're keeping it on ice, in case they decide to sue. Evidence. For some reason, they want to imply that the Springs was to blame for the fact that Audrey ran off, when clearly she was having problems at home."

"That would explain the tears in your office," said Bill, a tinge hopefully. "Teenage parent problems. Happens all the time." It was almost as if he wished this were the case.

"Maybe," I said. But I wasn't convinced of anything anymore. I had to wonder why the Armats would have gone to such lengths to hide a simple argument with their daughter. And her medical records didn't point toward a simple argument with anybody; they seemed to indicate a chronic psychological problem—which could be rebellion, or something else entirely.

Colonel Simms stood in the corner, huddled over the phone. Suddenly he looked up. "I have something here," he said. "The front gate didn't see Audrey, but Mort was taping over at the driving range this morning. There may be something there. He thought somebody may have stolen a car. He's on his way over."

Mort is our resident media expert. He designed our

state-of-the-art multimedia center and supervises the performance videos of our clients, often manning the camera to shoot a golf swing or tennis serve for later analysis. Mort knows everything there is to know about media and technology, including such fine points as the difference between 3-D and 3DO, whereas I still cannot program my own VCR. Small in stature, with a well-trimmed beard, Mort is probably the least athletic person in the entire Springs complex, as his button-straining physique reflects. Mort's idea of physical exertion is setting a light meter. He drives around in a golf cart/mobile video center stocked with equipment, including cameras, monitors, microphones, ladders, lights, cables, battery packs, and playback machines for instant analysis. By splitting or overlaying video frames, Mort can show you an image-for-image overlay or side-by-side comparison of your stroke, serve, swing, putt, or shot.

"At dawn this morning there was a group of corporate clients on the driving range, and Mort spent several hours taping and playing back their swings. He thinks he may have gotten something by accident," the Colonel explained as Mort walked in and unloaded a stack of videotapes from his backpack.

Mort flicked on the villa's TV and VCR. He popped a tape into the machine and scanned it on fast forward. The images were almost a blur, but he seemed to know what he was looking for. "I'm not sure where anything is on these tapes, or even if I got something," he said, peering at the screen. "But I remember one of the Jeeps was going where it shouldn't have been and I sort of made a mental note. I saw it out of the corner of my eye. Maybe I got it on camera."

The first two tapes revealed nothing but a cross-

section of clients with bad golf swings. By the time
Mort had fast-forwarded through three tapes, my eyes
were crossing. Then, on the third tape, Mort hit pay dirt
and abruptly froze the frame.

"Got it," he announced. "Jeep, one o'clock north in
the frame." It was small and a bit blurry, but there. Off
in the distance, beyond the golfer, was the faint but def-
inite back end of a white Jeep, heading across the golf
course toward the edge of the grounds.

"They're off-road, that's why I noticed them in the
first place," said Mort. "If it hadn't been one of our
own cars, I'd have called security, the way this guy was
tearin' up the turf and driving over the fairway. You
know, unless you count the cable car, there's only one
way out of this valley, and they were headed for it,
making a beeline for Highway 111 at the far end of the
golf course."

"They?" asked Gus.

"Well, I'm actually not sure about how many people," Mort said, squinting at the screen. "I'm gonna
have to blow this up a few times. But the license plate
will be clear. What happened? Somebody steal this
Jeep?"

"Right now our priority is to identify which Jeep it
was and who was in it," said Bill. "And can you tell the
time, Mort?"

Mort nodded. "Sure. Every tape is time-coded to the
second. See the numerals down in the corner? This was
five forty-five A.M. Want to know how fast they were
going? We can tell that, too. Take the speed per second
of the tape, you've got twenty-two thousand frames per
minute . . ."

"That won't be necessary yet," interrupted Gus.

"Let's just confirm who was in the car, if we can. Mort, could you please take this back to the A-V room and enlarge the picture for us?"

Mort nodded as he ejected the tape from the VCR.

"On my way. And if you'd like, I can print out a still picture from the video, for the files."

"Do it," said Gus. "How long will that take?"

Mort shouldered his backpack. "Fifteen minutes?"

Joan begged off, but the rest of us followed. In the cool, dark, Naugahyde-padded video studio, Mort was in his element. He knew every piece of equipment, what it did, and how to run it. I'd often sympathized with him—the only overweight, out-of-shape guy in a sea of fitness fanatics, Olympians, and others whose cholesterol counts, pulse rates, and muscle tone were professionally perfect. But here, seated at a control panel that would have given a 747 pilot second thoughts, Mort was clearly in charge, and the rest of us were merely his audience.

"Okay, here we go," Mort announced, pushing a button that froze a frame, then activating an electronic pointer that boxed off the area to be enlarged.

"Once, twice, three times," Mort intoned as the picture jumped larger, then larger again. You could clearly see the pink of Audrey's warm-up suit. She was wearing a baseball cap, and she was with a dark-haired driver, presumably E.J.

"We can verify this more exactly," said Mort. "But it looks like they were doing sixty miles an hour, at least. Moving fast, at any rate. Here, I'll scan out a still of this frame."

"But where'd she go?" I wondered aloud.

The mood in the darkened A-V room was glum, as if

this proof of Audrey's escape from the Springs was hard evidence of a failure, even though we knew that wasn't the case.

"She'll turn up," Bill predicted.

"Don't be so sure it'll happen so fast," cautioned Gus. "She was obviously under a great deal of stress and, as her mother pointed out, she's not used to handling her own life. She's unpredictable at best, at this point."

The phone rang sharply. Mort answered and handed it to Bill. After a few brief seconds of monosyllabic conversation, he hung up and leaned back against the wall. "Well, here it is," he said. "That was Ted Robb at Global Sport. The Armats called them from the airport. Nobody's taking this thing lightly, and we shouldn't either. To have that kid escape from under our noses, and blaming us! Well, one thing's clear. She'd better turn up, or we're talking lawsuit."

"But they couldn't win," I said. "There's no cause."

Bill shrugged. "That's immaterial. The damage the accusations would do to us in court would be enough to keep clients away in droves. And the press would have a field day—celebrity runaway, the whole bit. They'd say we brainwashed her, who knows?"

"Can't Global Sport help out?" I asked.

"Global Sport is going to protect its asset—which isn't us. Ted made that much clear. We're facing a damage control situation here. We've got to find her." He brightened imperceptibly. "And, on the upside, if we find her before the Armats do, we can be in the position of returning their daughter to them. We'd be heroes. We could turn the whole thing around."

Mort handed each of us a paper printout of the video

frame. I looked at it. A girl in pink running away. That was all. Who knew from what?

Bill was good in a crisis. He hadn't been on all those corporate boards for nothing. "Gus, what do you think—won't Jordan have the edge here in a fact-finding situation? She can get behind the scenes in the tennis community and get some feeling for what the real story is. Maybe somebody knows something that can help."

"I say this calls for a professional," insisted the Colonel. "This whole thing sounds like a bunch of egg-shells just waiting to be walked on. You'll need somebody with experience. I'd better handle this."

"You've got the experience, all right," said Bill, "no questioning that. But, let's face it, Colonel, you'd be pretty conspicuous in a women's locker room. Jordan has a real reason for being there, she's one of them."

"I think the Colonel's right," said Gus. From the restless way he was standing, I had already been able to tell that he was about to disagree. "Look at what's happening in tennis today—the Monica Seles stabbing, the stalker who was after Steffi, weirdos coming out of the woodwork, like the creep who hid in Chrissie's closet at Wimbledon. For God's sake, the guy *lived* in there for a week before they found him. Who knows who or what is really going on here? All we really know for a fact is that we don't know the facts, that the facts have been purposefully twisted. Jordan's not a trained investigator. And if the Armats decide to dig in, they could cut her off from professional tennis, word would spread, and we'd be no better off than if they sued, when you come down to it. You know how this works—if the top players or their families don't like somebody, that person is virtually dead in the tennis community. Gone. I think we have to draw the line, set limits. It's a no-win situation, Bill."

"Oh, this is great, just great." I rubbed the palm of my hand across my forehead, hoping there was another way out of this. "Mrs. Armat already hates my guts. Now I've got you guys deciding what I ought to be doing."

"Well, I thought this was a group discussion. Come on, Jordan," said Gus. "We're just trying to work this out."

"Look at it this way," Bill interjected. "Jordan's really the only one who can find out anything without waving a giant red flag. Nobody else in the organization knows the tennis world. But if you're really uncomfortable, nobody's going to force you to do this." He stared at me, eyebrows arched expectantly, waiting for a response.

I *was* really uncomfortable, but I wasn't about to let them talk about me like I wasn't there and then send me a memo about what they decided. It was obvious to me what had to be done. I don't pretend to have an explanation for everything, but nobody had to spell out the fact that the Springs was a young business in a precarious position and could not afford being at the receiving end of a major scandal. As Bill clearly realized about sports stars who liked their endorsements—they tended to avoid scandal, and they certainly weren't going to pay money to associate with it.

On the other hand, what if I failed? If I couldn't get to Audrey before the ranks closed around her again—and the odds were likely that this would happen—we'd be in a bad position. Or, less likely but much more unthinkable, what if Audrey were in serious trouble? Then I surely would be in over my head. But I preferred to be optimistic. My guess—admittedly risky—was that in the end, Mrs. Armat would still hate my guts but, due to whatever was the real subtext of Audrey's note, they'd all have a strong interest in making the surface appear as smooth as possible.

"Wait a minute," I said, slamming my hand down. "Halt, hold it! Nobody's thinking about Audrey here. Everybody's out to protect their own skins. Well, I saw a young girl in tears yesterday, and there was a reason for it, and if I can help her I will. She's the skin that counts here, and that's the only reason why I'm going to get involved with this." That, and, for some reason, I was starting to feel like this was my chance to give something back to the sport that had given so much to me. When I was playing, I'd been too wrapped up in myself, and then after the accident, I'd spent a long time curled up in a ball in some corner licking my wounds, literally and figuratively. Now I was ready to move beyond that, go out on a limb for maybe the first time. I looked toward Gus, as I tend to when I want him to understand what I'm saying without having to explain. Since I left tennis, Gus has taken on the singular role of replacing an entire cheering crowd. I'll admit it's a big role, but this time he wasn't applauding, or if he was I couldn't hear it.

"I vote no," said Gus. "This is crazy. We're not even sure what kind of problem we're dealing with. Audrey could be back home by now, watching TV in the family room. I think Jordan has enough real work here at the clinic, without sending her off to reenact *The Fugitive*."

"Think this through, Jordan," urged the Colonel.

"You know, little lady, you'll be doing that girl a favor if you let the experts do the job. You don't see me taping any ankles."

It was the "little lady" part that did it. I saw Gus cringe, knowing as he does that I'm neither little nor much of a lady. "I'm going to look for Audrey," I said evenly. At this point nothing else made sense. "Or at least do what I can to figure out just what went on here." I started toward the door.

Gus shrugged. He appeared to be nominally resigned. Our relationship appeared to be entering the down phase of its up-and-down cycle. "Just do me one favor, please, Jordan, if you will?"

"What?"

"Don't go falling off any mountains."

"Oh, excuse me. Since it's doctor's orders, I promise not to go over twenty feet above sea level."

I was holding the door open for A.M. to scoot out when someone stepped behind me—nobody had to tell me who.

"What, Gus?" I didn't turn around.

"I don't think this is a good idea for you, Jordan."

"And why not?"

He moved in front of me and put his hands on my shoulders, and I froze. Touching wasn't fair, not fair at all. It wasn't like Gus was just a boss, a slot on an organizational chart who ran my department and gave me a performance review once a year. That would have been simple. His touch meant so much to me—healing, listening, teaching, exploring, loving—it was all there in those hands. I remember when I was in the rehab hospital in Vail after the accident, lying there, my leg a patchwork quilt, basted together and in traction, my body broken, my mind a mess. Everything I had worked for all those years had come to an abrupt dead end. The jackpot at the end of the rainbow was simply to endure the pain another day in hopes of sometime moving, maybe walking.

I lived through a relentless cycle of doctors, physical therapists, rods, pins, microsurgery, stitches, painkillers, monochromatic meals on trays. Athletes will do almost anything to shore up their bodies, because they *are* their bodies. I'd heard that Boris Becker supposedly had bees' blood injected into his knees. But when the fine points of physical finesse were beyond my comprehension, much less my capability, I had ceased to exist. My life was twenty-four-hour television, a bodiless monster suspended on the wall above my bed that taunted me with snippets of a dreamworld I had left behind, where people ran and jumped and moved without wheelchairs and walkers and crutches. By comparison, winning at Wimbledon or the U.S. Open seemed such a paltry exercise. Then I knew what it really meant to be tough, to have guts, and I had neither.

What I had was Gus. I looked up from my horizontal haze of self-pity and he was standing by my bed, arms folded, tapping his foot. "Well," he announced. "Progress! You're looking a hell of a lot better than the last time I saw you."

I think I looked back at the TV. Lucy was scamming Desi again. "Oh. Have we met?"

"Well, 'met' is probably stretching it. We had an encounter." He sat on the edge of my bed and explained how he had visited me in the ICU, but I was too out of it to remember. Then he told me that Mariska had sent him the first time, but he'd come back on his own.

And he never left. For all the long months of surgery and therapy, Gus was my guide, my inspiration, and my drill sergeant. At first he pushed me so hard I hated him. I screamed and ranted, blamed him for anything and everything. But it was as if he were deaf. He just plugged ahead, and eventually I followed, if only out of pride. And the day I was released from therapy, almost a year and a half after the accident, he took me to dinner. "Not as a patient," as he'd made clear. "You're not a patient anymore. I would never get involved with a patient," he'd said as we ordered the wine.

Gus showed me that there was another way, another life. He let me into his world, and I became fascinated. I didn't merely want to share it, or watch over his shoulder, though—I wanted it to be my world, too. It felt wonderful to see people respond to therapy, make physical progress, gain back their pride. I knew it first-hand. For the first time in my life I was interacting with something other than a ball, and it was a heady sensation. So just when our relationship seemed to be at its best, I left to get my degree in physical therapy and athletic training. It was the beginning of a new career for me and, in a way, I suppose, the beginning of the end of my relationship with Gus, or at least the beginning of the decline. Frankly, here's how I see it: as I recovered, I was never quite as worshipful, or as deferential, or as unquestioning. The dynamics changed accordingly. Among other things, I was no longer flat on my back and literally looking up at him, no longer holding his hand as I inched my way along in his powerful wake. He, on the other hand, might accuse me of losing my empathy, becoming prematurely cocky, straining at the bit, putting him down, where once I had applauded him.

And, in a way, he'd be right. This kind of conflict is relationship nursery school, but we couldn't seem to get out of it. We started to fight over little things—like who had the most chances to do what they wanted on weekends in the past month and keeping a tally sheet, who didn't call whom back—which always means that there are big things. We tend to handle this by distancing ourselves from each other, because neither of us wants things to get to that terminal state, because we know there's still something there. To his credit, Gus has always been professionally supportive. It's our personal relationship that's suffered. In fact, I almost didn't take the job at the Springs because of it, which probably would have broken my heart. I can't imagine working anywhere else. My job is my life now, just as tennis once was. The staff are my family. Where Gus fits in is hard to categorize. Right now, the passion seems to have diverted itself into our work. Now we're like two magnets, circling each other, alternately attracting and repelling. Today was no exception.

"You've got a job to do here," Gus insisted. "Running after Audrey isn't a job. It's a wild-goose chase."

"I think I can help."

"And maybe you can. You know, tennis used to be your world, but this is your world now. Jordan, don't you see?" He began to sound exasperated. "You're finished proving something to those people in tennis. But you're just getting established in this field—you've worked so hard for this, and you don't need to be in the full force of a frontal attack by the Armats. Something like that could seriously damage your career."

"Not looking for Audrey could seriously damage my career, too. I appreciate your concern, Gus, but I really think I can handle this, and I'd appreciate your support."

"You know you have my support. You always will. But professionally, I have to tell you, this is not your responsibility and I think this is not the way to go."

"What's your real agenda on this? Why are you so afraid to let me go out and do something on my own?"

Gus's hands dropped from my shoulders, and we looked at each other for a minute.

He was probably right about a lot of things—Gus is usually right, or at least he's the master of the good point. But it didn't matter. What was the difference if I observed the professional proprieties and Audrey suffered? Or if I didn't make waves and somebody drowned? There are no handbooks or rules for this sort of thing. You just have to do what you feel in your heart is right. I felt like this was one time that I had to push the limits. A young girl was missing—she just happened to be a top tennis player. This was something I had to do—for Audrey, and for the Springs. And I had to do it for me. Gus should know that in a way that nobody else could, and it infuriated me that he couldn't give me at least a token vote of confidence. Did he still think of me as his apprentice? Besides, if Corinne Armat had really wanted me out of the picture, she couldn't have chosen a worse approach. She'd turned this into a contest, a match. And if there's one thing I've never been able to do if I can help it, it's lose matches.

Within twenty minutes, A.M. and I were back at our town house, packing.

FIVE

"**Y**ou're looking at a dead man," whispered the young tennis assistant. Courtside in a wheelchair sporting an oxygen tank, Paul Cranston was pushing a star player of a Florida college tennis team through her drills. At age eighty-five, Paul had suffered several debilitating strokes, hip-replacement and cataract surgeries, and his body was riddled with cancer, but that didn't stop him from struggling onto the court every morning—always immaculately attired in whites, with his trademark straw fedora at a rakish tilt.

"I don't know how he does it," the assistant, Jamie something, marveled. "He's got a routine—hits twelve balls from the ball machine, then we help him back into the wheelchair, and we mike him up." Jamie pointed to his earpiece. "We go on court and play, while he gives us the orders through this. Hank down there is wired, too." He chuckled. "*He's* the dead man. Paul's running him all over the court."

Indeed, the student assistant charged with chasing down and returning the girl's powerful ground strokes looked ready to drop, not surprising given the heat and humidity in Florida this time of year. I knew how he felt. I'd been on court under Paul's direction myself, when he'd once briefly anointed me as one of his chosen. "What's your job?" I asked.

"When I'm not on court? Stay out of the way. Get water. Figure out how this guy does it. His legacy, he calls it."

"So how does he do it?"

"First you gotta play for thirty years, then coach for fifty. I think I have a way to go."

It had been forty-eight hours since Audrey Armat disappeared. At least, we had to assume she was still missing. According to Gus, the Armats refused to take calls from him or Bill. All Audrey's agents at Global Sport would say was that it was an extremely serious situation. We were assuming the worst, and the first person I wanted to see was Paul Cranston. They call him "The Keeper of the Secrets" because he's seen and done it all. I'd heard that he was introduced to tennis in the south of France, where he met and became the confidant—and, some say, lover—of the legendary Suzanne Lenglen. During World War II, he was supposedly a spy. He played at Forest Lawn and officiated there for thirty years. At Wimbledon, he was a protocol expert and an unofficial ambassador to the international media. The greats he's coached included Alice Marble, Tony Trabert, and Arthur Ashe. He designed a line of tennis clothes, wrote three books and a tennis column. The Duke of Windsor, Charles Lindbergh, and Douglas Fairbanks were among his friends. Women players were his specialty, and he could still take a young talent and mold her for greatness. At one time or another Paul has touched virtually everyone in tennis, and his phone lines buzz nonstop as his many friends, associates, and media contacts keep in touch from all over the globe.

Still, Paul doesn't take himself too seriously. After his last operation, so many floral tributes flooded the hospital that he hired a hearse to take them home.

Paul is like a giant computer, with everything that has ever happened to anybody in tennis programmed into his brain. Of course, he may not choose to tell you what he knows, but he is sure to know something about anything or anyone. And he always cuts to the quick of an issue, never walks around the middle of it. So he was, logically, the first person I talked to about Audrey. A.M. and I had flown into Tampa and rented a zippy turquoise Mazda Miata, and this morning we'd shot on over to the Floridian campus to pay a call on Paul.

Practice ended, the player squatted down to towel off her sweat-drenched body and pack up her equipment. Paul radioed an order to his assistants, who converged to take the girl through some stretches, and I made my way over to him. A.M. got there first. She and Paul have always hit it off.

"Ah!" he exclaimed. "A.M., my favorite dog, named for the lovely Alice, one of my favorite players. There was nothing like her at Wimbledon in '39. Can your owner be far behind?"

"Hello, Paul." I stooped to kiss him under the hat, and was pleased to see that he hadn't abandoned his diamond stud earring, an accessory he'd adopted decades before it became fashionable. The wheelchair in no way diminished the impact of his willowy six-foot-six frame. A.M. and I perched on a bench as he sipped from a thermos with a straw.

"It's good to see you," I said.

"Damn good you made it before the funeral."

"Paul, you are immortal, you know that." I squeezed

his hand, genuinely unable to imagine the world of tennis without him.

He eyed me sharply, his eyes watery blue behind thick glasses. "Is this a social call, or are you going to get out there on that court where you belong, girl?"

"Not unless I can borrow your wheelchair. How about a little lunch?"

"Excuses, excuses. If you insist, there's a little French restaurant just down the road," he said. "It won't put the Hotel du Cap out of business, but it's presentable."

Jamie materialized to help Paul to his specially equipped van, push the wheelchair onto its pneumatic lift, and drive us the short distance to the restaurant. Actually, the wheelchair was somewhat of an improvement over Paul's previous mobility. For all his athleticism, he had always been one of the clumsiest people in sports, continually tripping or falling over the stairs, a scrap of carpet, or, most often, his own feet—and usually sporting some kind of scrape on his nose or scratch on his face as a result. People were somewhat relieved that he didn't want to be an umpire anymore, because to get him off the umpire's chair was always an adventure that caused all involved to hold their breath.

I invited Jamie to join us for lunch. "I'll just take A.M. for a little run," he said, indicating that he'd be waiting in the parking lot in case he was needed.

Over iced tea and salads, Paul and I caught up on the gossip. Paul was a champion gossiper, and often a vicious one—you certainly didn't want to get on his bad side.

"They're going to be putting some sort of tribute on for me at Wimbledon," he said, gruff but obviously pleased. "I hope you'll be there, Miss Myles. Even if I'm not." He sighed melodramatically.

"I'll try to be more optimistic than you are," I said, thinking that Wimbledon was still a good month away. I hadn't been back since my days as a player.

When I was fifteen, Paul had taken me under his wing and singled me out for special coaching. Even more helpful was his word of mouth, as good a reference as you were going to get in this sport. Everybody knew that Paul said it like he saw it. There was no bull, no candy coating, nothing but the bare, blunt truth as Paul saw it. If he said you were good, you were—or you'd damn well better become good fast. Nobody crossed Paul.

"So you're a doctor now?" he asked, his hand shaking as he laboriously conveyed the salad from his plate to his mouth.

"Not a doctor, a physical therapist."

"Same difference. You could've operated on my hip and done a better job than my surgeon. Stuck me in this damn chair." He whacked it with his heel. "Well, get to the point. I want to hear what you have to say while I'm still conscious."

"Paul, do you know Audrey Armat?"

He finished his bite of salad. "Audrey. Talent, ten; brains, three."

"You don't think she's smart?"

"I think she has no common sense. She listens to that father."

"He must be an okay coach—she's gotten to the top ten pretty fast."

"Who knows where she'd be if I'd coached her. And don't think I didn't try."

"You wanted to coach Audrey?"

"Parents shut me out." The sprig of mint fell into his lap as he raised his iced-tea glass. Liquid sloshed precariously over the side. "Damn!" he whispered.

I wanted to help him, but I knew that Paul's dignity wouldn't stand for it. So I waited patiently as he sipped. Finally, he shakily lowered his glass to the table.

"This girl has God-given talent. No question. It's like most of them. The problem's not the player, it's the people around them. I remember this one entourage—it was like the court of Louis XIV. Two coaches, four dogs, a cat, a nutritionist, a preacher, a PR person, a motivational music programmer, a girlfriend—and that was just for practice!" He broke into a coughing fit and clapped his napkin to his mouth. "God, I hate this," he gasped. I forgot about my salad and wondered if I should reach for the oxygen tank, but he continued as if nothing had happened. "Anyhow, Audrey. Well, she's quite your little performer."

"Yes, she's a wonderful player."

"That, too. But that's not what makes a star. Let me tell you, the most incredible competitors are usually great actors and actresses. Excuse me, Jordan, you were a fine player, but this was something you could never do. You are what you are."

I couldn't tell if this was a compliment or an insult.

"What actors do is bring to life the emotions called for in the script. Athletes who are great performers do the same. The script is clear—to project confidence, high energy, positiveness, fight, spirit, determination, regardless of how they personally feel. If a Jack Nicholson or a Meryl Streep has to go in front of the camera and play a part, nobody cares if they have a headache. To perform, they have to become somebody else, and the audience has to believe it. That's what makes a star—on camera, or on court. Everybody else is really just a bit player or a character actor, supporting the stars." Paul was lecturing, in his element now. "But take Kelly Kendall. That America's sweetheart thing. Sure she was a world-class player. But she was also a world-class performer. Her real personality is nothing like what she projected on court, that girl-next-door act. Ha! How about the time she won the Ladies' Singles at Wimbledon, then got drunk and threw up into the trophy at the Players' Ball! You can bet your bippy that never hit the press. But Kelly created a persona the fans liked, and she acted the part, totally. The media knows what the public wants to read—and if they want to sell stories that's what they'll give 'em. If she'd worked in Hollywood, Kendall could have won an Oscar. And then there's the men. McEnroe was supposed to be a brat, so he was. What a performer! And you think that didn't sell tickets? People paid to see the show as much as to watch the game. Alex Bracht, well he plays the bad boy, too. Audrey—don't you think she's not the same. Maybe more so."

"I don't know Audrey well, Paul, but I don't think she's throwing up into any trophies when we aren't looking."

He shot me a look. "You know, when you're talking, you can't listen, and when you're not listening, you can't learn."

"What do you know about Audrey?"

"She's young. There's time."

"Time for what?"

"To put it all together. There's the performer self, the

talent, and now she's got to figure out who the real Audrey is. Right now, her parents are taking care of everything. She's in a hothouse environment. But if the real Audrey can't be taken care of, if her personal needs aren't met, things might come apart. Sommelier! The wine list, please."

"That's a fascinating theory." I wondered if Paul should be drinking wine. He was probably on medication.

"It's not a theory, it's a fact, girl. Didn't they teach you that in medical school?"

"I didn't go to medical school."

"Well, maybe you should have. They need good doctors. The medical profession is overrun with quacks."

Minutes later, as the waiter poured the wine, Paul proceeded to demonstrate the finer points of his hip operation, using a steak knife and a broiled half chicken.

"So, Paul," I said as he dissected the thigh socket. "Are you saying there's a side of Audrey that we don't know?"

"Of course."

"She doesn't seem very happy."

"Understandable."

"Actually, Paul, there's a probability that she may have disappeared."

The knife wobbled in midair. "What?"

"Run away, we think. But I'm not sure. I need to find her. Can you help?"

He nodded. Paul knew more secrets than anyone else in tennis. He licked his lip and took a quivery sip of wine. "I knew something wasn't right," he said softly. "If I'd been a few years younger, maybe I'd have figured it out. You trying to help?"

I nodded.

"I wish I had something to tell you," he said sadly.

I patted his hand. "You did, Paul."

He squinted through his thick glasses. "Try Bracht. He might know something."

"Yes, he's her boyfriend."

"So to speak." He speared an asparagus.

"What's that mean?"

"Talk to him, that's all. Now. Are you going to Eastbourne? Because I'm not. The doctors told me to save my strength for Wimbledon. I told them, if I die before, sell my diamond earring and use the money to cremate me and send my ashes to England for my testimonial. I absolutely refuse to let them use a little thing like my dying as an excuse to cancel it."

"You're not going to die, Paul. You have a lot of Wimbledons ahead."

He put down his silverware and waved his hands. "I told you! You're a terrible actress. God-awful. Waiter, the dessert cart!"

Suddenly, Paul toppled sideways in his chair and gasped for breath. Instinctively, I grabbed the oxygen tank and slipped the mask over his nose and mouth. He sank back and breathed heavily, and soon regularly, his eyes blazing with rebellious refusal to acknowledge the inevitable.

After Jamie and I settled Paul comfortably back at his apartment—where, to my relief, a live-in nurse was in attendance—he dropped A.M. and me back at the Miata. It was a nice day, so I put down the top and we headed for the next stop on my itinerary, the Women's Tennis Association in St. Petersburg. I managed to make a few calls on the car phone: my voice mail, to check my messages and confirm that Audrey hadn't turned up yet and that so far the Armats still hadn't filed a lawsuit; my mother, to tell her that her daughter was still alive; my friend Annie in Palm Springs, to tell her I wouldn't be there to make it for Chinese and the movies tonight; and the person I was on my way to see—my old friend Carolyn Rice, who is a primary health-care provider with the WTA, a job I once had. I'd seen her signature on a number of Audrey's injury reports. Carolyn is a rock-solid person, totally dependable and completely committed to her work and to women's tennis. She travels constantly to the tournaments and is on the road, as I had once been, some thirty-three weeks a year, racking up more air travel miles than even the players. We used to joke that with our air miles we could travel around the world and back three times for free—except the last thing you wanted to do when you had some time for yourself was more travel. I was lucky to catch Carolyn in town and in her office. We made a date to meet for drinks at the Stouffer Vinoy, the five-star resort that's the player home of women's professional tennis.

As I drove past the airport and into St. Petersburg, I felt pretty good. How many times had I made this trip? A.M. propped herself up on her baby blanket with her front paws and hung her head out the side of the car, the wind raking her ears back, and I pushed my hair up under my baseball cap and sang along with my k.d. lang tape. Ever since I first got my license, driving fast, surrounded by wind, music, and a hot, Technicolor sun, has always made me feel like I could handle anything. I felt like Thelma and Louise, except A.M. was Louise.

Traveling with dogs has its distinct advantages and disadvantages. They are never backseat drivers and will happily accept any plans or change of plans. You tell them anything, and they will listen indulgently. On the downside, some establishments are not thrilled to welcome members of the canine family. For that reason, A.M. has become adept at hiding silently inside a gym bag, nestled among the towels, to be smuggled into some of the finest restaurants and hotels in the world. The way I see it, my dog is a much more desirable guest than a lot of people I know. A.M. has been to the governor's mansion in Puerto Rico, Versailles in France, the Roman Forum, and to the top of the Empire State Building. She's traveled on the Concorde, in her own Louis Vuitton carrying case, which my friends gave me when I left the circuit. Although I always pack dog food, she holds out for room service. When I traveled on the tour, one hotel in San Francisco used to give her dog cookies, her own monogrammed hotel dog bowl, and a towel with her name on it. Of course there's always the potential downside, like the time we were in Rome for a tournament and I had to stay up all night with A.M. at an Italian-speaking vet's. One minute she was chasing a cat and the next she couldn't move, she was comatose, for no apparent reason. It turned out that she'd eaten rat poison in L.A. four days earlier, and it took that long to affect her system and attack the white cells. A.M. had a transfusion and vitamins to counteract the poison, and she pulled through, but I was a wreck, and God knows how I played the next day. Another time she ran away in Chicago, and I got her back only because the fans mobilized a citywide flyer dragnet and somebody on a street corner recognized her from the flyer. Then there was the time A.M. got loose an hour before a final. She ran out of the locker room and onto the middle of the court and pooped in front of five-thousand people. I'm usually proud that she's my dog, and I don't mind cleaning up after her at all, but that time I asked the locker-room attendant to go out there and take care of it. I was totally humiliated.

We'd just pulled off the highway and stopped for a stop sign when, with a jerk and an unmistakable crunch, somebody managed to hit me from behind, toppling A.M. onto the floor of the car.

First, of course, I made sure A.M. was all right. She was still wagging her tail, so that was a good sign, but how do you know if a dog has whiplash? I walked wearily around the car, hoping I'd remembered to check the box for insurance coverage at the Hertz counter. Sure enough, a red Taurus four-door had made a nasty connection with my rear right bumper. There was a fair-sized scattering of shattered glass from his headlight on the pavement. An overweight man in a lime-green leisure suit, the three remaining hairs on his balding forehead combed sideways from ear to ear, was climbing laboriously out of the Taurus, pen in hand.

"You should drive more carefully," I said sharply. "It's not like you couldn't see me."

"Sorry, I was lost," he said. "This is a rental car. I'm from Indiana." His glasses had clip-on sunshades, and a camera dangled around his neck. He looked like a conventioneer in search of a name tag. We exchanged the perfunctory information, then extricated our cars. From the looks of the Miata, the damage was going to cost. I didn't have time to be messing around with returning the car, so I decided to live with a crunched fender for the time being. Irritating, but Carolyn was due to leave on an evening flight, and I knew she wouldn't have much time. I had to move on, and hoped this wasn't a bad omen.

At the Stouffer Vinoy, Gaby Sabatini was on her way out as I was coming in. Friendly as always, she gave me her radiant smile, and we exchanged hellos. Carolyn was waiting at an umbrella table on the deck that overlooked the tennis courts. She jumped up when she saw me, and we hugged.

"Good God, Jordan. Look at you! You actually ran in here. That's great!"

"Yeah, watch out. I'm mobile again. Well, you've changed your hair. Looks good." Her formerly long brown hair was now in a Dutch-boy-type bob.

She flashed her diamond-ringed left hand at me. "I had to spruce up for the wedding. You better come. It's here, in October."

"After the season, of course."

"Of course. Tennis first," she said, laughing. "George is used to it." Everybody in tennis was always used to it. You squeezed in personal time when you could—even weddings, births, and, if you planned to die, you'd better schedule it a year ahead. It was amazing that Carolyn had found time to meet somebody, much less develop a relationship.

But, of all people, Carolyn could probably figure out a way to swing it. She had adapted to the gypsy lifestyle better than most and, now that I thought of it, she'd always had a domestic streak, propping her hotel rooms with family photos and even scented candles to humanize them. That was what I remembered most about traveling with Carolyn: opening her hotel room door to a waft of vanilla or lavender or cinnamon spice. My room, on the other hand, usually smelled like Lysol. Carolyn was now in her forties and had always seemed to be married to tennis. She'd worked hard and done it by the book, starting in college at Purdue, where, she told me, she'd gotten into the athletic training program by cleaning the training room. From that point on, while most girls juggled studies and dates, Carolyn's life had revolved around training programs and game days, which meant early classes, weekends on duty, and traveling with the school teams. With her master's degree in athletic training finally in hand, Carolyn had been recommended to the women's tennis program by one of the university coaches. From there she'd worked her way up.

In the athletic world, medicine works differently than on the outside, where you simply go to the doctor. For professional tennis players, the first, most immediate, and most constant point of contact is often the physiotherapist or trainer, who is on the scene at a tournament from an hour before play begins till hours after it's over. There is a tour physician on call, but not always on-site. The world watched in horror when Monica Seles was stabbed on court by an assailant. The first person at her side, the person who went to the hospital with her, was the tournament trainer, who stood by as Seles was examined and X-rayed and assisted medical personnel in monitoring her vital signs. Clearly, this is not a job for anyone who is less than totally knowledgeable and dependable, and it requires a focus and dedication that I recognize and appreciate, having been there myself.

Carolyn has always been known among her fellow physios as the Rock. When things are in total disarray, she's in control. When everybody else's paperwork is backed up to the ceiling, her desk is clean. When there are players on fifteen courts at once, any one of whom can and does need her, she never seems rushed. And although tennis is an individual sport, Carolyn's approach is always that this is a team and we are all on it. Whatever needs to be done, she does it, whether it is talking her way through customs with an extra hundred kilos of luggage or figuring out how to handle blisters on fifteen pairs of feet. Carolyn, the detail queen, isn't the type to miss any nuances. I hoped this would mean that she'd noticed something about Audrey.

We settled in at the table, ordered drinks, and I gave A.M. a glass of water. "She's a little shaken up," I explained. "We were just in a fender-bender."

"It's good to see you," said Carolyn. "But I take it this isn't entirely a social call."

"Not entirely," I said. "Can we talk for a minute about Audrey Armat?"

"Sure, but of anybody on the tour, I'd have to say I know her least."

"But you signed a bunch of her injury reports. And there were an unusual number of them."

"Tell me about it." Carolyn rolled her eyes. "She has a million and one problems. To listen to her, it's amazing she can even walk."

"You don't believe her?"

Carolyn frowned and traced the lip of her glass with her finger. "I'm not saying she's a liar, mind you. A symptom-magnifier is more to the point. How did you see those reports? Are you treating Audrey at the Springs?"

"I was," I said, and left it at that, taking Paul Cranston's advice to listen for a change.

"I don't know," Carolyn sighed. "This is a tough one. You've been there—you wonder where to draw the line, where it's not appropriate to dig any deeper. You're really supposed to wait for them to come to you. I don't know." She shook her head, and it was a minute before she spoke again. "I did what I could. I treated the injuries."

"Were they legitimate?"

Carolyn picked at her cocktail napkin, tearing off little damp pieces and rolling them into balls.

I leaned closer. "You have to tell me your opinion," I said. "This girl may be in trouble. Please."

"Off the record, what I really thought, Jordan? What I really thought was that Audrey used these complaints as an excuse."

"For what?"

"Oh, in case she lost, or hoping they wouldn't let her play. I have a feeling there were repercussions if she lost."

"What kind of repercussions?"

"I saw some nasty bruises on her." Carolyn's voice was a whisper. "More than once. On her back and breasts. Once on her legs. And some suspicious burns."

I gasped. "Why didn't you say something?"

Carolyn leaned away suddenly, and I could sense gates slamming. She was, above all, a team player. "There was no way to prove anything. Audrey certainly wasn't talking. She claimed she fell, or dropped a cigarette—we all knew she didn't smoke, and how do you get a cigarette burn on your buttocks? If she wasn't going to stand up for herself, who could do anything? Besides, she kept winning. She was Audrey. There was a lot of pressure . . ."

"From whom?"

"Everybody. Listen, Jordan, there's thirty-three million dollars in prize money at stake out there in the women's tour, and some sponsors that need a lot of hand-holding. Do I have to tell you, of all people, how hard we've fought for women's tennis? Sixty-two tournaments, twenty-one countries. Nobody wants to turn the clock back to the sixties and see this sport slide back to women playing in high school gyms for no money. Who's going to rock the boat, especially with the number-one crowd draw?" Carolyn's mouth was tight. "What if I did say something? Because I did, you know. But you know the drill—nobody could prove anything, nobody could do anything, and one hint of suspicion and Corinne Armat would pull her daughter from your tournament."

"Carolyn, believe me, I don't want to put you on the spot." I knew all too well that if she were honest, she could lose her job. If she made any kind of accusations that weren't ironclad, the Armats could easily threaten to play exhibitions and boycott the tournaments, citing Carolyn as their reason and effectively slashing the profits of the women's tour by eliminating their daughter, a key crowd draw. "Nobody's blaming you or accusing you of anything," I assured Carolyn. "I've been there myself. That's not the point." It wasn't easy to be objective about these things. Part of your job is to know the players, but if you know somebody, or if you're in an awkward position because of politics, it's easy *not* to be objective. It was always strange, the way the world saw one side of a player, which we didn't know, and we saw another side, a side nobody else ever saw. I wasn't sure how I'd have handled the situation if I'd been in Carolyn's place. I wasn't even sure how to handle it now.

"Let's face it," sighed Carolyn, exasperated. "Legally, I can't do much. I have to wait for the player to tell me—I can't coerce information out of her. And then I have to document it. I'd have to be really, really sure before I said something. And even then, I could only make suggestions; we can't give advice. I'm not in a position to speculate, and neither are you, my friend."

"Believe me, I know this is a tough position. I'm only trying to help Audrey. She's just a kid."

"That! The terrible part. The kids. You know, Audrey did mention one thing. Her mother put a lock on the refrigerator, and she kept the key."

"Good God."

"I'll tell you what," said Carolyn. "Let's go back to the office. I'll check my files. Maybe there's something in there."

We settled up and walked back out of the open-air restaurant, past the bar, and toward the exit, tension still in the air. At a table near the bar, a lime-green leisure suit caught my eye.

"I have an etiquette question," I said to Carolyn. "Is it appropriate to wave to the man who just rear-ended your car?"

"You know, I thought he knew you. Your back was turned, but I saw him watching you the whole time we were talking. Maybe he wants to buy you a drink."

"Spare me."

"Well, he was taking your picture."

"What?"

"Yours, and a lot of others. The decor, people passing by, that kind of stuff."

I looked back over my shoulder, but he was gone. Thank God.

The WTA building was a few minutes away, a modern renovation in a sedate part of town, quiet, not many cars on the street. It's an unassuming place that could be anything—you'd never guess it's the hub and heartbeat of an international sports business with twenty-three members who earn more than a million dollars a year. We took the elevator up to Carolyn's floor and walked past the low-key reception area to her office.

"I can tap into the main computer from here," she said. "We have every player's file on-line. Wait. Here's something. Just a note. Shanna, one of the physios at the Lipton, told me she'd treated Audrey at several of the recent tournaments and she thought she might have some eating problems. There's nausea noted a few places in the files . . ."

"Nausea?"

"There was talk that when she thought nobody was looking, she'd stuff herself—nachos, candy, whatever—then go into the locker room and throw up. And apparently she did that a lot."

"Bulimic?"

"You can't rule it out. Maybe that's part of the reason why her game fell off. Her chemistries could be way off. Her vision and stamina would be affected—she'd never be able to stay strong for an entire match; she'd poop out early. It's not unheard of. You know as well as I do, there's more than one woman in the top twenty with an eating disorder of some sort. Look what happened to Daisy Sheffron."

Daisy Sheffron was a beautiful young Australian player who had become anorexic to the point where she weighed ninety-six pounds and had to be hospitalized. Bulimia. Burns. Bruises. I was starting to feel sick. We'd done blood work, though, and anything unusual would have shown up there. I'd have to make sure a doctor looked over the chemistries and have Tony fax them to me.

"Do you know if Audrey has any friends?" I asked. "Somebody who might know her well? Somebody she might go to visit?"

"That's the thing," Carolyn said. "She was so self-contained, for a kid." She thought for a moment. "Well, of course there's always E.J., her twin brother."

"Do you know him at all?"

"Nobody does."

"Girlfriends?"

"Not that I've seen. But, you know, so many of the younger girls aren't American and they don't even speak English that well. It's probably harder than ever to make friends." She glanced at her watch, and then at a pile of paperwork.

"I know you've got to get going," I said. "Maybe I can just tag along for a few minutes while you pack up?" Packing up was no small task, as I well knew. You never could be sure what they'd have at a tournament site, so you just finessed it by bringing everything. I parked A.M. on the sofa and followed Carolyn to the storage room while she went through her checklist: ultrasound and electrical stimulation machine; eight cases of 1- and 1½-inch white tape; six cases of elastic tape; four cases of various other tape; eyedrops; first-aid cream; medical supplies, but never Band-Aids—you make your own; two or three 25-yard rolls of sterile gauze; splints; neoprene sleeves; and so on. That was what you sent ahead. Then, of course, you carried your immediate kit with you, sort of a mini-hospital in a carryall. I used to keep mine stocked with bottles of hydrogen peroxide, first-aid cream, a roll of tape for emergencies, scissors, thermometer, and a sphygmomanometer to measure blood pressure. Forget about traveling light—and you can imagine what fun airport security was.

Carolyn and I finished inventorying the cases for shipping and she slung her bulging bag over her shoulder. "Well," she said. "Give my regards to Audrey. And grab a fact sheet. My number in Eastbourne is on it." Fact sheets have all the tournament details, including the tour staff and their hotels and phone numbers.

"I wish it were something simple, like a sprain," I said. Carolyn and I agreed to keep in touch, and A.M. and I were heading down in the elevator when it stopped and Kanga Cheyne got on.

Kanga, so nicknamed because she is Australian, was impeccably dressed, as always, in a white piqué suit and navy sling-back heels with white wing-tip toes, her skin a golden tan, her lipstick sprightly coral. A navy and white clutch bag was tucked neatly under her arm. Personally, I've never known how she manages to look so pulled together, especially with her schedule, but she always does. During trophy presentations Kanga was often on the presentation committee, always a striking figure in the congratulatory photo. But it isn't her looks that keep Kanga in this demanding job—she's very smart, and she loves what she does. I knew she'd been a Rhodes scholar and spent much of her early career in Europe, where she'd learned to speak several languages. Kanga used to say she was an international junkie who just happened to love sports. She'd landed a glamorous job with a Spanish sports promoter, had a disastrous affair with him, then segued back to the U.S. for a job in sports event planning in New York. Nobody even called it sports marketing then—she was just selling small-tournament sponsorships, or trading them for early-round tickets. Because of her language skills, she managed to pick up work in spurts as a player liaison at the Grand Slams, where she translated the various demands of the Spanish-speaking players, of whom there seemed to be increasing numbers. After a few years she signed on with Imperial Foods, the umbrella tour sponsor, handling tour promotions and sales events, which ultimately led to her position as player coordinator of the Women's Tennis Association. Frankly, I've always felt that in spite of her qualifications, which were beyond dispute, one of the reasons that Kanga had taken the job was because she hadn't seen Marion Stryker's alter ego. The public Marion charmed the promoters and the sponsors with smiles and graciousness, but behind the scenes she ruled the backstage of women's tennis with an iron fist and brass knuckles.

I liked Kanga from the first time I met her. She is efficient and bouncy, like her nickname, and she manages to keep a flock of often disgruntled players, coaches, and families not only in line, but satisfied. Ms. Fix-It, that's Kanga. Once, when I was a player, I mentioned that having some Perrier on court would be nice. Kanga ran to the grocery store to get it for me, and even taped over the logo before she handed me the bottle so I could drink it when the TV cameras were rolling, because Perrier wasn't a sponsor. Whatever a player wants, there is one sure way to get it, and that is to open your mouth and yell "Kanga!" During the time I'd traveled on the tour, at one time or another I'd personally seen her materialize an incredible grab bag out of thin air to satisfy a player's whims: courtside tickets to Chicago Bulls games; a New

York deli platter complete with pastrami and cheesecake at two A.M. in Paris; a playpen for a player's rambunctious dog; transportation for a player's mother; a professional photographer to shoot a player's son's Little League baseball team; a complete line of promotional items, including twenty-five each of sweatshirts, T-shirts, bags, and buttons for an entourage member with a yen for freebies. Kanga is nothing if not resourceful. Her only real difficulty on the tour was the fact that she reported to Marion Stryker. But then Marion is a walking brick wall with attitude. It was anything but easy for her to accept a bright, pretty, ambitious young woman, a prejudice that had in the past materialized in an inordinate amount of orders to do menial jobs, like collating press kits.

As usual, Kanga lit up at the sight of an old friend. "Jordan, what brings you here?" she beamed.

"Oh, A.M. gets nostalgic for chasing sea gulls from time to time." I wondered if she knew why I was really here. I supposed not.

"How's Marion?"

"She's got me on T-shirt detail."

"Typical."

"That's okay. We sold two hundred thousand dollars' worth of T-shirts in one day at the Lipton." She held up a shopping bag full of the merchandise.

"Congratulations."

"Well, when you've stooped to trading tickets for tablecloths, you get to know the tricks."

"And you know them all. By the way, have you seen Audrey lately?"

"No, but I heard she was resting her leg. And she did call in."

"Oh? You talked to her?"

"No, Marion did."

"Oh, isn't that interesting? Did Marion say where Audrey was?"

Kanga frowned, concentrating. "Hm, not that I can recall, but then I didn't ask for the details."

"When exactly did she call in?" I tried to keep it casual, but I really wanted to know.

"I'm not sure. I think yesterday, maybe. At any rate, Marion mentioned it to me yesterday."

"She actually talked to Audrey, or did she talk to her parents?"

"I'm sure she said she talked to Audrey herself. At any rate, Marion says everything's going just fine, and Audrey should be in top form for Wimbledon. It should be quite a show, her and Mariska. The match of the decade, Marion is calling it. The press is already going berserk."

"I can imagine." I was still not sure of the whole call-in thing, but this was vintage Marion. The press had a way of dramatizing rivalries to make matches more exciting, and if that brought more fans out to see a match, or more sponsors to the tour, all the better for the sport—that was Marion's theory. Kelly and Mariska had been promoted as legendary rivals, but since Kelly's retirement the feelers had been out for a replacement. Audrey fit the bill nicely as being diametrically different from Mariska, everything she was not—all-American, sweet, the girl next door. It was a match made in PR heaven. But I had to wonder where all this hype was going to lead. If Audrey was out of the draw, there was still good tennis and some exciting women players, but none of them were American and there wasn't a focal point for tournament officials to promote. So much weight had been put on Audrey's shoulders, and that was just one more pressure for her to bear. What if she couldn't handle it this time?

The elevator doors opened and Kanga stepped out. "See you in England!"

I felt relieved that at least Audrey had checked in with somebody from the tour office. Still, I wasn't any closer to finding her, or the answers I needed. My next stop had to be Mac Haskell, in Boca Raton. Haskell customizes the rackets for 90 percent of the top players, and is usually in constant touch with his clients and their coaches. He is always a good bet for some information.

It was early evening now, time for dinner. I was driving along, debating whether to stop for dinner at a restaurant, get a hotel room for the night, or pay a surprise visit to my former roommate, when I got the feeling that I was being followed. I'd never been followed anywhere by anyone before, so I decided I'd better be certain and took a deliberately circuitous route, zigzagging nonsensically until I reached the Boca Beach Club. I pretended to pull in, then, at the last minute, swerved. So did he. That's when I got nervous. I peered into the rearview mirror, trying to distinguish the car and the driver, but he was just far enough back to stay unidentifiable, hiding behind his lights, or, to be exact, light—he only had one. My stomach contracted. I am absolutely no good at this sort of thing. Luckily, however, I am an excellent driver, especially at high speeds. I convinced myself that if I didn't get killed this could be an interesting test of my driving skills, and floored it.

S I X

I sped off toward U.S. 1, purposely going absolutely out of my way as I headed toward Fort Lauderdale. The headlight followed. Who could be following me, and why? And what would happen when they caught me? There was no question that they would, because I wasn't about to reenact the chase scene in *The French Connection*. A.M. seemed to sense that something was wrong and cowered on the floor mat. What if somebody was trying to force us off the road and rob me? In my rented car, I looked like a susceptible tourist. Rummaging in my backpack, I found my key chain with its miniature emergency can of mace, which Tony had given me last Christmas as a present. I checked the road frantically for police, but naturally, since I was now going almost ninety miles an hour with a terrorist on my tail, they were all off giving parking tickets. Quickly, I analyzed my options. The best, I decided, was to see what I was up against. After some maneuvering, I was finally able to dodge between traffic and get a better look at my pursuer. It was a red Taurus. *The* red Taurus, complete with crumpled fender and smashed headlight.

Enough was enough. I swerved off at the next exit,

which was a steep ramp, pulled over on the shoulder of
the road, the way police do when they are hiding and
want to nab you with their radar, and started to count.
One one-thousand, two one-thousand ... On the count
of four, the Taurus flew down the exit ramp, and I shot
out from my hiding place and pulled up right behind
him, leaning on the horn and flashing the lights, clutching my Mace between my knees and my phone in my
left hand. He slowed down a bit and I pulled up beside
him, lowered my window, and leaned out, brandishing
the phone.

"I'm calling the police, you maniac!"

We both screeched to a stop and I sat there asking
myself if I had lost my mind. What if the guy had a
gun? His car door opened and out stepped Mr. Lime-
Green Leisure Suit. If there wasn't a law against following me, there ought to have been one against having
to look at that outfit three times in one day.

"Well," said Leisure Suit. "We meet again."

A.M. growled threateningly, which would have been
helpful if we were being attacked by a sparrow.

"You're not going to tell me this was another accident?"

He propped a green elbow on the edge of the open
car window. "No. Because it wasn't."

I tried to see his face more clearly. He didn't look
like anyone I knew, although that's certainly not a qual-
ification to join the weirdo club.

"So what are you doing—following me?" I spoke
carefully. You didn't want to rile these types. Sometimes confrontation was not a good idea.

"You might say that."

I cursed myself for not calling the police earlier, when this guy first ran into me.

"Relax. I was just drafting you."

"Boy, what a relief." I fervently wished that A.M. had some Rottweiller blood.

The next thing I knew I was being accosted by a business card. In the eighteenth century, people carried swords, then it was guns, but these days cards are the weapon of choice. Somebody's always sticking one in your face. This one said *Noel Fisher, Private Investigator*. There were some other details, but that was as far as I got.

"I'm working for Global Sport. The Audrey Armat case."

Global Sport. Of course—Big Brother is always watching. I scrutinized this guy. He certainly didn't dress like Columbo. "I didn't know it was a case."

He shrugged. His jacket opened and I could see a shoulder holster under the leisure suit jacket. "They're all cases."

"Did Global Sport tell you to follow me and wreck my car? Or was that your own idea?" I was getting angry now, clutching A.M. to my chest, banging my hand onto the steering wheel.

"Sorry. I just followed a little too close, maybe. You were really moving for a while there. I didn't want to lose you."

"You gave my dog whiplash and you almost ran me off the road."

"I apologize, Ms. Myles. I'm very bad at chases. Got a depth perception problem. And I guess I'm out of practice. It's been a few years since I was in the department."

"What department? The Department of Sanitation?" I waved the Mace. "Just leave me alone. Jerks like you lurking around the tennis community are not going to help either Audrey or your client." I wondered where they dredged up this guy. If this was Global's idea of protecting their investment, they might as well file for bankruptcy now.

"Let's not be coy, Ms. Myles. Do you want to find this girl or not? We have a mutual interest here. I'm not saying you're not going to find her first. You know the territory. That's why I'm tagging along. I was on your plane—did you see me in coach? Terrible lasagna. Anyhow, I figured Jordan Myles knows these women. She knows this game. You played it too, right? Maybe we should team up." He grinned, and his face had the look of a melted candle—broad brow, drooping jowls, thick, overhanging brows. "In fact, that was sort of what I had in mind."

"So Audrey's still missing?"

"And Chairman Mao is still dead."

"Well, your scare tactics aren't going to work, Mr. Fisher. Tell your client, let the Armats sue if they want. Tell them to sue me personally. But don't terrorize me. Now excuse me."

I shoved the car into gear and it leapt away. This time Fisher did not follow. I looked back and watched him in my rearview mirror until he dropped out of sight, just in case. And just to be safe, I called Tony from the car.

"Tony, could you do me a couple of favors?"

"It's never a question of if, it's only a question of what."

"What would I do without you? First, my plants—"

"Yes, I will make sure they're watered. Does A.M. miss Uncle Tony? Put her on."

"She's pining, but she can't come to the phone. The other thing is, there's this guy Noel Fisher. He says he's a private detective working for Global Sport, but he's a flake. Could you maybe run a background check on him?"

"Consider it done." And I did. Tony had proved many times that, given the need, he could do anything, from making an emergency gelato to hacking into a high-security computer program.

Don't ask me how, but the next morning the Fish, as he deserved to be called, pulled into the parking lot within thirty seconds of my arrival at Mac's. Dealing with this guy was like having a piece of tape stuck to the heel of your shoe. Definitely the dogged type. I imagined the Fish could probably guess all the letters on *Wheel of Fortune*, maybe even win an RV. For a few seconds I contemplated blowing his cover to get rid of him, but then I realized that wouldn't work. First of all, and this was the main thing, nobody would believe Noel Fisher was a private detective. However, he seemed to compensate for his image inadequacies by being a fast learner. For example, he was now making a special effort to blend in with the Florida environment by wearing a blue velour warm-up outfit. Although the outfit accentuated his resemblance to an upholstered couch, I had to hand it to him. He was a person who looked absolutely, convincingly like anything except what he was, which in his field had to be a major professional advantage. Also, if there was a scene in the parking lot and Mac Haskell thought this was anything other than an informal visit from me, he would almost certainly shut down, and nobody would learn anything, which wasn't going to help Audrey if she was really in trouble. Then there was the fact that if Fisher was as determined as he appeared to be—albeit unsubtle—it was possible he could be of some use. On the downside, of course, was his recklessness and apparent stupidity. I made a flash decision, and when I saw Mac waiting to welcome me at the glass doors in front of the building, I propped A.M. on my hip and purposely fell into step beside the Fish as if we'd planned it. He in turn pulled out his camera and snapped pictures in the manner of any self-respecting tourist.

"This is Dr. Fisher," I said, introducing him to Mac. "A dentist and family friend." Actually, he did look like he could have handled a few root canals, if you had sufficiently gassed the patient.

The Fish caught on right away. "You know," he said as Mac escorted us down his glass brick entrance hall, "I keep telling Jordan that good dental hygiene is the foundation of physical fitness."

Mac nodded politely as he scratched A.M. above the eyebrows, where she particularly likes it. Really, it wouldn't matter what you said to him—he'd heard it all, and he was beyond reacting. Whatever the circumstance, both Mac's brow and his trademark plaid sport coat remained unwrinkled. As long as I'd known him, whether the wind was thirty miles an hour or the thermometer over ninety, his gray hair remained perfectly in place and his glasses unfogged. In the midst of a panic, even when a top player forgot to request tournament rackets until the last minute, Mac never moved quickly, raised his voice, or betrayed the slightest anxiety.

We followed Mac down a hall lined with autographed photos of virtually every tennis star imaginable. If they played during Mac's lifetime, their picture was hanging here. There were also pictures of some of the top golfers, with a group of golf bags standing at attention directly beneath them.

"Golf fan?" asked Fisher.

Mac grinned. "Dr. Fisher, tennis is my profession, but golf is my passion." He gestured to an interior glass wall that looked into an expansive room lined with cubbyholes stacked with rackets. "Those are Jordan's rackets up there—top row, third from left, green suede grip."

Fisher pulled a small bag of potato chips from his pocket and ripped it open as we walked into the room. "Lunch," he said, shrugging apologetically, although it was only ten forty-five in the morning. He tipped back his head and shook the entire contents of the bag into his mouth, leaving a flotilla of crumbs scattered across the front of his jacket. A.M. trailed behind, scavenging.

Mac pointed out Mariska's rackets, four rows down from mine, then Alex Bracht's, Steffi Graf's, and just about everybody else's in tennis.

Fisher nodded thoughtfully as he chewed. "What about Audrey Armat?" he asked.

Mac gestured to the two young men in shorts and T-shirts who were systematically clipping strings. "Those are hers, in fact, that pile that Steve and Gary are working on."

Snap. Snap. Snap. With the clip of small hand-held wire cutters, the face of one of the world's most expensive and exclusive tennis rackets was systematically shredded, its seventeen-gauge, .047-inch-thick gut strings—so fine most stringers couldn't even thread them into a racket—clipped off, yanked out with pliers, and unceremoniously drooped onto the floor, where a stack of identical, seemingly brand-new rackets awaited the same fate. Next the frames would be inspected for cracks, checked for deflection changes, regrommeted, restrung, cleaned, and regripped. The handles would be checked for shape problems and reset with weights and balances. Then the rackets would be restenciled with the sponsor's logo, bagged, and shipped—perhaps to win, or lose, a championship.

When tennis is your career, the difference between even the best mass-merchandised tennis racket and a Haskell racket is beyond comparison. The manufacturer's name appears on the equipment, but it's a nonsecret that the handiwork of Mac Haskell's rarefied group of sports artisans makes it world-class and, maybe more important, makes sure each player's racket is absolutely identical to the others he or she owns in every way, to the millimeter and microgram. Consistency is the key. You have to know precisely how your equipment is going to respond every time, so that your only variable is you.

In his fifteen years in the business of supplying the top players with customized rackets, Mac Haskell had never let a client down, even if it meant jumping on an all-night flight to Europe himself with twenty rackets under his arm and special customs permissions forms in his pockets, then turning right around and flying home. The fact that a player was currently number one or two in the world was incidental; Mac gives the same kind of service to every client on the tour—as he had to me, when I was surfacing somewhere in the double digits of

the rankings. In fact, he still insists on making my practice rackets, for a fraction of what they're worth, which
is lucky for me. Once you've played a Stradivarius, it's
hard to go back to a ukulele.

Mac's people, guys like Steve and Gary, train with
him for years just to learn the fine points of how to
string, clean, and balance a racket—an apprentice
can spend an entire year refining his or her string-
straightening technique. Haskell can take a standard-
issue sponsor racket and customize it from the handle
up, or they can refit and refurbish it after every use so
it plays like new each time. That's a lot of rackets,
when you consider that many of the top players use a
racket only once before they feel it needs to be completely restrung and returned. On a four- or five-week
tour, a player may go through a hundred customized
rackets, each handle made to his or her own specifica-
tions and measurements. After each one is used, the
player's assistants air freight it back to Haskell before it
goes out again and into play. Some especially particular
players, like Lendl, were known to change rackets for
every change of balls, so that the sensation of play was
always exactly the same. And these rackets have a short
life cycle; a racket can be restrung only once.

It was a sure bet that Emilio Armat would have settled
for nothing less than a Haskell racket for Audrey.

"Sure," Mac had said when I called from the road.
"Audrey's been a client since she was nine years old.
Sweet little girl. When Wexner became her sponsor this
year we had to do a little more work, because she grew
up with a Wilson. She didn't want to adjust to anything
new, so we customized a Wexner racket with a Wilson-

type handle recast especially for her two-handed back-hand."

One thing—when you have your racket customized, you have to be there. You have to be on court to play-test it, and your hands have to go into the plastic to make the mold for the handle. They can't do it by proxy, and your agent, coach, or father can't do it for you, even if they want to. So this would have been one of the rare times when an outsider had the chance to spend time close to Audrey. I kept thinking about my own short time with her at the Springs, how she'd seemed so silent and tense, as if the simple act of speaking would shatter a composure as delicate as hand-blown glass. But when you're working with a player one-on-one, you can't cut off their head—or cut out their heart. Mac or one of the guys in his workroom might also have seen, overheard, or even sensed something. Maybe there was something that seemed trivial to them, but that might help other pieces of information fit into place.

"Did Audrey just send in these rackets?" I asked Mac. Maybe I could find out if Audrey was secretly off practicing somewhere. Of course, Mac is very close-mouthed about his clients, which is why everybody trusts him.

"Emilio did. We have to get forty-five of them ready for Eastbourne and Wimbledon. It's the usual—take them apart, inspect them for cracks, put them on the machines, look for deflection changes, put in new grommets, restring, clean, regrip, check for handle problems, reset the weights and balances, stencil them, bag them, and ship them to Paris Monday. I've already talked to DHL, customs, and the hotel concierge. Except we're doing an extra-tight inspection on these. Emilio Armat thinks something might be off in the rackets and affecting Audrey's game. And, well, you know how she's been playing."

"What did you find?"

"Nothing. But of course, we can't assume that that's what we'll find. We're problem solvers. It's up to us to interpret what you players are really saying."

"I'm not a player anymore, Mac," I reminded him.

He put an arm around me. "Once a player, always a player. Believe me, you can't assume anything. You guys are like the princess and the pea. Take Mariska. Once, we accidentally wrapped a piece of paper tape into the handle of one racket. This tape was something like half an inch long, but she felt it in there and sent the racket back."

"Half an inch?" Fisher asked dubiously.

Mac held up a tiny piece of paper to demonstrate. It was smaller than his little fingernail. "The top players can feel variances plus or minus fourteen hundredths to eight hundredths of a gram. The average factory variance is five grams. What does that tell you?"

Fisher thought for a minute. "If they were my patients, I'd give them novocaine before I cleaned their teeth."

Mac stared at him in stupefied politeness.

I decided to cut this short. "Did you find anything unusual about Audrey's rackets?" I asked.

"It's as much psychological as anything else. If she thinks she's got a problem, she's got a problem. It's not up to her to verbalize it. It's up to us to figure it out." He tossed the shred of paper into the wastebasket. "Things used to go along pretty smoothly, but suddenly, when she hit this little slump, she started having problems with everything. Everything and nothing, if you know what I mean. She can feel the butt cap; the tension is off; something's off with the racket face at two-o'clock. But we never find anything. It's always possible that something could turn up, but at this point I have to say I don't think it's an equipment issue."

It sounded all too familiar. "Speaking of psychological," I said, trying to sound casual, "when she was at the Springs a few weeks ago she seemed unusually distant, even for her." I picked up a racket and tried out the grip.

"I know what you mean," Mac said, frowning. "Even the guys commented on it, and they're closer to her age. Usually they can get a conversation going with the players, particularly the young ones—have a few laughs, kid around, have some fun. But not with Audrey. Of course, she didn't have much chance to talk." He tossed a small white cube of wax to Gary, who ran it along the strings of the racket he was working on. "Her mother never left the kid alone, even when she went into the bathroom. I'm not kidding—she actually went into the ladies' room with her, swear to God. I heard that at tournaments it's worse—Mrs. Armat even goes into the stall. She acts like the kid is in some kind of protective custody. But that's no secret."

That, and worse, I thought, but I wanted to let Mac talk.

"I always tell our clients, 'Come out without the entourage,' but we're not talking about a guy with a masseuse and a coach and a manager and a girlfriend and the usual menagerie of hangers-on—this is an underage kid. You can't keep the parents out; the parents are the mouthpiece. Which is fine, it's as it should be, except some of these parents are really all over the place—they try to do everything for the kid except hit the ball. And sometimes I think they're convinced they could do that better, too."

"What about Emilio Armat? Was he there, too?"

"Of course he was there. He's okay, at least he tried to be nice. But that mother—"

Shaking his head, Mac walked over to the computer, tapped the keys expertly, and brought up Audrey's file. "Here she is. Wexner RQ-180 Widebody; eggshell color; no bumper guard; technifiber string; gray string strip; small white Wexner butt cap; Wilson-type grip. She's got leather overlapping the butt cap so she can't feel the edge. Plays with both sides of the racket, so there's no up- or downside. We've got her exact gram weights and millimeter balances on here, too." He noted the screen.

On the other side of the room Steve and Gary had rotated to the stringing studio, where each was stringing a racket clamped in a standing viselike device. They worked in a rhythmic pattern—weave, spin the vice, clamp; weave, spin the vice, clamp—a dance of expertise.

"We developed our own stringing machine," Mac said proudly. "And you're looking at intestine," Mac explained to Fisher.

"What?"

"The top pros all use animal intestine as opposed to the nylon strings they use commercially. Ours is made in France."

The Fish grinned. "No guts, no glory."

I cringed, but the ever affable Mac chuckled. "I guess

you could say we're a bit detail-oriented. You're talking about four hundred fifty-five thousandths of an inch. Well, we had one of those time and efficiency experts in here once. We told him we spend five or six hundred hours a year on each of our players' rackets. He told us we were nuts." He looked around his sleek, state-of-the-art premises. "Well, he might be right. All I know is I've got seven of the top ten players in the world, men and women, waiting for their rackets, and it's our job to get them right, every time out."

"Mac, do you think we could talk in private?" I asked.

"Sure thing."

I put A.M. down to roam the premises, and the three of us walked into his glass-walled office, which offered a desk, a couch, two chairs, and a clear view of the goings-on in the studio. As we walked, Mac slipped his arm around my shoulders.

"What's happening with you, Jordan? Thinking about a comeback? You could do it. You know, your only problem was you were too good. In school, I mean. You weren't like some of the others—you had a real choice. Could have gone either way. You had the talent, but then you also had the education. You were just at the point when you could have had it all, and boom, it was over." He leaned forward. "And I don't mean that accident. That was a tragic thing, but let's face it, that's not the whole story."

I squirmed uncomfortably. "I'm not here to talk about me, Mac. You won't get off that easy." Actually, even the thought of serving filled me with panic.

"No? I'm disappointed. I thought I could get you

back on the court." He patted me on the shoulder. "No pressure, Jordan. You know that."

"Thanks, Mac. What I really wanted to do was talk a little more about Audrey. It's ... part of her therapy program."

Mac eyed Fisher. "Is this for publication?"

The Fish held up his hand as if to inform us that sensitive situations were his specialty. "I'm a doctor, sir. I'm sworn by oath to keep everything I hear confidential."

Fisher was just plausible enough to get by, if you didn't know the fine print of the Hippocratic oath, or the fact that he had never taken it, and probably never even read it.

"Very well, Doctor. Something very strange happened the last time Audrey was here, Jordan, and if you hadn't probed specifically and if we hadn't known each other for so long, I wouldn't mention it, but ... well, it's bothered me a lot since it happened. And I'm glad to hear that Audrey's in your therapy program because, otherwise, I just don't know."

Mac seemed on the verge of tears. I couldn't imagine what he was going to say.

He took a deep breath. "The last time she was here, she got a hold of a car—I won't go so far as to say she stole it, but it wasn't hers. That mother probably wouldn't give her the keys to her own car. You know, she has that Mercedes that Milt Bevins gave her. Anyhow, this car that wasn't hers drove off with Audrey at the wheel and there was an accident."

"She totaled it? In a joyride?" It seemed so unlike Audrey.

"Well, that was the on-the-books explanation—which,

of course, was kept very quiet—a little teenage indiscretion. But I saw that girl in the hospital afterward . . ."

"Hospital?"

"Yes. She'd been knocked unconscious and they took her to the emergency room. Since the car she borrowed—well, I did leave the keys in it—was one of mine, they called here, and I went right over of course."

"And?"

"And." He paused, and he appeared to be debating whether to go on. A few moments ticked in silence, except for the dull buzz of ringing phones outside the office and the muffled music from the studio. Finally he continued, his voice soft. "And I think she tried to kill herself."

"What?" I was stunned. Running away was one thing. This I wasn't prepared for. "But how do you know?"

"Well, her parents arrived at the hospital just when I did. I stepped aside, of course, and I heard Corinne Armat chew her out: 'Did you hurt yourself? You have to practice!' And then Audrey said—I heard this—she was crying, and she said she wished she were dead."

I shook my head sadly.

"These teen things need to be taken seriously, Jordan," Mac said insistently. "One kid down here killed himself in the driveway of his parents' house and left a note apologizing about his grades. You have to take these things seriously these days. I'm speaking as a father now, not as an expert. Which I'm not."

"God."

Fisher sat frozen, finally out of his depth.

Mac sighed. "It was as terrible a thing as I've ever witnessed. And you should talk to Gary. He saw something, too. I wish we could have gotten involved. But how?"

"What happened then?"

"Two days later Audrey was back on the court practicing six hours. And it was like nothing had ever happened. She was sweet, nice, she was Audrey again. It was like the Body Snatchers had taken over for a few days, and now that was over. But there's more to it. Let's talk to Gary. I'll get him." Mac picked up the phone, and the Fish and I exchanged uneasy glances. I was certain this wasn't going to be good.

Mac escorted us to his Tennis Racket Hall of Fame, a room lined with rackets that his notable clients had given him after winning matches, each with a small brass plaque beneath it detailing the player, the match, the tournament, and the date of the win. It was like being in a tennis museum. Gary came in wiping wax off his hands with a towel, which he then tucked into his waistband. With his short hair and Stanford T-shirt, Gary looked like a college student, not far from Audrey's age. A.M. bounced at his heels.

"Tell them about what you saw when you delivered those rackets to Audrey," Mac directed.

Gary seemed nervous. "Are you sure?"

"Jordan's trying to help. And Dr. Fisher here might have a medical opinion."

"It wasn't a good thing," Gary said uneasily. He stood up and sat on the edge of Mac's desk. "I had to deliver some rackets to Audrey at Amelia Island. There was some kind of delivery screwup, so I went personally. Audrey lost her match, and in the parking lot, her mother threw a gym bag at her. Hard."

I was stunned. "You saw this, and they knew you saw it?"

"No, they didn't see me. But afterward, I went up to Audrey at the dinner that night and I asked her about it. I told her to report it. And she said, 'What can I do? My parents love me. I can't do that to them, after all they've done for me.' She's a really nice girl. It's just sad."

"Do you know where Audrey is now?"

"Sure," said Gary. "Her father left a message with our service about her rackets this morning. She's practicing."

Or was she? "Where?" I asked.

"He didn't say," Gary said. "At home, I assume."

Home being a summer house in Connecticut at which the Armats had installed state-of-the-art tennis courts and training facilities.

The Fish nodded. "What would happen if, say, you called her right now? Let's say you had a technical question. Think she'd come to the phone?"

Gary shook his head. "No way. You have to filter everything through Mr. or Mrs. Armat. Sometimes it's really hard to get through the layers to these stars."

"Yeah, I can picture it." The Fish stood up and grabbed a racket that was propped in the corner. "Say, do you guys suppose I could get a racket custom made for myself? What would it cost?"

"You play tennis?" asked Mac.

The Fish looked like the most exercise he ever got was pushing the butter dish across the table.

"A little. In fact, I've been thinking about spending some real time on the courts. What kind of racket should I get?" The Fish lobbed the air. His form was nonexistent.

"Don't quit your day job yet," I mumbled.

But Mac answered him as seriously as if he were a world-class player. "I always tell people, we never make that decision. We don't know. What we do know is how to put you in a rackets clinic, so you can make your own decision. Would you like to try a little play-test out on the court with the boys, Dr. Fisher?"

For a minute I actually thought Fisher was going to go for it. I was wondering how I was going to save him from himself when my beeper propitiously went off. "Oh, well!" I conspicuously turned the beeper off. "Sorry to cut this short, but, well, I guess we'd better be going."

"Come back anytime for that play-test," said Mac as he shook hands with the Fish. I promised to keep in touch.

"You should do more than that, Jordan. You should try to play more, just for fun."

"Now, there's an oxymoron," I laughed, brushing his cheek with a kiss. "Tennis and fun. Well, you never know."

"Still afraid?" Mac challenged, purposely trying to bait me.

I didn't rise to it. "Still an armchair psychologist?"

"What's this about being afraid?" the Fish asked as we walked out. As we approached the lobby, I noticed Andre Agassi's coach coming in and was grateful that he didn't know me and I wouldn't have to introduce him to Fisher.

"It's nothing. Just a joke."

He snapped a picture. "Then why are you getting angry?"

"Because it's none of your business, that's why." I tend to get irrationally emotional when people ask me about tennis, I'll admit. But I have my reasons.

"I was going in there, with or without you. And you knew it. If you'd stop being so stubborn for a minute, you'd see that maybe we can get more done together. We're both here for the same reason. And we got some information in there." He pulled a small box out of his pocket and shook it. "Chiclet?" He poured out a handful of little white peppermint squares, stuffed them into his mouth, and started chewing. "The fact is, Audrey's rackets are still coming in like everything was on the upsy-daisy. Supposedly she's back practicing. My client, Global Sport, will be happy to hear this. Case closed."

"I don't know." Perspiration was dribbling down my hairline. It was too hot to keep the top down, so I closed it, turned on the ignition, and blasted the air-conditioning full force.

The Fish rambled on. "You heard it. The parents are strict, but the kid loves them. Maybe they had a little spat, but she's back, she's practicing. If you're going to make any allegations beyond that, you better have it airtight—witnesses, the whole shot. And Audrey'd have to give sworn testimony." He squinted at the sky. "I wonder if I can get a tan before this heat kills me." He unfurled a large handkerchief, mopped his brow, and patted the three remaining hairs on the crown of his head.

"We haven't actually talked to Audrey," I said uneasily. "So I'm not sure of anything until that happens." I kept thinking of Audrey being hit with the gym bag. Her mother rationing the car keys. Audrey in the hospital.

The Fish folded his handkerchief, then refolded it into a small square. "Face it, my friend. You and I both know there's something wrong with this picture. Maybe you and I aren't the only ones who know it, but until somebody else is elected, we're the ones who are in a position to do anything about it. And as I see it, there's a girl in trouble out there. Personally, I'm bothered, and I think you are, too. Now, what do we want to do about it?"

The car had cooled off a little, so I motioned A.M. inside while I checked my beeper. It was flashing Gus's number, so I turned my back on the Fish and called him on my mobile phone.

"Hi, Jordan. Where are you?"

"The parking lot from hell."

"Spare me the details. Listen, about those blood chemistries. They're back. Nothing abnormal."

"Really. Well, I guess I'm going to have to look a little harder. I was hoping they'd show something. Anything else?"

"Well, good news, actually. Audrey's turned up. Global Sport called. She's back and she's training."

"So I heard down here."

"We want you to come home. The Armats' attorneys have been in touch. They're not filing suit. Thank God. Maybe now things can get back to normal. We've got the Davis Cup team coach coming in, and we're going to need you."

My stomach churned. "I can't come back, Gus. I've got to set this straight, and I can't do that from a training room."

"What's there to set straight?" Gus said tensely.

"Audrey's back. She's training for Wimbledon. They're not suing."

I tried to make him understand. "That's not the point here, Gus. I don't care about suing or not suing. Well, I care, but—Gus, I've found out enough that I'm really worried about Audrey. I think she may need help, and I can't walk away from that."

I could envision Gus pacing in his office. "Well, you better run, not walk away, Jordan, because the Armats know you're poking around in their business. If they find out you're in Florida asking about them, there'll be hell to pay. And what I didn't tell you is that their lawyer said if you don't lay off and leave their daughter alone, they will bring an action against you personally, for what he called improper practices and failure to use accepted methods, resulting in mental anguish and intentional inflicting of emotional distress. And I quote."

"Gee, I'm scared. That only proves that they're worried."

"Worried about you causing problems," Gus said exasperatedly. "Listen, Jordan, I know nobody can tell you what to do, but I'm making a strong professional suggestion here."

"Professional?"

"And personal, too. I hate to see you get yourself into this kind of a mess. The Armats are taking a hard line. Now, when can we expect you back?"

I momentarily wondered if I was doing the right thing. It made sense to go back. But it didn't feel right. Not yet. Not until I knew for a fact that Audrey was safe, and I could get to the bottom of this. Even if she was back with her parents, it wasn't good. In fact, it was worse.

"I don't know, Gus," I said. "But, believe me, I don't want to do anything that's going to cause problems for the clinic. I'm taking a short leave of absence, as of now. Off salary."

Silence. Then Gus said, "I think you should reconsider." His voice was tight.

"Thanks for the advice. See you." I clicked the END button and the call was over.

I turned and looked at Fisher, who was trimming his cuticles with a pocket clipper. "I guess I'm on vacation. Maybe you are, too. They say Audrey's really back."

"Mind if I use your phone?" He punched some numbers and stood with his ear to the phone for a few minutes, frowning, saying nothing. Then he handed the phone back to me. "I'm off the case," he said. "Global Sport left word on my voice mail that Audrey has returned and there's no longer a need for my services. So I guess we're both on vacation now."

"What about Audrey?" I asked.

"Somehow I don't think she's having much of a vacation," he said.

"Neither do I. Nobody seems to care what's really going on with her." I knew I had to get to the bottom of this, but I wondered how I was going to handle it alone.

"Where to next?" the Fish asked. "I'm thinking Happy Meal and Thick Shake. My treat." He sauntered back to his car, unloaded a garment bag and a duffel, and tossed them into the passenger side of the Miata. "I'll call the rental company from your portable and tell them to pick up my car. I think it's undrivable."

Well, I was wrong about one thing at least. There was no way I was going to be alone.

SEVEN

If there's one thing I hate, it's the smell of grease in my car. But with the Fish spreading his Big Mac and large fries all over his lap, it was pretty unavoidable. "It's one thing to be chauffeuring you around," I said. "But do I have to wallow in grease?" We had a two-hour drive ahead of us, but I stared at I-95 in hopes that Miami would suddenly appear at the other end. In Miami was my old friend Cassie Heller, a sports reporter for the *Miami Journal*.

I'd met Cassie when she was a fledgling reporter and I was trying to blast my way into the top ten. It was a lonely place to be for both of us. People always think one of two things about the women's tour: that it's a glorified sorority, full of close friendships and off-court socializing, or that it's a hotbed of lesbianism. In fact, neither scenario is the case. There are probably no more or fewer gay women than in the population at large—but those who are gay tend to be in the limelight and attract more than their share of opportunistic relationships and press attention. And while you do make some close friends, most of the players are not just athletes, but self-contained entrepreneurs, each focused on her own individual goal. The practice and travel schedules and the necessary level of commitment don't leave much room for off-the-cuff socializing. Even so-called free weeks don't end up being that, by the time you factor in getting to and from wherever you're going, plus workouts and practices, and usually an exhibition or two thrown in for good measure. After a tournament, everyone heads their separate ways until the next time, and the silence in the women's locker room can be deafening. But sometimes, as you see the same people over and over again in the same role but different settings, you strike up a conversation, and sometimes something sticks.

When Cassie and I first met, I was the rising star and she was the junior reporter—one who stood out from the very beginning by the nature of her interesting and decidedly nonformulaic questions. I was her first exclusive. I still remember meeting her grudgingly for a ten-minute interview that was so interesting it turned into half an hour. Next time our interview became a real conversation, and then there was a dinner interview, and I had a new friend. Soon the two of us were the scourge of the women's tour, as immature as two twenty-one-year-olds were capable of being. We specialized in juvenile practical jokes, like having thirty pizzas delivered to somebody's hotel room. For a while Cassie and I would alternate holidays at each other's homes. Cassie was even with me when I met Tim, although she now denies introducing us and claims her only regret was not short-circuiting his blow-dryer when she had the chance. And when Cassie got engaged to Rob Pernice, a coach on the men's tour, I was the first one she called. Still, there had always been an awareness of our respective roles. I was the player, she was the press. It wasn't always an easy dynamic, drawing the line between a private conversation between two friends and something we both knew could lead to career recognition for her. Invariably, Cassie chose our friendship. She knew where the lines were drawn, and she always knew a lot more than she ever printed, which is probably true of most good reporters. I suspected that if anybody was reading between the lines about Audrey Armat, it was Cas. And then there was the fact that Rob, her husband, was the coach of none other than Alex Bracht.

The Fish spurted ketchup onto his burger, smeared it around with his thumb, then licked his fingers. "This is good, healthy American food. Can I help it if you prefer to eat brooms? What you need is a nice helping of my mother's brisket." He shook the fries under my nose. "Help yourself. I understand potatoes are vegetables."

"No thanks. You know, serving politically incorrect food in this car is grounds for being dumped on the side of the highway."

"Believe me, I'm undumpable. Milk shake?"

"Do you know where milk shakes come from?"

"Cows?" he asked tentatively, as if he wasn't sure.

"Yes. And do you know that while a normal cow has a life span of twenty-five years, dairy cows only live ten years? Why? I'll give you a clue. They inject them with hormone enhancers, and when they give birth they take the baby away—which, if it's a male, they kill for veal—and then they artificially inseminate them two months later, so they spend most of their lives pregnant. And they never see the light of day. Did you know this? How can you drink a milk shake?"

He slurped through his straw. "Chalk it up to moral bankruptcy."

"Where are you from, anyhow?"

"Wilkes-Barre, Pennsylvania." He broke a piece off the hamburger and fed it to A.M. who, unlike her owner, responded with relish. "That's originally. Now I live in Queens."

"Family?"

"My mother."

"No wife or girlfriend?"

His face clouded, and he cleared his throat. "I was married once. Had a little girl."

"Divorce, huh?"

"She left me. Not that I blame her. It's a hell of a life, being a military wife. She didn't like travel, hated moving. One day she just moved out and took Tracey with her."

"I'm sorry."

"Well, don't be. She got married again, to a guy with a chain of dry-cleaning stores, and he was home by six every night, they had a house, and Tracey had the kind of life I couldn't give her. Sisters and brothers, a neighborhood, the whole shot. It's better for kids that way."

Having spent most of my teens without a father myself, I wasn't so sure, but I didn't say anything. And from the look on Fisher's face, I had the feeling that it was better to change the subject. "How did you get into the detective business?"

"For ten years I was on the Wilkes-Barre police force, until I got shot in the line of duty."

"My God. Shot?"

"I was breaking up a domestic dispute. These things happen. Well, at least I got pensioned with disability. But one thing leads to another. That funded my business."

"What kind of cases do you specialize in?"

"Whatever. They say I'm good at finding things—and people. A talent I picked up with the Special Forces."

This was astonishing information. "You were with the Special Forces?"

He nodded. "Green Berets."

"What division?"

"Motor pool."

"Oh."

"Well, that was at first. Then I went into the electronics unit. Intelligence, terrorist tracking, the usual."

"What's the connection with Global Sport?"

"One of the partners was in Washington with me. We kept in touch. Most of my work is corporate. I do a little pickup work for them now and then." He wadded up the McDonald's bag and dropped it onto the floor of the car. "Say, your tape is a little loud. Do you mind?" He reached for the dash.

"You're getting grease on the controls."

"Sorry, I just don't get this country stuff. Got any Tony Bennett?"

I swerved to avoid a station wagon that cut in front of us, and the Fish braced his knees in front of him and checked his seat belt. "What about slowing down? Could you maybe slow down? You're going over the speed limit."

"For someone in a dangerous business, you're pretty nervous."

"I was just trying to save you a ticket." He paused to noisily slurp his shake. "You married?"

"No."

"So you played tennis. Pretty well, too, it seems."

"Yes." I turned up the music and pressed harder on the gas.

"So you had an accident. Mountain climbing, was it?"

"Yes."

"Think you'll ever play again?"

"No."

The Fish nodded as if he understood, but he didn't try to turn the music down or complain about my driving. "You want to talk about Audrey?"

"Hey, there's an idea."

"I don't think Audrey's home practicing. I don't think that at all, do you?"

"And what if she is? I can't believe people knew something was wrong and nobody did anything about it."

"Human nature—nobody wants to rock the boat. So they let the boat sink."

"As soon as I get some concrete proof that Audrey's being abused, I'm going to report it."

The Fish guffawed. "To who? The girl has to cooperate, and so far she hasn't. The tennis people aren't exactly lining up—she's their big draw. My client—well, let's face it, former client—she makes money for them. They don't want to see anything blown out of proportion. It could hurt the entire business."

I felt my cheeks getting hot. "Oh, now I get it. You're into damage control." I swung over to the shoulder of the road, slammed on the brakes, and faced Fisher. "I think you should get out. Right now."

"Here?" He pointed to the cars and trucks whizzing past us with inches to spare. "It's too dangerous."

"You were a Green Beret. You can handle a little

danger. Out. Unless we are in total agreement about what we're here to do."

The Fish reclined his seat until it was almost horizontal, yawned, and closed his eyes. A.M. crawled unhelpfully onto his lap and closed her eyes, too. "You know, for a smart woman, you disappoint me," he said. "I told you. Once in my life, I lost a little girl. I'm not going to do it again. You can count on that." The car phone jangled, and he reached out and picked it up.

I yanked it out of his hand and heard Tony's voice. "Hello? Hello?"

"Tony!" I clapped the phone to my ear.

"Hi, Jordan, I'm glad I got you. That Noel Fisher check came through. Didn't take too long. Want to hear?"

"What?" I asked guardedly.

"The guy is a corporate security consultant and he lives in Queens."

"And?" I eyed Fisher, who was pretending to sleep. He now had A.M. enfolded in his arms, her head on his chest. All they needed now was a lap robe.

"Highly decorated war hero. Pentagon attaché. Law degree. Surveillance expert."

"Are you sure?"

Tony continued, "Yes. The report says, chief of police in Wilkes-Barre, Pennsylvania. Pensioned on disability. And here's the interesting part."

"I can't wait."

"He holds four patents."

"For what?" I was truly astonished.

"I'm getting the details. I'll fax you. Oh, personal data—he's divorced, had a daughter. She died in her teens. Car crash."

My breath caught.

"Where are you, Jordan? Gus wants to know."

"I'll call back, Tony."

"So, Mr. Fisher," I said, tapping the wheel with my fingertips. "You're an inventor. What did you invent?"

Without opening his eyes, the Fish reached into his pocket and handed me a pen. "It's yours," he said. "Free sample."

"A pen? You did not invent the pen."

"I invented a technical variation on the ballpoint that comes in particularly handy. As you will see for yourself."

I put the pen into my bag. This much was obvious: a Pentagon-trained surveillance expert would hardly have run into my car, allowed himself to be spotted in a restaurant, then let himself be caught by the likes of me. A man who was still castigating himself for his daughter's death—however she died, I didn't have the courage to ask—had something personally at stake with Audrey Armat.

The Fish opened one eye and squinted at me.

I pulled guardedly back onto the road.

"So where are we headed?" the Fish asked.

"I'm meeting a friend who is a Miami sportswriter. You can sit in. We'll take it from there."

For the rest of the trip, Fisher snored noisily in his tilted-back seat with A.M. on his lap. I had plenty of time to study him. His clothes were certainly a disaster—obviously, Elements of Style was not a course taught by the Green Berets. For that matter, it seemed clear that the Special Forces and their fifty-six weeks of basic training were a long time distant. Fisher was at least forty pounds overweight, which did not sit aesthetically well on a man of medium height. His every feature and limb was padded out with a soft layer of excess flesh, like a puffy slipcover that had been made for a face two sizes bigger. The extra layers on his cheeks rustled when he exhaled, and his complexion had the pasty look of someone who rarely left flourescent lighting and barely moved. He seemed like an inflatable land tortoise, on its back and out of its element in this car, much less, God forbid, the Pentagon. Well, I had made the decision to let him stay with me, but time would tell if it was a wise move or the stupidest thing I'd ever done—although a lot of events in my life vied for that honor.

When we hit the causeway to Miami I turned the music up an extra decibel and started to sing along with the Supremes to "Baby Love." Sure enough, the Fish moved. One eye opened, then the other, and he stretched in his seat. "What? Are we there?" He winced and rubbed his ears, but made no comment on the music.

I called ahead and reached Cassie just as she was leaving the office. "You're in town and you give me no notice," she complained. "Typical. I was just heading over to my place. We've moved to South Beach. I meant to send you a change of address card, but things have been wild the past few weeks." She gave me directions and we agreed to meet at her apartment.

"It's above the Palmetto Café on Ocean," Cas said. "You can't miss it."

Looking for a parking place, I immediately saw that South Beach had undergone quite a transformation since my brief stint in Miami. In the not-so-many intervening years, it had made itself over into a swirling Art Deco vortex of color and sound colliding head-on with a relentless phalanx of fashion designers, models, res-

taurants, and avant-garde types. I actually had to carry
A.M. to keep her from being trampled in the onrush of
hipness that surged down Ocean Avenue. The Fish's
head fairly swiveled off his neck as we forged our way
through the trendy, multiethnic crowd that thronged the
beachfront: flocks of beautiful six-foot-tall girls in
microshorts and midriff tops, their legs as tan as they
were thin; couples on in-line skates, weaving through
the pack; photographers and clutches of assistants and
equipment; street musicians on harmonicas, guitars and
steel drums; tourists and children; a woman in rhine-
stone-studded glasses carrying a bright red wig on a
Styrofoam head; sprinkled in, the occasional business
type; and a dark-skinned Rousti with a boa constrictor
coiled around his shoulders and a sign that offered to
take your picture with the snake for ten dollars. On the
other side of the street, beyond the bumper-to-bumper
parked cars, were the beach and the ocean, white and
turquoise and tranquil, and the palms, standing witness
to the scene.

Cassie's apartment was in one of those renovated ice
cream–colored Art Deco buildings that probably had a
life cycle of being first a classy hotel for northern vaca-
tioners in the forties, then a seedy hotel for one-nighters
and less, then an abandoned wreck, then a home for se-
nior citizens, and now an expensive and exclusive
apartment building with a celebrity watering hole on the
ground floor. The entrance was on the side street. Both
names, Heller and Pernice, were on the directory. Cassie
buzzed us in, and a small, painfully slow elevator jerk-
ily took us up two floors. She was waiting at the end of
the hall, in front of her open door. Her long frosted hair
tumbled in curls to her shoulders, held back by clips.

Oversized silver hoops dangled from each ear. She wore black leggings, a long, sheer chiffon blouse, and high-heeled mules with a bunch of plastic fruit on them. No question, Cassie Heller had the most eccentric footwear in the history of sports journalism.

"Jordan! As I live and breathe," she yelled. Cassie, a transplanted Texan, was never one for subdued greetings. We exchanged a boisterous hug and she ushered me inside, looking over her shoulder at the Fish, who dutifully trailed.

"Who's this?" she whispered, leaning over to scratch A.M. behind the ears and receive her requisite lick. "New man?"

"Oh, my God, no. Absolutely not. He's an . . . associate."

Cas shrugged. "Well, you never know. Last I heard, you'd broken up with that doctor whoever, and . . ."

"This is Noel Fisher," I said, introducing them.

"Nice place," he noted. "Ocean view."

Cassie had fixed the place up in blue, lavender, and white to complement the sea and sky outside her wooden louvered shades. It was a one-bedroom apartment, but with a mirrored wall and clever decorating she'd made the most of it. A large-screen TV stood at one corner, opposite the round dining table, and piles of newspapers and magazines overflowed large rattan baskets in every corner. A white paddle fan wheeled slowly overhead. Framed pictures of Cassie and Rob filled an entire wall—their wedding, which I had attended; their vacations; holidays. They looked happy. Cassie's suitcases and several large cardboard moving boxes blocked the hallway to the bedroom.

"I have to get around to unpacking someday," she

apologized. "But by then we'll probably be ready to move."

"Sorry, Cas. Looks like you're taking off," I said.

"I'm always taking off, you know that. This one's one of those throw-everything-you-own-into-a-garment-bag nightmares." She kicked a suitcase out of her path. "I was supposed to go to Eastbourne, but my editor turned up an interview with a golfer in California. I had to file the story, then turn around and head back here, and I just got in last night. Eastbourne's over on Saturday and Wimbledon starts Monday, which gets me to London just in time if I leave tomorrow."

Cassie had one of the coveted journalist's passes to Wimbledon, which were rarer and, to some, more valuable, than the crown jewels. You didn't just show up and apply for a press pass. Wimbledon required an application months in advance, with accredited sponsors, like admission to the exclusive club it was.

"Oh, excuse me, I'm a terrible hostess. Would you like some herbal iced tea?"

"Great," I said.

"Beer?" she asked the Fish, who nodded with obvious relief. Her puzzled glance as she headed toward the kitchen told me that she had no idea what this man was doing here and was wondering how free she was to talk. The sports world is a very tightly closed circle. Everybody has credentials.

"Confidentially, Noel and I are working on a case together," I said. "Audrey Armat."

Cassie emerged with the drinks and set them on the coffee table. "I interviewed her once, when she was thirteen. After that, her mother doled out every press opportunity with tweezers. She's let it be known—if it's not a cover story, forget it. And, of course, she insists on final approval of every word. You call that journalism? I call it self-serving PR."

"Doesn't Rob coach her boyfriend?" I asked.

Cassie glanced uneasily at the Fish.

"Cassie, I have to tell you something nobody knows. This is completely, totally off the record, because among other things, it's still just a suspicion. We have no real proof one way or another at this point. There's a lot of contradictory information flying around. But Audrey may be in trouble. There were some big problems at the Springs with her parents. But I'm finding out that it's even worse than I suspected, and I need your help. Noel and I are working together to get to the bottom of this before it blows up in everybody's face."

"When it goes on the record, I have it first." Cassie stated this as a firm fact. "And if I hear anything anyplace else, I have to go with it, you understand?"

I nodded. The Fish poured his beer.

"I wonder about Audrey's relationship with Alex. Did they have some kind of breakup or fight recently that anybody can pinpoint? Anything that would make her act strangely?"

Cassie flopped back into the couch cushions and dangled one fruited mule from her pedicured toes. "Well, I could ask Rob, but, frankly, he's never mentioned much about it."

"No gossip about the relationship?"

"Well, no—but Rob's not the type to notice things like that. A player's serve, yes. His girlfriend, no."

"Do you know Alex?"

"Somewhat. Talented, and a very charming guy. Bit of a rebel. Rides a motorcycle. Lots of leather off-court.

Earring, the whole bit. He actively cultivates that teen-heartthrob image. Alex adores the press, as long as they spell his name right. He'd definitely be the type to hook up with Audrey. Miss Perfect would offset his image nicely."

"Are you saying this is a PR opportunity, not a relationship?" asked the Fish.

Cassie shrugged. "Well, he might like her, but he's a shrewd kid, and let's say he'd certainly see the added value in Audrey, versus some high school honey from his hometown."

The Fish reached into the basket of magazines on the floor beside him, pulled out a back issue of a tennis monthly, and flipped idly through it, glancing up occasionally.

"What about her relationship with her parents, particularly her mother?" I asked.

Cassie's eyes narrowed. "There have been some unconfirmed reports of things. What do you know?"

"Nothing certain yet. But nothing I like, either. Something is definitely driving that girl into a very bad state of mind."

"Well, I can tell you this. Rob gets faxes and calls all the time here at home from Corinne Armat, requesting, or I should say ordering, Rob to have Alex show up wherever. We joke that she thinks Alex works for an escort service." She got up, walked across the room, pulled back a long sliding door to reveal a complete office in a closet, and picked a piece of paper off the top of a stack of mail. "Check this out. It's the latest fax from Corinne."

I took the fax and looked it over. It was a typed schedule of engagements, drawn up for Alex and

Audrey four months in advance. Alex was supposed to appear with Audrey at this dinner, that press conference, various testimonials and sports functions. There was a joint interview scheduled for a teen magazine. Even Audrey's birthday was noted, with appropriate gift suggestions. It looked more like a press program than a young couple's dating schedule. Except for the Prince of Wales, I didn't know of any men who planned their dates—or, should I say, had their dates planned for them—with such military precision.

"But he goes along with this? I thought he was the rebellious type."

"Rob thinks he should tell the Armats where to get off, but Alex is just so good-natured. He always does it, never complains. I tell him he's a pushover. Then again, maybe he likes Audrey."

"Then why doesn't he just call her direct, like most guys?"

"Point," said Cassie. "Of course, who knows what they do when they're on their own? And he does seem to be one of the few people who actually gets along with the family. He and E.J. hang out at the tournaments. Ride motorcycles together, that sort of thing."

"What do you know about E.J.?" I asked. "He's a complete enigma. What kid would want to spend his life tagging along in his sister's shadow?"

Cassie shrugged. "From what I've seen, it seems like E.J.'s being trained to be a gofer when he grows up. It's too bad. Rob tells me he's not a bad player at all. Maybe with the same time and attention that Audrey got, he could have been a top player himself."

"But he doesn't have Audrey's ability to switch on the star power, does he?" I said, remembering Audrey's amazing ability to charm an entire stadium at will. "In the end, he's not the performer. She is. The Armats must have seen that much early on. And a cute little girl with a lot of ability—that's merchandisable."

"It's sad," Cassie commented, and I had to agree.

"If they're buddies, do you think Alex knows where E.J. is now?" I asked. "Maybe he's the key to this whole thing."

"Could be," said Cassie. "I think they keep in touch—or as much in touch as anybody keeps with one of the Armats."

"What about those unconfirmed reports," the Fish said, tossing his tennis magazine onto the coffee table. "What did you mean?"

"You're sure we can talk in front of your friend?" Cas said cautiously.

I nodded.

"Well, some people think Corinne Armat hits Audrey," Cassie said bluntly. "There's been some talk about it, rumblings. Nothing concrete. To write about it would have been irresponsible."

"It's dangerous territory," I agreed. "The main problem is Audrey herself. If she's being abused, why won't she complain? Forget about testifying against her parents. She actually defends them."

"A lot of women older and more mature than Audrey have struggled with this kind of thing," said Cassie. "You read about it all the time—battered wives, girlfriends. Everybody always says, 'Why don't these women leave?' But it's not that simple, not for the women. And Audrey's just a kid."

"Do you think Audrey's being abused?" the Fish asked.

Cassie suppressed a shudder. "That mother is some-one I'd hate to have waiting at home."

"Assuming she did run away—where would Audrey go?" I wondered.

"I don't know," mused Cassie. "It's not that easy for her to hide. She's been on too many magazine covers. And she's just a kid."

The thought made me very sad—a kid who had to run and hide from something or someone. How could you know what was in her mind? "Would she go home?" I asked. "People say that she's there practic-ing."

"That would make sense," Cassie answered, "since her father duplicated the Wimbledon grass courts, right down to the strain of grass, at their compound in Con-necticut."

"You're kidding," said the Fish.

"Oh, yes. He supposedly hired one of the grounds guys from the All England Tennis Club as a consultant and flew him over to supervise every blade of grass. The word is, it cost over half a million dollars. Armat wanted to work on Audrey's grass-court game, to make sure nothing got in the way. He wanted to duplicate Wimbledon match conditions exactly, right down to the last bounce of the last ball. He even bought a hundred dozen of the exact balls they use at the championships. If he could control the weather, he'd probably import the Wimbledon rain."

I laughed, because it always did seem to rain during Wimbledon. "Well, maybe that's where she actually is," I said. "Working on her grass-court game." There are so many intricacies to master that under ordinary circum-stances, that would make a lot of sense.

But Audrey was not your average Wimbledon contender. If anything was her challenge, it was not so much her game as her life.

Cassie brought out refills of the iced tea and beer, along with some rice crackers. "So how can I help?" she asked quietly.

"Tell me more about those unconfirmed reports of abuse."

Cassie tugged on her earring. "There was nothing I could ever go with. Nobody would come out as a source. But there were rumors for a while. Nothing overt, like in the case of Jack Mancini—no yelling and disrupting matches or obscenities or anything like that. Nothing that would cause the authorities to take action. This was much more subtle. But anybody who ever met that mother knew something wasn't right there. The woman has more than one screw loose, if you ask me. I'd certainly hate to be her daughter."

"Did Alex ever say anything about her?"

"No, she was actually pretty consistently nice to him, except for the command-performance stuff. But it was probably an act. Personally, it seems to me that the woman is incapable of any kindness that's not self-serving."

Cassie jumped off the sofa and disappeared momentarily into the bedroom. When she came out she was modeling a wide-brimmed hat. It was black, with a huge cluster of fake flowers cascading over the brim.

"So what do you think?" she asked.

"Perfect for Ascot."

"Come on—it's for Wimbledon, strawberries-and-cream time. Afterward, Rob and I are going to drive up through Ireland—the Ring of Kerry, the Blarney Stone, the whole bit."

"That sounds wonderful. I'm jealous." And I was. There was nobody who was ready to take off on a vacation with me. At this point I was lucky if Gus would even take my calls. I looked at Cassie's walls and all the pictures of her and Rob and wondered if I'd ever have my own wall like this. So far I was doing a fair job of isolating myself from everybody except the Fish. I was always married to my causes—first it was tennis, then it was physiotherapy, now it was Audrey. Relationships never panned out quite as well, because they always involved that major variable, emotions.

Cassie picked up A.M. and gave her a cuddle. "I love this dog," she said. "God, if dogs could talk . . ."

"Please, Cas, you know too much already."

"All the news that's fit to print."

"And some that's not. So can I have Alex's number?"

"He's in England. He went straight there from the French." She went to the desk, flipped through Rob's Rolodex, and scribbled a number on a scrap of paper. "This is his international pager number. You can get him anywhere in the world with it. Nobody has this number. Rob would kill me if he knew I gave it to you. But I didn't give it to you."

"Thanks, Cas." I tucked the paper into my wallet.

"And now for my pound of flesh. When this story comes to a boil . . ."

"I'll call you. Right away."

"Deal. Now, the couch pulls out into a bed, so you'll stay here tonight, and we'll get some food."

"You've taken up cooking?"

"What? Are you crazy? My only utensil is a Mr. Coffee. But the place downstairs has a great black bean soup and Cuban sandwich. They'll do a vegetarian version. And guess who's in town."

"Who?"

"Mariska. She's been training on grass at Longwood in Boston, but she skipped Eastbourne this year and came down for an exo on Key Biscayne. I know that's unusual for her, but I hear it's big money. It should be over early."

Exhibitions were usually pretty cut-and-dried. You were paid the same whether you won or not—usually fifty to seventy-five thousand dollars for a top player like Mariska, and in special cases up to a quarter million or more. You showed up, there was a cocktail party before the match where you mingled for fifteen minutes, sat down and signed autographs. Maybe there was a press conference earlier in the day, so it would make the five o'clock news. You played two or three sets. You left and collected your check. It was not unheard of for a player to skip a major tournament in favor of an exhibition if the money was right. One year, the number-one women's player sent her regrets to Wimbledon and played exhibition in New Jersey for a rumored half million dollars. The stakes speak for themselves. Agents usually push their players to take on as many exhibitions as they can handle, if the money is good.

"Let's drop in. We can swing by the locker room and see if she wants to have dinner with us." She dashed to the bathroom, returned with a towel, and tossed it on the floor. "Here you go, A.M. Veg out."

"I'm so hungry, that boa constrictor we saw on the way over here looked tasty," the Fish interjected.

"You want to stay around here or go with us for a

bite to eat?" I asked. "You can't come into the ladies' locker room regardless."

"What if I meet you at the restaurant," he said, reaching into his pocket and producing a Slim Jim, which he proceeded to unwrap and devour. "Maybe I can hang out, check out the area, and meet you girls at the café downstairs at, say, nine o'clock, nine-thirty?" He sauntered over to the window. "Quite a scene out there. I think I'll take a few shots to show my mother back in Queens. She'll never believe it." He started snapping flash pictures out the window.

"Just don't take any pictures of Mariska, okay?" I said. "She hates that."

Fisher looked up, indignant. "What do you think I am? Insensitive?"

"Well, let's keep dinner a low-key occasion, okay? We'll just relax."

He nodded. "Absolutely."

"A nice quiet dinner." I was looking forward to spending some time alone with Cas and Mariska. Just see old friends, have a good time, and forget about Audrey Armat for a few hours.

EIGHT

An hour and a half later Cassie and I were in Key Biscayne in front of a press trailer monitor on the grounds of the Tamiami Tennis Club. At a small beige metal desk at the front of the trailer, a young woman answered the phones and pinned messages to the bulletin board behind her. The back of the trailer was a maze of video monitors, cables, and technicians. The match was just coming to a close, and Mariska was losing 6–4, 6–2, 5–4 to Anke Hess, a young German sensation whose game consisted mainly of a serve clocked at 115 miles an hour.

"Oh, she's going to be in a great mood," I said. Mariska took every match hard, even exhibitions; but thousands of games into her career, some losses were more critical than others. The matches that really mattered to Mariska were going to be played on grass courts in England. And maybe that was part of the problem tonight. Some players walked through their exhibitions purely for the money. Others, like McEnroe, really gave it their all, no matter what the event. Tonight I had the feeling that Mariska's heart was already on the grass courts abroad.

A blistering forehand from the German ended the

match quickly, and Cassie and I scrambled out of the trailer and into the pink building that held the players' lounge, where we knew Mariska would return after her press conference.

Cassie had press passes, so we breezed past security. The Tamiami Club itself was luxurious, a fortress in old coral and older money, but the players' lounge was like most of the others that were not set up for Grand Slam events, which is to say, makeshift, with all the atmosphere of a waiting room. A bunch of utilitarian chairs that looked like rejects from a TV talk show set huddled on a cheerless carpet. A side table draped with an orange cloth held huge plastic-wrapped baskets of fruit, some plastic-wrapped bouquets with cards, a chafing dish of hot pasta, and buckets of ice and cold drinks. This was definitely not the glamour end of the business. A few people I didn't recognize lingered about. Matty Reardon, Mariska's coach, sat on one of the chairs drinking mineral water and watching TV, his girlfriend Wendy beside him. Matty was tan, blond, and very California-looking. He wore jeans, a pale yellow polo shirt, and Nikes. Wendy had stylishly rumpled hair and wore a studded western shirt, skintight black denim jeans, and cowboy boots. A turquoise and silver concha belt encircled her tiny waist, and her hand was on Matty's arm. Matty waved as we came in, and we walked over and exchanged kisses. Since Mariska hadn't won, the atmosphere wasn't very festive. Cassie and I sat on the couch, and within twenty minutes Mariska appeared in her warm-up outfit, her face stormy, her racket bag slung over her shoulder. The room immediately cleared. Not many people wanted to face Mariska after she'd lost a match.

Without acknowledging anyone, Mariska disappeared into the adjoining locker room. The door banged behind her. Seconds later, a series of resounding slams echoed through the door. Cassie and I exchanged glances. "I guess nobody told Anke that she wasn't supposed to win," said Cas.

We watched TV until Mariska appeared, dressed in jeans and a work shirt, her hair damp from the shower.

"Tough match," I said.

She smiled weakly, struggling between being furious at losing and pleased to see us. Cassie is one of the few journalists that Mariska really likes. Mariska is an avid reader, and has an appreciation for somebody who can capture the details.

Mariska sank into a chair and cupped her chin in her hands. "It only gets tougher," she said. "You know what I found myself thinking about out there? My dry cleaning!" She laughed joylessly, and Matty raised his eyebrows. "I kept wondering if I'd remember to pick it up. What does that say about my concentration?"

"You have it when it counts," I said.

"It always counts," said Mariska. "But when you're younger you don't have so much to think about. You have no responsibilities, you can focus one hundred percent. Not that my dry cleaning is a big thing, but I just think about other stuff."

Suddenly a boisterous crowd of people laughing and speaking German burst into the lounge, clearly the entourage of tonight's winner. Mariska stood up abruptly, unsmiling. "So, we're having dinner? I was thinking of this little Thai place on Washington Street."

"What about the Palmetto?" asked Cassie.

"I had lunch there," said Mariska. So much for the Palmetto.

The Fish would be waiting there, but maybe I could get word to the maître d'. On the drive over, I tried a couple of times on the car phone, but the line was always busy.

"That place is a madhouse," said Cassie. "Forget it, you'll never get through."

The Fish would have to understand.

We found the Thai restaurant just off the lobby of the wildly funky Coronado Hotel, a once-venerable institution that had recently reopened with a flourish of pink granite and wrought iron under the ownership of a British rock star. The crowd here was stylish—overflowing with exposed midriffs of models who appeared never to eat. The decor was spare but ultrachic: welded iron furniture, kidney-shaped fake coral tables, giant banana palms, architectural lamps, and one entire wall that was a giant fish tank stocked with every conceivable form of marine life, including a small octopus. Mariska, of course, was instantly recognized by the blue-jeaned and T-shirted maître d', who led us to the table with a certain hip deference. Seconds later he rematerialized with a waiter bearing a pocket camera.

"Please, it would be such an honor," he said, jockeying into position beside Mariska.

Mariska froze briefly, then flashed a Kodak smile, her standard fan-shot expression perfected over thousands of intrusions. Usually she allowed fans to take her picture if the encounter was brief. On the other hand, she almost always refused to give autographs. And she hated being interrupted during a meal.

We'd just gotten our drinks and ordered the food

when I noticed a man in a hat stroll toward our table. He looked remarkably like the Fish. On second glance, it was the Fish.

"Hi, everybody." He waved a fleshy arm amiably. I noted that he now sported a touristy straw Panama with a Day-Glo orange hatband.

"What is *that?"* Mariska lifted an eyebrow.

"Somebody I . . . know," I admitted. I couldn't imagine how he'd found us here. Then again, he'd probably been following us the whole time since we left the apartment.

The Fish pulled up a chair from another table and plopped into it. "For a while there I thought I'd missed you guys," he said. "Got the wrong restaurant or something." He shook his head, looking confused.

"I tried to leave word at the Palmetto," I said. "Their line was always busy. How did you find us?"

"You must have mentioned this place. Whatever—no harm done, the gang's all here now. Waiter, how about a martini." He squinted at the menu. "What's this? Pla Muk?"

"Squid stuffed with chili shrimp paste," explained Cassie. "It's excellent here."

"They have any American food? A porterhouse maybe? Nice and juicy, still mooing preferably."

"I didn't see porterhouse on the menu. Mariska," I interrupted, "this is Noel Fisher. We're working together. Sort of."

"What?" Mariska asked.

"I'm handling Jordan's root canal," Fisher answered. Cassie blinked in surprise.

"Your dentist travels with you?" Mariska was suddenly curious. She probably thought it was a fascinating new twist on the entourage, and she visibly brightened. To Mariska, anything even vaguely connected with the care and treatment of the human body is interesting.

I waved my hand to dismiss further questions. "It's ... complicated." Mariska would never talk openly in front of a stranger, much less a private detective. Her off-the-record remarks had ended up as public record once too often.

Mariska leaned closer. "Dr. Fisher, tell me more about how you work with Jordan. Personally, I travel so much, it's very difficult to find time to fit in visits to the dentist."

"I hear you," said the Fish. "For me, it's restaurants. When I travel, I never know where to eat. You must know them all. How'd you pick this place?"

He'd hit a nerve, I thought. Mariska loves to talk about food. The two of them were quickly in animated conversation.

Cassie smirked. "Come on, J.M. You snuck off when we weren't looking and called the guy. Admit it, you can't resist him."

"Spare me, Cas." The Fish was now talking with the waiter, indicating with his fingers the desired thickness of a hypothetical steak as Mariska guided him in some Thai suggestions.

The food began to arrive: Tofu-Todd, Ka-Nom-Chob, which was steamed dumplings, and a spicy satay—and the restaurant started to fill up.

"Don't look now," said Cassie from behind her menu, "but here comes another one of everybody's favorite guys."

Milt Bevins was walking in alone. Probably in town for the exhibition. Bevins had the means to fly to any tournament or match he pleased. Among other things, he had his own private jet and personal pilot. He nodded a greeting to our table and proceeded to a small table along the wall.

"This guy is too much," said Mariska, who was at last distracted from the Fish. "Did I tell you about him?"

"Didn't he try to give you a Porsche once?" I asked.

"Well, I didn't take it," Mariska said. "So he donated the equivalent in cash to one of my charities. It was amazing. But that was during the time that he liked me." She made room for a huge mound of noodles.

"He doesn't like you anymore?" I asked. "Is that good or bad?"

"It's good, I got rid of him. Kelly had him before me, and I guess I inherited him by default when she retired. But then Audrey came along and he glommed on to her. And now all he does is complain about me." She served herself a huge helping of sautéed string beans and passed the platter. "Audrey was grunting when she served at the French, and it was distracting to me, and after our match Matty complained to the officials. Well! Such a row you have never seen! Not with the officials, or even the Armats. They were all status quo. But Bevins! He actually tried to have Matty thrown out of the arena. Claimed he was using hand signals, illegal coaching from the sidelines. It was ridiculous!"

We all laughed, because everybody knew how the fans could get crazy. One pair of middle-aged sisters had spent a decade traveling to every one of Mariska's Grand Slam matches. They knitted her scarves, baked her cookies, sent her birthday cards and presents, and treated her like a member of the family, including instituting haughty feuds when they detected an imagined slight from anyone in any other player's entourage.

"Do you remember how Bevins used to run around the players' lounge with an iron in his hand?" I asked. "Ironing the blouse of whoever was his current favorite?"

"He doesn't know about dry cleaning?" asked the Fish.

"Oh, he knows," said Cassie. "The guy probably has two valets at home to take his own clothes to the cleaner. If he doesn't own the cleaner. You're talking old family money. Real old. Real money. Oil, railroads. The usual."

"I heard he gave Gina's parents a trip around the world for the whole family," Mariska said. Gina, who had since slipped to number twenty, came from a family of seven. "God knows what he has given the Armats."

"There was a rumor about a million-dollar check," whispered Cassie, taking a heaping spoonful of Pad Thai. "Poor guy. Not married, no kids, no family. Just a big, cold, lonely trust fund to keep him warm. You've got to feel sorry for him, trying to buy love."

"He can adopt me," said the Fish.

"Come on, Dr. Fisher," said Mariska. "Won't you have some dinner?"

"Oh, I will, I will," said the Fish, declining everything on the table. "Don't worry about me."

Through the open door I could see a delivery boy pull up to the restaurant on a bicycle. He hopped off and carried in a large package in an insulated bag. After a whispered huddle, the host directed him to our table, where he deposited the bag, emblazoned with AUGIE'S STEAK AND CHOP HOUSE, in front of the Fish.

"Porterhouse steak, rare?" said the delivery boy, brandishing a charge-plate imprint machine from a hook on his belt. We all stared in amazement as Fisher ran his charge plate through, signed, opened the bag, set out the steak on a plate, pulled a Swiss Army knife from his pocket, and flipped open a steak knife attachment.

One thing about Noel Fisher that I conceded right then: the man is resourceful.

"So, Mariska," I said, trying to be casual. "They're talking about you and Audrey at Wimbledon as the match of the century."

She gave a little laugh. "Every year is another match of the century."

I know how Mariska works. Her preparation for a match is as much psychological as physical. She might pretend indifference, but she and Matty would have spent a lot of time studying her opponents, and at this point it was a good bet that she knew as much about Audrey as almost anybody outside the family. "What do you see as her Achilles' heel?" I asked.

"Her Achilles' heel is in not letting her find yours," Mariska said, sipping her mineral water thoughtfully. She always drank it room temperature, never with ice. "If she finds anything she can go for, she will. She's very consistent. She'll stay back there at the baseline and wear you down with her power, if you give her a chance. And her mother is usually there in the players' box, screaming at you, trying to create a distraction. They use that, the Armats. They'll give you a problem, even if you don't have one. Or the mother will scream at Audrey, which is equally distracting. You can't let it get to you, or you're dead."

"Do you think Corinne Armat is an abusive parent?"

I glanced at Cassie. It was understood that this conversation would never appear in print.

"I think it's an act, but I'm sick of it. Everybody is. There's talk that she will be banned from Wimbledon. I certainly hope so. I think it would be good for Audrey. I mean, she has to know that her mother is over the top, but still, she's her mother, you can't escape it. I know that even at my age, I keep hoping for approval from my parents. I call them after I win, and sometimes my father will mention not that I won but that I missed some point, and it really upsets me, and I'm a grown woman living on my own for years a continent away. For a young girl still living at home, how can her mother not be a problem?"

"But did you say you thought it was an act?"

"For the mother, I just think she's nuts. The father, now *there* is an act. He is too slick for words."

"But why would he need an act?"

"I think they play good cop–bad cop. They can't both be terrible, or nobody would listen to either of them." She yawned, already bored with the subject.

The waiter appeared with a bottle of champagne. "From the gentleman," he said, indicating Milt Bevins. Bevins nodded and smiled.

"I guess he's trying to bury the hatchet," she said, summoning up a canned smile and nod of thank-you. It is always a tightrope as to how enthusiastic you are in a situation like this. Of course you want to acknowledge a friendly gesture, but being too friendly can result in an unwelcome addition to the table.

But Milt Bevins was already making his way over. He stretched out his arms, as if he wished he could embrace the table. "Mariska, the champion of champions."

He beamed. I received a slight nod of acknowledgment, but he clearly was focused on Mariska.

"Hello, Milt." She acknowledged him politely, he leaned down, and she reached out to shake his hand. Instead, he took her hand and kissed it gallantly.

"Wonderful to see you here," Milt said. His eyes swept the table. "All of you! Isn't this quite the in place these days? Now. Will I be seeing you all at Wimbledon?"

"I'm planning on it," said Mariska, as if it weren't obvious.

We sat awkwardly, our food cooling in front of us.

"Well!" Milt rubbed his hands together. "It should be quite a match, Mariska, you and Audrey. The young challenger versus the old warhorse!"

Mariska's eyes narrowed infinitesimally, but her smile didn't waver.

"I wouldn't miss it," Bevins continued. "Fine! See you there, then." With an elegant wave, he retreated toward the door, where he pressed a thick wad of bills into the maître d's hand on his way out.

The champagne was poured, but left largely undrunk as we finished dinner. It was getting late, and Mariska called for the check. "Will I see you in England?" she asked.

"I'm not sure," I answered. I hoped to have located Audrey by then, and I had no other real reason to go.

We disbanded at the door of the restaurant with a plan: I would spend the night at Cassie's, the Fish would put himself up in the hotel next door, and Mariska and I would keep in touch. Then it was back into the humidity of the Miami night for the short trip back to Cassie's place. It was a short walk around the corner to where the car was parked. When we got there, I couldn't believe what I saw.

The windshield was bashed in, heaps of chipped-ice glass fragments all over the hood. A brick was on the front seat.

We stood there for a minute.

"God, the crime in Miami is terrible," Cas said, shaking her head in disgust.

"At least it's a rented car," I said.

"They left the radio," said the Fish.

I quickly opened the car door and peered inside. Everything seemed in order except for A.M.'s carrier, the beautiful little Vuitton case. We mainly used it on airplanes, when I could pop her into the case and pretend it was a purse to smuggle her on board when I needed to. The case was so elegant and she was so quiet, people rarely suspected there was a dog inside. Now the case looked like someone had run it through a power mower. The only good thing was that A.M. wasn't in it. I shuddered to think what might have happened then. But it was an expensive piece of leather goods. I wondered if my insurance covered dog carriers.

"Very strange," said Fisher.

"Well," I said, "it's a sporty car with rental plates and something on the seat. I should have put the carrier in the trunk. They obviously thought they were getting a purse, and when it wasn't, they got mad there was no money and cut it up."

"Hm." Fisher inspected the dog carrier.

"I guess we better report this," I said.

Two hours later, after the police had duly arrived, a report had been filed, and the car rental company had been notified, Cassie and I said good night to the Fish and trooped, exhausted, back into her apartment.

A.M. was waiting expectantly. You didn't have to be an animal psychic to know what she wanted. A two-minute walk was the least I could do after abandoning her for the whole evening. This was a routine we did on autopilot: I picked up the leash, and she dashed under it so I could clip it to her little spiked collar. Our mission was short and direct, and once it was over I didn't plan to spend any time strolling the promenade. All I wanted now was a good night's sleep. A.M. would have to be understanding. "Back in a flash," I said to Cassie as I picked up A.M., tucked her under my arm, and headed out.

It was nearly midnight, and the crowd on Ocean Avenue was thicker and more colorful than ever. Music blared and beats throbbed from every available opening, a blistering cacophony in the hot neon night. It was exciting, a far cry from the tranquillity of Palm Springs. I couldn't imagine how Cassie slept every night with this circus going on outside her windows. Cars crawled down the street bumper to bumper as tourists gawked and kids piled in convertibles shrieked with the fun of being out for a good time. With A.M. still under my arm, I forged my way across the street to a small patch of sand surrounding a palm tree by the curb and set her down. I passed a shirtless man totally covered in tattoos. He was absolutely amazing. It looked like the entire ceiling of the Sistine Chapel had been reproduced on this person's body, culminating in his bald head, which featured a tattoo of an archangel with elaborately detailed wings outstretched to his temples. I put A.M. on the grass and stared. The next thing I knew, I felt something jerk A.M.'s leash out of my hand with a hard yank, and a violent shove pushed me off my feet and into the street. I stumbled into traffic. Horns blared, and a huge chrome-covered motorcycle jammed on its brakes and swerved, searing my leg with its exhaust pipe. Brakes screeched from both directions in the oncoming and following traffic, and there was the sound of crunching metal as two cars rammed.

I sat, dazed, in the middle of the street clutching my leg. I could tell I had a nasty burn.

"Lady, let me help you." The tattooed man leaned anxiously over me. I noticed that he wore silver rings in both ears, his nose, and his left cheek. "You coulda been killed."

The driver of the motorcycle, still astride, stood with his mouth agape, immobile in his leather and chains. Horns honked furiously all around us, and a police siren approached. The area cleared slightly as the squad car barreled along the beach, lights flashing. On the curb, a crowd had gathered.

"Can you move?" asked the tattooed man, extending a hand emblazoned with a butterfly.

"I think so," I said unsteadily. "He just grazed me. I mean, he didn't really hit me. I just got a burn from the exhaust." I ventured cautiously to my feet. My leg stung, but otherwise I was intact.

The squad car pulled up on the ocean side, and two uniformed officers jumped out, staticky voices bristling from their radios. They rushed over, directed by the tattooed man.

"It wasn't anybody's fault," I said, as they helped me limp to the sidewalk. "Somebody shoved me from behind. I guess the crowd got rambunctious. Can I borrow your flashlight?" I inspected my burn.

"Maybe you should get medical attention," said one of the officers. "Would you like us to take you to the emergency room?"

"No, thank you. I'll be fine. I've got some medical training. I don't think I need the emergency room." It looked to me like a second-degree burn. It would blister and weep a bit, but they couldn't do anything at the hospital that I couldn't do for myself with a tube of ointment.

One of the police officers stepped into the middle of the street and got traffic moving again, and within seconds Ocean Avenue had resumed its usual rhythm. Suddenly I remembered A.M., and the yank on the leash that had jerked it from my hand. With horror, I dashed back to the street. The tattooed man grabbed my arm and yanked me back.

"Lady, what are you—suicidal?" he yelled.

"It's my dog," I said, my teeth chattering now in spite of the heat. "I had my dog, and somebody pulled the leash out of my hand, I'm sure of it!"

"You're in shock, lady," said the tattooed man. "Sit down here on the grass for a minute and catch your breath. We'll find your dog."

I didn't want to sit down, although I had to admit I needed to. I looked frantically around, but there was no sign of A.M. I had a hideous vision of the slashed dog carrier, and then I really panicked, pushing my way through the crowd. In the dark and the confusion, I had no idea how I was going to find a tiny dog; I only knew I had to. I lowered my head, shoved my shoulder into the crowd, and bulldozed my way through the human jungle, pushing people's hips so I could get a better look at the ground. "Everybody look down!" I yelled. "There's a small dog missing!"

Then I turned my head and there was A.M. on a patch of grass, calmly doing what she'd set out to do in the first place, as if no excitement had happened whatsoever. She was at least a block away from where I'd last had her on the leash. The leash was completely missing. A.M. was smart, but she could not unclip the leash by herself. Someone had taken it off, probably the person who'd grabbed it. I had a feeling I knew what happened: A.M., when under pressure, has been known to bite. She'd probably nipped her dognapper, and he'd dropped her.

The tattooed man, whose name, as it turned out, was Paul, insisted on helping A.M. and me back to the apartment. "I don't want any road kill on my conscience," he explained.

I didn't have keys and I was limping, so Paul walked me to the door, carrying A.M., and after Cassie buzzed us in, into the elevator and then to the apartment door. I knocked lightly, and Cas opened it and froze when she saw Paul's tattoos and earrings.

"This is Paul," I said.

Cas wrapped her arm around me and whisked me inside. "Where've you been?" she hissed into my ear. "The tattoo parlor?"

"The street," I groaned, limping to the couch. I pulled up my pants leg. An elongated red blotch throbbed on my calf. No panty hose for me for a while. "Ice," I said. "Give me some ice and a towel."

Cassie rushed into the kitchen while Paul settled A.M. next to me on the sofa. "Thank you," I said.

"You've been so nice. I'm sorry to have inconvenienced you."

He held up a rose-vine and snake–entwined arm. "No problem. I only wish I'd caught the guy who pushed you."

"You saw him?"

Paul nodded. "Yeah, I saw him. Ran after him, too, but he took off. He's a sicko."

"You mean you think he did this on purpose?"

"Sure he did. There are people like that down here." Paul shook his head, jangling about twelve earrings. "Lady, if I was you, I'd stay inside the rest of the night. There are some weird people out there."

"The person who pushed me—what did he look like?"

"It was a kid. A kid with a ponytail. That's about all I could see. It was dark, he had on a baseball cap. But I saw the ponytail. Dark hair, and he was about five-ten, five-eleven. Thin. Wore jeans and a T-shirt. The usual."

"I think he also tried to take my dog," I said. "He grabbed the leash, but then he unclipped it and let her go."

"What's this?" Cassie brought in the ice.

"I guess somebody pushed me into traffic," I said. "I burned my leg on a motorcycle, and Paul helped me. He saw the guy who pushed me. The same guy tried to take A.M., but he let her go."

"Jesus," said Cas. She knelt down and dabbed the burn with ice. "Anybody we know?"

I took a deep breath and let it out slowly. "I hope not," I said.

Paul gave me his business card. It was very professional. Apparently, he was a window display designer.

"If I see that guy again around town, I'll let you know," he said as we exchanged numbers.

"I can't thank you enough, Paul," I said. "But I hope you won't mind if I don't get up." He let himself out of the apartment, heading back out to Ocean Avenue.

Cas just sat next to me on the couch, wrapped in her bathrobe, with a worried look. "You're thinking about something," she said.

"Yeah," I said. "It's ironic. I lived in Miami and I never had any problems, and now I'm here for one night and somebody breaks into my car and serrates my dog carrier with a grapefruit knife, and somebody else tries to steal my dog and shoves me into oncoming traffic."

A.M. pushed her head into my lap and I stroked her ears.

"Who says it was somebody else?" said Cas, her mouth tight.

"You're a writer, you have a big imagination," I said. I, on the other hand, had no imagination. But I didn't need one to conjure up one very real young man about five-ten with a ponytail. Not that it meant anything. There were lots of young men about five-ten with ponytails. I decided to sleep on it.

The next morning the Fish appeared like a polyester tide rolling in. "Nobody called my hotel! Nobody woke me up!" he groused incredulously, waving a powdered-sugar Bismarck from a Dunkin' Donuts bag as Cassie pointed him toward the coffee. She was rushing around the apartment doing last-minute packing, reopening bags and haphazardly stuffing in a flurry of scarves, hats, and shoes.

"You never know about the weather over there," Cas

said worriedly. "It could be ninety degrees or it could be freezing. Well, I'll just have to bring everything." She hesitated a moment, then unzipped a large duffel and stuffed in a down-filled vest and a pants suit.

"Sorry," I said to the Fish. My ointment-smeared leg hadn't improved much overnight. I'd decided to let it breathe, so I was wearing shorts, which revealed the patchwork of scars on my legs, residual reminders of my reconstruction after the fall. Whoever thought that crossing the street to walk your dog could be almost as dangerous as mountain climbing?

The TV was tuned to CNN, as usual, but in deference to the early hour Cas had the volume off. Audrey's picture appeared on the screen, and I grabbed the remote control and turned up the volume. "In the world of tennis, the agents of teen sensation Audrey Armat have released a statement that following a recent rest to rehabilitate a knee injury, she'll be returning to the game at Wimbledon," the announcer said. "They have also announced that Audrey will launch her new perfume and cosmetics line at this Grand Slam championship tournament, perhaps the most prestigious in tennis. And in baseball . . ."

I turned the volume down again. "What do you think?" I asked the Fish.

"Did we see her make the statement on camera?"

"No."

"Then we can't be sure she made it, or it was made for her."

"By the agents."

"Or the parents."

It was seven A.M. in Palm Springs, but Tony always forwarded his phone home when he wasn't in the office.

It was the only way to work when you had clients in so many time zones.

"Where have you been?" he railed exasperatedly. "I've been trying to beep you."

"Oops. I left my beeper in my suitcase. There's been a lot of excitement. Listen, what's the deal with Audrey and the announcement that she's on ice till Wimbledon due to her knee? Did you guys hear anything?"

"Better talk to Gus," said Tony. "He's been looking for you in a big way."

"I'd rather not. I'm not sure we're speaking. But what are you saying?"

"Well, let me patch you through to the clinic. I'm sure he's there. And I'm sure he's speaking."

I heard Muzak, then Gus was on the line.

"Jordan." He said my name factually.

"Hi, Gus."

"I have some news. Audrey's pregnant."

"What? How do you know?"

"We reran the blood chemistries, just to make sure we didn't miss anything. It turned out we did. This was one test we didn't do last time. According to the hormone levels, she would have been about two months pregnant when she was here."

With the Fish sitting across the room, I was careful not to say anything too revealing. "Well," I said calmly. "That is very interesting. Now what?"

"Now you come home. It's obvious why she was so upset."

"What I can see is all the more reason to find Audrey. This thing is like the emperor's new clothes. Nobody seems to want to acknowledge the plain facts before their eyes. This girl is in big trouble."

"Audrey needs an obstetrician, not a sports therapist."

"Wait a minute, Gus," I said. "I'm pretty sure somebody tried to scare me off yesterday, or at least make my trip highly inconvenient. I think I know who it was, and they did a very good job, by the way. I have a very unattractive burn."

"You're hurt?"

"Motorcycle exhaust pipe burn."

"For God's sake, Jordan, how many times have I told you to stay off those things!"

"I wasn't on one, I was shoved in front of one. There's a subtle difference." It was amazing how Gus and I could turn any discussion into a personal altercation these days.

"Well, in that case you should definitely get on the first plane back here. Where are you, anyhow?"

"I have to wrap up a few loose ends. Please put Tony back on."

"With pleasure."

More Muzak. Then Tony again. "Don't tell me. You want me to water the plants."

"Tony, you must have ESP. Talk to you later."

I had to think this through again. I grabbed an orange, sat down, and peeled it, being careful to take off as much of the bitter white membrane as I could. Pregnancy in itself is not unheard of among unmarried women players, even stars, although it is one fact that always somehow manages to elude the press. A rumor will surface that a certain unmarried player is pregnant, and then it will drift off, unaccounted for, unresolved, unexplained. But nobody seems to have the babies. Unlike movie stars, you certainly don't see the top women tennis players flaunt unwed pregnancies and single motherhood. It is an image that just doesn't seem to mix with sports, no matter how natural, not to mention the sponsorship implications and the impact on a woman's game.

How much did Audrey's parents know, I wondered as I sectioned the orange with my fingers. And it was always possible that Audrey was no longer pregnant at this point. Maybe she'd had a miscarriage or an abortion, which also could have explained her disappearance. At any rate, nothing was as it appeared. I decided not to share this news with the Fish. It was confidential medical information about my client.

Leaning against Cassie's desk, I wondered if Gus could be right. Maybe it was time to call it quits. Once the Armats learned what we knew, they might destroy their daughter. Certainly, Audrey had nowhere to turn. She was bound to be desperate. There would be a huge scandal if this got out, which it probably would. The only answer was Audrey. More than ever, I had to find her. But if I went back to the Springs, there would be a head-on confrontation, and I've never been one for off-court confrontations.

Cassie tossed me a banana from the kitchen as she grabbed her bags and headed out. "Breakfast," she instructed. "Lock up when you leave, people." The door closed behind her.

"So now what?" asked the Fish, stretching on the couch.

"Now I have to get to work." I sat down gingerly, rubbing my hand over my leg.

"That looks bad," said the Fish.

"It's okay." I leaned back and tried to figure out what to do next. Audrey was supposed to show up at

Wimbledon, play, hopefully win, then give a press conference to launch her new perfume and cosmetics line. Too much was at stake for her to miss this. It was virtually a command performance. She had to be there. And if I wanted to see her, so did I.

Enough chasing shadows.

"My office needs me to go back," I said.

The Fish swiped a hand across his face, smearing the remnants of the doughnut into a fine sugary paste around the corners of his mouth. "Oh. Really? Well, I guess I'll probably be heading home soon, myself. I mean, maybe you're right. I'm off the Global Sport payroll, and things must have straightened out, what with the TV announcement and all."

"Well, I'm not going back," I said defiantly. "I'm going to England. I'm no self-appointed vigilante, but if I went back, I'd feel like I'd left Audrey in the lurch. Somebody has to stand up to this, and if it turns out to be all blown out of proportion, then the worst that can happen is I'll have egg on my face." Or a lawsuit, I thought, suppressing that possibility.

"Good girl," said the Fish, with a nod. "Well, drop me a postcard. I believe you have my address."

I gestured to my leg. "I hope you'll understand if I don't get up and see you out, but I really have to get moving."

He pulled himself to his feet. "Well, sure. I understand." He ambled toward the door, then stopped. "Are you sure you don't need a doctor? I could take you to one."

"No, really, I'm fine. Thank you. You're okay with renting a car?"

"Yeah, I'll be okay. Actually, this is great timing. I

thought I'd take in Sea World. Shamu, Flipper, the whole bit. You just take care of that leg."

"I will. See you. It was—interesting."

He cocked a finger at me. "See you."

The minute he left, I made my action plan. This hinged on Tony's agreement to do me the favor of a lifetime, which was to go to my house, get my passport out of my top left dresser drawer, and make sure it got on the last FedEx pickup tonight. I checked my address book for the latest number of Alison Crane, my former Miami roommate. She didn't know it, but she was about to become the temporary adoptive mother of one very loving dog.

NINE

Getting to England was no problem. I just bought a ticket and flew nonstop from Miami to London, carrying on the same bags I had brought to Florida. Whatever I didn't have I figured I could borrow from Cassie. I checked into the Gloucester, a player hotel, which due to a lucky last-minute cancellation was also easy enough.

Getting to Wimbledon, however, proved to be more difficult than I expected. When I was a highly-ranked player, every detail had always been prearranged for me—transportation, housing, equipment, food, schedule. I had a staff of my own, and I never needed to think about the practicalities. When I arrived at Heathrow I would be whisked directly to my brick house in the village of Wimbledon, SW19, which somebody else had rented for me. It would already be stocked with the foods I liked, cases of clothes, shoes, towels, and equipment from current and prospective sponsors, and a rented bicycle that I rode to and from the courts. Somebody else would take care of the hassle of arranging my practice time. The tournament provided food vouchers, my restaurant bills went on my charges, and the bills went to my accountant. If I needed to go anywhere, I could call for a car and it would take me there. For the major stars, everything escalated another level. Porsche routinely gave Mariska a car to drive for the duration of the tournament. And last year I heard that Alex Bracht had virtually monopolized the complimentary on-site players' beauty and grooming salon.

Even though it had been five years since I'd left tennis, and my years at school and the WTA had been a crash course in reality, I still sometimes found myself floundering, especially when I visited a tournament site that seemed to trigger preconditioned behavior. Now it was up to me to find my own way around. I decided to forgo the expense and traffic of taxis and cars and take the tube, which seemed both simple and timesaving. It did, however, require a certain knowledge of the London tube system, and I found myself sweating in the cool, damp air as I contemplated my tube map, which looked to me like a knot of multicolored spaghetti.

Eventually, I emerged at the Southfields station and walked the rest of the way down to Church Road, past the redbrick houses with their neat little gardens, then past Wimbledon Park to the tall trimmed hedge where the spire of St. Mary's Church, a clutch of press shuttle buses, and the thwack of balls signaled that I had arrived at the entrance for the competitors' practice courts of the All England Lawn Tennis Club. The championships didn't start till the next day, but the diehards of the queue had started to form up. This was the hard core of the so-called LQS, or London Queueing Society, among the hardiest, most loyal, and best-equipped fans in the world. They had converged from all over the globe to wait patiently for their chance at one of the six hundred tickets that would be going on sale for Centre

Court on a first-come, first-served basis, or at least a glimpse of their tennis idols. They had come with a staggering array of equipment, ranging from tents, lawn chairs, blankets, and down duvets to plastic bags. One man had constructed a mini-shrine to Steffi Graf right there on the pavement, decked out with hundreds of magazine clippings and a few treasured snapshots. Everyone was prepared to camp out for up to ten days. Bad weather or rain were but minor inconveniences. Nobody ever complained, and equally amazing, nobody ever got mugged. By four A.M. on tournament days, this line would stretch to Southfields and back along both sides of the pavement.

As I approached the bridge near the main gate, I noticed more fans with cameras, hanging over the railings as they awaited the arrival of the players. Since it was the Sunday before the main draw began, many of the players were coming in to have their photo pass made up and check the draw. The last time I had been here, I had been one of that elite group. Now I was just another person hoping to get into the grounds.

At the massive black iron gates, uniformed guards in crisp white caps, white shirts, and gray flannels maintained a polite barrier as a steady stream of official cars, trucks, cranes, forklifts, media and catering vans, and players with gym bags slung over their shoulders arrived and were scrutinized for security clearance before being admitted. Security is always tight at Wimbledon, and it is a known fact that the entire club and grounds are routinely searched starting three full months before the championships begin, and that key sections are sealed off weeks in advance for several reasons, including the anticipated attendance of the royal family.

A woman who looked like she was hunkered down for the millennium was reading from a guidebook. She was clearly a seasoned pro: dressed in jeans and a sweatshirt decorated with the words "I Queued for Wimbledon," she appeared provisioned to the hilt with a thermos, blanket, sleeping bag, stack of books, folding camp cot, and battery-operated TV complete with antenna. She and her friends had commandeered several street barriers and used bungee cords and tarps to form a makeshift tent community as the line approached the gate. " 'The All England Croquet and Lawn Tennis Club held its first lawn tennis championship in 1877, for a first prize of twelve guineas,' " she read, and it was clear from her accent that she was Australian. " 'Two hundred spectators observed for a cost of a shilling apiece. Now, re-situated on the grounds of Wimbledon Park, over four hundred thousand international spectators crowd the grounds and the stands in a highly civilized fashion to witness the most elegant tennis tournament in the world. Prize money has escalated to two hundred sixty-five thousand pounds for the men's singles winner and two hundred forty thousand pounds for the women's. The Championships have been a favourite of British royalty since 1907, when the Prince of Wales visited the old Worple Road grounds, watched the day's play until it was rained out, then accepted the presidency of the Club, which he held until he became King.' " A pizza delivery boy bicycled up and she waved him over, paid him, and took possession of her lunch without breaking stride as she continued to read. " 'Last year at Wimbledon, food and drink consumed included twenty-three tons of strawberries, twelve tons of salmon, two hundred eighty-five thousand cups of tea, and one hundred ninety thousand sandwiches . . .' "

As I edged past the queuers and fans toward the front of the line, an elderly woman in a straw boater bedecked with a huge bunch of purple flowers reached out a hand and grabbed my sleeve with a stern expression. "Now there, that's no way to handle things," she admonished.

I jerked to a halt. The woman had a viselike grip.

"It just won't do, dear. You'll need proper clothes. It's going to get quite chilly tonight, and it may drizzle." She gave me a pitying look and pressed a folded poncho into my hand. "Take this. I have an extra."

I tried to pass it back. "Thank you, but . . ."

She held up her palms. "I won't take no for an answer, now. We have to take care of each other, it's only neighborly. Now, clearly, dear, you're a first-timer in the queue. Come here, now. Let me give you a few pointers." Cornflower-blue eyes, tissue-paper skin, seventy-some years old, she was sweet, grandmotherly, smelled of violet cologne, and was hard as stainless steel.

"Thank you, but . . ." I tried again, only to have a bag of chips shaken under my nose.

"Didn't bring any food, did you, dear. Oh, you young people think you know everything there is, and we suppose we did too, once, didn't we, Thelma," she asked her equally elderly companion, who nodded. "But we don't come all the way from Ottawa every year for ten years to stand here and not be comfortable. So let us help you out—we all share, you know. Sometimes it's difficult for first-timers to understand. Now." She pointed up the street. "Should you need laundry, there's a local resident who will take it tonight and run it back next day, for a fee, of course. She should be making the rounds about six or so. There's an all-night stand for burgers, and someone will hold your place in line if you go for food. Somebody will surely have an extra pillow. And the end of the queue is that way." She jabbed a finger in the direction of the end of the line.

"Actually, I'm not waiting. I'm here on business."

She perked to attention. "Oh, you're with one of the players? Which one? My favorite is Alex Bracht. Used to be Lendl, but he's getting on, you know. Have to stay modern, support the youth. Such a cute bum, Alex has. I always judge a player by his bum." She picked up a thick, dog-eared notebook and patted it. "This is my Alex, right in here." She tenderly removed a candy wrapper from between the pages. "He gave me this candy bar last year. This year, maybe he'll get us tickets to the semifinals. We're waiting to see what his draw is, so we'll know what court to get tickets for tomorrow."

Thelma inclined in my direction. "Stella keeps a diary of all Alex's matches and everything he says in the press."

Stella nodded sagely and gripped my sleeve even harder. "And lots of things he doesn't say in the press. Phooey on the press! You want to know anything about the players, dear, don't waste your money on those books and papers. You come straight to the source. Ask us, any of us here in the queue. We know what's really going on. In the queue, people have friends who work in grounds maintenance, in the hotels, in the laundries, the restaurants, the bicycle shops, the golf course. We're here all day and all night. We hear things. Bits and pieces, and we put it all together, dear. Those press people are just doing their job. But this is our life! *We* know why Borg never came back. *We* know what broke up McEnroe's marriage. *We* know where Audrey Armat is." I had been trying to politely break free, but this last declaration stopped me. "You do?"

"Of course," Stella and Thelma chirped confidently in unison, nodding to each other.

"She's here, isn't she?"

"Oh, my dear. Tsk, tsk." They clucked at each other. "Where else would she be?"

"Well, you don't think we'd divulge that kind of information about our dear Audrey to a *stranger*, do you now?" bristled Thelma.

"Of course not," said Stella. "But by tomorrow dawn, we'll be best of friends, dear. That's how it works in the queue. We'll talk about it then, when we have a little history between us. Meanwhile, take this." She handed me a plastic rain hat. "It's the least I can do."

I thought briefly about telling her again that I wasn't sleeping in the queue, but the woman was clearly crazy and, fortunately, she'd released her grip. It was time to move on.

I circumvented the remainder of the crowd and moved closer to the gate, wondering how I would get in without a pass or a ticket. Nobody slips in here on a smile. Even Mariska, a six-time champion, had once been detained at the gate for twenty minutes when she forgot her pass. What the fan with the guidebook hadn't read, because it's never in any books, is that Scotland Yard and private security companies hired by the club are always on the alert for terrorist attacks. Few people realize that not far from Centre Court is an area specifically earmarked as a temporary morgue that can hold four hundred bodies. Inside the gates, I could see a squad of eight men in dark blue uniforms herding a pack of five or six Labs and English springers past the bronze statue of fifties champion Fred Perry toward the Tea Lawn—sniffer dogs to search for bombs or explosives. These days, it seemed, tea-and-crumpets extend just so far.

"Do you have a pass, miss?" asked the guard when it was my turn at the gate.

"No, but if you'll call the players' desk, perhaps Wendy Shelton will be there." In fact, I knew Wendy would be there. To the players, she was the face of Wimbledon, their chief contact. She worked on it all year long, but for weeks before the tournament started she never left the players' desk. "Please tell her that Jordan Myles is at the gate."

Five minutes later a young woman in blue culottes and a white knit shirt trimmed in stripes of Wimbledon green and purple and sporting the green Wimbledon insignia appeared. A laminate pass hung from a cord around her neck, and she beckoned me inside with a polite smile. As we walked together, I was impressed all over again by the beauty of the grounds. A village of green-and-white-striped tents fluttered against the sky, which was threateningly gray. Workers were busily putting the last-minute touches on the profusions of pink and white hydrangeas and pink, red, and yellow rosebush trees that seemed to line every walkway and balcony. Even the manual laborers had a genteel look—there were strictly enforced rules that contractors to the tournament weren't allowed to take off their shirts or listen to radios. We passed several flatbeds of flowers being rolled through the grounds, and weaving incongruously through them, groups of men in black suits and sunglasses with walkie-talkies.

"Security is unbelievable this year," I said as we passed the statue of Fred Perry and the ivy-covered South East Hall with the huge green logo over the entrance: ALL ENGLAND LAWN TENNIS & CROQUET CLUB. This was a club so exclusive, a member had to resign or die before a new member could be admitted. Here, in a kind of athletic Brigadoon, males were still "gentlemen" and females "ladies," and the club colors of green and purple reigned supreme. Flowers never died, grass was always green, and strawberries and cream were always on the menu.

I was escorted briskly past the security team who guarded the entrance to the Competitors' Building. This was a relatively new facility, pretty and modern. As I expected, Wendy was at the players' liaison desk, just inside the doors of the glass-fronted entrance, on the phone. A huge flower arrangement on the counter dwarfed her tiny frame. Her ash-blond hair was cut short with bangs, and she wore a Wimbledon green knit shirt with a black skirt, pearl earrings, and the ubiquitous laminate around her neck. Wendy looks like she is in her early to mid-forties, but it's hard to tell. She has beautiful English skin and seems ageless in an athletic sort of way. In forty-eight hours this desk would be swamped with players, coaches, and families checking in, getting schedules, leaving or picking up messages and passes, making requests. Just past the desk, a door in a wall wainscoted in light oak led to the Ladies' Number 2 Dressing Room. This is the locker room for all the unseeded women competitors. Their names were listed on a large plaque beside the door, and by the next day, I knew, a matron would be guarding the entrance inside and out. The women who were the top-seeded players and past champions would not come here. They dressed in the legendary Lady Members' Dressing Room in the club building. I had only been inside it once, when I was somewhat amazed to see an attendant drawing baths.

People of every sort were rushing in and out of the lobby. A group of young men and women stood chatting by the door. "Did you enjoy the dance?" one of the women asked a young man, referring, most likely, to one of the many championship parties. These included the International Club reception on the first Saturday; the Hurlingham garden party the Sunday before the championships begin, which includes spouses and children; the Wimbledon Ball at the Grosvenor House Hotel on the middle Saturday, which is a thank-you from the Lawn Tennis Association to its councilors and staff; one or two testimonials honoring somebody or other sprinkled about—this year's was for Paul Cranston; numerous corporate events; and, of course, the champions' dinner at the Savoy on the final Sunday night, attended by the gentlemen's and ladies' singles winners, their families, former champions, and organization people. Every competitor also got a voucher for two of the best seats in the house at the West End play of their choice.

"No," the young man said. "Twenty people who'd just been voted off the committee were at our table. It was awful."

"I thought the music was a bit too loud," said his companion.

A woman barged her way up to the desk, demanding

to be told where to go to get her picture taken for a photo pass. People streamed through to pick up the daily match schedules. Phones rang nonstop on the desk and in the office beyond. The scene was about one inch ahead of chaos. The first week of the championships is always the busiest. The second week, as competition winnows out the field, things calm down just a little.

Wendy hung up the phone and waved me over. "Jordan, how nice to see you. You don't come round much anymore, now that you're off there in the private sector. But you're looking terrific."

"Yes, the old leg finally got it all together. And I thought I'd swing by. See old friends. But, Wendy, it was sort of a last-minute decision, and I don't have a pass. Can you help me out?"

She immediately produced a book of passes for the grounds and Competitors' Building. "I'll have to work on the tickets, love. You know how that is. Keep checking."

"Who's been in today?"

"Well, Kelly's here—she's covering the matches for one of the networks. And Mariska flew in from the States Saturday night. Her assistant was in earlier to pick up her credentials, but I think she's in London at the WTA meeting. Pete's here, and, oh, most of them have checked in, as you can imagine, at this point. Anke and Steffi, of course."

"Any sign of Alex Bracht?"

"Bracht!" She snorted. "He sent a fax from some yacht off Sardinia. He wanted to know if we could handle a body wax at the grooming salon. For himself." She furrowed her brow with disapproval as she pinned several messages and envelopes to the bulletin board. "I don't know when he thinks he's going to show up—if it were up to him, probably just for the finals. Last year, well, can you imagine a defending champion—he drives in here a half hour before his match, he doesn't have his pass ..." Wendy frowned disapprovingly.

"Can you help me get a meal voucher?" a tanned man in his mid-forties interrupted.

"We don't give meal vouchers to coaches," said Wendy. Subject closed.

"So Alex isn't here," I said.

"I should say not!"

"What about Audrey? Any word from her?" I tried not to sound too interested or anxious.

"Oh, I think she's here, actually," said Wendy. "Her mother was in this morning, meeting with security, and E.J. picked up her credentials."

A player in tennis shorts and a windbreaker, a towel around his neck, came up to the desk. "The physios aren't going to be here today, are they?" he asked.

"Not till tomorrow," Wendy said. She handed him a schedule and he bounded out the door.

"When's Audrey's practice time?" I asked.

"I don't think she's practicing at the club. She's at Aorangi Park," said Wendy. That in itself is not unusual. Practice time is extremely difficult to get. To save the grass for the tournament, players aren't allowed on the All England Club courts for more than a half hour a day, so many arrange to practice elsewhere. Then Wendy said, "You know, there's been a death threat."

"A death threat? Against whom?"

"Several of the top women players have been targeted, apparently."

"I hadn't read anything . . ."

"Oh, they're keeping it quiet. But there have been some unsettling incidents already."

"Such as?"

"Well, somebody sent Anke a box of a hundred pairs of absolutely lewd panties. That's not dangerous in itself, but . . ."

"Creepy." I shuddered.

Wendy nodded. "And some anonymous person's been sending Audrey ten dozen roses a day here at the desk, which is a nice gesture, but unfortunately, these days I suppose we have to wonder even about that, don't we?"

"I suppose so."

"So many crazies out there since what happened to Monica."

"So many crazies out there, period."

The sniffer dog squad burst through the doors, tails waging, straining at their leashes. One of the handlers held a large floor plan of the building, which the others gathered around to consult. All of them carried walkie-talkies. A golden Lab raced over and stood on its hind legs against the desk. "Hello, Ginger, there's a good girl," said Wendy, producing a doggie biscuit from under the desk.

"What's the story on this death threat?" I asked.

"Well, they've offered twenty-four-hour security to all the women, but the Armats have hired their own private guards. We'll escort Audrey here and on and off the court, of course, but till she's on the grounds it's up to her parents, I'm afraid."

The sniffer dog contingent disappeared into the ladies' dressing room.

"Most of the agents this year are MI5 cleared," Wendy said.

"What's that?"

"Our version of the CIA. They did the G-7 summit and drove the prime minister and the president of the United States."

"I guess they're not taking this lightly."

"Not at all, dear, not at all. Security is really taking everything into consideration. They even sent all the courtesy cars back to the factory to be checked."

The phone started ringing again, and Wendy thrust a purple and green Wimbledon beach towel and a tote bag into my arms. "Here," she said. "Souvenirs. Oh! By the way, there's a message for you here. I wasn't sure you were even coming—nobody'd mentioned it. So I kept it under the desk." She rummaged through a drawer and pulled out a small white envelope, then busied herself immediately with the phones.

I had no idea who even knew I was here. I opened it. The handwritten note said, "Look outside." I turned and peered through the glass. On the other side of the window stood the Fish, waving cheerfully.

He moved up and tapped on the glass, miming that he wanted me to come outside.

"I'm glad you're here," he said the minute I stepped out the doors. "What with this death-threat thing, Global Sport put me back on the case."

"So you heard?"

"Naturally. What did you think I was doing here? Going to the tennis museum? Although, I must say, it looks very interesting from the outside, all those tennis greats. They got your picture in there?"

"Hardly. Listen, now that you're here, I'll make a

deal. I'll tell you what I know, you tell me what you know. Okay?"

"Why do I think I'm going to end up on the short end of this stick?" The Fish swiveled 180 degrees, scanning the area through the viewfinder of his camera. "Gotta catch this scene. This is my first time in Europe as a civilian. I'm documenting my whole trip, starting with the TWA departure lounge and the lobby of the Hilton. My mother's never gonna believe this. All these flowers. My mother and flowers, it's like ham and eggs. She'd go crazy for this place, forget about the tennis. Where does the queen sit?" He clicked off a few shots of court 2, opposite the Competitors' Building, then stuffed the camera back into his bag—the official Wimbledon tote bag, I noticed. "By the way, how's the leg?" he asked.

"Fine."

"By the way, did you keep the pen I gave you? It might be worth something someday."

"Yes, I have it."

"Prove it."

I sighed and rummaged through my purse. "There." I held it up.

"Let's see." He took the pen, examined it, and clicked the point a few times. "Seems in good working order." He handed it back. "Like I told the guys in the patent office, it's a good pen. Always keep it with you."

"I'll try to," I said dryly.

The Fish pulled a book of tickets out of his shirt pocket. "I got tickets for every day of the match. Let's see—tickets for Centre Court. Those are good, right?"

"Yes. And extremely expensive and hard to get, especially at the last minute. How'd you get them? Global Sport must have a very high opinion of you."

"Actually, these tickets are wasted on me. I don't really understand the game, you know. Never did have any feel for it—this fuzzy little ball flying through the air that you have to whack at. Now, bowling, there's a sport. You got a nice, big ball to work with, and a place to put your fingers."

"Now tell me what you know about Audrey. I need to talk to her as soon as possible."

He took out a box of film, opened it, and started reading the directions. "Well, we have death threats. We have a guy with a thing for lady's lingerie—or, let's be liberated—could be a girl. We have a flower lover."

The Fish covered ground quickly, I had to admit. "And Audrey?"

He shrugged. "They say she's here. In a house. Nobody's seen her. Although I did see her mother and her brother."

Just then, Wendy reappeared. "Another message for you, Jordan," she said, handing me an envelope. "E.J. Armat left it a few minutes ago."

"Where is he?"

"Gone. I think he just left."

"Damn!" I whispered. I would have given anything to talk to him. I opened the envelope, hoping it wouldn't contain a summons or some legal broadside from the Armats.

The note said, "Please meet me Tuesday at ten in the locker room. I will designate you my physiotherapist, so get a photo pass." Beneath was the address and Audrey's signature.

"What's that note?" asked the Fish.

"Nothing." I crumpled it up and put it in my pocket, as if it had no significance.

"Well," said the Fish, "in that case how about a tour?"

"I've seen the grounds," I said.

"But have you been behind the scenes? I've been getting to know some of the boys in security. Interesting group. You might like to see their setup. And maybe we could talk to them a little bit." He took my arm and propelled me behind the courts to a little road behind the Aorangi Park pavilion that was lined with cabins and trailers. Between the trailers were small groups of folding tables and benches. A security detail was meeting around one set of these tables.

"Prevention is one thousand times better than any kind of security," said a wiry-haired, strongly built man in a dark suit with a thick Scottish brogue. A laminate pass was clipped to his pocket, and he wore an earpiece. He held up a picture of a man I didn't recognize, captioned *Mr. Morton Minor*. "This man is banned from the grounds. Stop him from entering if possible. However, if sighted, he must not be challenged, but Control must be informed. Remember, if there is an altercation, talk him out. Negotiation is always the first move."

I smiled in spite of myself. Only at Wimbledon would a person who is banned be referred to by security as "Mr."

The meeting broke up, and the Scottish man, who was obviously in charge, came over to us and extended his hand to the Fish. "Yes, Mr. Fisher. Payin' us another visit, are you?"

I wondered how the Fish had gotten so friendly with security so quickly. It seemed like a monumental accomplishment for a man who didn't even know where the royal box was.

"Just thought I'd drop by. Jordan Myles, this is Harry Bruce, U.K. events manager. Jordan's a physiotherapist. Harry, well, he's sort of the link here between the police, the club, and the players."

"Well, here we go then, Noel," he said.

"The death threats?"

"Business as usual."

I left Fisher with his security cronies, and for the next hour I wandered around the grounds. I'd played here many times, first as a junior and then as a professional, and then I'd returned twice with the WTA. It seemed strange to be at Wimbledon as an outsider, with no real role. I went into the stands to look down at Centre Court: it was almost dreamlike, like being caught in a sense of déjà vu but knowing it was real. Wimbledon has eighteen grass courts, five red shale, three clay, one artificial grass, and five indoor. But only grass is used for championship play, and there is only one Centre Court. This jewel box of a site, the epicenter of the sports world for the duration of the championships, is used the rest of the year only for a few pre- and post-Wimbledon rituals, like the tradition where lady members of the club play a doubles match before the tournament fortnight starts to "raise the sap" in the turf.

The sap eluded me, but, as always, I felt energy just from the history of the place and the smell of the grass and the earth. Green—Centre Court is so many shades of green, from the deep bottle green of the seats to the variegated green velvet of the three varieties of grass, like the felt of a pool table. The best thing about Centre Court was that you never lost a ball there; it's so dark, with those big, high green canvases that dissolve into shadows. For a player, that's heaven. But it's overwhelming in another sense, touched by so many spirits and ghosts. I sat on a seat. It was cold and hard, like a dead body. Not at all the vibrant, breathing entity that was Wimbledon. Or was it just that Wimbledon was dead for me?

My first reaction was always, Oh my God! There's the royal box, there's the grass, there's the Slazenger signs. The hallmarks of Centre Court routinely unnerved me. So I devised a ritual. The night before the tournament started, I would sneak in and sit on the grass and meditate, summoning up those ghosts and spirits. Suzanne Lenglen in her diaphanous dresses. Alice Marble and her revolutionary—for women at the time—serve and volley game. The formidability and grace of Althea Gibson. Evert facing off against Navratilova. Billie Jean with her unsurpassed twenty titles. Then I would pluck a small tuft of grass and tuck it in my racket for good luck. It was always so quiet, only a few guards around. I would feel totally removed from the world sitting there, imagining the finals with fifteen thousand people in the stands and millions watching on TV. And one year it was me on Centre Court for those finals, I was number three in the world, and I had a piece of my own dream, playing the best tennis of my life.

The day of that match, I felt everything, starting with each drop of water in my morning shower. I remember standing there, hypersensitized, the water rolling down my skin and pooling around my toes as my body seemed to collect and prepare itself. I felt the porcelain under the soles of my feet, the roughness of the terry towel, the coolness of the tile. And when I picked up my racket, it was as if my whole self had been conceived and existed to do just that, like an animal with one purpose in life. I was aware of my hands, my fingers, the feel of the air. My vision seemed acute, my eye-hand coordination instinctive.

I had it all for one set. The strokes, the precision, the luck. I had time for every shot, and shots for every opportunity. I was truly in the zone. How many times have I relived that game, replayed it backward and forward in my mind? And how many times have I sworn to forget it? Was it the shock of being beaten, or the shock of being beaten by a girl so young she looked like she belonged on the playground swings at recess? I had so much to think about; she was a blank slate. I was ahead 2–6 after the first set. I had my opponent's back against the wall. This was when I needed to turn it on and step up my game.

I knew I was the stronger and better athlete. On grass the best athlete usually wins because the bounces are so irregular you have to be able to adjust and think so quickly, with precision eye-hand coordination. I knew I played a better grass-court game than Letty. I had one of the best two-handed backhands in tennis at the time, a weapon I knew would serve me well on grass, because I could adjust quickly and with more strength. Grass isn't like other surfaces, and my game and style suited it. On grass you have to be able to hit the ball low over the net, even if it has a lot of topspin. You have to be able to hit off bad bounces, make the ball dip earlier so it goes over the net at your opponent's feet instead of her shoulders, so she's forced to volley up and you have a chance to pass. And you have to have a good first serve, and a better second serve, so the other person can't attack it well. Otherwise, the point is over.

I knew what I had to do, and I knew I could do it. And in the beginning I did it. But this wasn't just any championship, this was *Wimbledon*. After I won the first set, I did the unthinkable and found myself thinking about winning instead of playing. It wasn't that I choked. Actually, it was worse. I started imagining curtsying to the duchess and taking the platter.

Little Letty Mandelson, meanwhile, didn't know this—but she knew she had nothing to lose, and she went for it. In the game of tennis, the momentum can shift in one or two points. I broke my concentration, Letty broke my serve, and I couldn't get back in the zone. For the record, I lost 2–6, 6–3, 6–2. My chances for a Wimbledon Championship blew away into that drizzly, overcast sky like an umbrella that caught a sudden gust of wind. My brief moment had given me a taste that was not to be sated that day, when it was the only day that counted. I can tell myself that making it to the finals at Wimbledon, not to mention my three previous Grand Slam wins, should be more than enough for any human being on this planet. But it wasn't nearly enough. I wasn't prepared to lose that day. It devastated me, and in spite of myself I lost my composure and found myself crying on the brocaded shoulder of H.R.H. the Duchess of Kent. It was a nightmare from which I never seemed to wake up, an indelible image. The media consigned it to history: for years they used that scene as a clip in the network sports coverage as part of the "Agony of Defeat" montage. My confidence was never the same again, never. Even now, I felt hot tears starting at the back of my throat. I bit my lip, hard.

"So where does the queen sit?" The Fish materialized behind me. "I don't see a throne."

I pulled a Kleenex out of my purse and blew my nose. "Allergy to grass," I said, clearing my throat. "There's no throne. Just seats in the royal box, although I'm sure they're more comfortable than most." I pointed to the area at the near end of the court, just behind the clubhouse. "They'll keep the royal family and honored guests in a special reception room until just before play begins. Serve them Pimm's Cup or tea or something. Then they escort them out."

"You ever play for the queen?" The Fish snapped pictures of every conceivable angle, the camera whirring as it automatically rewound.

I shook my head. "She's supposed to come this year, for the first time in ages. It's usually the Duke and Duchess of Kent. Princess Diana. For a while there, Fergie came. I did have to curtsy to the Duchess of Kent, though."

"You? An American citizen?"

I shrugged. "Well, it's a courtesy. A ceremonial kind of thing. I practiced first, in front of a mirror." I stood up and demonstrated. "It's painless. Besides, the duchess is very nice. The motherly sort. I didn't mind." I didn't tell him how I'd slobbered on the poor woman's suit. I wondered if he knew. There was probably a miniscule chance that he'd missed me on "The Agony of Defeat."

I yawned. Jet lag was starting to creep up on me. All I wanted was to go back to the hotel, leave a message informing Cassie that I was here, and sleep. I figured I could throw myself on the mercy of Annabelle, the transportation manager, and hop a ride back on one of the shuttles to the hotel.

We started walking back through the maze of empty

covered walkways that would soon be thronging with people. Our footsteps echoed on the damp concrete. Everything was dark green and shadowy, like a deep, mossy forest. For the first time, it seemed almost sinister.

TEN

Opening day transformed Wimbledon. Yesterday it had been an elegant stage, the sets and players in place, waiting for the curtain to rise. Today the show was on. As if on cue, the sun broke through, adding a sheen to the flowered dresses, pastel suits, and visored caps in every conceivable color, although just as many people in the crowd looked as if they could almost step onto the courts themselves in their shorts and knit shirts. The vendors were in full swing, and on the Tea Lawn people carried everything from champagne glasses to teacups to small paper cups heaped with ripe red strawberries, as fleets of people with push brooms circulated through the crowd to keep the grounds immaculate. At the Last Eight Club, a chintz and rattan enclave for past singles quarterfinalists or doubles finalists and their guests, former players reconnected with one another and savored the prestige and the memories over a Pimm's. Beyond the tennis courts and the croquet lawn, in the private marquee area, corporate and private receptions were in full swing. These were elegant events, and some guests remained there for the entire duration of their stay, glued to large-screen TVs and drifting among the smoked salmon, caviar, and champagne.

I headed for the players' lounge, which was on the top floor of the Competitors' Building, across from the prize-money office. I wasn't going to watch the matches—my goal was to hang around in the crowd and pick up whatever the grapevine had to say about Audrey. According to the draw, she was scheduled to play tomorrow. She would have to surface soon. I waved at Wendy and headed up the stairs. Looking up, I saw Marion Stryker in a sleek, pale gray Armani suit, heading down the stairwell. Her gray hair was in a smooth bob, every strand in place, anchored by black-rimmed sunglasses pushed on top of her head. Her mouth and jaw were firmly set, like those of a woman on a mission, which she always was. I looked straight at Marion but she didn't acknowledge me as she forged her way to the lobby. On the top floor, I went into the carpeted lounge area and ordered a bottle of water from a white-coated bartender. The atmosphere was low-key and somehow soothing—people relaxing on the comfortable upholstered chairs and banquettes, a few babies in arms, one couple playing backgammon, a soundless TV playing the coverage of the matches.

At the bar I saw Milt Bevins getting himself a Pimm's, complete with cucumber garnish. Of course, the Armats would have arranged a guest pass for him. Before I could sneak by, he spotted me.

"Jordan! Hello!" Milt was his usual immaculate self. He wore a beautiful lightweight navy blue sport coat over a pale striped shirt. His hair looked damp from the shower and freshly combed, and his nails were buffed. On his right hand, which he extended to me, he wore a gold and carnelian seal that had been made into a ring. I also noticed his cuff links. They were enameled replicas of the team insignia Audrey wore as a necklace, and they must have been a gift from the Armats.

"Hi, Milt."

"Can I get you something?" He spoke expansively, as if this were his personal house party.

"Not right now, thanks."

He tipped the bartender, then made his way over to me. "You know, Audrey should take it all here," he said.

"Well, it's possible."

"Possible!" He snorted. "They should put a statue of her on the lawn there, right by Fred Perry's. In fact, I think I'll suggest that. I hate the way they like players to be dinosaurs before they give them the credit they deserve. Being young should not be a handicap."

"No argument from me on that one, Milt," I said, looking for an escape hatch.

"I think you understand Audrey," Milt said, sipping his Pimm's. "You were a young player yourself. That's good. I told Corinne Armat that you understood, that you would never push a delicate young girl beyond endurance. Do we understand each other?"

This was getting uncomfortable. "You know, Milt, I have to meet somebody. See you."

As I turned, he grabbed my arm. "You know, it's common knowledge that there've been death threats. Audrey's received them, and it's horrifying. Don't you feel they should cancel the championships this year?" He sounded indignant. "As a safety measure? In fact, I feel a responsibility to recommend it myself, if nobody else does. You'd think they'd be concerned about the royal family, if not the players. Sometimes the obvious escapes these people." He shook his head in dismay.

"Milt, I'm sure they're covering the situation." I escaped through the sliding glass doors and found a seat at one of the balcony tables. Even here, the pink and lavender hydrangeas were out in force. Of course, none of the seeded players were here, but I did spot XuXu's family, several of the coaches, and a sexpot movie star in shorts, suspenders, and lipstick-red cowboy boots. On the adjoining balcony the press were gathering, and I kept an eye out for Cassie. Below, matches were about to begin on courts 2 and 3, and the bleachers flanking them were full, awaiting the arrival of the players from the concourse. A clutch of security guards escorted XuXu from the Competitors' Building directly across onto court 2, to scattered applause. She was up against Kyoko Oshimi, a highly ranked rising Japanese twenty-year-old who was very popular with the fans. Oshimi would be coming from the Lady Members' Dressing Room. Although it stood to be an interesting game, I didn't envy them playing on court 2. They call it "the Graveyard," because a conversation in the back of the stands carries word for word down to the players.

Then a scream. More of a shriek than a scream—high-decibeled, shocking, sudden. My head whipped around automatically toward the sound as pandemonium broke loose below. There was a stampede in the press box as reporters raced off and photographers jammed the rail, and I jumped up and tensely scanned the scene. Directly below I could see Kyoko slumped on the ground, surrounded by security, her coach motioning frantically. The word rippled through the crowd on the balcony: "Kyoko's been stabbed!"

I grabbed my bag and bolted inside, through the lounge and down the stairs, which were clogged with people heading up, down, or frozen in place. On the ground floor, Wendy stood grimly, the phone glued to her ear. Outside, security and police converged from all directions. Sirens began to wail. Within minutes the area had been cleared of spectators, and guards stood at the entrance of the Competitors' Building, allowing no one in or out. Several police vans and an ambulance arrived, and after a few minutes, a stretcher was unloaded. XuXu's mother raced from the Competitors' Building across to the courts. A hush fell on the crowd as Kyoko, motionless under a blanket, an IV in her arm, was carried out on the stretcher, a medic hurrying alongside, leaning on her chest. I noticed Carolyn Rice, my friend from the WTA, climbing into the ambulance behind the stretcher as the doors closed.

I made my way to the desk. "What happened?" I whispered to Wendy.

Her lips were tight. "Someone lunged from the crowd with an autograph book and what looked like a pen. But the pen turned out to be a knife. Some sort of stiletto. The initial report is severed tendons in her wrist and arm. There's a lot of bleeding, and the chest is involved."

"Oh my God. How horrible! Did they catch the person?"

"He ran into the crowd at court number one. There's a match in progress—Courier's playing Hilton. He got away completely. With all this security, I can't imagine—well, they're saying he was a professional. Nobody knows—there may be others, and they may go after other players, or even the royals."

"You could have total panic on your hands."

"We hope not." An official motioned Wendy over

and she hurried away. They huddled for a few minutes before she returned to the desk. "A total obsessive fan, most likely," she said. "But the imminent danger seems to be over, and the director's office has decided to continue with the matches. They're also putting all the top-seeded women under twenty-four-hour guard."

One of the top ten women players was now out of the championships, and there had been death threats against several others. Women's tennis at Wimbledon, the bastion of gentility, where an on-court glimpse of Gussie Moran's lace undershorts had once seemed the ultimate scandal, had become a vortex of senseless violence.

"You look like you could use a break." The Fish materialized at my elbow.

"I'm fine, thank you. But you're right. I could use a break from standing out here in the lobby with the rest of this crowd. I'm going into the physiotherapy room. Maybe somebody has heard a medical report."

I approached the locker-room door, where a wall of guards now stood. "I need to speak with somebody in the physiotherapy room," I told the matron who sat closest to the door, her feet, in their sensible black oxfords, crossed like gates.

A female guard escorted me inside, and I recognized the attendant at the desk. "It's all right," she said. "Miss Myles may come in."

"Antonia, it's nice to see you." We hugged across the desk. Antonia had been head locker-room attendant for the unseeded players for more years than I'd been alive. She was a veritable institution.

"Terrible thing, isn't it?" she said.

I nodded. What was there to say?

"Jill's back in there. Go on in." She motioned toward the door of the physiotherapy room.

The players were dressing and undressing silently as I crossed the locker room. It was fresh and pretty in shades of green and peach, with a long bisecting banquette. The only sound came from the two televisions broadcasting the matches, the showers in the next room, and the whine of a blow-dryer from the dressing room. I didn't know anybody in the dressing room. They were all young; many spoke Spanish or other foreign languages. A new generation of players, to which I did not belong.

Inside the physiotherapy room, Jill Converse sat on the edge of one of the two tables, in front of a huge wall chart of the hip, knee, shoulder, and elbow. Jill and I had worked together when I was with the WTA. Tall, with short, curly reddish hair, Jill is usually a lot of fun. Now she was uncharacteristically quiet. We dispensed with the social pleasantries.

"I saw Carolyn get into the ambulance," I said.

"I know. She called from the hospital. She did what she could. Kyoko's in surgery."

"What about the rest of the girls?"

"Some of them seem to be almost in shock. They had to sedate XuXu."

The door swung open and a player came into the room. "Can you take a look at my ankle?" she asked Jill.

I left the room and went back through the locker room into the lobby. "It doesn't look good," said the Fish. "I hear she's in bad shape."

"Absolutely not, absolutely not!" The voice of Corinne Armat preceded her into the room. She stalked across the floor in an Easter-egg-yellow Chanel suit with a short chiffon skirt and black-and-yellow jacket. On her head was a beret made entirely of fake flowers. Twenty or thirty chains and pearl necklaces clanked around her neck. She swung her quilted black bag with a vengeance and deposited it on the counter in front of Wendy as if she were delivering an anvil. "Audrey cannot play in this atmosphere of uncontrolled terrorism. A championship is not worth my daughter's life." She thrust her chin out at Wendy, as if she were personally to blame for the situation.

"Mrs. Armat, if you'd like to go to the director's office . . ." Wendy said.

"Why? I have nothing to say to the director. What's he done for this tournament? Direct traffic? That's about all he's good for. There is absolutely no security."

"Quite the contrary, Mrs. Armat. Let's discuss the measures we're taking." Wendy kept her voice calm. "And tomorrow, you know, the queen is supposed to attend for the first time since 1977. So you know security will be at the absolute maximum. Why won't you just permit us to assign security to Audrey, and—"

"I don't trust your so-called security, and obviously I was right. Let the queen trust them. Us, we have our own. The people who guard the Saudi royal family. Well, you warn them. One more incident and that's it, Audrey's out. Now. Here's the press conference schedule for the perfume launch. Make sure it gets to the media. Revlon's reserved an entire marquee, and they're unveiling a rose named after Audrey." She turned on her heel and screamed at the unfortunate public relations minion who was following her, carrying a stack of glossy press kits. I hoped she wouldn't see me.

"You!"

Too late.

"What's she doing here? She's totally unqualified to be around professional tennis players." She glared at me. "You can't play yourself, so you try to wreck my daughter's career. Well, you'll be held accountable, and I'll see to it personally. You and that Mickey Mouse clinic of yours."

The PR minion grabbed Corinne Armat's arm and dragged her out of the building, her protests echoing. "Let go of me, you little creep. You work for me, and don't you forget it!"

I stood frozen, swallowing dryly, envisioning the fall-out from this as the entire room stared at me.

"Nice lady," said the Fish. "Retiring little thing. How about some tea and crumpets?"

"Everybody's going to remember this. I've just destroyed my company," I said morosely.

"Wrong. Nobody's going to remember it," said the Fish.

"Oh, come on. Please. I can't stomach pandering."

"They're going to be talking about something else," he said. "Kyoko's dead. I heard from Bruce."

"But she was in surgery!"

"She died on the table. The knife went right through her arm and into her heart. Severed an artery."

I gasped with horror.

"They'll be announcing it soon. They're taking the royal family out first, very quietly. They can't have panic, but you're talking moving forty thousand people quickly out of a restricted area. Let's get out of here before the shit hits the fan."

I felt stunned, numb. This was tennis. This was

Wimbledon. Green, white, and purple, now red with blood.

We walked outside into a solid wall of people with cameras, down the concourse and out the gate. "I thought I'd go into town for a drink," said Fisher. "I saw a pub. Or we could walk down to the Global marquee. The heavyweights don't get in till next week, but there's probably somebody around."

"I'm not in any mood for dealing with people."

In a matter of minutes, I knew, Wimbledon was going to become the focus of the international news. Media from every country would converge here, adding to the already news-glutted environment. There would be questioning, inquests, a trial. Tennis lost its relevance to the horrifying fact: a girl was dead.

The queue was in an uproar. Everyone seemed to have an opinion on what was going on inside. Several people brandished papers with headlines that read DE-RANGED STALKER TERRORIZES WIMBLEDON. Thelma, my self-appointed queue buddy, saw me walk through the gates and yelped. "Dear! Is it true what they're saying in the queue? There was a stabbing? Kyoko was stabbed, poor little thing? I'm just distraught."

"Yes, Thelma. I'm afraid it's true."

"It's not safe anymore," said Thelma emphatically. "There's a stalker on the loose." She thrust the newspaper at me.

She leaned over and whispered into my ear. "Our sources at the hospital say Kyoko's dead. Imagine the tragedy! Of course we haven't heard anything from inside the gates, but Stella has a cousin who is an X-ray technician there." She pulled a mobile phone from her pocket. "We've been in touch. Of course, you don't always get through, but . . ." She sighed. "Poor Kyoko. And poor Audrey in Earl's Court. Poor, poor Audrey."

Stella elbowed her in the ribs.

"Ouch! Stel, the dear girl's practically one of us! Well, fine, have it your way." She folded her arms, dropped onto the curb and pouted, refusing to say another word.

"What's this about Earl's Court?" I asked.

Stella leaned over, cupped her hand to my ear, and whispered, "We have a friend of a friend who's a chambermaid. That's all I can mention."

I had no idea what she was talking about. "See you later, Thelma, Stella."

"What do you suppose she meant about poor Audrey?" asked the Fish. "It's Kyoko she should feel bad about. And what's in Earl's Court?"

"I have no idea. She said something about a chambermaid. She's obviously missing a few marbles, although you'd be amazed what these people in the queue seem to know."

We agreed to call each other if anything important came up. The Fish headed up Church Road toward his pub while I wondered what to do. Everything felt surreal. With murder in the picture, I didn't want to wait a day to see Audrey. Absently, I flipped through the newspaper Thelma had given me. On page 2 was a map of the Wimbledon area, pinpointing the locations of the tennis stars' rented homes, a variation on those Hollywood Maps of the Stars. The Armats were on Newstead Road. I headed there.

The charming houses around Wimbledon range from the neat and cozy, with roses and trimmed hedges fronting immaculate brick façades, to upper-crust Georgian mansions that cost from one to four thousand pounds a week. Although the security factor is clearly more difficult to control, many players prefer to stay in a house a convenient bike ride away from the courts rather than travel an hour in traffic in the player van from a London hotel, or endure the lack of privacy of a fashionable Wimbledon hotel like the Cannizaro House. Also, a larger house can hold a player's entire family and entourage. Ivan Lendl, for instance, moves in for the fortnight with his wife, children, nanny, manager, coach, dietitian, and personal racket stringer. Houses are a big thing in Wimbledon, an entire subeconomy. Not only players, but also agents, corporations, and sponsors rent them. Cooks, maids, business services, and all the amenities are, of course, available to round out the package. Smaller fish, like linesmen, umpires, and aspiring junior players, stay in local townspeople's spare rooms for twenty-five pounds a night or so.

The Armat house was not ostentatious, but it was very private. A high brick wall and locked iron gate surrounded the premises. There were no signs of life in the house and, amazingly, no security guards. I knew the typical layout of the local houses; there was probably a large garden in the back, off the alley. I circled around to the end of the block and behind the building.

I peered over the adjoining walls into the Armats' backyard. A typical English garden: roses, geraniums, lighthearted ivy-print cushions on white wrought-iron furniture, two bicycles leaning against the wall. There was a small birdbath, but no bell, no way to get inside. I wandered down to the end of the alley.

I was met by the glare of high-intensity lights, blinding me for a second. From the darkness of my peripheral vision, I heard someone say, "Cool it, it's not her!"

The lights went out. I blinked and found myself looking into the eyes of my ex-husband, holding a microphone and backed up by a cameraman, a sound man, and a UKB crew in a mobile news van.

"Oh, for God's sake, it's only Jordan!" Tim sighed, and the cameraman swung the videocam down from his shoulder.

"*Only* Jordan? Gee, Tim, I thought you'd be back covering the swimsuit segment of the Miss America Pageant."

"Very funny. For your information, all hell has broken loose in tea and crumpet land."

"I know. Kyoko. It's terrible."

"And the latest is somebody's sent a note threatening to kill Audrey Armat."

"God, the place has gone crazy."

"We're here to get her comment."

"Well, more likely, your being here has driven them away. The place is deserted."

"Well, we're gonna get an exclusive, one way or another," Tim said decisively.

"Here's an inside tip that's right up your alley, so to speak—I think the Armats' garbage is out back there. Go for it." Without a backward glance, I turned and left.

Back at my hotel I thought I'd get a few hours' sleep, but my jet lag caught up with me, and when I woke up it was the next morning. I showered, changed, and called Cassie.

"Can you believe it?" she said.

"I don't know what to think," I said. There wasn't

much point in talking about Kyoko. "Do you think they'll play today?"

"They say so. They'll play the middle Sunday to make up yesterday. Imagine if they canceled Wimbledon. It would take World War Three. But they did announce this morning that the queen wouldn't be attending. Scotland Yard put their foot down. So I guess I'll leave my tiara at home today."

"Knowing you, I'm sure you packed one."

"Alex hasn't heard from Audrey, by the way. They were supposed to do a photo-op together, a fashion shoot, but she canceled. Have you connected with her yet?"

"I was supposed to see her before her match today, but since that's canceled—I don't know. I don't feel good about Audrey. It's weird that nobody's seen her for so long."

"But Marion has."

"Marion?"

"Sure. I asked specifically about Audrey at the press conference. She said she'd met with Audrey about the fragrance launch, and that Audrey's just keeping a low profile for security reasons. You know, Jordan, maybe you should go home. It's nuts here. What are you going to find out, anyhow? Go back to where you can at least help some people."

"Well, I'm taking this as a challenge. And you know me and challenges."

Cassie sighed. "Unfortunately."

ELEVEN

Two hours later I hopped a player van and by 9:30 was back at Wimbledon. It was overcast, with clouds so low and heavy they looked like you could wring them out. The atmosphere on the van was subdued—none of the usual chatter and gossip. I went straight from the transport parking area to the Competitors' Building to get a cup of hot water and lemon. The place was empty—the matches didn't start till 12:30, and the grounds didn't officially open till 10:30.

"They're all upstairs watching TV in the lounge," explained the girl at the desk. "The Armats' agents are making a statement."

I dashed up the two flights of stairs, edged my way into the crowded room, and claimed a corner of carpet on the floor. Ted Robb of Global Sport was on the screen, standing at a podium in front of about two dozen microphones. "We wish to announce that due to security considerations, our client Audrey Armat has regretfully decided that she must withdraw from the All England Lawn Tennis Championships at Wimbledon. Audrey had hoped to keep her Grand Slam dream alive here this season, but as you know she has been the target of death threats, and in the current hostile environment she and her family have decided it would not be wise for her to continue. Audrey is also postponing all marketing and endorsement activities, which are to be rescheduled at a later date to be announced. Audrey Armat and her family wish to take this opportunity to extend their deepest sympathies to the family and friends of Kyoko Oshimi. Thank you very much." A blast of questions exploded immediately from the press, but Robb held up his hand. "We have no further comment, ladies and gentlemen."

The cameras cut away to Tim standing in front of the Armats' rented house. "Here at the Armats' temporary home, there has been no sign of the much sought-after Audrey Armat. She is supposedly in seclusion under heavy guard, with her family. No word yet on whether or not they plan to remain at Wimbledon for the remainder of the championships . . ."

"There goes her ranking," said a well-dressed American man standing next to me.

"Maybe they'll make an exception, under the circumstances," said his companion, who carried a briefcase.

"And if they don't? Will you renew her contract?"

"Very iffy. Our client wants winners in his commercials."

"Yeah, but she'll get the sympathy vote. And even if you never heard of Audrey Armat before, you will have now. As I see it, this should put her Q-scores over the top . . ."

The two men moved off toward the bar.

The TV reverted to the matches in progress, and I got up and pushed my way out of the room. From the doorway of an office across the hall, I heard the unmistakable voice of Marion Stryker and the equally unmistakable Australian accent of Kanga Cheyne in a heated discussion.

"We have to be open about this, Marion," Kanga was saying.

"We are being open," Marion snapped. "Audrey has withdrawn from the tournament for valid security reasons. Period. It's an extenuating circumstance. And I am going to recommend that she keep her ranking—and her visibility. Between now and the Open, Global Sport will line up an exhibition match for her with Mariska, maybe something on pay-per-view."

"Marion, that's not fair to everybody else. That's sweeping the Audrey problem under the rug."

A group of people surged past me up the stairs, and the conversation became inaudible. I wondered exactly what the Audrey problem was. I stayed at the top of the stairwell, pretending to rummage through my purse, until I could hear more.

"Listen here," Marion was hissing, "you don't understand marketing at all. This sport needs Audrey Armat. Especially now. What have we got here . . ." Her voice dropped and I strained to hear. ". . . all this bad press . . . girl dead . . . disaster . . ."

There was silence, and then Marion picked up the cry in full. "My sponsors don't think about violence on a global scale; they think, 'Bad investment.' Checkbooks slam shut from here to China. If you follow your line of thinking to its logical conclusion, we will have no sponsors and no Association as it exists."

"Marion, I think you're overstating—"

"I am being quite reasonable to stand here and listen to you, after all my years of experience. I will not have you or anybody else tear down what some of us have taken the better part of our professional lives to build."

"But the girl's probably terrified—"

"That is your opinion, not her parents' or mine. I spoke with Audrey yesterday. Of course she's upset, we all are, but we have to look forward. Audrey Armat will be at the U.S. Open and it's imperative that she keep her ranking and that the tour continue to showcase her. Meanwhile, we have to exercise damage control. See if Kelly can fill in at the sponsors' reception. They all love Kelly. And if you can't agree with the best thinking of the management of this association—"

The door banged shut.

What, I wondered, was "the Audrey problem"? Or, more accurately, which of many problems were they referring to? There was obviously a hidden agenda, but I didn't know what it was. There was a chance she would still show up to meet me in the locker room. I had just enough time to get my photo pass and meet her there.

"Sorry, miss. She's not here," said the guard at the door of the Lady Members' Dressing Room. "We haven't seen her at all. You know, she withdrew from the championships this morning. But there is a note here for you."

The typewritten note, on Audrey's letterhead, said, "Meet me at the north exit to Centre Court. A."

I walked quickly to the stadium area and jogged through the overhung passages, my feet padding softly on the cement. In a half hour spectators would throng into the complex, but for now the place was deserted. At the north exit, I checked the stairwells and the exit doors. It was 10:10 according to my watch. I heard footsteps—a guard, or was it Audrey?

"Audrey?" I said.

The answer knocked me flat: no pain, just a blinding blow, a white flash behind my eyes, falling over. In my dizzying fall I saw a man behind me, and I clutched at him, grabbing at his shoulders. He wrenched away, but the fabric of his jacket was in my hands, and I felt it rip as I fell. We struggled, and he grabbed my hands with his own, which were gloved. I looked up and saw his face. Except it wasn't a face, and in the shock of seeing that, I let go of the jacket. The figure lunging at me wore a ski mask, a knit sort of thing with only a sug- gestion of features leering from behind the holes for eyes, nose, and mouth. I heard his heavy breathing and I clawed at the mask and missed as I went down. I re- member falling, then nothing.

"Jordan? Jordan!"

Now there was pain. A colossal throbbing at the back of my head. I struggled to open my eyes. My cheek felt cold and bruised. My eyelid scratched against some- thing: the concrete floor. I was lying on the floor. Just ahead, I focused on a tennis racket. There was blood on the frame. Suddenly, I realized it was mine.

"Don't move her!" It was the Fish's voice, as if from a distance.

I struggled to sit up. "God, what happened? Did something fall on me?" I touched the back of my head. It was matted and wet. My hand came away bloody.

"Yeah," said the Fish. "From the looks of it, this ten- nis racket fell on you. Of course, a person was at the other end of it at the time."

"But I was meeting . . ."

"Somebody met you, old buddy. Somebody you weren't expecting, I'd say."

Two medics in white coats arrived. One looked in my eyes with a light while the other snapped a blood-pressure cuff on me.

"Do you feel dizzy?"

"My head hurts. But I think I can stand."

"Better not yet, miss. Looks like a few stitches might be in order. Should we call for the stretcher?"

I groaned. "I think I can walk."

Fifteen minutes and a short ambulance ride later, I was lying on my side on a sheeted cot at St. George's Hospital, having my head stitched up. The Fish, Harry Bruce, the head of Wimbledon security, and a police officer sat outside the examining room, occasionally glancing in.

"If you feel any nausea tonight, or if the headache gets worse, call the tournament doctor or your hotel doctor," said the stitcher. "It's possible you have a mild concussion, but I don't think you need to be hospitalized. Your pupils aren't dilated."

I felt a series of little tugs on my anesthetized scalp.

"Twenty stitches, then," the doctor continued. "Don't wash your hair tonight. The stitches should come out in about five days. If you're still here, stop by and I'll clip them for you. You may want to take a couple of aspirin tonight."

He helped me sit up. I dangled my legs over the edge of the cot, then eased myself down. "Thank you. I appreciate it."

"Well, well, what have we here," said the Fish as I made my way out of the examining room.

"I wish I knew," I mumbled. "None of this makes sense."

"Do you know of anyone who would purposely try to harm you, Miss Myles?" asked the police officer.

"Not really. But apparently a line is forming."

"We're looking into the racket," said the security man. "It's a custom job, apparently."

"Mac Haskell," I said.

"Is he a suspect?"

"No, he's the man to ask about custom rackets. If he didn't make it, he'll know who did. He's in Boca Raton, Florida. You should definitely be able to trace a custom racket."

"I got the address," said the Fish.

Harry Bruce pulled out a chair for me. "So, who would want to connect a lob to your head, now, Miss Myles?"

"I don't know, but it might be the same person who pushed me into traffic in Miami Beach." These episodes were starting to annoy me. I hadn't survived falling off a mountain to die in the stands of a tennis stadium.

"Lucky Mr. Fisher came along," said Bruce.

"Truly lucky," I said. "In fact, how can I be so lucky that in an entire stadium complex, you found me?"

The Fish shrugged. "I was looking for a hot-dog stand."

In spite of my headache, I was beginning to reassess my opinion of the Fish, who was emerging as a real talent of sorts. Unquestionably, he had a genius for following people, or at least for following me. On the other hand, that meant that I did all the trailblazing, while he coasted. He seemed to have mastered a sort of mental judo—using the other person's moves to his advantage.

"This guy wore a ski mask and gloves," I said. "Do you think he's the same person who killed Kyoko?"

"Hard to say," said Bruce. "That man was definitely a professional. He had a plan and a purpose, which was to terrorize. Terrorists are not muggers. And you're not in the limelight, like Kyoko was. There are differences. The question is, who would want to do this to you?"

I thought for a minute. "I really don't know. Audrey Armat's mother isn't too fond of me right now, but other than that . . ."

"I told Miss Myles to take it easy for the rest of the day." The doctor walked back, waving off my audience. "Luckily, it was a relatively superficial laceration."

"I'm worried about Audrey," I said. "I was supposed to meet her. She left a note to meet her at the north exit to Centre Court. Somebody knew about that. I think they tried to stop it."

"Would you like us to assign a security guard to you, Miss Myles?" asked Harry Bruce. "You seem to have been through it."

"Too many loonies out there this year," said the police officer.

"All I want to do is talk to Audrey. It's all I've been trying to do for weeks."

"Well, that's going to be difficult, I'm afraid," said Harry. "She left this morning, her agent told us. The whole family left."

I sighed. "Fine. I guess I might as well go to sleep—and go home."

Harry patted my shoulder. "Take care of yourself," he said. "Listen to the doctor. I have to go. Mariska is going onto Centre Court. We can't risk any more difficulties."

He and the detective departed.

"You need to go back to the hotel and rest," said the Fish.

"Maybe I'll just watch a bit of the match from the lounge TV," I said.

The Fish smiled. "I know somebody with tickets to the match."

"I don't think I'm up for that," I said.

"But you were going to watch it on TV."

"That's not the same as sitting there," I said.

"I thought it was supposed to be better."

"Not to me. I've got too much on my mind already."

"You know, they got jelly doughnuts here. A little sugar would probably do you some good about now. You know how they put the jelly in the doughnuts? I've always wondered, myself. I think they use hypodermic needles."

Fifteen minutes later we were ensconced in the players' restaurant—which was actually more of a cafeteria— munching jelly doughnuts and watching the action on the courts below. It's a family sort of place, packed with robust young men and women in nylon windbreakers and logo T-shirts, their parents, coaches, and young children, chattering in a montage of languages. On one side is a utilitarian cafeteria of the high school variety, with everything from salads to stir-frys. On the other are comfortable wooden booths and a wall of glass overlooking the outer courts. A soundless video monitor mounted on the wall listed the results of the matches in a typewritten crawl.

"See?" said the Fish as I mechanically ate a doughnut. "I told you. You feel better, right?"

"A little."

"Sugar. There's nothing like it." He washed his

doughnut down with a swig of diet Coke. "You sure you don't want my tickets? Maybe for tomorrow?"

"No thanks."

"So who do we have to thank for this?" asked the Fish.

"God, I wish I knew," I said. "A guy in a ski mask, jacket, and gloves. That's all I know."

"You don't think this is a coincidence?" the Fish asked.

"No, but I don't see the link, either. And I hope nobody else has to get hurt before it becomes clear—especially me."

A voice came over the loudspeaker: "Attention please. Mixed doubles closes at six o'clock today in the referee's office."

"You probably wish you were playing, like you used to, instead of watching," said the Fish.

"Not really."

"Come on, it has to be like detective work. Once you get it in your blood you can't let it go."

"I let it go. Okay?" My voice was edgy.

"Oops! Stepped on some pinkies there, did I?"

"It's just ... I had some good times here, and one time I'd like to forget."

"Oh yeah, you mean 'The Agony of Defeat'?"

I groaned. My head hurt worse. "You saw it?"

"Sure. So what?"

"I lost in the finals."

"At Wimbledon. A little hearts-and-flowers music, here. How many people even make it that far?"

"It's more than that. I didn't really get that upset because I lost. I just knew at that moment that match on

Centre Court was probably the best I would ever be. I knew I'd peaked."

"Maybe not. Maybe you were just hitting your stride. You don't seem like a quitter. Why didn't you give it another shot?"

"I went on a vacation by myself before the U.S. Open to clear my head, and I was climbing a mountain and I fell. My leg was broken in three places, my ankle was shattered. By the time they put me back together, I was lucky I could even walk. Twelve surgeries on my leg and ankle. A year of rehab. That was the end of tennis, of life as I had known it. After that, I went to school." I chomped on my doughnut.

"So why are you mad? You look like you could strangle that doughnut with your bare hands."

"I'm mad at myself. I took the easy way out."

"Falling off a mountain is easy?"

"Well, it was more complicated than that." Somehow it just came tumbling out. "I'd just reached the point where if I was going to go for it, I had to make a total commitment to tennis. Quit school, go the whole bit. If I'd done that—who knows? Maybe I'd still be out there today, like Mariska. I never gave it that chance, though. I even took that break in my training for the Open to go mountain climbing. Then after the accident I told everybody I couldn't play anymore because of my leg, and you know what? Nobody wanted to believe me. Nobody could relate to me without tennis. But I was secretly relieved. I needed the excuse, because I didn't see any way out. The more you try to escape, the more the walls cave in on you. Nobody understands what it's like. Normal, layman things don't have any value or respect in that world. I mean, in pro tennis, you go to an international press conference every day, but in real life, who's listening to you?"

I picked angrily at my cuticles, pulling the skin until my thumb started to bleed.

"I used that accident as a cop-out, so I wouldn't have to face myself. Or maybe I was too programmed to make one goddamned decision on my own: the decision was made for me; end of problem. That's the truth. And that's why I can't watch that match on Centre Court. Not because I blew it—everybody does that sometimes—but because for me it was the beginning of the end." I laughed dryly and wadded up my napkin. "I can't even enjoy watching tennis as a game at all anymore. The joy is gone. Every game, it's like putting myself through therapy."

"Until you get through it, and you will," said the Fish.

I couldn't believe I'd told him all this. The man was a stranger, an inventor of pens. Maybe even a spy. Who knew? Here I was, being like my clients—people I barely knew spilling their life stories in the training room. "Listen. All I want to do now is help Audrey, so she doesn't have to doubt herself like I do—did."

The Fish nodded, listening intently. For once he wasn't snapping away with that infuriating camera.

"You know, I think half the reason I stayed in tennis as long as I did was because other people wanted me to. There were always so many people concerned with getting me out there on the court, working me, keeping me match-tough, keeping up my level. You're propped up on all sides. Nobody lets you grow up emotionally, and then they say you're spoiled. There's a whole community of people feeding off you; their entire identity in

life is being your mother, or your coach, or your agent
or boyfriend. Say you decide not to play. Who are they
then? And if you're a kid, how do you get away from
that, from the guilt of maybe letting them down? And
what's it worth? Is it worth the prestige, the endorsements, the money? What's the currency—your childhood, your innocence? Tell me, is it worth the trade?
You can get pretty desperate. Believe me, I can sympa-
thize with Audrey. If she needs to talk, I can hear her.
She thinks she's alone, but she's not." I glanced down
at the courts and, beyond, St. Mary's Church. A blimp
floated overhead, casting a shadow on the courts.

The Fish stared evenly at me. "Give yourself a break.
Isn't that what you'd tell Audrey?"

"Yeah, I guess so." My head was really hurting now
that the local anesthetic had worn off.

"Ready to go?" The Fish blotted his lips and crumpled his napkin.

"Yeah. I guess I'll be heading home tomorrow."

"Rest a day, maybe. You'll feel that head tomorrow.
We'll get you a car back to your hotel. I'll come with
you."

"I'm fine."

"You were unconscious less than two hours ago.
Don't push it."

"I can get myself back to the hotel."

The Fish insisted on walking me to the transportation
office.

"When do you think they'll know about the tennis
racket?" I said.

"They're air-freighting it out. I'll stay on it."

"Do you think there's any hope for Audrey?" I asked.

I felt so frustrated. I couldn't even protect myself, much less her.

"You do what you can do," said the Fish.

Back at the hotel, I double-bolted the door, took the sedative the doctor had given me, told the operator to hold all calls and admit no guests, pulled the blackout shades, and fell into bed. From the pillows, I reached for the phone.

I dialed Gus at the clinic and told him what happened.

"I'm not going to say I told you so," Gus said.

"Well, okay, I'll say it—you told me so."

"So how did I know you were going to do this, and how did I know you were going to get yourself into trouble?"

"Psychic, I guess."

"Therapy would be a little less dangerous. You've got to work this thing through for yourself, Jordan, not channel it through Audrey Armat. I know why you did this. But to put yourself in danger . . ."

"Whatever I did, it didn't work out like I thought it would. All I got was a hit in the head."

"Jesus, we'll hire a security guard this minute."

"Believe it or not, I've got this guy who's a former Green Beret." Details were best left unspoken.

"Well, that's a relief. The important thing is, you're out of it now. Get out of there. Take a week off. Rest. Then come home to . . ."

Why couldn't he just say it? For a psychologist, he couldn't even recognize his own commitment phobia.

". . . to us. Let the police figure out this mess. And don't be alone for a second. If you think you're in trouble, I'll fly out personally."

Home. The idea sounded pretty good about now. Gus sounded pretty good, in spite of everything. He understood me. He always had. "I have to pick up A.M. in Miami. Why don't you meet me there?"

He missed his cue again. "We'll get Tony to handle that. You come home." He was getting insistent again, but the sedative was kicking in and I was too woozy to argue, or even speak. This he mistook for assent. "Great. Then we'll see you next week."

"Mmm ... See you ..." I dropped the phone onto the bed beside me and fell immediately asleep.

I dreamed of Audrey, her face floating in the night, just out of reach. Her mother's screeching, her father's silky voice, somehow more frightening than the Mercedes and the tennis racket, because those were weapons I could understand.

A huge ruckus outside my door awoke me. Pounding, yelling, kicking. I staggered to the door, opened it a crack, and peered through the chain.

"Jordan! Thank God!" Cassie stood in the hall, two hotel security men restraining her. She wrenched away. "Let me go, you idiots. This is my friend! For God's sake, Jordan, I've been trying to call you for hours, ever since I heard what happened to you. I thought—well, let me in."

"It's all right." I nodded to the security guards and unlatched the door.

Cassie flew into the room and threw her arms around me. "You poor kid, let me see that cut."

"It's pretty much hidden in my hair," I mumbled. "Sorry. I took a pill last night and it really put me out."

"Well, that was smart. If somebody tried to break in here, you couldn't hear them. Get back into bed. Why didn't you call me? I would have come right over. How do you feel? Do you need a doctor? Maybe you need a second opinion. Now, I've contacted the embassy, and—"

"Cas, I'm fine. Relax."

"But whoever did this is on the loose. They could come back. You've got to get out of here. You shouldn't be alone."

She had a point. Yesterday I'd been too dazed to be scared, but it was beginning to sink in. Cassie fluffed my pillows, hopped onto the bed next to me, kicked off her shoes, commandeered the phone, and called downstairs to room service for fresh juice and tea.

"Shouldn't you be working?"

"This is an emergency. Now tell me what happened."

I went through the story, which wasn't much of a story since I had no idea who hit me or why.

"Do you think this has any connection to what happened to Kyoko?" Cassie wondered.

"Well, she's on the circuit, I'm not."

"Who would want you out of the picture?" Cassie asked. She picked up a pad and pencil from the bedside table and started making notes.

"Well, let's start with Corinne Armat. She hates my guts. But she's more the type to smear you in court than do something physical."

Cassie made a note. "Anybody else?"

"I have my doubts about E.J. The guy who pushed me in Miami had a ponytail."

"Him and a couple thousand others. Next."

"Well, I overheard some weird stuff involving Marion Stryker yesterday. She never got over the fact that I screwed up her plans and didn't turn into America's sweetheart. And she's trying to cover up something involving Audrey, I think. She might have gotten wind that I've been following up on Audrey, and now she's trying to stop me."

"Marion has a lot to lose if somebody finds out something and Audrey's career falls apart," said Cassie. She chewed on the pencil. "Her career depends on keeping women's tennis in the forefront, and Audrey's her ticket."

"Marion's always been a bitch, and everybody knows it," I said. "But she's so self-absorbed, I wonder if it would occur to her to consider me a threat."

Breakfast arrived, and Cas forced me to eat and drink. "Stress is very debilitating," she said. "You have to keep your strength up. Where's your vitamins?"

I picked up the remote and flicked on the TV just in time to see the matches at Wimbledon interrupted by a special news flash. A British newscaster stood somberly in front of a small stone town house as a covered body on a stretcher was carried out by police. "Teen tennis star Audrey Armat allegedly jumped this morning from the roof of a bed-and-breakfast here in Earl's Court. Authorities believe she was killed instantly."

Cassie and I froze.

"Authorities are at this time unsure of the motive for the apparent suicide, but an autopsy will be performed and an investigation has been launched into the circumstances." A file clip cutaway showed Audrey last year, winning the French Open. "Miss Armat, the fourth-ranked woman tennis player in the world, had a spectacular career at an early age, winning her first Grand Slam tournament at age sixteen. She was considered to be a leading contender for this year's Wimbledon

Championships." Back on the live scene, attendants closed the doors and the ambulance drove away. "Miss Armat, who had been forced to withdraw from this year's tragedy-fraught tennis tournament due to death threats, had been registered at this bed-and-breakfast in the Earl's Court area under an assumed name, possibly for security reasons. She is the second top-seeded women's tennis player to die under tragic circumstances in what seems to be the curse of the Grand Slam circuit."

TWELVE

"Burnout," whispered one of the reporters at the reception after the memorial service, a squat little guy with a comb-over hairstyle and a weekly column in the sports pages of one of the major newspapers. "Like I said in my piece, Audrey Armat was a bright comet in the sports firmament whose star shone too brightly for too short a time."

"Bullshit," murmured Cassie as we wandered through the marble foyer of Global Sports' New York headquarters. It had only been two weeks since Wimbledon. "Total speculation. Emmet just likes to hear the sound of his own voice. The whole thing is just too goddamned mysterious. You'd think this was Marilyn Monroe, with all this armchair theorizing."

Everybody had a theory on the tragedy of Audrey Armat. Scotland Yard had ruled her death a suicide, but the motive remained unclear. Burnout was the favorite school of thought, but pressure and depression over her losing streak and unrequited love were others—and the press was making much of "The Curse of the Grand Slams."

Cassie had come in for the memorial. She'd brought A.M. up with her on the plane, and we'd had a happy reunion at the airport. I had bought a new canvas carrier that looked like a purse, and A.M. fit in very unobtrusively, so she was attending the reception too.

The GS headquarters is actually an elegant turn-of-the-century mansion in the Seventies just off Central Park that had been built by an oil baron for his family and is now a National Historical Register showplace, with the original limestone façade, ornate plasterwork, polished marble floors, and mahogany paneling intact. It is the scene of some of the biggest sports transactions and talent networks in the world, and seven-foot basketball stars, broad-shouldered baseball players, and cauliflower-eared boxers find themselves signing eight-figure athletic-shoe contracts under rococo ceilings in rooms where liveried butlers had once served tea to society matrons: Michael Jordan meets Edith Wharton.

Loudspeakers piped through Audrey's favorite Mariah Carey songs. Dark-suited waiters circulated with trays of drinks, there was a buffet in the paneled dining room on the third floor, and everyone in the world of tennis was there, eyeballed from the walls by oil portraits of the impressive Global Sport client roster. Several people were red-eyed. Marion Stryker was somber in black, her eyes sheathed in black sunglasses, gripping a pair of black lace gloves as if they were a lifeline. The younger players from the women's tour stood in a clutch, talking quietly. Twelve-year-old Angel Martinez, the hottest new phenom in tennis, had flown in from Los Angeles with her parents to make a rare appearance. I was curious to get a look at her because she was scheduled to spend a week at the Springs later this month. Shy, tiny, just clearing five feet, her knees knobby and hair frizzy, Angel looked like a skinny kid in braces and ankle socks, which she was. Although she'd been pursued by agents since she was ten years old, her parents had so far shielded her from the glare of the spotlight. I had to wonder why she was there at all. The mysterious death of one young star hardly seemed like an auspicious occasion to launch the career of another.

Most of the top-ranked men players were there as well, and an infusion of celebrities from outside sports. David Dinkins, the former mayor of New York and well-known tennis buff, was there, as were Wilt Chamberlain and a number of movie stars. In fact, the star quality was almost a replay of the awards show earlier this summer. Outside, a battery of media vans, photographers, and fans waited to catch a shot or a glimpse of anybody who was "somebody." However, there were no young people who might be personal friends of Audrey's. Not one. And Alex Bracht was a conspicuous no-show.

Corinne Armat was the centerpiece of the second-floor parlor. She sat on an oxblood quilted leather couch, buried in a black veil that covered her face and was draped over a pillbox hat in the manner of Jackie Kennedy at Arlington. At her side was E.J., in black leather from head to foot, in spite of the summer heat. In the funeral procession, he had escorted the hearse on his motorcycle. Hovering nearby, ferrying drinks and mourners and acting as a de facto member of the family, was Milt Bevins, immaculate in a European-tailored black suit. The word was, he had chartered the Concorde to fly the Armats back from England. Across the room, leaning against a wall, was Emilio, paler and thinner than I'd remembered him. His piano-key smile was frozen in bas relief on his face, but the drink in his hand trembled. He glanced past me and looked right through me. An old woman sitting alone on a chair sobbed openly. Cassie told me she had been Audrey's baby-sitter.

As devastated as I was by Audrey's death, I can't say I'd really have volunteered myself to attend the memorial reception. I had my own share of problems. I'd planned to get home and back to my routine, and I was equally sure that Corinne Armat did not want me around as a reminder of her tragedy. But, surprisingly, Global Sport had specifically issued a formal invitation on behalf of the Armats for me to attend the memorial. At this point, Bill said, with the possibility of a lawsuit hanging over our heads, the Springs legal counsel did not feel it would be wise for me to do anything that could be interpreted at this emotional time as hostile to a goodwill gesture from the Armats.

I'll admit, politics is something I've never really understood. To me, Audrey was gone—there was nothing further I could do for her. Even Noel Fisher had veered off to other pastures—he sent me a fax from Queens informing me that he had moved on to his next case, locating a tax evader for the IRS, although he would be keeping his pipeline open to Harry Bruce in London in case of further developments. The inquiry into my own assault was still open, pending identification of the "weapon," but with the frenzy about Audrey's death and my own return to the U.S., it seemed to have fallen into back-burner status.

As I tried to make myself inconspicuous among the mourners, Kanga Cheyne gave me a sympathetic smile. She walked up, took my arm, and steered me to a quiet corner. "I know you wanted to help Audrey," she whispered. "You were right. What happened here was a crime. They sold Audrey out, and she couldn't take it. I tried to stop them, but—"

"Kanga, what exactly was Audrey's problem?"

She bit her lip nervously. "I have no real evidence of anything, Jordan. Everybody wanted a piece of her, till there was nothing left. People went nuts. People got— killed."

"Who exactly went nuts?"

"I just have my suspicions." She gazed pointedly at Marion Stryker. "You know, I'm no longer with the Association."

"No. I didn't know. That's too bad."

"No it's not. You can't imagine what she put me through. She's crazy. She's a vindictive, dried-up no-talent, and she doesn't have a clue. All she's got is her pet players and her schemes." Kanga lifted her chin and straightened the lapels on her black cotton suit. "But at least I've got my dignity."

"Where will you work?"

"Maybe CNN. I'm interviewing."

"Well, good luck."

As I turned away, an arm slipped around my waist. Buffed, manicured nails, a chunky gold vintage watch. Mickey Mouse cuff links, which I recognized because I gave them to him. Tim.

"I've been worried sick about you, Jordan."

"You didn't call."

"Call where? I had no idea where to reach you."

A stunning redhead oozed up, a fixture on a game show, where she excelled at turning letters while wearing sequined dresses. "Timmy, is this a friend?" she asked, smiling a little too brightly.

"A very old friend, Jessica." He gave me his insider's smile. "Be a sweetheart and bring me a Pellegrino, would you? With lime." He sent her off with a pat on the butt. "So how's the head? God, you're the most accident-prone person I know. You could injure yourself on an electric blanket."

"It wasn't an accident and you know it." I wondered if he was trying to be funny. Tim had always been very bad at humor.

"What's the story on who did it?"

"Nothing yet." It was time to leave. "Gotta run. Plane to catch." I waved to Cassie, who was talking with Kelly. As always, Kelly looked calm and unruffled, radiating poise. That was her greatest gift, the deceptive air of calm that cloaked her true emotions. She had a great mental capacity for discipline and self-control. It was an aura that made her difficult to read as a person, impossible to gauge as an opponent, and, in the end, a world-class champion with her own niche in the history of women's tennis. When I was coming up on the circuit, the media used to pit Kelly and me against each other as arch-rivals. It made for good copy. She was fair and cool, I was dark and hotheaded. Off the court, however, we were friendly, if not friends. Few people could really be friends with Kelly, especially fellow players— she was just too competitive. Kelly had been a textbook teen tennis sensation herself, but, of all of us, she had survived with the most dignity and stature. She now had a happy marriage to a Wyoming rancher, three little kids, and a solid career as a horse breeder, commercial endorser, and manufacturer of her own namesake sportswear line. Insiders like Paul Cranston knew that Kelly hadn't been quite the Pollyanna that was her public image, with her legendary string of not-always-storybook romances and her over-the-top partying, but it didn't matter. She was bulletproof. In perspective, Kelly's was quite a success story, in no small way because her ultimate success was personal as well as professional.

"Come on," Cas said. "Have dinner with us later. Maybe you could talk to Kelly about Audrey."

I was sure I wouldn't learn anything that way. Even if she had any insight, Kelly wasn't the type to share it. And she was always aware—a master, really—of the PR angle on everything. Still, it would probably have been fun. Kelly was always good to laugh with. But I'd had it. I begged off.

Mariska caught me on my way out. "I'm sorry to hear what happened to you at Wimbledon. I didn't get a chance to tell you."

It hadn't surprised me, and I hadn't expected to hear anything from Mariska. During a tournament, she remained totally focused on her goal: winning. Nothing ever intruded on that, even life or death.

"Did you see Kelly?" she asked.

I told her I had.

"She's lining up people to appear in her charity tournament, and somehow I found myself telling her that of course I'd come." Mariska grimaced. "I can't believe I agreed to that. But you know, Kelly never changes. I remember, in Rome in 1979, we were about to go on for the finals, and Kelly got her first period fifteen minutes before. She ran around telling everybody she hadn't had her period before—I mean, she was that young, she'd barely hit puberty—so there was this big flurry while everybody hunted down a Tampax, and then she couldn't get it in, she didn't know how to use it, and we could hear the crowd outside, slow-clapping because we were a half hour late. And then we finally started the match, and I was beating her 6–2 in the first set. Then, in the changeover, I asked her if she was okay because she'd been so upset before the match, and she said, 'No, I'm fine,' and then proceeded to kick my ass, 6–2, 6–1. And here I was closer to menopause than she was to even having her period." Mariska shook her head, still amazed. Kelly was always Kelly.

Mariska and I agreed to call each other later, and I walked outside wearily, feeling totally drained.

"Ms. Jordan Myles?" A man stepped in front of me from the crowd of fans and media, holding out an envelope.

I took it automatically, pulled out the pen that the Fish had given me, signed my name, and handed it back. I still occasionally get requests for autographs, and since Wimbledon my name and picture had been back in the press—accompanied by an unwelcome revival of the "Agony of Defeat" clip.

He handed the envelope back. "Let me clarify," he said. "I'm serving you with legal papers." He turned and walked away, leaving me holding the envelope in the vortex of camera coverage. In the upper right-hand corner was a string of four or five names: Somebody, Somebody, Somebody & Somebody. A law firm. He was a goddamned process server. No wonder Corinne Armat had issued me a gold-plated invitation to the memorial. I was like a butterfly in a bell jar; all she had to do was spear me with the pin. I put A.M. down in her carrier and ripped open the envelope. Most of it was indecipherable legal jargon, but I figured out that I was been personally sued by A², the Armats' corporation, for many millions of dollars in damages. When Audrey had died, the case had come back to life, and by the five o'clock news the world was sure to know it.

This time I really did take the next flight home, stitches and all. Tony was waiting at the airport. A.M., sensing she was home, licked his hand through the window of her carrier.

"Am I glad to see you," Tony said, wiping his brow dramatically. "If you weren't on this plane, my orders were to go to New York and bring you back personally." He frowned distastefully. "I wouldn't have wanted to do that. All those hours strapped in a seat next to you, with you ripping me up and down? No way."

"This is infantile," I said.

"Well, I must admit your picture in the *New York Post* didn't do you justice," he said. He reached into his pocket for a dog treat and fed it to A.M. "Here you go, big puppy."

"They picked it up? God, it just happened this morning. They must have planted the piece in advance. This is obviously a PR ploy. I didn't even tell Bill and Gus yet."

"Oh, they've got the drift." He unfolded a piece of paper from his pocket and handed it to me as we walked to the baggage claim.

It was a faxed page from the *Post*. "Who sent this?"

"Joan Gribbens at IBM." IBM was Bill's major new corporate client. "When she canceled."

I groaned. My picture, juxtaposed with Audrey's at

the top of the article, was blurry, but you couldn't miss
the headline: ARMAT FAMILY SUES FORMER TENNIS PHENOM
OVER AUDREY'S DEATH. In a half-page story, "a source
close to Audrey Armat's distraught parents" was quoted
at length about my professional irresponsibility. No specifics, of course—just a lot of innuendo that could be
attributed to grief-stricken parents and that could ruin
my career and damage the clinic's reputation, even if it
didn't hold up in court.

"I'm going to sue them for libel," I said.

"This could get mean."

"Mean is an understatement, Tony. It's a matter now
of survival. Literally. Not to mention fairness."

We picked up the bags and drove straight to the
clinic. On the way, Tony gave me an update.

"The place is wild," he said. "Lawyers coming and
going, lawyers on the phone, lawyers on the fax, Global
Sport throwing their weight around, reporters sniffing,
clients canceling."

"Who else canceled?"

"A coach from Notre Dame pulled his player. A couple of corporate clients—"

Not good. This sort of thing was like pulling stones
one at a time from the bottom of a rockpile until it fell
on you. I felt a cave-in coming.

I left A.M. at Tony's desk, which was fine with her.
Tony kept a highly tempting assortment of rawhide
chew toys in his top drawer, behind the paper clips. It
felt strange being back at the Springs, a place I'd always loved to work at, with this threat hanging over our
heads. I spoke to a few secretaries and account executives as I made my way down the halls, but people
seemed strained, subdued, reluctant to look me in the

eye. Even Sharlene, the cleaning woman, scurried out of my path. I should have known what awaited me.

Everyone was holed up in the conference room. This was another bad sign, because it was used only for the most serious business discussions. Our meetings tended to be in one another's offices or in hallways. I walked in to a lineup of grim faces, most of whom I didn't recognize. The table was cluttered with folders, empty coffee cups, soda cans, water bottles, glasses, and sandwich wrappers: signs of a siege. The worst was, they were all in business suits, even Gus. Gus owned only two suits, which he usually hauled out of the back of his closet for weddings and funerals, which he would then attend smelling faintly of mothballs. Gus had left an empty chair next to him, and I took it.

"The board of directors," he whispered.

"Really?" I whispered back. "I thought they were Mount Rushmore."

"Ah, Jordan." Bill smiled. "Welcome home. How are you feeling after your terrible experience at Wimbledon?"

"I'm doing fine." I felt worse sitting here.

"Wonderful. That's wonderful." He adjusted his cuff links. "Well, we're meeting here with our board, and let me make the introductions." He went around the table: a banker from Los Angeles; a health-insurance executive from Connecticut—the only woman on the board; the president of a major car company; the former United States surgeon general; and the retired quarterback of three legendary Super Bowl–winning teams. Also at the table were two of the clinic's lawyers and Jillian Edwards, PR director for Desert Springs.

"Well, Jordan, as you're well aware, this is a tragic period in sports, and we all have to come to grips with our personal emotions about that. We also want you to know that we stand firmly behind you with our complete and unqualified support. We've called this meeting today to see how we can help you. Explore the avenues. And, of course, how we can keep the professional integrity of this organization—our family—intact. Jillian?"

Edwards passed slick white folders to everyone at the table. I hadn't seen her since the day that *Twenty-First Century* did a show on the Springs and she'd escorted the camera crew around. Jillian was on retainer to us. She had her own PR firm in Los Angeles and flew out for meetings on an as-needed basis. She was supposed to be the best, with an uncanny instinct for turning any kind of debacle into a promotional opportunity. Her clients included former presidents, movie stars, a major art museum, and people who paid handsomely to keep their names *out* of the press. Gus had told me that she was reportedly not above such image overhauls as reshaping the occasional ex–white collar felon/tax evader/junk-bond insider trader into a vaunted pillar of the community. Jillian stood up, resplendent in a tailored black and white silk suit. She had a gold pen and a French manicure. Her hair was short and businesslike and looked like it had been trimmed one follicle at a time by a surgeon. Her face had that subtle, no-makeup, natural look that took dozens of expensive cosmetics and expert application to achieve. Her jewelry was understated but expensive. She was the picture of composure. I stared across the table at her, my khakis and T-shirt wrinkled from my cross-country flight, feeling like a wayward schoolkid who'd run away and was about to be taken to task by a very refined headmistress.

"Let's review the situation," Jillian said calmly. "The

Armats are claiming that the clinic, specifically Jordan, failed to provide adequate supervision or use proper practices and accepted methods, which resulted in mental anguish, or intentional inflicting of emotional distress, which, in turn, led to Audrey's death."

I felt sick. I'd read the summons on the plane, but it was a lot of legalese. This really put it in front of my face.

"They're asking actual damages for lost projected income for Audrey's lifetime career earnings, had she lived, and also punitive damages."

"Excuse me, but I didn't understand that part," I said.

"According to our lawyers," said Bill, "punitive damages can be any amount a jury believes is fair to—well, punish the perpetrator and hold them up as an example to the community. Our lawyer also threw in the fact that California has what he calls a liberal policy on punitive damages."

"Oh my God."

"Plus," Bill continued, "they're claiming damages as a result of Corinne and Emilio Armat's mental anguish. What we're dealing with is an action against the Springs for sixty million dollars."

"It's obvious," I said hotly. "This whole thing is a sham. The Armats are just looking for a new meal ticket, and we're it."

Jillian held up a blowup of the headline piece. "This article in the *Post* is obviously an insider plant and is designed to create a sympathetic environment for a lawsuit."

"Or to divert attention from the real issue," I interrupted.

"I'd like to hear what that issue is, in your opinion, Jordan," Bill said tensely.

So much for his "complete support."

"Since you've been pursuing it on your own now for some time," he continued, "why don't you enlighten the group?"

I pushed back in my chair. "Something was very wrong with Audrey before she died. I suspected it from the time she was here. I have strong reasons to believe there may have been abuse involved. Her parents are control freaks. They held a whip over her head. I think she was bulimic. She had a weird relationship with her boyfriend. He didn't even show up at the memorial. We know she was pregnant when she was here. And the brother is apparently without a life of his own. So it could be any one of those issues, or a combination."

Jillian cleared her throat. "To continue, the issue from a public relations standpoint is, who is the focus here? The Desert Springs Clinic, or one of its employees?"

"Partners," I corrected.

"Well, what I suggest is a simple solution. Until this unpleasantness blows over, perhaps Jordan should take a sabbatical, or a vacation."

"What!" I couldn't believe what I was hearing. Every nerve in my body suddenly felt electrified. Jillian was suggesting they pass the buck to me. Let me be the straw dog. There was no other way to read it.

Bill raised his hand. "Let's hear Jillian out, please."

With difficulty, I restrained myself.

"Thank you, Bill. Now, Jordan, let me reposition this. Perhaps I was unclear. I'm not suggesting this for any reason other than your own personal welfare. I under-stand you've suffered an injury, and I'm sure you could benefit from a little respite. Your doctors would certainly agree that you're not physically in condition to deal with a major lawsuit right now, and—"

"Forget it," I said quickly. "Absolutely out of the question."

"Okay," said Jillian. "Fine. But have you considered this: with your ongoing involvement in the Audrey Armat situation, Jordan, you are making yourself a target. A legal target and a media target. No matter what you do or say, right or wrong, the ghost of a dead sixteen-year-old girl is always going to come out on top here. The facts of the case aren't going to change human nature. This is an image issue. We have to deal with that." She turned to the group. "Perhaps Jordan could be more involved in the less high-profile aspects of the work here at the clinic, like the Honor Badge summer camp program for handicapped children. That's a very positive association for Jordan, and it's low-profile and noncontroversial."

Honor Badge was a special two-week sports clinic we put on for handicapped children from all over the country. It was a wonderful event, but it was not a full-time job, and it was certainly not the job I had come here to do. Now I stood up. "Wait a minute. Are you saying I should be sidelined? Shuffled off to the camp like some rah-rah junior counselor? You've got to be joking."

Jillian placed her palms on the table and leaned forward. "I'm not suggesting you should be sidelined, Jordan," she said evenly. "I know this is a sensitive issue. Don't misunderstand me. I'm suggesting you step back and consider the welfare of this group as a whole. It makes sense as a corporate strategy. And it makes sense for you."

"I'm not going to hide behind some kids' skirts. Period. I have nothing *to* hide. Don't you people realize that somebody is out to get me, one way or another? If they can't kill me, I guess they're going to sue me to death."

"Honor Badge is a very fine program, something we're all extremely proud of," interjected Bill. "And you need to get off the firing line for a while, Jordan. Literally. We don't want anything else happening to you. This is in your best interest."

I felt my face flush. "Wait a minute," I said. "Let's be honest here. I can't believe that one person at this table seriously believes that I mishandled the Audrey Armat case. Or am I wrong?"

"That is accurate," said Bill. "Of course."

"So the Armats are suing, and I am the scapegoat. Is that the situation?"

"Actually," Gus said, "the situation is that corporate sponsors and clients are bailing out left and right and we're going to lose the confidence of our financial supporters. We may lose our shirts, actually. So do we take the PR route and throw Jordan in, or do we go with a united front and go one-on-one with these people?" He shoved his chair back from the table. "You people are a bunch of chickenshits." He got up and walked out of the room.

I shook my head sadly. "We're in the business of showing people how to play from strength and win," I said. "I can't believe we're incapable of following our own advice. How's it going to look for future business if I hide my head in the sand when the going gets tough? My God, Bill, you were an Olympian. We need to face this now, head-on. We'll win, because we're right. And because Audrey needs to be vindicated. She's the real victim here, not me—can't you see that? I don't matter. I never did. I can take care of myself, and I don't need to run and hide to do it. Sure, I'll help out with Honor Badge, and not because it's the right move for spin control. I'll do it because I'm proud to, I want to. They're wonderful kids. They've faced something a lot worse than a little media pressure, for God's sake. I hope to learn something from them. But you know what? I'll do it along with my job, not instead of it, thank you. Don't expect me to go fade into the woodwork for PR purposes. That's not the way I care to work. Or *can* work." I sat back down.

Bill nodded. "If that's your decision, Jordan, we respect it."

One of the board members, Steve Ott from the bank, nodded tentatively. "This is a very delicate situation. Once business starts walking out the door like this, you have to stem the tide."

"I'm aware of that," said Bill.

"You know, a producer from one of the tabloid TV shows has already called my office about doing a piece on the clinic," said Jillian. "With these people, that amounts to an exposé."

"Good grief," shuddered Ott, his eyebrows disappearing into his hairline.

"I told them we would not cooperate, but they're going to go ahead anyway. When they show up here, which could be anytime in the next few days, refer them to me. Meanwhile, send out a memo immediately to the staff that says nobody is allowed to speak to any member of the media or any person asking questions about Desert Springs, its employees, or its clients. But don't expect it to hold them off for long. These tabloids pay big money to their so-called sources. It's tempting."

A muscle twitched in Bill's jaw, and his lips were a thin, dry line. I supposed he was envisioning everything he'd worked for, his life's dream, slipping away from him. In a way, I wouldn't have blamed him if he'd sacrificed me.

"We stand behind Jordan," said Bill firmly. "Now. Anybody feel like a little food?"

The meeting was adjourned. I stayed in my seat as they all filed out. As he passed my chair, Bill squeezed my shoulder. "Hang in there," he said.

Tony came in to help clear the table. "Tough meeting," he said. "Gus told me."

"I don't suppose I have any clients on the books this week?"

"You did, but they all canceled except for a Mrs. Silverman from Chicago."

"Who's she?"

"Some woman with a country-club game of tennis who wants to perfect her mixed-doubles techniques so she can win the club championship."

"And the Honor Badgers?"

"We got twenty of them due to check in in a week."

I sighed. "I'll be there. But only because I want to be, for as long as I want to be."

From the conference room I went straight to Gus's office. "Thanks for sticking up for me in there," I said. "It turned out okay. For the time being."

"It doesn't look good," he said. "But we're in this together."

"Thanks. Now, somewhere in your dim past, you have a medical degree, am I right?"

"Somewhere."

"Ever perform surgery?"

"No."

"Okay. Forget live people. Ever dissect a cadaver?"

"Once."

"Then this should be a piece of cake." I lifted my hair and leaned over. "Could you take out my stitches? I'd do it, but I'd probably end up scalping myself."

He laughed. "I don't carry the equipment on me. Unless you want me to use the staple remover."

"Try the supply room. There should be gauze, scissors, and alcohol in there. If not, I have it in my kit."

My beeper went off. I looked at the phone number it was registering. Area code 718. Queens, if I was not mistaken.

"It's the private detective that Global Sport hired," I said.

Gus frowned. "What's he want?"

"I don't know. He's a weird guy. He was off on another case, some income-tax-evasion thing." I dialed the phone while Gus went to the supply room.

"Jordan," said the Fish's voice. "Where are you? I sort of lost track of your comings and goings."

"I didn't see you at Audrey's memorial."

"Well, I can't say I actually knew her. Besides, the office is nuts, I was out of town so long. Say, I showed my mother the pictures I took. She can't believe it. I think she's disappointed I didn't get one of the queen, though."

"I'm sort of in a meeting, so . . ."

"Oh. Yeah. Right. Well, you know what? They finally traced the racket that hit you. I thought you might be interested."

"Who?"

"Audrey Armat."

"But how can that be? Audrey's family were the only ones who ever got near her equipment, and that's a known fact. She never even autographed tennis balls for fans. And every one of her rackets was always accounted for and sent back to Haskell for restringing after her matches. I don't get it."

"Well, according to your buddy Haskell, it checks out. That's all I know."

"What does this mean? You don't think that Audrey tried to mug me." I couldn't imagine it.

"Well, somebody did."

"Any more news on Audrey herself?"

"Not yet. They're working on it."

"Thanks, Fish. Let me know if you hear anything else."

"Sure. Meantime, I thought I'd send you a few of these pictures. I got some good ones."

"Thanks. Fine."

"Are you still using my pen?"

"Got it right here."

"That makes me feel just wonderful. Keep it with you, okay, like a good-luck charm?"

"Sure. See you." I hung up.

"What was that all about?" Gus asked as he walked back in.

"Audrey Armat owned the racket that hit me. They just identified it."

"No kidding."

I sat on Gus's couch and aimed a gooseneck lamp at my head. Gus sat beside me. The operation could now begin.

I parted my hair with my fingers, took a big clump from the back, and fastened it to the side with a rubber band. "You know, I had my weaknesses on the court, but I was always pretty good at strategizing. There were lots of players better than me, but if I worked at it, I could outsmart them."

"Meaning?" Gus poured some alcohol into a glass. I could hear the utensils rattling around in it.

"First of all, we have to stop letting this situation control us. We have to control it, or at least how we're responding to it. Let's analyze this like you would an opponent on the tennis court. Ouch!" I felt a twinge at the back of my head. "Be gentle, will you?"

"I'm removing stitches, not giving you a pedicure."

"Let's put it under the microscope and look at the strong points and the weak points. There have to be some weak links here, and I think I have a pretty good idea who they are." I heard the scissors clipping and felt the tugs on my scalp. I felt like a tennis racket being restrung.

"And?"

"And their names are Alex Bracht and E.J. Armat. Talk about a low profile! E.J. is practically the invisible man, a person who always lived in the shadow of his twin sister. He has to be really hurting now. And Bracht, the boyfriend, didn't even show up for Audrey's memorial."

"Actually, he's not far from here now; he's in Rancho Mirage," Gus said. "There's a two-hundred-thousand-dollar exhibition at the Burning Tree Country Club for some big athletic-shoe sponsors tonight. We got some comp passes." I felt a final twinge. "That's it. Let me clean it up with some alcohol." I felt a cold swabbing on my scalp. "All done. You won't even see the scars. It healed nicely."

"Well, that's a relief. I assume there's no permanent brain damage. Feel like going to an exo tonight?" I patted my hair back into place. Gus didn't have a mirror, but I had one of those hairstyles that always looked the same—styled or uncombed, wet or dry.

Gus gave me one of his looks. "Oh, no. Don't even think about it."

THIRTEEN

Alex Bracht was arguing with the chair umpire, insisting that the line judge be removed. He didn't like his calls, he didn't like the judge, mainly he didn't like the fact that his opponent, Terry DiLio, was winning. DiLio, an underdog, had made the mistake of taking the match seriously and was giving it his all. The crowd loved it.

Bracht was clearly a showman, born to court the crowd. He looked the part, and he played it. He wasn't so much handsome as riveting to watch, a spectacle in motion. His fans, mostly teenybopper girls, screamed with delight at his every motion, and Bracht made sure there was a lot to look at. His gestures were broad, his tennis clothes were iridescent neon colors, his hair bleached platinum and buzz-cut. Today, out of respect to Audrey, he wore a black mourning armband. His shirt, however, was unbuttoned almost to the waist in his usual style, showing off the chiseled muscles of his waxed-hairless chest, and between sets he tossed his sweatbands to screaming girls in the crowd. His secret weapon was his smile—disarmingly boyish, dazzling, surprising given his frowning, glowering attitude. Luckily for him, he had the talent and flair for the game to make good on the image. Alex's attitude was appealing because it seemed sincere; you could almost touch his desire to win. He didn't give a lot of interviews—his love affair was with the fans, not the press—but his record stood for itself, without apology or explanation.

At nineteen, Alex Bracht was the number-three-ranked player in men's tennis, a natural and fierce competitor when he wasn't engaging in on-court dramatics. He was a strong backcourt player with a surgically precise serve and an ability to return any kind of shot from almost any angle or player with scorching speed and accuracy. Temper tantrums were a way of life with Bracht. He was like a two-year-old, thrashing around to get himself noticed on the playground by the big kids, and he got his wish. His reluctance to give interviews only made him more intriguing, and the tragic denouement to his romance with Audrey Armat was sure to give him a Heathcliff-esque aura.

I knew that the argument with the umpire was practically scripted, so I slipped back to the press area to intercept Alex after the match.

The press conference was perfunctory. Alex seemed tired, less than his usual dazzling self, as if his fire had been extinguished by DiLio, 6–2, 6–4, 6–4. One of the reporters asked a question about Audrey. Alex's response was a curt "No comment." He rose from the podium and pushed through the curtains, escorted by exhibition officials, Rob Pernice, and a bodyguard.

I stepped up and intercepted Rob.

"Jordan! Great to see you. Cas told me you were at the memorial. Sorry I missed you in Miami."

We exchanged hugs.

"Rob, would you do me a favor? I need to ask Alex something."

"God, he just lost the match. He's not going to be all sweetness and light."

"That's okay."

We caught up with the group and Rob introduced me to Alex. He smiled his stage smile. "Hello, nice to see you, but I have to change now." He was still in his warm-ups.

"I'd like to have a word with you, please."

He started walking, and his group moved with him. "It's been a bad week, if you don't mind."

"I knew Audrey. She was my client." I was jogging backward in front of him.

He stopped warily. "Yes?"

"We have to speak privately, Alex. It's very important."

One of the men in his group looked on curiously. He wore a badge from the athletic-shoe company. A sponsor.

Alex smiled again. "Excuse me one second, gentlemen." He shot Rob an impatient look, stepped aside, and leaned close to me. "Now what the fuck is this all about?"

"This is all about the fact that I know and you know that Audrey had some big problems, and I think you might have had a lot to do with that."

His eyes flashed. "Oh, come on. Let the poor kid rest in peace. And what's it to you?"

"Let me put it bluntly, since I can see you are in a hurry. Somebody tried to kill me with one of Audrey's tennis rackets at Wimbledon, so I have a vested interest. As I see it, you are one of the very few people who had access to Audrey's tennis equipment."

"So let me follow your logic. You're saying I got

hold of one of Audrey's rackets and I was the one who tried to kill you? Give me a break, lady. I don't even know you. Right now I can understand why somebody might like to knock you off, but believe me, unless you continue to bug me I would have no reason to kill you, so why don't you get lost?" He started to walk away.

"You have a reason," I said quietly. "Two reasons. Maybe more."

He stepped back. "This had better be good."

"It is. Reason number one, you were defending Audrey, protecting her from me because I was asking too many questions. And you had access to the Armats and Audrey's equipment. Didn't you sometimes practice with her brother? Reason number two, Audrey was pregnant right before she died."

His face didn't move. "Oh? And how would you know this?"

"My clinic ran the blood tests. We have the records. Is there any chance you might have been the father?"

"No. Is this some sort of joke? Because this is laughable."

"We'd better talk." I nodded toward the sponsor and waved. "Or I'll talk to them." I opened my purse. "I brought the lab tests. They're right here, and I took the liberty of having them notarized, and . . ."

Alex strode quickly over to Rob and the entourage, said something, and came back to me. "Let's go."

I nodded to Rob, who raised his eyebrows curiously.

Alex put his hand in the small of my back and pushed me along until we reached the back entrance. A clutch of fans was waiting, and a motorcycle was parked by the door—an old Indian, beautifully restored.

"Nice bike," I said.

"It's transportation." He shrugged, his nonchalance unconvincing. The guy would have had a heart attack if there had been so much as a smudge on the finish. "I have it shipped wherever I go. Makes me feel at home." He stopped and signed a few autographs, then raised his arm to the cheers like conquering Caesar. Win or lose, Alex always acted like the champion to his fans. "Get on." He gunned the engine and the bike leaped forward.

After about ten minutes of harrowing stops, starts, and a run down Highway 111 designed to scare my lights out, we pulled up in front of a bar in Cathedral City called the Crank Case. I'd driven by this place before, but never gone inside. It was in the gay district of town, a little lattice-fronted shack noticeable mainly because of the vintage cars that were usually parked in front. Tonight there were a Cord, a gull-wing Mercedes, and a 1956 T-bird. Palm Springs is known for its collector cars, but I couldn't tell if these were props or actually belonged to customers. I followed Alex inside and into a booth at the front of the dark barroom. There were other customers, but they were purple shadows, mostly buried in the back of the room. Music was playing—some sort of nondescript jazz.

"Drink?" Alex asked.

"Just some red wine, any kind."

He went to the bar and returned with a glass of Burgundy and a bottle of Japanese beer.

"So what's this shit?" He picked at the label on the beer bottle with his thumb, tearing off a strip of damp paper.

"Like I said, Alex, Audrey was pregnant a week or so before Wimbledon. She was also highly distraught. You sort of have to put two and two together. She left our clinic rather suddenly. Did she go to see you?"

"Me?" he snorted. "No way."

"Why not? You two had been seeing each other for a fairly long time."

"So?" He rubbed the top of his pale head with the palm of his hand.

"So let's not be coy, Alex. There's got to be some chance you were the father. And that could open up a lot of avenues here, you might say."

"Au contraire, Miss Know-It-All, this is a dead end. Zero. If I were you, I'd drop it."

"Well, Alex, I'd like to, but somebody has tried to kill me or at least hurt me at least twice that I know of, and this is sort of self-defense at this point, do you understand? And the police know that somebody used one of Audrey's rackets to put a nice little dent in my head at Wimbledon, and Audrey herself didn't make it out alive, so where you fit in here is not something I'm going to drop, because I like my skull in one piece, thank you. And the police won't drop it, either. There is also a private detective looking into this, so somebody is going to make this connection, and it can either be private, right now, between us, or very, very public. Let's start with why you weren't at Audrey's memorial?"

"I had a prior commitment."

"Oh, come on."

Alex looked toward the bar and motioned to a man, who walked over to the booth and sat down. "This is Jackson Marshall. My personal manager."

Jackson nodded imperceptibly. He was in his thirties, with wire-rimmed glasses and an impeccably cut sport coat and jeans. He wore a white shirt buttoned up as far

as it could be buttoned. His black hair was combed
straight back.

"I have no secrets from Jackson, so let's continue our
conversation," said Alex.

"You're sure?"

"Positive. I can't wait. Because, as Jackson here will
attest, Audrey Armat and I had a business deal, not a
romance."

Jackson frowned anxiously. "Alex . . ."

"Shut up, Jackson. The fact is, Emilio engineered the
whole thing. And Corinne." He finally poured his beer.
"It was all part of the show. The Alex and Audrey
show." He laughed. "What a joke. We'd trot out for the
press, for a photo opportunity, and that would be that. It
served both our purposes."

"You fooled a lot of people then."

"Duh, that was the point, butthead."

"But why the charade?"

"If I was supposedly Audrey's quote-unquote boyfriend, nobody else came sniffing around. Emilio didn't
have to worry about some guy getting in her pants. Or
into her head."

"And what was in it for you?"

Alex blinked innocently, his eyes wide: Impudence
'R' Us. "Oh, who knows. What do you think, Jackson?"

"I think you'd better cool it, Alex." Jackson was nervous.

Alex chortled as if he'd just heard a very funny joke.
"Wait till you hear this one. Jordan Myles here thinks I
got Audrey pregnant. That maybe I killed her out of unrequited love." Alex burst out laughing until he
slumped over and banged the table with his forehead.
Finally he rubbed his face in his hands, then sat up.

"Well, Jordan Myles, let me tell you, neither of your little romantic scenarios is worth my time or yours, because you see, Audrey didn't interest me." He leaned forward across the booth. "*Women* don't interest me. Am I making myself clear, or do you need a demonstration?"

I looked at Alex, and at Jackson, and it was now perfectly clear.

"Oh."

"You were a player," Alex said. "Let's get real here. How long do you think my sponsors would stick around if they knew the facts? You're friends with Mariska—ask her. And for men, forget it." He took a long drink of his beer. "This has nothing to do with ethics—it's business. I have an image and I work damn hard to keep it. Audrey was part of that, although she was a nice kid, Jackson and I liked her. I didn't know her though, not at all. I don't think she wanted anybody to know her, and nobody ever did. That's why nobody could ever psych her out on court. But she knew the score. She played her part."

"There are clauses in Alex's contracts," Jackson said. "He's expected to conform to certain standards of behavior. And we have to look ahead, to future movie deals. Alex has a big future in Hollywood."

"People aren't as liberated as they'd like you to think—is that any surprise? They wear their red lapel ribbons, they support their little P.C. causes, but, man, that is it. When it comes to business, they're gonna lay those dollars right straight down the fucking middle of the road. It doesn't take much for them to back off. I don't know anybody who'd exactly warm to seeing their star client dragged into some assault case, either,"

Alex said. "So let's just drop this right now before it gets out of hand. If Audrey was pregnant, I'd suggest you talk to her parents. They're weird dudes. But they knew every move she made."

I can't say I wasn't stunned. The macho bad boy of tennis was all an act. And Audrey had been acting, too. Paul Cranston had been right. She was more than a great tennis player, she was a great actor.

"Audrey went along with this charade?"

"Sure. She did whatever the parents told her to do."

"And what about E.J.? Didn't you hang out with him?"

"No more than anybody else on the tour. But I'll tell you this much, just to get you off my back: E.J. is a nice kid. He's the one who didn't buy into any of this. Everybody thought he was jealous of Audrey, but he wasn't. He loved her, he was always looking out for her. He wanted to spring her. Just before Wimbledon, E.J. called me. He said he and Audrey had split. The parents had the bloodhounds on their trail, so he asked if they could come and hang with me until things blew over. I wanted to help them, but I couldn't get into it. I have enough problems without harboring a runaway, or whatever. And Corinne Armat, she's a vicious bitch, she would have found out and strung me up. It would have been all over. I couldn't get involved. I never called him back." He sighed and dropped back against his seat. "Now I guess I should have. Who knows? Maybe Audrey would still be alive."

"You can't blame yourself, Alex," said Jackson.

"Then who was she seeing?" I asked.

"Believe me, she saw nobody."

"Do you think Audrey was abused by her parents?"

"I think Audrey was fucked by her parents."

"Meaning?"

"Meaning just that." Alex stood up. "Now if you'll excuse us, our friends are waiting." He gestured to the room. Then he walked away with Jackson, stopped, and turned back. "Listen. Don't get me wrong. I feel really bad about Audrey." His face was suddenly and unexpectedly sincere. The bad-boy mask had slipped, revealing a vulnerable young man.

"I believe you."

"You need a ride home? I can call Rob to pick you up."

"Don't bother. I'll call a friend."

I knew Gus would be working late, because he always was. He was your typical workaholic—up at five-thirty every morning to work on his next book, working after-hours to keep up with the latest research developments. I called him from the pay phone.

"How about a late-night snack and some company?" I said. "You bring the snack, and I'll bring the company."

A half hour later we were in my living room, eating McDonald's drive-up fries from the cardboard container.

"What happened to strictly health food?" Gus said.

"We all have our weak moments. At least potatoes are vegetables."

I told Gus about Alex Bracht. "So Bracht was just a decoy."

"Mr. Macho Man, huh?"

"This whole thing only gets weirder and weirder."

"Teenagers are very emotionally needy. The question

is, how were those needs being met for Audrey? And
what was she reacting to?"

"Well, if your parents were abusing you, wouldn't
you react?"

Gus shook his head sadly. "It's just so ironic—Audrey
really held all the cards, and she never seemed to realize
it. Without her, the Armats are going to have a tough go
of it, I'd predict. They lost their meal ticket."

"Well, they've got us to pick on now. Do you really
think they can drive us out of business?"

"They seem to have the press on their side."

"But they won't have the law."

"Well, if they're coming after us for the big bucks,
they've got their strategy down. They've filed for depositions in New York, conveniently starting during and
just after the Open, when tennis is on everybody's
mind. This case is bound to be a supertabloid special.
There'll be innuendo and more innuendo, and by the
time there's actually a ruling from a judge or a jury, I
wonder if what happens in court will even matter.
That's the bad part."

"I refuse to think about that," I said. "We're right.
That's what counts."

"All the public knows is that a girl died and we had
something to do with it. That's enough. You know, I put
a few things into the computer—maybe I can come up
with a behavioral profile. Or at least something to go
on."

A.M. begged for a fry, but I wouldn't give in. Why
pump cholesterol into the veins of a defenseless animal?
Better to clog my own arteries and let her lick my fingers. It didn't look like I had much of a future, anyhow.

"You're not going to keep eating those fries after that dog licked your hand, are you?" Gus recoiled.

"Why not? Human mouths have more germs than dogs'." Gus could be very anal at times. It was a big problem in our relationship. "Here, give us a kiss."

"Dog germs," Gus teased. We kissed anyway, so I thought he might have been coming around. Unfortunately, that's as far as the romance went for the moment, because I fell asleep on the couch while Gus was throwing out the french-fry containers. He must have covered me up with a blanket and let himself out, because that's where I found myself the next morning—on the couch and alone, except for A.M. The story of my life.

The next day I paid my bills and balanced my checkbook, a nightmarish experience brought on by seeing the words "Final Notice" stamped on a few envelopes that I opened randomly. My desk was a mess. It had gone beyond desk into the category of receptacle. Tony had brought in my mail periodically, but envelopes were stacked a foot high, important things mixed with junk mail and Victoria's Secret catalogs. I felt like my career was on final notice, like those bills—maybe even my life, if whoever pushed me and whacked me ever got it right. I thought about how much I loved my little house, and how much I wanted to keep it. And how much I loved my job, felt rewarded by helping people and cared about the people at the Springs. The possibility that it was all falling apart seemed surreal and frightening, a hideous hallucination that only got worse when I closed my eyes. I tried to focus on my work, to concentrate on something else for a while.

Later I went into the office and read the charts of the kids who were in the Honor Badge program. This year there were twenty, ages nine through sixteen. These kids made our problems seem minuscule by comparison. They all had serious illnesses or handicaps, many arriving in wheelchairs, some on IVs or with surgically implanted pumps or shunts. Several were undergoing chemotherapy, or were struggling with low blood platelet counts, or had survived comas; most had life-threatening illnesses. And yet they were all looking forward to coming here and enjoying getting outside, making new friends, and participating in sports. Some were returning from last year; others were new. A few I remembered from last year's program were too ill to come back, and I wrote letters to each of them, tucking in a picture of A.M. I lost myself in working on charts for each child's case, and for the first time in weeks, I felt productive.

I worked through lunch and then decided to check out the camp equipment to see if any adjustments needed to be made. Heading down the hall toward the door, I was so engrossed in my notes that I almost ran into Gus.

"Sleep well last night?" he said.

"Fine. Thanks for the snack and the tuck-in."

"Good, because you're not going to sleep well tonight after I tell you this."

"What?"

"Angel Martinez's parents canceled her time here."

"Oh, God, another one."

"And that's not all. Guess who they've just announced will be her new coach, as of today?"

"I can't imagine. Anyhow, I hate guessing games."

"Emilio Armat."

"Well, that explains why the Martinezes were at

Audrey's funeral. The Armats don't waste much time, do they? Audrey hasn't even been dead a month, and they're replacing her."

"Emilio was quoted on the news as saying that Audrey would have wanted him to continue his work with young people."

"I suppose E.J. will sign on as hitting partner."

"The Armats are a package deal, aren't they?"

"And Angel's parents?"

"They don't have any money. They look on this as a godsend, most likely. Angel's going to be moving out of her home and in with the Armats. They'll take over her schooling, her training, everything. Emilio said in the interview that they would treat her like their own child."

"Poor Angel. Somebody should put a stop to this. It's like hiring a bank robber to be your cashier! Audrey was traumatized by being the Armats' child. She was an abused kid. The same thing could happen to Angel, couldn't it?"

"Well, if Emilio is transferring his emotions and his professional vision to Angel, there's certainly that chance."

"This is not a good thing. I wonder if her parents have a clue. Maybe we should contact them."

"You just love those lawsuits, don't you?"

"Well, we can't just sit back and let those monsters destroy another child for their own selfish purposes. At least I can't."

"Jordan, stay out of it, at least until things are clarified about Audrey. I hate to break it to you, but in this country people are presumed innocent until they're proven guilty."

"Thank you, Perry Mason. I'll try—but I'm not sure I can."

For the next few weeks, at least, I *was* able to stay out of it. At one point, pulling into the parking lot, I noticed a minicam crew parked at the front door, no doubt lying in wait for an ambush interview, so I veered off, went in the back way, and left it for Jillian to handle. Otherwise I was able to resume some semblance of a professional life. My time and attention were on the camp and the kids. I supervised the physical therapy program along with the program's pediatricians and specialists, and conducted the tennis clinics, basking in the joy in the kids' faces when they finally scored a point, connected with a ball, or even just held a racket in the sun. I gave out awards for everything—best grip, best ball toss, best sprint, best serve, best return, most improved over yesterday, best winning attitude, even best loser. A.M. was camp mascot, of course, and as usual she made even more friends than I did. The kids got together and hand-painted a special bandanna for her, which she wore around her neck with great pride and panache. At night we roasted marshmallows and told ghost stories, my specialty being the continuing tales of the Hound of the Palm Springs Baskervilles, complete with appropriate spooky howling. By the tenth day of camp, I think I was having more fun than the kids.

I was in my Honor Badger T-shirt, shorts, and visor, heading for the tennis courts, when I ran into Bill in the hall between our offices. He waved a letter at me. "We have word that you're first on deck for the New York depositions in the Armat case," he said. "They've timed them for the Open."

"I heard. Maximum publicity value." Angel wouldn't

be in the Open, so this was a way for the Armats to remain in the spotlight and also keep public sympathy on
their side.

"Probably. Nonetheless, as we knew, yours is the primary deposition. You don't need to worry—our lawyers
in New York will be preparing you the previous few
days."

"Preparing?"

"Well, just so you won't have any surprises. This
kind of thing can be unnerving if you haven't been
through it before. But we have the utmost confidence in
you, Jordan. Can you arrange your schedule to leave tomorrow?"

"Camp's not over yet."

"Well, this is an unusual circumstance. There's a legal summons involved. You've done a terrific job with
the camp, especially under the circumstances, but we
have to face it, if we want to have another camp next
summer ... Besides, you should have visibility at the
Open. We don't want anybody to get the mistaken idea
that you're hiding from anything. You'll have seats in
our corporate box."

I imagined there were a few vacancies in the box,
now that most of our sponsors and clients had bailed.

"I'll be there myself," said Bill. "We don't plan to
roll over on this, I promise you. They'll have a fight on
their hands."

"I welcome it, to tell you the truth," I said. "Audrey
couldn't fight for herself when she was alive. But if
there's any justice in the world, or after, she'll be
watching this."

FOURTEEN

In the cloyingly hot and humid days that seem always to accompany the U.S. Open, many of the top players like to practice two or three hours at New York's East Side Club, a high-rise sports gym and athletic complex on the Upper East Side. It was one of the few locations in this space-starved city where you could find two full floors of tennis courts, another floor of exercise rooms, and an Olympic-sized pool and state-of-the-art weight room on the glassed-in roof. There were food and drinks and a smoothie bar in the lobby where, as I signed in at the front desk, I saw Todd Henley, a top-seeded singles player, discussing an endorsement contract with a manufacturer's agent. With one hand the agent was thrusting a clipboard holding what looked like a contract at Todd. With the other, he was demonstrating a hand grip exercise device.

Players gravitated to the East Side Club for the convenience of the facilities, and also because it was a private club, which limited outsider access to your practices. At least you knew that the smattering of people pressed against the wall or sitting cross-legged on the floor at the fringes of the composite courts were members or their guests. This was where I staked out a place to watch, leaving my sunglasses on and pulling down my baseball cap to blend into the background. The bare wooden courtside benches heaped with gym bags, warm-up jackets, plastic drink bottles, towels, and spare rackets in their cases were the status seats here, reserved for players' coaches and friends. Mariska was practicing at East Side today, as was XuXu Lopez. I was glad to hear that XuXu seemed to have recovered from the shock of the events at Wimbledon. I sat quietly out of Mariska's sight lines and watched her practice with her hitting partner, a black man who had an incredible serve. She was having trouble today, and she was sweating and swearing during the changeover.

"I can't see the goddamn ball coming out of there. It's really pissing me off." She bounced her racket onto the court, plopped onto the bench, and drank from a pink plastic bottle.

"That's not an auction racket, anyway," I heard Matty, her coach say. He was talking quietly to a friend as he unwrapped a fresh racket from its plastic cover. "So, listen, I had Courier four–three serving. On clay."

"And what happened?"

"Lost six–four. I really had him. But every time I served the biggest serve of my life, he just tapped it back. So of course I kept on serving big serves, and he wiped me out."

Mariska didn't seem like she was in the mood for visitors, so I meandered around the courts to check out Anke. I slipped behind one of the dividers and onto a court occupied by Angel Martinez and Emilio and E. J. Armat.

Angel was hitting balls with E. J. At thirteen, she was too young to enter the Open, and it had been announced that she'd be playing the juniors in the second week. As when she appeared at Audrey's memorial, a more primary purpose of Angel's presence was visibility. It didn't take a nuclear physicist to figure this out, given the fact that a writer and photographer from *People* magazine were recording her every move as she hit with E.J., spurred on by Emilio's coaching. It was fascinating to watch him in action, to the point where I almost forgot about Angel. His face was intense, set. Every time Angel so much as moved, he had a response that bordered on psychodrama—shouted cheers and encouragement, emphatic body language, a range of facial expressions that could move the back row of any theater. In his hand was a rolled-up magazine which he used like a conductor's baton, making sweeping and pointing motions, orchestrating the court. He put his whole body into his coaching, pacing, balancing on his toes, jumping up, rocking his weight, waving his arms, miming Angel's moves. He was doing everything except playing the game. Occasionally he barked an order to E.J., who responded instantly. It seemed a very distracting technique to me, but I could see Angel seeking out Emilio's eyes for approval and, when she got it, beaming happily. Her game was astonishing for such a young girl. She had a crosscourt backhand like a heat-seeking missile, unexpected in someone so small. Her footwork was light, agile, and precise, and she had some nice saves off her backhand volley, right off her shoe tops. Her strokes were flawless, her return game so aggressive she reminded me of a pit bull, her talent obvious. Even more apparent was Angel's total enthusiasm and eagerness for the game. She was so eager to play and make the most of her time on court, she raced to pick up every ball and ran to the net to talk to Emilio. Immediately, I could see the contrast with Audrey. Angel was there because she wanted to be, not because her parents wanted her to play.

Watching E.J. was almost as interesting, for other reasons. It was clear that he was a very competent player, but he was like a painter who had all the brush strokes but could only paint by numbers. He seemed to perform by rote, like a windup toy. I got the impression that when the key wound down, he might just stop cold. There was no emotion in his work, no happiness in his attitude. It disturbed me that a person this young could have lost so much of his spark and his essence, but then, his twin sister had died, and now their father seemed to be in the process of replacing her. It had to be excruciatingly painful for him.

Angel was playing on the court next to Mariska, but after a few sets the entire group picked up and moved across the club. I figured Emilio didn't relish having this fresh green shoot of a girl in a side-by-side comparison with a living legend who'd won every title in tennis. As they got up to move, I tried to duck out of sight, but then Emilio headed straight toward me while the photographer headed off to take some posed shots of Angel.

"Jordan," he said, twisting a towel between his hands. The dazzling smile was back. "It was so kind of you to come to the memorial."

"I didn't get a chance to tell you how sorry I am," I said. "I hope you realize that."

Emilio lowered his eyes, dropped his chin to his chest, and took a deep breath. He was silent for a minute. Then he raised his head and looked back into my eyes. "Thank you." He nodded. "I appreciate it." He draped his arm across my shoulders and guided me to an empty court behind one of the heavy rubbery curtains that bisected the hangarlike room from floor to ceiling. "What do you think of our little Angel?"

"She's impressive."

"You know, going by the book, the rule to play at the Open is you have to be fourteen, and Angel is going to be fourteen on Wednesday. So, as I see it, technically, she could enter and not play until Wednesday, when she'll be fourteen. I proposed this to the officials, but ..." He shrugged and tossed up his hands. "They had to be sticklers. What are you gonna do? We had to settle for the juniors this year. But next year, it'll be a different story."

Emilio didn't miss a beat.

Suddenly he put both hands on my shoulders, leaned so close I could smell his woodsy-scented cologne, and said in a quiet voice, "I have to tell you, this legal business is no good. I have told my wife, we must make peace, and she agrees. This animosity is eating us apart—my family, your company. No healing can happen. Audrey would not have wanted it that way."

I nodded. What was he getting at?

"It's time that Audrey rests in peace, God bless her soul." He crossed himself. "We are going to drop the lawsuit against the Springs. Now that I see you, I have decided."

"I ... Well, that's good news."

"My work with young players—that will be my living memorial to Audrey. Perhaps we will establish a scholarship."

"Good. Wonderful."

Emilio extended his hand. "Let us put tragedy behind us and move forward. The past is past. Best of luck to you."

I shook it, attempting a smile, but I was somewhat perplexed by all this sudden global warming. It was hardly consistent with the events to date. Actually, I was finding it hard to trust anybody anymore. This whole experience had been such an emotional roller-coaster, I couldn't think rationally. I wondered what the real agenda was here; there had to be one.

I decided to call back to the office. Maybe the law-yers had some advice. I got in the elevator and headed down. At the second floor the doors opened and E. J. Armat got on. For an instant I was startled by his re-semblance to his sister.

"Hello, E.J." I supposed we should speak.

"Hi. Um—can we talk for a minute?" He looked un-easy, fidgeting in place as he stood. One knee jiggled disjointedly, and he gnawed at a cuticle. His hair hung limply, which could have been construed as a fashion statement, but he looked pasty beneath his tan.

"Sure. I wanted you to know how sad I was about your sister. I know you two were really close."

The elevator doors opened, and E.J. stepped in front of them so they wouldn't close. "You're a physical ther-apist, right?"

"That's right."

"I got an injury. Maybe you could take a look at it."

"Of course, but . . ."

"Maybe you could meet me back here in the weight room, just before the club closes tonight. I'll be work-ing out." His face was blank, expressionless, like a piece of paper with nothing on it. A dusting of blemishes was breaking out on his shiny forehead. The irises of his eyes were like cracked ice.

"Listen, E.J., I need to ask you ... did you try to meet me at Wimbledon, and ..." Before I could finish, he was gone and the elevator doors had closed behind him.

It didn't seem like a good idea to meet E.J. for much of anything at this point, even now that a peace offering had been extended by Emilio. I was sure there was no real injury. If there was, he wouldn't ask for my particular help. But E.J. seemed to be reaching out, trying to connect, and he was clearly traumatized by his sister's death. I knew he'd been the one to drive the car when she bolted from the Springs. For all I knew, he could have been involved somehow in her death. But looking at him, I saw Audrey in his face, the brow line, the soft lower lip. I looked at this kid and I saw the plea in Audrey's eyes that I'd never be able to answer, heard her voice, quivering, replayed the scenes of her smiling as she tossed those rolls of tape to A.M. I'd be there.

I spent the afternoon walking in Central Park, watching people rowing on the lagoon, rich kids with remote-control boats that could have won the America's Cup and street kids on Rollerblades and skateboards. I was tempted to try a pair of Rollerblades myself, but I knew my poor patchwork leg would hardly be up for it. The scars from the motorcycle burn were just starting to fade. So instead I bought a pretzel and an Orangina from a vendor, spread out a napkin as a seat, sat under a tree below the Great Lawn, and watched a company baseball game—it was the mail room versus the executives, or something like that. Occasionally the ball rolled in my direction and I fielded it. The sun was hot, and by four o'clock I was ready to go back to my room at the Inter-Continental for a shower and a rest.

Dinner was no big deal, but I was looking forward to it. I decided to stop in at a deli next to the hotel for some real New York coleslaw and garlic dill pickles. It was one of those time-warp places with quilted red leatherette booths and linoleum floors. I'd been coming here for years, since I was on the circuit, and it had never changed. The lighting was one solid fluorescent ceiling, the plasticized menu extensive. I noticed that there was a new addition to the usual deli standbys, a trendy international smattering of Thai, Italian, and Mexican dishes. Scanning the menu, I halfway expected to see them serving dishes like "The Cisco Kid Reuben" or "Matzo Mama Mia."

Dinner wasn't glamorous, but at least the company was exclusive. I had coleslaw and pickles, then went back to my room. There was a fax from Gus: a stupid cartoon of a dog that resembled A.M., with a balloon that said "Miss you." For Gus, this was the epitome of romance. He'd drawn it himself, so it made me smile. The dog looked more like a one-eyed porcupine with a complex. Gus is a terrible artist. I thought about the fact that before the days of the fax machine, we'd never have made it. We were apart so much, the fax was often the conduit of the entire relationship. Before the fax, we'd have had to settle for being pen pals. For now this was fine, but eventually, I knew, things would either escalate or die off. As I got older, I occasionally thought about settling down, having a real family and kids, especially when I was alone in a hotel room, like tonight. I knew that when that happened I'd have to be ready to change my life even more radically than I already had.

So far, they hadn't figured out how you could get pregnant by fax. But no matter how wistful I sometimes got to feeling, I knew I wasn't ready yet. A dog was about all I could handle right now. That, and myself.

The East Side Club closed at eleven, so at ten I took a cab over. The club had slowed down now. The blender bar was closed and the lobby was dark and almost empty, the shadows of the large indoor ficus trees dappling the walls. E.J. had left my name at the desk, so I went straight up to the weight room. It was stylish in the stripped-down fashion of the upscale health clubs—gray low-nap wall-to-wall carpet, shiny chrome equipment, racks of weights neatly stacked according to size, broad expanses of smoky glass darkly reflecting the city lights outside.

E.J. was there, sitting on the bench in bleached denim shorts with jagged, unraveled rips that exposed tan patches of thigh. The sleeves of his Greenpeace T-shirt had been rolled up, revealing muscular arms. Elbow locked on his thigh, he was practicing perfect flies in the mirror on the ceiling. He wore a headset and a Walkman clipped to his waistband. A waist-high rack of free weights was between us. Across the room a lone man, thirtyish and sweating, was plodding away on the StairMaster. Otherwise the place was empty.

"So you came." He spoke to my reflection in the mirror.

"I'm glad you asked me to," I said. "If there's anything I can do to help . . ."

E.J. set down the weights, dropped the headphones around his neck, and shifted his position on the bench. "So did Emilio tell you he's your friend now?"

"Well, not in those words, but . . ."

"Fuck him."

"What?"

"I said fuck him. You can't believe anything he says."

"E.J., whatever you think, he's your father." You should never run down a kid's father in front of him, even with the truth.

The guy on the StairMaster passed us on his way out of the room, padding slowly across the carpet.

"I just wanted to tell you, watch out," said E.J. "Emilio never lets anything go. Ever. Or anyone. He'll get you. Like he got my sister." E.J. said this simply, without emotion, as if he were commenting on the weather. He stood up, picked up another weight, and started doing reps of curls, watching his form. He clearly liked what he saw in the mirror. For a second he smiled. "Curls for the girls," he said. Quickly, he was serious again. "Not that I give a shit about you. It's Angel. I don't want him to get her, too. And maybe you can help Angel—like you didn't help my sister." He glared at me.

"Now wait a minute. Audrey never asked for my help. And I might have been able to help her, if she hadn't vanished. Split. In a car driven by you."

"Oh yeah, that." He dropped his arms for a second, holding the weights as if they were ballast. Then he stood up, walked to the rack, and carefully put them back. He stood there for a second, facing away from me. Then he walked back, sank onto the bench, and blinked up at me. His mouth opened, but no sound came out. Finally, his eyes flooded with tears.

I rushed to his side and sat on the bench beside him.

"What happened?" I whispered. "I know you want to tell me. Please tell me."

"It's my fault," sobbed E.J., his voice catching on every word. Tears spilled down his cheeks and splashed onto the shiny chrome weights. He rocked back and forth slowly on the padded bench. "I told her I'd help, I told her we'd run away, but then I couldn't do it. I didn't know how to do it. She had to do it on her own. I couldn't even help her."

"Maybe nobody could have helped her, E.J.," I said. "People have to help themselves."

"She was my sister, man, my twin sister, get it? I felt it. I felt everything she did. We were born together, we'd never been apart. I could always read her mind, you know? If she was happy, I felt it, if she cried, I was unhappy, too. And it was always the same for her. When she died, right when she died, she was in pain, I know it. And he killed her."

"Who?" I whispered. I wanted to hold this kid, somehow to ease his agony, but his fierceness kept me at bay.

"Emilio. He killed her."

I held my breath, waiting, listening. E.J. turned to me, really looking at me for the first time. "Do you think he pushed her too hard?" I asked.

"He wanted to own her," E.J. said angrily. "So he did. He forced her to . . . he had sex with her. Since we were little kids." He wiped his nose on his T-shirt. "All my sister ever wanted was for people to love her. She was such a great kid. She'd do anything for love. And that was his hold on her. I told her not to listen to him, not to let him touch her. But she couldn't stop it. Because she didn't want him to stop loving her, and if that was what it took . . ."

Suddenly the whole hideous picture fell into place. The frantic mother. The icy aloofness. The bulimia. The accidental and imagined injuries. The bogus boyfriend who was gay. The horrifying fact of the pregnancy, most likely her own father's child. I wanted to race to the phone, call the police, have Emilio arrested for what he had done to Audrey. On another level, I wanted to kill him myself. Emilio Armat deserved to be destroyed, as he had destroyed his daughter. I wanted to weep for Audrey, trapped as she'd been in that cycle of silence. The ice princess had hidden all her emotions behind a mask, because they were too crushing to face. The girl had been one walking cry for help. She'd cried out plenty, in her own way, but she'd been too good an actress, in the long run. That was one major problem with being a star. People made allowances for you, sometimes too many. You were supposed to be gifted, chosen, golden. If you weren't normal it didn't matter, because nobody expected the chosen ones to be—they would have been disappointed if you were. No one wanted to look too closely. Nobody wanted to be the one to step in and break the spell.

"She didn't want to win, you know." The words ripped out of E.J., as if from a tear. "She didn't even want to play. The sex thing was his sick idea of a reward, and she didn't want it. She hated it. She tried to make him stop, but he wouldn't. So she tried to make him not like her. She tried to lose. She tried to stop eating. But it had to be that he stopped wanting her, that was her plan. Because she didn't want to hurt him. Can you get that shit? *She* didn't want to hurt *him*." He sniffed loudly. "She thought it was all her fault."

"Couldn't she go to somebody?"

"She did. She told Corinne. Corinne called her a liar. She slapped her for it. Really slugged her. I saw the marks."

Everyone thought Corinne was a bitch. But she was worse, she was an enabler. Emilio could abuse his daughter, and her mother allowed it to happen.

"I tried to talk to Corrine, but it only made things worse. She called me a liar, ungrateful, spiteful, jealous. Called me everything she could think of. Slapped me. Threatened to throw me out on my ass." He stared at the ceiling. "I should have gone then, and taken Audrey with me. But we were fourteen years old. Where were we gonna go? We couldn't even drive."

"E.J. . . ."

"And then I thought about calling the police. I wasn't stupid. I knew how bad this scene was. But I couldn't do that to my sister. She was already famous. Everybody knew who she was, and not just in America. Her picture would have been plastered all over the place, with headlines about sleeping with her father. I figured there would have probably been some sort of trial, she'd have had to testify. It would have wrecked her life. All because of me."

"Don't blame yourself, E.J. It wasn't your fault," I said, trying to think of something to say to him, anything I could give him to hold on to. I wondered if I should touch him, offer comfort or sympathy, or if it was better just to let him be. But he was oblivious now, talking as much to himself as to me, his voice cracking, taking on shades of hysteria and desperation.

"When Alex started seeing Audrey, I thought, great, we'll get him to help us. I tried to be his friend, his buddy. But it didn't work, just like nothing ever worked. He's just a selfish jerk, out for himself. He never really cared about Audrey, or about me, either. All he cared about was his fucking image." E.J. yanked off his gloves. "Then I tried Bevins. The guy's a fucking billionaire, I figure. He can't drool over Audrey enough. But will he help? Hah!" E.J. laughed bitterly. "He said he had this place, a cabin in Connecticut, on some lake—and we talked about going there, hiding out, you know? He said it was all stocked up and we wouldn't even have to go out, that nobody would find Audrey there, or even see her. But when we made the break, where was he? Off in Fiji or something on vacation. I couldn't believe it, I couldn't even get him on the phone. Yeah, there was nobody but Audrey and me. We were gonna help each other. And we couldn't do thing one. And me—I was a zero."

"E.J., I can only imagine how you must feel. But these are serious accusations."

He laughed. "Oh, I'm scared. Yeah. What the fuck do you think?" he shouted angrily.

"Did you know Audrey was pregnant right before she died?"

E.J. shook his head numbly. "Then I guess it's better that she's dead. At least now she has no pain. She's free. Her and the kid. Maybe they're better off than me. At least they got out." He sighed, drained, and then slid down onto the carpet, where he rolled over and lay facedown, his arms over his head. For a few moments he was quiet. Then he said, "She killed herself. I couldn't believe it, after all we'd agreed to do. We were

gonna split together, we really were. I was working on
it. It wasn't gonna be much longer till I had a plan for
us."

"Was she ever actually in the town of Wimbledon,
E.J.?" I asked, as gently as possible.

"No," he said into the carpet, rolling his head slowly
from side to side. "Everybody covered for her, especially me. I helped her hide. Our idea was, she'd freeze
them out at Wimbledon. Not show up. To really fuck
Emilio just once, leave him holding the bag. She figured he'd really hate her then, and she'd be free. He'd
be so mad, he wouldn't even try to find her. We were
gonna wait for Bevins, go up to his cabin."

I had to strain to hear E.J., he spoke so softly.

"Where did you stay?" I kept my own voice low and
calm.

"Some hotel in New York, near Times Square. We
paid cash. They never looked twice at us. We just
stayed in the room and watched TV. Then Audrey decided she wanted to go to Wimbledon after all. But
without Emilio. She wanted to show she could handle it
herself. And I think she was feeling guilty, what with
the perfume thing and all. So we went over on our
own." He pounded the carpet with his fist. "Then she
got sick, real sick. Now I know why. She didn't even
tell me about being—pregnant. She must have lost it, or
taken something to get rid of it. I don't know. One day
she disappeared for a long time, and when she came
back, she just stayed in bed and cried. After that she
just gave up. She didn't want to live. She told me that.
And she didn't. She was like a zombie. I kept telling
her she'd snap out of it, that when she saw how much
everybody loved her, she'd be okay. I ran around and

organized stuff, but I had to leave her alone too much. I should never have let her out of my sight. The day she died, I got back just in time to see them taking her away. She had already jumped. But the way I see it, she didn't kill herself. He killed her."

"How can I help, E.J.?" I asked. I tried to be as gentle as I could. This boy needed professional help. I felt so bad for him. He was just a kid, and he'd had this terrible secret to carry for all this time.

"Angel," came his muffled voice. "He's gonna get her, too. I see it. Maybe you can do something. I sure as hell can't. I couldn't even save my own sister."

I reached down and touched his shoulder. "Please, E.J., you can't blame yourself."

"If I had helped her better, she'd be alive now," he said. His back trembled.

I knelt beside him and pulled him up. "It'll be okay," I said. "You're very brave to tell me this." The first thing I wanted to do was call Gus and get him out here. He'd know how to handle this, where to get help for E.J. I blotted his tear-streaked face with his towel. "Take it easy, now," I said. "Go rinse off your face and drink some water. Then we'll figure out what to do."

E.J. nodded numbly, then picked himself up off the carpet one knee at a time, slowly and painfully, like an old man with cement limbs. Then he walked slowly out of the weight room and out to the central hall that led to the rest of the club. I noticed he'd left his gloves and his bag. I leaned over to pack the gloves into the bag and zip it and to pick up my purse, when I became aware of another pair of feet standing behind me. There was just a vague recognition, that feeling you get when someone is watching you, although you don't know who it is. Fleetingly, I thought about the guy from the StairMaster, or the attendant. The room was about to close down for the night. Already, they were dimming the lights in the hall beyond the glass wall. I sat up and had just started to turn around when a towel dropped around my face. I didn't even have time to wonder what it was all about before something slammed against the top of my skull. It was crushing, heavy. I felt myself reeling, tumbling forward toward the floor. Then, darkness.

I came to, dimly and throbbingly, with a vague awareness of being carried. The towel was still over my head. I had no idea where I was. I wanted to scream, but couldn't. My mouth was taped, my voice immobilized. The towel covered my eyes and made it hard to breathe. I didn't think about who had hit me or who now carried me. All that mattered was escape—and survival. I knew I was alone, on my own. Nobody knew I was here. There was no way I could be found. Instinctively, my body struggled. My arms were fixed at my sides, tied down somehow, or maybe paralyzed. I wrenched myself, left, then right, trying to turn and break free. Then, suddenly, I did. Whoever or whatever held me released me, simply let go, and I felt myself sliding, falling. Disoriented, I hit not ground but, with a splash, water—warm, with the heavy smell of chlorine. *Don't panic,* I told myself. My clothes sopped up water like a sponge, weighing me down. I knew I was sinking, not floating. I struggled to kick my legs, but they seemed paralyzed. Still, I tried to find my way to the surface. In the back of my mind I knew I was a good swimmer, I had good wind capacity. I wasn't sure, as I floated toward oblivion, which was worse—being under the water or out of it. What would happen if I got to the surface—who would be waiting—didn't occur to me. I reflexively sucked a breath through my nose, and took in water instead. Water went up into my sinuses, down my throat, exploded into my ears. I tried to blow it out, but that meant expelling precious air. They say your life passes in front of you at times like this. That hadn't happened when I fell off the mountain, and it didn't happen now. Still, the sensations were similar, familiar. I'd been here before, on the edge of breath and death. Time elongated. There was no up, no down, no light or dark. Just a strange, almost womblike nothingness in suspended animation, a moment in time between living and dying, a precipice awaiting my arrival on one side or the other. My lungs started to burn. I choked, gagged, breathed in more water, then passed out again, without even time or presence of mind to wonder if I was going to die.

When you almost drown, it is only fitting that you should be rescued by someone called the Fish.

"Come on, girl, come on," he was saying. At first, lying there, wet and shivering with my eyes closed, grateful to be on land and breathing again, I thought I was dreaming, hallucinating. But it was definitely the Fish's voice, and I was definitely alive.

While he was talking, he was slapping my cheeks. "Ouch!" I complained.

"Sorry. Gotta get this tape off you. They taped that towel around your neck, you know. Looks like they taped your arms up pretty good, too."

I moaned. "Is it really you? What are you doing here?"

"I decided to get rid of my gut, join a health club. I thought you'd be proud."

"God, my head. I got hit." I reached up and touched the top of my head with my newly freed hand, then looked at it. No blood, just a gigantic headache and a throbbing lump. The towel must have blunted the blow. But I knew I'd been unconscious. The hit at Wimbledon had been a dress rehearsal compared to this. I still felt dizzy and disoriented, and my head throbbed.

"Don't move," said the Fish. I disobeyed his order, moved my eyes upward, and looked at his fleshy and heaven-sent face. To me, he looked positively beautiful. He pulled off his sweatshirt and placed it carefully under my sopping head. "There's a phone over there. I'm calling 911."

Lying there, I realized that I was beside a swimming pool. I wondered how long it had been since I'd been in the weight room with E.J., and what had happened to him. Did he try to kill me? There was no second-guessing this one. Somebody had tried it. They would have found me underwater in the morning, when the club opened. And it came close to working. Before, I had been annoyed. This time, I was really scared. Somebody knew every move I was making. They'd followed me from continent to continent, city to city. Or— the thought occurred to me now—maybe I was following him. Or her.

Only E.J. had known I was at the club. E.J. had asked me to meet him. What had happened to him? Where was he now? And if not E.J., who? Emilio? Had he followed his son and overheard what I'd been told? Suddenly I was terrified for E.J.

The Fish reappeared and bent down over me. "The

paramedics'll be right up, and club security is on its way. Jesus, kid, didn't your mother ever tell you not to swim alone after a full meal?"

I groaned and closed my eyes. No point in trying to act heroic. I couldn't summon the energy regardless. "I was talking to E.J. He told me Emilio molested Audrey. They told Corinne, but she refused to believe them. Audrey got pregnant, she ran away, she lost the baby, or maybe had an abortion. She couldn't go back and she couldn't stay away. I guess she was too conflicted to handle it herself, and nobody was there to help her. Anyway, she killed herself. E.J. was real upset talking about it. He blames himself. He went to get some water. Next thing I know, I'm whacked on the head."

"Did you see anybody?"

"Just a pair of shoes. White Nikes." I tried to sit up.

"Hold still, will you? You have a head injury. And here come the paramedics and the security guys."

I heard the elevator door open, punctuated by a ding when it landed on our floor. It was a loud ding, and I hadn't heard it when I was talking to E.J. I propped myself up on an elbow. "Hey!" I yelled to the uniformed security man, who was approaching at a trot. "When do you lock the stairwell to this floor?"

He knelt down in the puddle beside me. "It's always locked, miss. You can go out, in case of fire, but not in. Now where's the injury?"

You could go out, but not in, and I didn't hear the elevator. Which meant that the person who attacked me was already on the floor. "Check the club sign-in sheet, Fish," I said. "See who signed in and not out. Not that anyone would leave a calling card. And maybe it was somebody who was here earlier and came back without signing in. There was a guy on the StairMaster."

The paramedics swarmed in. They took my pulse and shined a tiny high-intensity light into my eyes.

"Her pupils are dilated," one of them said. Then I found myself lifted onto a rolling stretcher and wheeled toward the elevator. The Fish walked beside the stretcher.

"When are you going to tell me how you happened to be here?" I asked.

"You lose your purse?" he said. I noticed he was carrying it.

"I guess it was in the weight room," I answered.

"Yeah, I found it there when I came looking for you."

I looked up at him from the stretcher. His face looked bleary, but I wasn't sure if that was the fault of his features or my vision. "How did you know I was in the weight room, or even at this club?" The Fish's habit of always being able to locate me was getting out of hand, although I had to admit that this time, his appearance was welcome.

"Mind if I open your purse?" We were in the elevator now.

"Fine, but if you think I'm going to tip you for this, forget it."

He rummaged briefly, then pulled out the pen he had given me and held it up over the stretcher where I could see it.

"I don't get it."

"The pen. My invention. It has a microchip homing device. That's what the patent was for. It operates by satellite, like a TV channel. The satellite beams a signal that sweeps a certain area—say, New York City." He pointed to a briefcase at his side. "There's a computer in here." He snapped it open, and I saw a keyboard and a screen. "I can call the satellite and tune in to the frequency—like on a computer modem. Same idea. The frequency gives you a map and all the coordinates in a digital signal, right down to the street corner. I developed it for the Green Berets." He beamed proudly. "Clever, huh? You saved your own life without even realizing it." He snapped the briefcase shut.

The elevator doors opened. "You're serious?" I couldn't imagine the Fish as a technological genius, but obviously—and luckily—my imagination was limited.

"Sure. I get royalties off the software. There's maps for all the major cities now. I tracked you to the club, and then I found your purse there on the floor of the weight room. I figured, if I know women and their purses, you weren't about to go off very far without it. The pen, though, that was the key. How else could a guy keep up with the likes of you? Guys like me, we're not too fast. We need every advantage we can get."

The stretcher was rolling through the club lobby. My stomach was queasy. I focused on the ceiling tiles, and they whirled until I closed my eyes. "But how did you know I was even in town?"

"I was trying to get in touch with you. Your assistant Tony told me you were in New York on business."

We were on the street now. I could see the flashing red lights of the ambulance at the curb. Four police officers had joined the group as well. I had quite an entourage.

"So what do you think? Do you think Emilio did this?" I said as the stretcher was lifted into the back of the ambulance.

"Nah." The Fish climbed in after me.

"God, the man's sick. He could have."

"No way."

The doors slammed shut and the siren started to wail.

"How can you be so sure?" The ambulance leaped forward. I hoped they would run all the red lights. I felt it was my due, after all the times I'd pulled over for ambulances.

"Because he's dead."

I really thought I was hearing things. Why not? My ears were ringing, and then there was the shriek of the siren. "What do you mean, dead? I just talked to Emilio today."

"Well, he's dead. I was on my way to the airport for a little R and R in Atlantic City. Had my police radio on, and I heard the report. That's why I was trying to find you. To tell you. And when I heard how he died, I knew I had to get to you. So I hope you'll forgive my little invasion of your privacy."

"How'd Emilio die?"

"Nasty. Shot in the face."

F I F T E E N

After the police report had been filled out and signed, and the nurses at Mount Sinai Hospital had helped me change out of my wet clothes and into one of those ridiculous hospital gowns with the flap in the back, my head was X-rayed and I was admitted for what they called overnight observation. My room was typical Early Hospital: drab green, with a beige curtain divider separating me from the next patient, a woman who'd had hemorrhoid surgery. My diagnosis wasn't too bad, considering what it could have been: I had a mild concussion, and a nasty lump on my head, probably caused by a blow with a heavy weight. The police had found a fifteen-pounder lying loose on the floor in the weight room, and since I distinctly remembered E.J. putting the weights he was using back into the rack, that had as good a chance as any of being the weapon, although naturally there were no fingerprints.

The Fish refused to leave my side for a minute, except for when I changed into the hospital gown. Even then, he sat right outside the door.

The doctor came in, motioning the Fish to join him at my bedside, where I was propped up on pillows watching the late news. She looked so young, I could hardly believe she knew how to read a thermometer, but according to the name tag on her white coat she was an M.D. "You're a lucky woman, Ms. Myles," she said. "You only received a glancing blow. And you suffered a mild concussion, but that seems to be the extent of it. Fortunately, you're in excellent physical condition. That's what really saved you from serious damage in the water. Tomorrow morning we'll take another look, but my guess is, you'll be going home."

"Don't release her too soon, Doctor," the Fish cut in. "She's had a shock."

"I can handle myself," I growled; then trying not to appear ungrateful, I added, "most of the time. So who killed Emilio?" I asked the Fish. "Can't you tap into your sources?"

A nurse briskly tucked a thermometer under my tongue, momentarily ending all conversation. Everybody stared at the digital thermometer until it beeped.

"Normal," the nurse proclaimed. She was a large black woman with the arms of a sumo wrestler. She positioned a plastic pitcher of water at my bedside table, showed me how to use the TV and the nurse call button, and handed me a menu to fill out for breakfast. It was a new feeling, being taken care of without being so terribly sick that you didn't notice or care. I decided I could get used to it, although there had to be easier ways to replicate the experience—say, going to a spa.

Suddenly I was very tired. I closed my eyes. But I couldn't let myself sleep. "We have to find E.J.," I said, struggling to sit up. I was frantic, unsure whether to be afraid of him or to fear for him.

The nurse gently but firmly pushed me back onto the

mattress. "We can strap you down, you know," she chided.

"Yes, Nurse Ratchet," I said.

"Doctor's orders are, you stay in this bed." She turned to the Fish. "And you. Visiting hours are over, sir, unless you are immediate family."

"I'm her uncle, a dentist," he said, not missing a beat. But the lights were going out. The last thing I heard before I fell into an exhausted and dreamless sleep was the comforting, crinkly sound of cellophane emanating from the chair at the foot of my bed. The Fish was unwrapping a Twinkie.

I've always found that when, theoretically, you should have the chance to sleep late, it never happens. But this time I not only slept, I was out cold. The exhaustion of the night before probably helped, but I didn't wake up until noon the next day, when I was greeted by a blood-sucking, thermometer-wielding nurse.

The Fish was snoring in his chair, using a newspaper as a blanket. My roommate was incommunicado, her bed shrouded in the hospital curtains.

I got up and tiptoed to the bathroom, where I splashed water on my face, rinsed out my mouth, and combed my hair with my fingers. My head was still too tender to risk approaching it with a comb or brush. I walked out of the bathroom to face a wheelchair pushed by an orderly, which I was supposed to sit in.

"What's this?" I said.

"We're going to X ray," he answered.

"I can walk."

"In." He pointed to the chair.

"I'm going for a cup of coffee," said the Fish. "Oh,

hope you don't mind—I ate your breakfast. You didn't miss anything. See you later."

Later turned out to be quite a bit later. X ray on a nonemergency basis involved a two-hour wait in the hallway until it was my turn. Then it was back to my room to await the doctor's prognosis. By four o'clock he still hadn't shown up, so as I saw it the next order of business was to check out, but first I had to get out of the stupid gown. I still had a headache, but I was going to be fine. I wasn't sure I could say the same about E.J. Clutching the back closed, I grabbed my clothes. They were still damp and reeked of chlorine, but that was better than the ridiculous gown. I wadded the damp underwear into a ball and stuffed it into my purse. Then I gritted my teeth and wriggled into my jeans, and slipped my T-shirt over my head. It felt clammy, but all it had to do was get me back to the hotel.

When I left the bathroom, the Fish was again ensconced in the chair. "Feeling better?" he asked. He rubbed his eyes and stretched in his chair. The newspaper dropped to the floor.

"Nothing a few trips through the spin-dry cycle won't cure." I sat on the edge of the bed and poked at the remains of lunch, which had a certain resemblance to coagulated wallpaper paste. "So what are the details about Emilio? I can't believe you fell asleep!"

"Why not? The word I overheard on the police radio was murder."

"They're sure it's murder?"

"You knew the guy. Would he ever have shot himself in the face? Besides, there wasn't any gun, and you don't go running around disposing of weapons if you're dead."

"Now I'm really worried about E.J. He's in real trouble, Fish. He blames himself for everything that ever happened to his sister."

"Maybe you should blame him for what happened to you. Ever think of that? Hey, toss me that jam."

I lobbed a small prepackaged tub at him and he caught it. "I guess I can't rule it out. But he just doesn't seem violent. If he were, he'd have taken on Emilio a long time ago. Now tell me about Emilio."

"A maid found him in the Armats' hotel suite, at the Inter-Continental. Apparently he was alone. Corinne wasn't there, and neither was E.J."

"Where are they now?"

"She turned up and they put her under sedation."

"Well, you know she had a motive. And I might have even understood."

"She also had an alibi. Apparently she was shopping. Had the sales slips to prove it. They didn't mention E.J., but that doesn't mean he's actually missing. We can check it. Let me play devil's advocate for a minute," said the Fish. He stood up and walked over to the window, then pulled the shade open a crack. It looked like the day's heat had not abated. Outside, Central Park was coming to life. Joggers and pushcart men crisscrossed the sidewalks, and traffic was starting to build up.

"We've got the Japanese girl. You. Audrey. And Emilio. What could possibly be the common thread for all this?"

"Well, there's tennis," I said. "Everyone had a link to tennis."

"So who is there with access to everything in tennis?"

"Any of the players, of course, plus their coaches and

families. The administrators, like Marion Stryker, I suppose, or even Kanga Cheyne. They're feuding now, and Kanga thinks Marion is nuts. She forced her out of her job, I think. And I heard them talking about the 'Audrey Armat problem.' Marion definitely has something that she's hiding. It could be her. She's probably pretty desperate to protect her job and her players. But I don't see her risking her neck to actually do something violent. She might leak something to the press, or stab somebody in the back politically. But why would she sabotage players? It only hurts her. And, for God's sake, she would never risk an image or a sponsor. No, not her. She had better reasons to try and kill me years ago, when I left the circuit. And Kanga? She already quit. She has nothing to prove anymore, and she's already cut her ties. She'll be okay. She'll get another job in PR or something. She's good at what she does."

"What about the mother, Corinne Armat?"

"God, definitely feasible. The woman is certifiable. She didn't even mind if her own daughter was abused, as long as she got what she wanted."

"Okay. She's on the list. Now what about E.J.?"

I thought for a minute. Just thinking about E.J. made me sad. And guilty. He reminded me of how I hadn't been up to helping Audrey, how I'd let her slip away. And he reminded me of all the people who, for their own personal purposes, had "overlooked" Audrey's problems. People had their suspicions, the evidence was there, right in their faces, but nobody had stepped in.

"If we'd known in time, do you think we could have put Emilio away?"

The Fish let his breath out slowly, like a balloon deflating. "I wish I could say, Yeah, sure, we could have gotten him, we could have saved her. But the truth is, it wouldn't have been easy. First off, you can't charge rape without the victim's cooperation. Or, let's say Audrey hadn't cooperated, because that was the drift. Then you have to have a technical eyewitness to the crime, a competent witness who can testify."

"E.J.?"

"Depends on exactly what he saw. He'd have to have seen details. Not necessarily actual penetration, but some pretty nasty specifics. And even if he'd seen it, it was a lot to ask of a young kid to say about his sister and his father. That's why so many of these cases go unreported."

"You can't blame E.J.," I said. "But everybody else . . . God. Nobody wanted to lose the golden egg, so they let the goose die." It made me sick. It almost didn't matter how Audrey died. She was lost long before.

"Wait a minute." I grabbed my computerized address book out of my purse, turned it on, and punched in the first three letters of Kanga Cheyne's name. Her phone number, address, and fax number came up on the little screen. Then I grabbed the phone and dialed her number in Florida, praying she'd be home.

"Hello," said an Australian accent.

"Kanga, it's Jordan Myles. I hope I'm not disturbing you, but I have to ask you a really important favor."

"Hmmm," she yawned. "It'd better be really important. I'm officially out of the business, you know. What is it?"

"Kanga, it's not tennis business. It's much more serious. You ran the big charity auctions, didn't you?"

She groaned. "If you want me to do an auction, my

dear, the answer is flat no, and I'm quite cross about being asked about it."

"That's not my point, Kanga. I think whoever hit me with Audrey's racket at Wimbledon may have gotten it at a charity auction." I covered the phone with my hand and motioned to the Fish. "Do you still have the serial number in your records?" I whispered.

He nodded and pulled a spiral notebook out of his pocket, the kind with a cardboard cover that kids use in school.

"I wonder if there's a master list somewhere on some database that keeps records of what player donations raised for charity. Maybe on the WTA computer. Do you still have your office key?"

"Well, I threw my key back in Marion's face, I'm afraid. But I may have a duplicate somewhere."

"Here's the favor. Could you please go over, now, and check the database and see if any of the charity rackets match the serial number, and if so, who won them?"

"Darling, I suppose I could call a few favors, but in this case I don't think I need to," yawned Kanga.

I looked over at the Fish. He was scribbling a number on a piece of paper, which he ripped off and handed to me. "I've got the number here," I said.

"Jordan, listen to me. What I'm telling you is that at every charity auction for the past three years, almost all of Audrey's rackets were bought by the same person, one person."

"Who?"

"Why, Milt Bevins, of course. Even if he wasn't there in person, he phoned in bids."

"Are you sure?"

"Absolutely one hundred percent positive. I could never forget it. He asked that he remain anonymous, of course. But the bids were so outrageously high—the last time around, he bid one of Audrey's rackets up to a hundred thousand dollars. Can you imagine! For a tennis racket! It was such a record high, it made the national press. I thought everybody'd read about it. Whatever and wherever the charity, Uncle Miltie'd be in the bidding. We used to joke that he had a racket fetish. Although he also bid high on her clothes. On anything of Audrey's, actually. Just like, before Audrey, he used to bid up Mariska's donations."

"Can you double-check this number against your records?" I pleaded. I read her the serial number.

"Jordan, if Marion finds out I got involved . . ."

"Please, Kanga, could you do it now? Say you left something in your office. And if it gives you any added incentive—not that you care, but first of all, Emilio Armat is dead. Probably murdered. And if what I suspect is proven to be true, Marion Stryker will be out of a job posthaste."

The silence that followed that statement was electric. "You think she did it? Or had something to do with it?"

"Not the murder, but some bad stuff. I think we both know she was involved in a cover-up, Kanga. Let's not mince words. But I think it was worse than anybody thought, and everything has to come out in the open right now, or a lot of people are going to look very bad. Listen, Kanga, you've been the soul of diplomacy, but I know for a fact that Marion Stryker covered up that Audrey Armat was being abused by her father. Sexually abused."

For a moment there was silence on the other end of the phone. Then Kanga said, "Jordan, I tried—"

"I know you did. I don't know how much Marion knew, but she knew enough—there had been suspicious reports from the physios, for one, and she did not help that girl. We're not going to make a similar mistake."

"I'm on my way," Kanga said breathily.

"If you find out anything, call me at the Inter-Continental in New York." I put the phone down and looked at the Fish. "Uncle Miltie," I said. "I don't know why it hadn't occurred to me before."

"Uncle Miltie?"

"Milt Bevins. The rich superfan. Trust-fund junkie, a joke on the circuit. He was at the Thai place in Miami when we had dinner with Mariska, do you remember? White hair, distinguished-looking."

"If you don't mind, I'm a sick woman, I'm in pain, and I'd like to get some sleep," yelled a raspy, Brooklyn-accented voice from the next bed, behind the curtain. "You are the most inconsiderate people I've ever met. Nurse!" she called out. "Nurse!"

The Fish pressed his lips together. I leaped off the bed, leaving the rumpled impression of my body on the covers. It was time to get out of there. It took me about thirty seconds to grab my purse and tell the nurses' station at the end of the hall that I was checking myself out.

"It'll be without medical authorization," said the head floor nurse in her most disapproving tone. "They'll be making rounds in a half hour or so. Why don't you wait till then, or let me page Doctor—"

"I'll risk it. Where do I sign?"

Downstairs on Fifth Avenue the Fish's car, a battered

black 1980 Volvo wagon, sported a hundred-dollar parking ticket, and a tow truck was closing in fast. The Fish unlocked the driver's side door, then leaned across and let me in.

"While we're driving, open the glove compartment."

"Why?"

"I still have my pictures from Florida and Wimbledon in there. I was going to take them to show my mother, let her pick her favorites, get copies made."

I popped open the glove compartment, and ten or twelve photo envelopes fell onto my lap and the floor.

"I got a photographer's loupe in there, too," said the Fish. "Just dig around the glove compartment. It's buried in there someplace."

"A loupe?"

"Yeah, for checking out details. In case you want to order an enlargement or something, an eight-by-ten glossy, whatever." He veered down Fifth Avenue, dodging the taxis. "Jeez! These guys are maniacs. Is your seat belt on?"

"Listen, Fish, I didn't survive a concussion to get a whiplash." I opened the first envelope and flipped through the pictures. They were color four-by-sixes of the WTA building. There were a few of the exterior, several of me going into the building, two of me leaving, Kanga Cheyne and others going in and out. And one of Milt Bevins. I couldn't tell if he was just going in, or strolling by. There were also a few misshots, like the sky and the floor of the car, featuring the gas pedal. The Fish was a lousy photographer.

The next envelope was mainly pictures of the Stouffer Vinoy—the tennis courts, the front of the building, the open-air restaurant where I'd met Carolyn for drinks.

Plenty of shots of Carolyn and me drinking and talking. An out-of-focus, overexposed shot of a club sandwich with an olive garnish on a plate. A shot of Gaby Sabatini, minus her head.

"See anything you want for your album?" asked the Fish.

I flipped back to the tennis-court shots. There was a small group of people standing off to the right of one of them. One of the men, wearing a golf hat, looked familiar. Bevins. I rummaged through the glove compartment, found the loupe, cleaned it on my sleeve, and held the picture up to get some light as I peered with one eye through the lens. "Bevins," I said. "He was in St. Petersburg."

"Do tell," said the Fish.

"You knew this," I said. "You checked these pictures."

"Yeah, but to tell you the truth, I wasn't sure what I was looking at. You tell me what you see."

With a sudden clamping feeling in my gut, I stuffed the pictures away and tore into another envelope. These were shots of Mac Haskell's place. The parking lot, the waiting room. I adjusted the loupe again and scanned the cars in the parking lot. There was a red Porsche, a person inside. It was part of the background, blurry and out of focus, but it was Bevins. I remembered his appearance at the Thai restaurant in Miami, and the way he showed up in my booth at the deli. "He was following me," I said grimly.

"Boy, you were some popular girl. Two guys on your tail." The Fish leaned on the horn as we slammed to a stop. "Jerk!" he barked out the window at a turbaned truck driver, who yelled back in a mystery language.

I flipped to the Wimbledon shots in another envelope. They were the usual tourist-type shots—even worse, if possible, than the Florida pictures, because the lighting was so bad due to the overcast skies. There were some taken from the balcony off the players' lounge, overlooking the courts. Squinting into the loupe, I scanned the crowds. In the twelfth picture I found Bevins. Of course, this was Wimbledon, millions of people were there. But I felt chilled at the thought of this man knowing every move I'd made on two continents.

"Audrey wasn't at Wimbledon," I said. "She was in England, so she must have given it some thought, maybe tried to force herself to show up. But it was all a PR thing engineered to cover up the fact that she wasn't going along with the program. They used security as a convenient excuse. Marion Stryker, as the Director of the WTA, knew about it, I'm convinced. She went along with the cover-up because she didn't want to lose any sponsors. I don't really think anybody knew where Audrey was, except her brother. The two of them were alone, they were in over their heads. It's my bet that Bevins was looking for her. And he knew I was, too, because he probably knew she'd been at the Springs."

"He got around, that's for sure," said the Fish. "Maybe he thought you'd lead him to Audrey."

"He didn't need me for that. E.J. called Bevins himself. He saw him as a potential guardian angel. But things didn't work out." I suddenly thought about Bevins and the way he made a life of following tennis players around. At what point, I wondered, did being a fan become being obsessed? "Bevins worshiped Audrey. Maybe he was trying to get rid of her competition—but

Kyoko wasn't real competition for Audrey, who routinely beat her."

We inched past FAO Schwarz and toward the Plaza Hotel, with its plume of a fountain and flurry of brightly colored international flags. Usually I enjoyed this trip down Fifth Avenue, but now I was so preoccupied I barely noticed. "Well," said the Fish. "I'm still not clear on what Bevins was after. There's still no motive that could link him to Kyoko—or to you, for that matter."

"I think it had to be a smoke screen. He—and a lot of other people, including Marion—wanted Audrey to keep her ranking, and he didn't want anyone to know that Audrey was bailing out, or waffling, or having a breakdown—all of which she was probably doing." I shivered, imagining Audrey alone and adrift in her room in the bed-and-breakfast, feeling increasingly desperate. "These threats and attacks on the women players could have been entirely orchestrated by one man rich enough to pull it off, couldn't they?"

"Possibly," the Fish conceded.

"Here's what I think. I think these threats, and the attack on Kyoko, allowed Audrey to stay out of the game without attracting attention to her personally. If there was danger on a large scale, well, that was a security issue, not an Audrey issue. I mean, even the queen canceled out of Wimbledon at the last minute. Nobody questioned it, under the circumstances—circumstances set up by Bevins."

"But Audrey couldn't stay out indefinitely."

"I think he thought he was buying time for her." I shuffled absently through the remaining packs of photos, without really looking. I'd seen enough.

"And do we think he tried to do you in, too?"

"We do. Or at least, I do. Actually, the guy gave me too much credit. He thought I knew more than I did—or do. But he knew that I knew something, that there was a major problem involving Audrey, and that I wasn't letting it go. I'm sure he encouraged the Armats to sue me. Probably financed the suit, sent in his law firm. If Audrey turned up in bad shape, he had his fall guy—me. But then I guess I poked around too much. I was the only one out there who could tarnish the golden girl, maybe because I was the only one who didn't need anything from her who was actually trying to do something for her. That was my kiss of death."

"Well," said the Fish, "that's an interesting theory." He swung off Fifth Avenue, following a garbage truck. "Now all we have to do is prove it. And while we're at it, figure out who killed Emilio Armat, and why."

I looked at him. "Global Sport isn't going to like this. Stuff like this is bad for the endorsement market. Don't you work for them?"

"Sometimes. But they're concerned, too. Nobody likes this kind of thing. And how I spend my personal time is my own business. This I call personal time. Let's say I'm just a tennis fan." He pulled up in front of the hotel, stopped, and looked at me. "But I'm a tennis fan who'll be damned if one more kid is going to get hurt."

"Now what?" I asked.

The Fish tossed the keys to a uniformed doorman. "Now I think you change into some dry clothes, I wait downstairs and make a few calls, and we take a little trip out to Flushing Meadows."

The hotel lobby showed little evidence that a brutal

murder had taken place in one of its pricier suites not twenty-four hours earlier. Flower arrangements were elegantly positioned, the concierge stood at attention, and uniformed employees glided silently across carpeted floors. Business travelers lined up at the front desk to check out, tourists with carts of luggage crisscrossed the lobby checking in or heading to their rooms, groups of people in shorts, jeans, and sun hats surged toward the doors, obviously on their way to the Open. The Inter-Continental was a big player hotel, and many of the players from all levels of the tournament made it their home for two weeks. Healthy young men and women with burnished tans and tennis bags slung over their shoulders clustered near the doors, waiting in the air-conditioning for the player vans to take them to the courts. I wondered how the hotel handled the discovery and investigation of Emilio's death without alarming the guests. I knew Emilio would not have been happy if they had taken him down the service elevator, even if he was dead. I went to my room, picked up the phone, and asked the operator to connect me with the Armats' suite. The phone rang twice, and a man answered.

"Detective Smollens."

"Detective, I'm looking for E. J. Armat," I said.

"Who is this?"

"Jordan Myles. Is E.J. there, or do you know where I can find him?"

"Are you a member of the immediate family?"

"No."

"Then I'm afraid that I can't help you. This is a crime site."

"What about Mrs. Armat?"

"I can't give you any information."

"Detective, I have the name of someone I think you should question. A possible suspect, he—"

"Are you a police officer?"

"No, but—"

"Well, we're very busy here with police business, so if you'll excuse me—"

"Officer, please. Someone tried to kill me last night as well. There's a man named Milton Bevins who I have reason to believe was involved, and E. J. Armat may be in danger."

"Thank you for your interest, ma'am. I'll make a note for the file."

He hung up. So much for that. The Fish would probably have better luck, if he could get through to somebody at the top. He seemed to know somebody everyplace. But there was no time now to plow through red tape. I yanked off my chlorine-soaked clothes, took a one-minute shower, and changed into fresh jeans and a Gap T-shirt. My head still hurt, but looking into the mirror, I saw my pupils were normal. No brain damage. I grabbed a bottle of mineral water from the minibar and slugged down a couple of Tylenols with codeine, which I keep for migraine emergencies, to take the edge off my headache. I could eat a banana from the complimentary fruit basket on the road—I didn't want to take medication on an empty stomach. I was peeling the banana on my way out when the phone rang.

"Jordan?"

"Kanga! Great! What did you find?"

"There were four Armat rackets auctioned off in a series of charity events last year, not all of them to Milt Bevins. One went to a doctor in Encino. Another one went to a high school coach in Chicago. The other two went to Milt Bevins—those were the hundred-thousand-dollar bids. I don't have the serial numbers in our file, but if you want me to do a little more checking, I'm sure the Armats have records."

"You're terrific, Kanga. Could you please make me a printout of whatever you find and fax it to Tony at the Springs? Thanks so much."

It had to be Bevins. I wasn't the detective, judge, and jury here, but I had serious doubts that the doctor in Encino or the high school coach in Chicago would be mugging me at Wimbledon. At least Bevins had to be taken out of circulation and seriously questioned. What if Bevins had E.J.? And could he be linked to Emilio's murder? There were too many loose ends, too few answers.

It was getting late, almost six. Night play at the Open started at seven-thirty, but the traffic would be horrendous. If we were going to get out to Flushing Meadows before midnight, we would have to take the subway. I knew Bevins would be there. He would have the best box money could buy. And he would have all the confidence of an escaped murderer. I wasn't going to sit around and let him come at me again. Next time he might succeed. If I was looking him in the eye and in the middle of a crowd of a couple hundred thousand witnesses when I took him on, at least I might stand a chance.

On the other hand, if I was wrong, Bevins would take over where the Armats had left off, and a nuclear test site after the blast would look good compared to what he and his money could do to my credibility, my career, and my company. You know what they say—money talks, shit walks.

But I had to risk it.

SIXTEEN

If Wimbledon is glorious and genteel, the U.S. Open veers recklessly between grit and glamour. Frantic, raucous, hectic, hot, with smells, noise, and garbage accosting you even on the court, it's totally unpleasant. The players dislike the outside courts the most, because the food smells are the strongest there. Food and garbage have had their place in the history of the Open: fans sometimes lob beer cans or cigarette butts onto a game in progress; and in the early eighties, play was suspended when a garbage bin caught fire and belched smoke. Waiting in the tiny locker rooms or the crowded players' lounge, space converted from indoor courts, you have no place to go, no windows, no sense of the outdoors, no idea if it's sunny or pouring rain. You feel like a rat in a trap. The players' food stinks, costs a fortune, and anybody with any sense brings their own. Except for the nursery, which players with kids seem to like, amenities are minimal. I remember there used to be a whirlpool tub in the women's locker room, but it never worked, so they took it out and put in two more toilets.

It's not easy to be comfortable. You're always either cold or hot. No matter what the temperature outside, the

air-conditioning keeps it so freezing inside the players'
areas that some players use plastic bags and towels to
cover the vents as they sit there shivering in their warm-
ups, before heading off into the blast furnace of the
courts. Then, on center court, the place transforms and
becomes big-shouldered, powerful, and in spite of the
size of the stadium, the crowd looms close, almost inti-
mate, and carries its energy to you as you stand there in
the eye of the needle. The fans demand your best, and
you give it, and they respond. The fans at the U.S.
Open are the most demanding in the world, but it's
give-and-take. You're in a relationship with them. They
don't put up with whiners, but they recognize effort and
reward you faster for it than anywhere else. That's what
makes it all worthwhile, what gives you goose bumps
when you walk out on center court, what keeps you
coming back. At night it's like a stage out there, with
the glamour and the lights and the crowd, and it's an
event, and suddenly you love it.

Of course, taking the subway is hardly the same experience as going in as a top player, but even the subway has its turbulent and tragic place in Open history.
A few years ago, the parents of a young tennis fan were
accosted by muggers in a downtown Manhattan subway
station as they returned from some night matches, and
the fan was killed. After dark, it didn't hurt to keep that
in mind.

The Fish and I took the No. 7 Flushing subway from
Times Square to the Shea Stadium/Willets Point station,
got off, and walked across a long ramp to the grounds
entrance of the National Tennis Center. The subway was
air-conditioned, but we were sweating through our
clothes before we even made it to the gate. The air was

still and overcast, with no night breezes, and as the sun faded, the ground seemed to radiate the remains of the day's heat. Blazing floodlights banked the way, and Louis Armstrong Stadium, huge and looming, seemed to glow in the dusk. I had my tickets from Bill, who would probably be in the box tonight. No doubt he was expecting me to show up in attire suitable for entertaining whatever clients or prospective clients we still had left, sit in the box, and make authoritative comments for their benefit.

"So where would Bevins be sitting?" asked the Fish as I turned in my tickets at the main gate and we pushed through the crowd, across the asphalt, and toward the blue-and-white-striped tents of the food court at the edge of the stadium. The aromas of fajitas and burritos, hamburgers, Buffalo chicken wings, hot dogs, popcorn, and french fries hung heavily in the air—a melting pot of food.

"Bevins would probably be behind the players' box," I said. The quarterfinals was always a big night, and the women were playing first. There were a few people milling around the area, loading up on snacks, but most were inside. I checked the huge video monitor that showed the match in progress: XuXu Lopez was playing Anke Hess. We dodged a man in a bright orange T-shirt pushing a huge cart loaded with bags of ice toward the Champagne Court. "If he's not in the players' box, Uncle Miltie will be right at courtside," I said.

"As soon as we spot him, I'm going to tip the police," said the Fish. "We have enough information to make it known that he's a security threat, maybe get him into custody."

"It's not going to be so simple," I said. "We don't

have anything concrete or on paper, this isn't a court of law, and the guy could probably buy the stadium." All I wanted to do at this point was find out what happened to E.J.

We passed a mini-trattoria in a trailer, with ropes of dried peppers, onions, and garlic hanging from the awnings, and the Fish gazed longingly and drifted in that direction, as if the grease were magnetized. I firmly steered him away. "Scrape your tongue up off the ground," I said.

The usher had pointed out our seats and we walked down several flights of steps toward them, center court looming at the bottom of this crater tiered with people. There were no empty seats at all. The players were between sets, sitting in blue and white canvas deck chairs at the side of the court, flanking the referee's chair. Sponsorship logos ringed the blue canvas that surrounded the court: Fuji Film, Cappio, Imperial Foods, Infiniti. The linesmen were in the traditional khakis, with shirts in blue, purple, and black. The net linesman wore a helmet. The press was massed—network TV cameras, and what seemed like more than the usual contingent of photographers with long-lensed still cameras at the edges of the court. The Fuji blimp floated overhead, and I knew that it was broadcasting, too. The "Curse of the Grand Slams" had brought them out in force tonight.

As I made my way down the stairs, I saw a familiar face coming toward me: Marion Stryker. She had on her trademark black-rimmed glasses, and she was chatting with a man in a business suit, but I couldn't help myself. Marion, of all the people in tennis, had known the most and done the least. I stood on the step squarely in front of her. "Excuse me, Marion."

"Oh, Jordan. How nice to see you." She smiled politely and totally insincerely.

"Well, I wish I could say the same, Marion."

"Excuse us for a minute, please." She smiled to her companion, pushing him along. Then she turned to me. "How like you to say the inappropriate thing at the inopportune moment, Jordan. You're blocking my way," she said firmly.

"I'd like to block you right out of this sport, Marion," I said, "after what you did to Audrey Armat." I knew that it was not the most diplomatic time to have this discussion, but what the hell. "You want to talk about inappropriate? Fine. Let's talk about inappropriate. You were one person who could have stepped in, and you didn't. I guess you figured it was . . . inappropriate. You pulled off a world-class cover-up at Wimbledon, but you ended up burying Audrey. You have to live with that. Personally, I don't know how you can. And I wonder what other people will think when all this comes out."

Marion turned sideways and edged past me, her face set icily.

"Enjoy the match, Marion," I called after her.

Ahead I could see Bill's back and, beside him, Gus. I wondered how much they knew about Emilio Armat's death. I started to rush down the crowded stairs, but the Fish grabbed my shoulder and pointed. Glancing to my left, I saw what had diverted his attention—a box marked with huge letters: THE HON. RUDOLPH GIULIANI, MAYOR OF NEW YORK. The mayor was in attendance in the front row, chatting animatedly with action movie superstar Max Headley. Also in the box was Donald Trump. Sitting two seats away from Mayor Giuliani and Max Headley, wearing a white straw cowboy hat, was Milt Bevins.

"Well, well, well," said the Fish.

"I guess we won't have to worry about alerting security," I said grimly. "They've got to have plainclothes people swarming around the mayor's box, and maybe in it." I could see a pair of security officers in white shorts heading back from the courts, where they'd stood during breaks in play, to the press area. "The only problem is, their job is to keep people like us out."

"They've got a couple dozen guys in the tepee," said the Fish, squinting into the crowd. "You just can't tell."

"What are you talking about? What's the tepee?"

"The security area flanking the aisle where the players come on court. It's triangular-shaped, like a tepee. So that's what they call it."

"How do you know?"

"I did some consulting once for a security company that was doing some event here."

It drove me crazy that Bevins was sitting there in the mayoral box, chitchatting away like he was in the cabinet or, even more deceptive, a normal human being. It struck me as obscene. There was about as much chance of getting through to the mayor's box at the U.S. Open as there was of having tea and crumpets with the queen at Wimbledon. I wondered how Bevins had schmoozed his way in, although it's a known fact that six-figure campaign contributions tend to make a lot of friends in politics.

"I'm going over there," I said, pushing past the usher and taking the stairs two at a time. When I reached the interior of the stadium, I ran down the cement corridor to the entrance of the aisle that would lead to the mayoral box.

"Time. Seats, please," the P.A. announced, as we surfaced into the outdoor arena. We now had to sit down or leave the area and go back inside the stadium. "Quiet, please."

I watched as Hess bounced the ball, flipped her racket, then aced her first serve, but it was as if the game were a commercial on TV, something of which I was marginally aware, but nothing I cared to focus on. The only thing I was really watching was Milt Bevins.

For a moment I wondered if I should involve Bill and Gus, but I quickly dropped that thought. It looked like there was a client with them, and besides, if the mayor was going to have me arrested, I could truthfully say they weren't involved.

An usher approached. "May I see your tickets?" he asked.

"We were just leaving," I said. The Fish and I retreated back inside the stadium.

"Look," said the Fish. "Bevins is with the mayor. He's on national television. He's not going anywhere for now. I'll go down to Stadium Operations. I can drop a few names; it might help."

I sighed helplessly. "I'd hate to see him get away," I said.

"Jordan, do me a favor and don't play bounty hunter," the Fish said. "There are people here to handle this."

"I'll be right there by the gate," I said. "I'll just keep an eye on him."

"You do that," said the Fish. He disappeared into the stadium crowd and I went back outside to watch

Bevins. I slipped by the usher and stood at the top of the aisle. It was almost dark now, but Bevins was close enough to the courts that the lights illuminated him. For ten minutes or so I watched him follow the game through his binoculars. Lopez won the set, and two security guards came out to watch the players. It seemed to me that extra security materialized around the mayor's box as well. Several people in the box got up and either moved or left the box. Among them was Bevins, who stood up, mingled with, then blended into the group, then disappeared.

I stared at the box, at the mayor, at Bevins's empty seat. I figured he'd come back soon, but the match resumed and there was no sign of Bevins or the white cowboy hat. Then a woman in a suit took his seat and leaned over to kiss Max Headley—obviously a friend. Suddenly it occurred to me that Bevins had just been visiting the box, not sitting in it permanently. *You're an idiot,* I told myself. I took off at a run. Maybe I could catch up and follow Bevins so that I could at least tell security where he was sitting.

I dashed down the hall, dodging people carrying hot dogs and Cokes. My elbow hit a man's box of popcorn and it went flying. "Hey!" he yelled after me, but I was already gone. I didn't know the stadium that well from the inside, but I approximated where I thought the mayor's box was, about a quarter of the way around from where I'd been. I was standing in the hallway, just heading toward the opening, when I saw Milt Bevins, in his white straw hat, emerge from a men's room precisely across from me.

He saw me at the same time, and a tight smile crossed his lips. For a fraction of a second, time seemed

to hang in the air as we stared at each other. It was one
of those telephathic moments; each knew precisely what
the other was thinking. I was thinking that I was going
to grab the first security person I could find, under any
pretense I could concoct. He was thinking that he
wanted to kill me. I swear to God, that's what the man
was thinking. I could see it in his eyes, in the clenched
quality of his face, which was like a fist. Instead of returning to the box, or even the stadium, he turned
quickly and headed toward an exit.

I followed, padding behind, never taking my eyes off
him, but watching peripherally for a security officer. It
occurred to me that the Fish wouldn't be able to find
me. Since we were together, he hadn't brought his
tracking equipment.

Ahead, I could see Bevins leaving the stadium. This
was not good. I picked up my pace and followed him
out, but he'd disappeared. Suddenly the Fish appeared
beside me. "Thank God," I said. "He's out there. He's
trying to get away. I'm sure he knows we're after him.
Where's the police?"

"They went to the box," he said. "I got up there just
as you were leaving. I was following you following
Bevins. Where'd he go?"

"He headed toward the main gate. He could have a
car out there somewhere, or maybe he's going to blend
into the crowd at the subway."

"Shit," said the Fish. "Next stop, JFK Airport." He
scanned the darkness. "Now, you wait here. Don't go
exploring, will you? We don't know what this guy is capable of. I better go tell these guys. If I move fast, they
can seal off the exits before he can get out." He took off
at a trot.

Then I remembered the press trailers. Dignitaries, VIPs, and stars arrived that way, unheralded and unbothered. I raced outside, where the grounds were moonless and starless, a darkness washed only by clusters of high-intensity lamps. The color was gone—it was like running into a black-and-white movie, all light and shadow. I could hear the applause from the stadium, and there was a strange distance between that massive waterfall of sound and the catch of my own breathing and soft padding of my rubber soles as I ran. I passed the blue-and-white Final Eight Club tent, which was empty, and the food-court area, also empty except for a few people who cared more about food than tennis. An ice cream vendor stood forlornly, the last outpost of culinary civilization at the tournament, ready to pack up for the night. Around the side of the stadium, I found myself ducking cables and equipment. There were cranes and stacked pallets and seats.

And there was someone following me.

I froze. I couldn't see him, or hear him, but I knew he was there as surely as if I could touch him. It was a feeling that made my skin contract, as if it were too small for my body. I whirled around, suddenly realizing that I'd gone farther than I'd intended. Being alone in this no-man's-land behind the stadium in the dark wasn't a highly intelligent move. Ahead I could see the press trailers: CBS operations, USA sports, CBS personnel, USA graphics, the press food trailer. It wasn't far. And there were hundreds of thousands of people in the area. Still, I might as well have been a million miles away, it was that deserted where I now stood. The stadium entrances weren't even visible. I tried to calculate whether it was better to retrace my steps or try for the

trailers. Or maybe it was my imagination that I was being followed. Sweat needled its way down my sides;
my hairline dripped.

"We meet again," said Milt Bevins's voice. He
stepped from behind a crane. His white hat gleamed in
the dark but left his face in shadow. A length of cable
was in his hand. "You know, you really shouldn't be
here. There's a lot of heavy equipment. Exposed high-
voltage wires. People are careless. Accidents can happen."

I swallowed. "Milt . . ."

He didn't hear me. He was swaying slightly from side
to side, lost in his own reality. "I loved Audrey. She
was everything to me. I would never have harmed her.
I tried to protect her—from that monster of a father."
His voice was shaking.

I tried to keep mine even, speaking slowly, clearly.
"Milt, I tried to help her. I did everything I could." I
stopped myself short. What good would it do to try to
talk rationally with someone this irrational? I decided to
buy time to figure out how to escape, or attract someone's attention. "Why are you trying to frighten me?"
As I said this, I looked around to examine my options.
In one direction we were at the end of the line of media
trailers, probably an equipment area that wouldn't
become active again until after the matches tonight,
if then. In the other direction was the heavy machinery,
then darkness. Sporadic waves of applause erupted from
the stadium, alternating with the roar of jets taking off
from La Guardia Airport.

"No one must know!" Bevins whispered fiercely.
"No one will know!" He fingered the cables, and I
stepped back, imagining them around my wrists or

neck. He was protecting Audrey, even now that she was dead. "Emilio?" I said, taking a calculated risk.

"He ruined her. Emilio Armat was an animal! He had to be destroyed. He had no sense of decency."

"There are legal avenues," I said, trying to string out the conversation, although I was aware that I was arguing with a madman.

"You are so naïve, Jordan. These days the law is unpredictable. He could have pleaded that he ate too many Twinkies, that he had been an abused child himself. Who knows? He didn't deserve to live, after what he did to Audrey. I exacted justice on her behalf. It was up to me. She was so pure, so perfect." For an instant a faint smile played across his face, a reverie; then he snapped, "E.J. told me about—*him*." Bevins's voice dripped disgust. "I tried to help Audrey. I wired from Fiji, I begged them to go up to my cabin. I told them I'd fly back immediately, wire money, anything they wanted. But—it was too late. They'd already left for England." His face was anguished.

I could imagine E.J., desperate, running after Bevins as a last resort. If I'd been him I might have, too. Bevins had money, interest, influence. And he might have helped Audrey, if he'd been able to. The very fact of his failure to do the one thing that could have made a difference in Audrey's life—possibly save her life— might have driven him over the edge, as it almost had E.J. The difference was that E.J. loved his sister; Bevins was obsessed.

"What Armat had been doing to that precious girl—it made me physically sick. But, after all, he was the parent, I had no real proof, the police wouldn't have acted, and I knew I had to bide my time, pick the right moment. I wanted to leave Audrey out of it, spare her. Of course, I couldn't blame Audrey for not wanting to play after what she'd been through. But I had to protect her, help her keep her ranking. Who else was working on her behalf?"

"So you killed Kyoko?"

"Oh, Jordan, of course not." He was patronizing now, condescending. "The point was just to create a diversion, a reason for Audrey to withdraw. But what can I say about people you hire? The man was supposed to be a professional—I paid him enough—but he turned out to be an imbecile, incompetent. I told him to scare her, maybe a little cut, nothing harmful. It was a freak thing that he hit an artery. I feel terrible about it. But Audrey had to be protected, don't you see?"

"Listen to me, Milt . . ." I began.

"No!" he said roughly. "You listen to me. You and all those others who think they know so much about Audrey. What were you doing, snooping around, dirtying her name? What you found out is for no one to know, do you hear me? *No one!* And you won't let it go, will you?" He was trembling with anger now. "Audrey was an innocent. She died a pure and perfect innocent. A sports legend. Her name must not be dragged through the mud by you and all your selfish professional motives. And it won't be! Not by you or anyone else." He was crazy, insane. But he was utterly determined.

"E.J.," I said quickly. "Where is he?"

"He is safe," said Bevins, struggling to calm himself. "He is a piece of Audrey. He's all I have left of her."

I wanted to grab Bevins, scream at him, shake the information out of him, but I stayed as calm as I could under the circumstances. "Yes," I found myself saying soothingly. "Yes, of course. It's good that he's—where did you say he is?"

"Somewhere," said Bevins flatly. "And you're not invited. In fact, I'd say you are distinctly uninvited."

He lunged for me and I jumped aside. In the shadows, something metallic glinted. A gun? In spite of the heat, I shivered, backing up cautiously, but he moved closer, gliding in and out of the shadows. I focused on his white hat, which was easiest to see, and surveyed my options. It wasn't fear I felt now so much as a heightened sense of alertness, as if every nerve ending in my body were exposed to any movement or sensation. I took it all in instinctively, marking the area around me, siphoning the close-up sounds from the din of the stadium crowd. At my back was a forklift truck. To the side was a stack of pallets. In one quick motion I scrambled backward up and into the forklift. Blinking in the dim light, I could see a paper cup resting on the control panel—and the keys. The operator had either left on a break or been in a hurry at the end of his shift. Hoping that the forklift drove at least remotely like a car, I turned the key in the ignition, and, thank God, the engine started. Almost simultaneously, I pulled a lever to the right of the steering wheel, which must have been the hand brake. The forklift immediately began to roll down the slight incline as I stomped on the gas pedal. The forklift surged toward Bevins, who was running ahead now, within inches of being impaled on the huge metal forks. Suddenly, I realized that I could kill him. It flashed through my mind: *Which is worse? To kill or be killed?* I pulled my foot off the gas, swung the wheel, and blindly groped for the controls, afraid to take my eyes off Bevins for even a second, hoping I could stop before I gored him or sheared him in half.

"Hey, what's going on over there!" yelled a guard. The bright beam of a high-powered flashlight swung in my direction, temporarily blinding me. I squeezed my eyes shut for an instant and slammed on the brake. When I opened them, Bevins had disappeared.

"Follow that man!" I yelled, leaning forward and standing on the gas pedal with my full weight. "Stop him! Call the police!" The forklift rumbled ahead like a yellow tank as the guard pounded along behind me, barking into his walkie-talkie. I thought I saw a shadow, or a form, dodging behind a T-shirt booth just ahead of me, and I swerved toward it, then crashed into it. The booth fell over with a terrible crash as wood splintered, metal crunched, and the forklift jerked to a stop against the crushed booth, throwing me against the windshield of the cab. I left the engine running and leaped to the ground. Pushing my sweat-soaked hair out of my eyes, I whirled around, gasping in the humidity, scanning the area, but there was nothing but the crumpled booth, the stalemated forklift, its engine still racing, and about two hundred T-shirts scattered across the pavement like fluttery white ghosts. "Bevins!" I called, but my voice was drowned out by the roar of the crowd and the grind of the forklift engine. I started running. I seemed to see him in every shadow, yet he had disappeared, evaporated into the night. Trailed by the guard, I ran until I reached the food court, where I ran into the Fish and a squad of security people.

"Okay, we got her," announced the guard who'd been running behind me. He grabbed my arm, and I realized from the look of relief on the Fish's face that everyone had been looking for me, not Bevins. "She tried to vandalize a forklift."

"Let me go!" I furiously tried to shake off his hand, telling myself that if I didn't think about what almost happened, I might be able to keep myself together. But I was short of breath now, not from the effort of the chase but from the horror of the encounter with Bevins, and I found myself gasping even as I tried to sound authoritative and professional. "Bevins is out here someplace. He has E. J. Armat—I don't know if he's alive or not. Bevins killed Emilio. He admitted it. He's on a vendetta for Audrey. You have to find him before he gets out of here. He has a gun, and he's absolutely nuts."

The Fish reached over and removed the guard's hand from my arm with a reproachful look. "They've got people at the stadium exits, the subway, and the parking lots. All the player vans have escorts, and each top-seeded player has been assigned a guard. They've already got the mayor out of here, and they're closing down this side of the stadium. Everyone's going to have to leave through one gate and parking-lot exit, and they'll be monitoring that." I could see a wall of uniformed men forming along the entrance to the stadium, and lights flashed as about twenty police cars swept past the gate and onto the grounds. Several helicopters hovered overhead, and one landed in the parking lot, the wind whipping trash and papers across the pavement.

"Let's go," said the Fish, touching my shoulder. "It could get nasty when they find him. And they will find him. This place is vacuum sealed."

"Who's in charge?" I demanded, refusing to move. The Fish resignedly pointed to a blond man in a suit.

He was going over a diagram of the stadium with some uniformed officers, but I broke in. "Bevins kidnapped E. J. Armat—he as much as said so." I was starting to feel frantic now. I remembered E.J. telling me about the cabin in Connecticut, and I told the police about it now. "I don't know exactly where, but it's on a lake," I said, as they scribbled notes.

One of the officers scribbled down what I was saying in his report notebook, but he was frowning. "Nobody has reported him missing."

"He's a kid. His sister is dead. His father was just murdered. His mother is under sedation. Who's there to report him?" I snapped. I wanted to get into the helicopter, grab the controls, take off in it, and go search for E.J. myself. "Just find him," I pleaded. "Please, find him." My heart was lurching with frustration. And I couldn't do one damn thing about it.

SEVENTEEN

The next day, the day of the semis, they found E. J. Armat—alive, locked in a toolshed on the grounds of Milt Bevins's house on a hill above Lake Waramaug, in a rural area of Litchfield County, Connecticut. The place had been laid in for a siege. The windows were boarded with plywood. There was six months' supply of food and water, a grab-bag arsenal of guns, ammunition and knives, chains, and locks. Heavy chain restraints had been attached to all the bedposts and rafters. Listening devices, motion detectors, and video cameras had been installed inside and outside the cabin. Numerous pictures of Audrey Armat and articles of her clothing and tennis equipment, obviously collected over time, were stashed throughout the place. There were also cases of vintage champagne, fine crystal and china, a complete service of sterling silver flatware, and several cases of Miss Clairol's Maxi Blonde lightener.

E.J. was hot and dehydrated. He had a fistful of splinters and a sore throat from pounding on the walls and screaming to be heard. His hair had been bleached blond by Milt Bevins, to better resemble his sister's, but otherwise he was all right—physically. Thank God. Psychologically—that's another matter. E.J. told the police his story of Audrey's abuse by their father and his mother's unresponsiveness, and action was immediately filed by the district attorney to make him a ward of the court until a thorough investigation could be undertaken. He was not returned to Corinne Armat, who was under psychiatric observation in a state of what was described as nervous collapse, but she did make a statement that her husband had been a sick, abusive, and violent man, that she'd stayed with him only out of fear, and that in her opinion he deserved to die.

After all this it was pretty hard to think about tennis, which is, after all, just a game. You have to wonder what it is about a game and the people who play it for a living that makes other people care enough to love them, hate enough to kill them. I put this very question to Gus as we sat in the Springs box, along with the Fish. Bill had flown back to the clinic to handle the calls that were already starting to pour in from all over the world. A Japanese electronics firm wanted to book a big motivational seminar, IBM had already rebooked, and the Olympic Committee had sent a fax. It seemed we were back in business. Just getting to the box had been like running a congratulatory gauntlet.

"I think it's two things," said Gus as we waited for the match to start. XuXu Lopez and Shelley McClain were warming up, and I found the thwack of their tennis balls comforting. "Money and familiarity. We all know what big money does. And familiarity, that's the key here, I think. In sports, we have a chance to feel like we're virtually part of the lives of the players, like we know them. We see them on TV and in the papers in our living rooms, our bedrooms, every week, and they become part of our lives. We're up close and personal, as they say, on a first-name basis. That gives some people an emotional toehold to have a claim on these sports figures. It escalates from there."

The Fish nodded. "What would have happened if Bevins had gotten away with kidnapping E. J. Armat?"

Gus waved his hand from left to right. "He was transferring his emotions from the sister to the twin brother—look at the bleached hair. Very powerful and very frightening. It's amazing. When I ran the computer profile of the possible suspect for all this, the traits that came out described Bevins perfectly: control freak, perfectionist, emotionally dependent loner. I just didn't know it was Bevins."

"Do you think E.J. can come through this?" I asked.

"He'll have therapy. It will help," said Gus. He sounded as unconvinced as I felt at this moment.

"I don't know how anybody could treat their kids like the Armats did. When I think of Emilio . . . it makes me sick. He was her father."

"It's terrible," Gus agreed. "You know, a male coach is a father figure even when he isn't the actual father. This was doubly incentuous."

"Audrey and E.J. were basically nice kids, and they were really vulnerable," I said angrily. Hell, it was like using Bambi for target practice. I'd never forget the look in Audrey's eyes.

Gus looked sadly resigned. I knew he felt as helpless as I did. As we all did. There were so many maybes. Maybe if we'd gotten involved sooner, maybe if somebody had treated Audrey like a kid, not a star, maybe whatever.

"Well, the rebels aren't as likely to get victimized," Gus said quietly. "They'll fight. It's the gentle, submissive ones, the most vulnerable ones, who are the most dependent. The ones who have the most intense need to be loved and cared for. Those are the sitting ducks."

"The worst thing of all is Bevins. I can't believe they didn't catch him."

"This is a huge place," said the Fish, scanning the top rows as if he half expected to see Bevins up there with a program and a beer. "He could have slipped out almost anywhere."

"He's probably in Europe or South America by now. Or counting the money in his Swiss bank account from the Riviera."

"They would have stopped him at customs," said the Fish.

"Maybe not," I said. "Money talks. Maybe he made himself a new passport. Maybe he's getting himself a new face."

"You watch too many movies," said the Fish.

It made me crazy to think that Bevins was still on the loose. With all the charges against him, he was unlikely to surface of his own volition, but when a person was that insane you couldn't predict. I, for one, would never rest easy until Milt Bevins was behind bars where he belonged. It seemed obscene that Kyoko and Audrey had to suffer, to die, that even Emilio Armat couldn't be pinioned by a judge and jury, while Bevins bought his way out. It infuriated me.

"Think on the positive side," said Gus. "It's just a good thing they found E.J. when they did, thanks to you."

"I didn't do anything," I muttered, pulling down my visor and smearing No. 20 sunscreen on my nose. My nose always burns. I was still frustrated by the fact that

I hadn't prevented more tragedy than I had. But I guess you can only do what you can do. I'm trying to come to terms with that. In tennis, if you practice at it and work harder, if you have the right approach and mental attitude, you'll usually see a difference in your game. That's not always so in life, and sometimes it isn't easy for me to admit it, because if you can't make a difference—well, to me that's failure, and that is the one thing that's absolutely out of the question. It's not so much winning as not losing. That's what it's always been about for me. As Gus knows.

"So what's she doing now?" asked the Fish, taking aim at the tennis court with his camera and snapping off a few shots of the players. "I never figured out how to keep score—that's why I don't play this game."

"They haven't started the game yet," I said. "There is no score."

"Oh. Okay. Now I get it." He passed me a box of popcorn. "It's not buttered."

"You know," I said, "I could never have gone all the way, like Sampras."

"But you almost did," said the Fish. "Come on."

I shook my head and ate a handful of popcorn. "No. I was too scared of not being the best. It wrecked things for me. I couldn't even sit back like I am now and watch a match. It's a good thing I became a physical therapist. I would never have been a world-class champion."

"That all depends," said Gus, fanning himself with his program. I moved forward to catch a bit of the breeze. Otherwise, the air wasn't moving.

"There's lots of different kinds of champions," said

the Fish. "Soft drinks! Over here." He waved down a vendor with a five-dollar bill.

"It's fine," I said. "I can actually sit here on the sidelines and enjoy this game."

"The sidelines, huh?" laughed Gus.

"No, really, I'm really looking forward to it," I protested, punching his arm. "I don't have to punish myself anymore because I'm not *in* it."

It felt pretty good. Maybe I wasn't winning any trophies, but I was doing some good things. I had a life outside tennis. It was rewarding and sometimes, like recently, even a little too exciting for my own good. I had to try—to force myself—to adapt, compromise, settle. Because it's a fact, you can't win them all.

NEW YORK POST
Late City Final
ALLEGED MURDERER ICED AT OPEN
by Martin Lutz

In a bizarre development in the recent "Curse of the
Grand Slams" story, in which a string of violent
crimes and misfortunes has stalked the world's top
tennis tournaments, the body of multimillionaire en-
trepreneur Milton H. Bevins was found this afternoon in a storage freezer on the grounds of the U.S.
Open in Flushing Meadows. Bevins, 64, son of the
late Stanford and Michelline Hanford Bevins of Ra-
leigh, N.C., inherited the bulk of his father's tobacco
holdings upon his death in 1969. Last night, Bevins
had been in attendance in the box of Mayor Rudolph
Giuliani before an alleged confrontation with former
tennis star Jordan Myles precipitated a grounds
search for him that caused hundreds of thousands of
tennis fans hours of delay in leaving Louis Armstrong Stadium. Bevins has been implicated in the alleged murder of the father of late tennis star Audrey
Armat and the kidnapping of her brother, Emilio
Armat, Jr., whom Connecticut State Police and the
F.B.I. found unharmed earlier today in a locked
cabin near Lake Waramaug in New Preston, Connecticut.

Bevins's body was discovered at three o'clock this
afternoon by a concession employee inside a ten-by-
ten-foot aluminum walk-in freezer that held five
thousand Häagen-Dazs ice cream bars. The freezer
had been padlocked for the night at 9:00 P.M. yesterday. Bevins's body was reportedly frozen solid. The

temperature inside the walk-in freezer was estimated at 10 degrees Fahrenheit. Police report that a .22 caliber pistol and a six-inch mother-of-pearl-handled stiletto were found on the body. The gun is being tested to see if it matches the weapon used in Emilio Armat's death. From marks and chipped ice inside the freezer, authorities speculate that Bevins was alive when he entered the freezer, became locked inside during the police search, and unsuccessfully tried to pry open the door.

"I didn't know anybody was in there when I locked it," said Häagen-Dazs concession employee Manuel Diego, 18. "I was just locking up for the night." Dr. Michael Chandler, the Queens County Chief Medical Examiner at the Elmhurst Hospital morgue, interviewed exclusively for the *Post*, said, "Preliminarily we believe that there are no suspicious circumstances and that Mr. Bevins succumbed to hypothermia, became unconscious, and froze to death. An autopsy is being performed on the body to determine the exact cause of death, and as soon as it is concluded we will release a statement with a confirmed result."

A police investigation into Bevins's involvement in the Armat murder and kidnapping is under way. Sixteen-year-old Audrey Armat was the number-four-ranked female tennis star in the world when she was found dead in England under mysterious circumstances in July.